A WIT'S WORLD

A WIT'S WORLD
Six Novellas

STUART R. SCHWARTZ

ARCHWAY PUBLISHING

Copyright © 2022 Stuart R. Schwartz.

All rights reserved. No part of this book may be used or reproduced by any means, graphic, electronic, or mechanical, including photocopying, recording, taping or by any information storage retrieval system without the written permission of the author except in the case of brief quotations embodied in critical articles and reviews.

Archway Publishing books may be ordered through booksellers or by contacting:

Archway Publishing
1663 Liberty Drive
Bloomington, IN 47403
www.archwaypublishing.com
844-669-3957

Because of the dynamic nature of the Internet, any web addresses or links contained in this book may have changed since publication and may no longer be valid. The views expressed in this work are solely those of the author and do not necessarily reflect the views of the publisher, and the publisher hereby disclaims any responsibility for them.

Any people depicted in stock imagery provided by Getty Images are models, and such images are being used for illustrative purposes only. Certain stock imagery © Getty Images.

ISBN: 978-1-6657-1754-0 (sc)
ISBN: 978-1-6657-1752-6 (hc)
ISBN: 978-1-6657-1753-3 (e)

Library of Congress Control Number: 2022900527

Print information available on the last page.

Archway Publishing rev. date: 04/14/2022

CONTENTS

The Unlikely Mentor 1

On The Tracks 35

Lambie 77

Survivors 125

Pyramid 215

Hair Shrink 271

THE UNLIKELY MENTOR

A NOVELLA

BY

Stuart R Schwartz

I was a little girl then. At least, at the age of 12, I considered myself a little girl. Life had not yet blossomed into a virtual world. As I sit here recalling those days, 30 years ago, I wonder what my response might have been had I been told that in 25 years, I could walk around with a device in my hand, one device that would allow me to call my friends and family and even send them messages. And, the device might even tell me what the weather will be for the next 10 days. I probably would have said that it is all science fiction. Yes, I knew what science fiction was back then. It was TV shows that had space ships flying around that looked like someone had pieced some cardboard together and flew them around on barely-visible threads. Yes, that WAS science fiction. Science fiction was rods that doubled for guns that made ZZZZZZZZZAAAAPPP sounds when the trigger was pulled. Sometimes the ZZZZZZZZAAAAPPP didn't sync with the pulling of the trigger, but to me it worked, and it was science fiction.

I wasn't very intelligent back then and I am not sure that I can consider myself intelligent now. But, but, but, I am smart. And even if I wasn't smart back then, I became smart in a real hurry. I surprised myself at how smart I became. I didn't do very well in school. I got by, but it wasn't easy. But, I became the smartest little kid in the class. I know that.

My story is nothing more than recalling that which made me an adult by the time I was 13. Up until that time, life was pretty routine. Every morning, Mom or Dad would tap on my bedroom door. Sometimes I would acknowledge it, sometimes I would ignore it, and other times, I was so sound asleep that I didn't even hear it. But, the familiar knock was the advice that it was time to prepare for school, or on Sundays, church. Saturdays were my day off, my Sabbath, just like my Jewish friends. Except, some of them had to go to their temple on Saturday. Breakfast came first and it was always the exact same thing. A glass of orange juice filled to the lower part of a pattern that started three quarters of the way up the glass. And, of course there was always a bowl of cereal, usually Rice Crispies with sugar and milk. That was assuming that Johnnie, the milk man, had made his twice-weekly milk deliveries. If it snowed badly or the roads were icy, Johnnie was nowhere to be found, so Mom would make toast with jelly instead of the bowl of cereal.

Speaking of Johnnie, I am still mad at him 30 years later. I should have forgiven him by now, but he scammed me back then. He took advantage of my lack of "smart" and played a nasty on me that lasted all of these years. You see, the TV was always going and on one particular Sunday, there was a TV commercial for Argyle socks that you could buy via telephone. There weren't any credit cards, so the sock company would ask you to mail them either a check or cash, and then they would mail you the socks. It seems simple enough, but it was hardly the most conventional way to buy socks. Well, the very next day, Johnnie knocked on the back door to hand me a bill for Mom and Dad to pay. I happened to notice that he was wearing argyle socks. So, I asked him, "Hey Johnnie?" To which Johnnie responded "Yes, little girl?" I asked, "Did you happen to buy those socks on TV?" Of course Johnnie immediately replied, "Well yes, little girl, I sure did". He smiled, handed me the bill and asked me to give it to Mom or Dad. He then turned around, walked down the 3 steps and left. For a few years, I was so pleased with myself about how I had guessed out of the blue that Johnnie had bought those socks on TV and what a coincidence it was that he was actually wearing those socks the very next day that I had seen them. But, one day, I realized that "Holy Crap, Johnnie was full of shit!" He had scammed me and took advantage of my naiveté. Johnnie has likely passed on, so I have gotten by this episode (barely), but my days of being a naïve little girl were soon behind me.

So, back to the routine. Breakfast was OK but nobody talked. Dad would read the daily newspaper that Timmy had delivered prior to heading to school. It was okay with me because Dad had explained that his insurance business office was so busy all day long, that there just wasn't any chance to catch up on the news. And besides, Dad would say, it really didn't matter if he read the newspaper at work or not because it was the same old shit every day. And, of course, Mom would admonish Dad for saying "shit" in front of me. To be honest, I never really gave a shit that Dad used the shit word around me. I had been hearing that shit for several years, so much in fact, that I couldn't understand why it was considered a bad word. Shit, shit, shit! "He's a shit, the dog shits, the movie was shit, teacher eats shit, I've gotta take a shit, nobody gives a shit, Holy shit!, shit for brains, cafeteria food is shit, and it goes on and on. It was a "shit culture". Everybody was a part of it, but we were all chastised for speaking it and thinking it.

Mom wouldn't talk during breakfast either because she was busy making my sandwich for lunch, specifically for the school days. There were three sandwiches for me. I was never surprised to open my lunch pail. It was either peanut butter and jelly..surprise, surprise; or bologna and swiss cheese with mustard; or bacon, lettuce and tomato. And, of course the fruit of the day was an apple, an orange, or a banana. I didn't mind peeling the banana, but I hated peeling the orange. The orange peeling made my fingers smell like oranges all day long. Looking back, maybe I should have washed my hands more often. But, I hated going into the girls' room because there was a chance that Margie was in there smoking one of her disgusting cigarettes. Didn't her mom notice the daily depletion of cigarettes from her stash??!!

I should probably skip all of the other routine "stuff" as most have lived it. But, you guessed it.. family visits, Sunday rides in the car with dad always yelling "They should keep those Sunday drivers off the freaking road". I wondered why he would always say that because that was what HE was ... a Sunday driver. Dad rarely ever said "fuck" but "shit" was flying out from his vocal chords daily. And, of course, if I behaved, ice cream would be in the future of the Sunday ride. And, there was church. That too bored me because I never understood what they were talking about. I did go to church school while Mom and Dad were in the chapel. They now call it bible study. I hated it. It all seemed like fairy tales back then with people doing harm, forgiving, blessing, eating weird shit, walking around with weird outfits, camels, and other stuff which none of us in the class gave two shits about. See, there we go again with the "shits". "Aunt Suzie is the shits". In its day, that was a good thing for Aunt Suzie.

In church school, they always talked about "the virgin birth". I had no clue what in the hell that meant until Frankie told me one day. Frankie had all but beaten Mom and Dad with the "birds and the bees" lecture. But I was pretty sure I knew what was coming. "Ohhhhhhh ... that's how it happens? If THAT'S how it happens, how can a baby appear on the scene, if it didn't happen." Frankie would say, "shut up Maria, you sound like a Jew". "Oh really Frankie??, How in fact do Jews sound?" "Maria, Jews don't believe in Jesus. In fact, they killed him". Well, for a time, I thought that nothing could have been crueler than to kill someone because his parents didn't have sex. I later learned that the Jews' take on the incident was a little different from Frankie's but I'll save that for later. I now have my own views of what really happened there. But, I wasn't there, so do I really know? In fact, do the people that were actually there really know too? That was a rhetorical question.

So, routines being what they are, my life was pretty uncomplicated. Vacations with Mom and Dad and the family dog were at the family cabin in the mountains. Our mountains were more like hills but it was serene and relaxing. I was one of those kids that enjoyed relaxation. I would play fetch with "Spot" for hours on end. Mom and Dad liked that because "Spot" was so tired at the end of the day, he would sleep through the night. Oh, we named our dog "Spot" because he was all white with one spot over his left hip. It was likely the least original name we could call him, except for maybe "Fido", but nobody seemed to care, especially "Spot". "Spot" shit in the woods too. I had to throw that in because dad was so proud that "Spot" knew to do his business in the woods. "Hey look, Maria, Spot knows to take a shit in the woods". "That's marvelous, Dad". Mother: "Would you please STOP using that word??!!"

After a weekend at the cabin, I was usually happy to return to school, even though I did not do that well there. Remember, I am not that intelligent. But, smart I am. School was a place where I could bond with friends, look at boys, (even though I was only 12), play in the school yard, and scribble in my note book when I was bored with what the teacher was trying to convey. Looking back, we probably never realized how good we had it when we were in school. Think about it. For most kids, you have a bed in a house, you have a room with toys, there's breakfast, dinner and a lunch to take to school. In school, there is no money to waste because somehow it is all paid, and best of all, sometimes you learn stuff. I actually enjoyed learning some stuff. Gym was good. Some history was cool. Math sucked. Literature could have been better if it didn't include poetry. Science was very cool, especially when Margie burnt her cigarette-holding hand in the middle of a science experiment. That incident may have been the first time I had ever heard the following words muttered …"MUTHER FUKKER!!!!"

It all changed shortly after my 12th birthday. If I was heading home after school rather than to hang out at a friend's, I would walk home and take a shortcut through a park. We lived in an upper-middle class town, so there were usually no surprises in the park. There was one unsavory character that I would spot now and then, but he never wore anything abnormal, like a raincoat and sneakers, so I felt quite comfortable walking past him. He was usually accompanied by a brown paper bag and I could see that the top of some type of bottle peered through the top of the bag. I did in fact wonder what he was drinking, but I was too young to think it was anything more than a Coke. The bag was too large for it to have been glue, so that notion was out. I knew about glue sniffing because some of the kids would sneak their airplane glue into their lunch sacks and sniff it during class. One day, Tommie Roberts started laughing his ass off (as little as it was) for no apparent reason. The teacher asked Tommie to share the gist of his outburst with the class. He couldn't respond. Tommie had no earthly idea what in the hell he was laughing at. If he were brave, he should have said, "Oh nothing, it's just the glue". But, in his case, bravery would have gotten him a suspension from school and a beating from his parents. So, he just sat there and giggled.

Well, as I was saying, I headed home one day and in the park, on a bench, was an old woman. She was looking at a magazine. I couldn't tell her age, but I knew she was old. Kids do not have much of a perspective on age. A person older than 40 seemed quite old to a 12-year old. My parents seemed old. Grandma and Grandpa were ancient. I once saw Grandma and Grandpa making out on the front porch. To me, there was nothing more hideous than that. Now I pray that I'll be making out on a porch at their age. So, digressions aside, I walked by the "old woman" and slowed down a bit. Yes, I was curious. She looked up and provided me with a sincere, but wrinkled smile. I am not one hundred percent sure, but I think she was reading *"Life Magazine."* And, by the looks of it, this was no recent edition. I could see that on the cover was a photo of a movie star. But, it was a movie star or some other celebrity from years gone by. I smiled back and kept going.

That night, as I lay awake waiting for sleep, I thought about the old woman. Who was she? Why had I never seen her before? What was she reading? Why did she smile? Did she know who I was? Does she have a family? Those and many other questions crossed my mind. I was very curious. And, most importantly, when she smiled, there was something about her eyes, something alluring, and something that spoke to me. It was more than a twinkle. It was a "statement". I had to know. Each day following, for an entire week, I took the same path home, solely to seek out this old woman. But, she was not there. I decided not to give up. I had to see her again. A week passed, and I made my daily trek through the park, and finally she was there. She looked the same. Nothing changed. And, it was the very same magazine.

As I approached, I stopped. She looked up at me and, again, there was the wrinkled smile. Her eyes glared right through me as if she were entering my mind with her eyes. I said, "hi". She said, "hello". I wanted to continue walking, but I could not. I told her that my name is Maria. Her response was limited to, "well, hello Maria". I wanted to know her name but was afraid to ask. But finally, "what is your name?" "Well", said the old woman, "you can call me Alice". "Is that your real name?", I asked. Not surprisingly, she said "No, but you can call me that, yes, call me that. I would like that. Alice".

"I'm walking home from school, Alice. Sometimes I walk through the park". I had no idea how to start a conversation with her but that was my "ice breaker". Alice didn't respond. She looked down at her magazine and opened it to a page. It was as if she were saying, "OK, that's all I have for today". So, I nodded, turned around, and walked the rest of the way home.

I could not sleep. Somehow I had to know who Alice was. I would figure out a way. The next day, I decided to gift Alice. I prayed that she would be in the park on the bench. One of my teachers always had a bouquet of fresh flowers on her desk. In the beginning of the school year, she had told the class that she brings fresh flowers each week. The purpose was to brighten the room and brighten our spirits. Rather than to simply "lift" a flower, I asked permission to take one. The teacher asked if there was any special reason, and I decided to be somewhat honest. I told her that it was going to become a gift. "Is it for a boy?" asked the teacher. I wanted to respond by asking her if she had lost her mind because, for shit sake, I was only 12. "No", I said, "it is for someone else". And, without any further inquiry, the teacher invited me to take whichever one I wanted, and I did.

That day, on the way to the park, I prayed, in my own special way, that Alice would be at the park. And, she was. This time Alice looked up as I approached and she beamed. Somehow she knew that I was on my way to see her. In her hand was the same magazine. Her clothes were similar but not the same. I handed her the flower and she looked up into my eyes without saying a word. But, I heard everything she had to say without her having to say one word. I smiled and walked away. After a few steps, I stopped and turned around. Alice was looking at me as if to say that she felt special that day. Mom used to say that "a picture is worth a thousand words". Well, so is an expression.

Who was this Alice? How could I get to know her? Should I tell anybody else about her, or should I keep this interlude between Alice and me? And the magazine? It was time to know. I had to know. I am not sure why, but for some reason, I just knew that Alice was about to change my life. It was a Friday. I had the weekend ahead and it was time to leave school. I headed off to the park, walking at a brisk pace. I couldn't wait to see her again. I brought the orange from my lunch pail and when I saw Alice, I gave it to her. She accepted it, put it in her pocket, and looked into my eyes. I just never realized until that moment how beautiful an old woman she was. Courage was not my greatest attribute, but I made the decision to ask her if I could sit down on the bench with her. Alice responded, "But of course, Maria, please do sit". I was quite surprised that she had remembered my name.

"Alice, can I ask you some questions?" Correcting me, Alice said, "Sure, Maria, you "may" ask me some questions."

"Okay then, Alice, do you live here?"

"I do now".

"You didn't live here before?"

"No, I lived quite far away from here."

"Well then, why did you move here?"

"That's a difficult question for me to answer Maria, but let's just say that was time for me to be here."

"Uhmmmm, why do you sit in the park?"

"It is a good place for me, Maria. Do you have any other questions?"

"Well, I probably have plenty of questions. But, I really would like to know if you will be my friend?"

Alice turned and looked at me for at least 30 seconds before she responded. "Yes, Maria. I would enjoy being your friend. But you are a young girl. Don't you have school friends?"

"Well, I do, Alice, but they are not like you".

"You do not know anything about me, Maria".

"Alice, I know that you are beautiful and you always have the same magazine".

Alice looked down at the magazine, blushed, and smiled. She stood up, turned, and looked at me. She told me that she needed to be going and that she would hope to see me on another day.

During the weekend following my brief conversation with Alice, I concluded that I needed her. I needed Alice more than anyone including my friends and my family. How did I know this? I do not know, but I knew it. Alice had something to share. She wanted to share it with me. I was sure of that. And, like me, she didn't know how. That was it! I was sure. Alice needed me as much as I needed her. I decided to make it my project. Get to know Alice. But, it wasn't that easy. The first time I saw her again after our brief discussion, I asked her if I could sit down with her again. She asked me to forgive her but she needed her "alone time". For a few minutes, I was hurt that she didn't respond as I expected. But, after thinking about it, I realized that "alone time" is something I craved quite often. Yes, my family was important to me, but my time by myself was cherished.

I let a few days pass then headed to the park again. This time, to my surprise, Alice stood when she saw me and waited as I arrived. She greeted me and asked if I would like to sit with her. So, I did. After a few minutes of quiet, she finally began talking.

"Maria, you are such a pretty little girl. When I first saw you, I didn't understand why you would want to be friends with me. I am old, and yes, I am lonely. All of my friends are gone, but you have a world of friends. I was surprised that you are not enjoying the after-school hours with your friends or your family. But then I saw that you were curious about me. And, when I looked into your eyes, I saw more than a friend. I saw a pretty little girl who was reaching out. Please do this for me, Maria? When you go home tonight, please think about your friends and your family. Think about what you know about them and what you do not know. Tomorrow after school, come to the park. I will be here. I want to know more about you. Is that OK?"

I was thrilled that Alice had finally reached out to me. I made it my mission to think about my friends and family, the good and the bad. I wanted her to know. I had so much on my mind, and who better to share with than Alice. I went to work and made notes, thinking, thinking, making more notes. I finally felt comfortable that I knew what I would tell Alice the next day.

I arrived at the park at about the same time as always. Alice was there with her magazine. She smiled and stood as I approached. "Hi Alice" I said as I approached, feeling the warmth of her smile. "Alice, I have thought about what you asked me to do", I said. I went on to tell her about my family and how I believed they were trying to mold me. I told her about school, my teachers, and my friends. When I spoke of my friends, I suggested that, unlike the other kids, I didn't attach myself to one particular friend or group. I wanted to be friends with everybody, but that was impossible. They all seemed to have their own little groups. If I joined any particular group at the lunch table, I was generally ignored. It hadn't really bothered me except for the time when I heard one of the girls say "here comes weird Maria". I am not sure why she may have thought I was weird at the time, but, looking back, it was OK. The boys didn't like me sitting with them either. It was a pride issue with them. Even at the age of 12, they could be macho, or at least try to appear macho. I was confused about the "implied rejection", but not terribly offended. I still had my family and "Spot". But, when I told Alice about my family and the lack of interaction, she simply nodded as if to say "I understand". I told Alice about church and how everything I was learning was either boring, sounded dumb, or just wasn't something I wanted to add to my repertoire of knowledge. I told Alice that I didn't feel as if I could be accepted anywhere than to just be "another little girl". When she responded with a simple "why", I told her that I believed I wasn't very smart. Alice interrupted me, "stop right there, Maria". I was somewhat surprised by the exclamatory nature of her request that I stop, but I decided to shut my mouth.

Alice looked at me very intensely, sternly, and began. "Maria", she started. "Let's talk about you first. When people prioritize, you usually hear a list like this: Family, God, Friends, in that order. Do you want to know who made up this list? Don't answer because I will tell you. It is made up by anyone who believes what their priorities are, not yours. So, going forward, I want you to think about what is most and least important to you. But, if I might make a little suggestion, put yourself and your personal aura on top of the list. You are the most important priority in your life. Your well-being and your health all fall into the category of "self". What could be more important to you? If you are not around, there is no list. Maria, the list of priorities will change as you age. Sure, it is fine to put things of importance in order of the magnitude of importance, but there are so many factors that affect the way you feel about yourself and others. Always, always be aware of these factors."

Alice was starting to lose me. When I looked at her quizzically, she said, "I know, Maria, it is a lot to absorb, but just think about it. What matters most to you?" She waited for my response. "Well, I just would like to be happy". Well then, Alice said, "do the things that make you happy, but always think about how your words and actions affect others. If you are not hurting anyone by what you say and do, then just simply go for it. Being accepted is not important. Your continual happiness IS important. And, if you are always happy, you will be accepted, because "smart" people will respect you because you are an individual. You are doing what makes you happy without hurting others in the process. This is what generates respect. Never forget that. If you want to be respected, don't mold yourself into someone who is trying to make everyone else happy, mold yourself into what makes you happy. It's a simple concept which most people lose sight of".

I asked Alice about church and the expectations that my family had. They believe strongly in God and his Son Jesus. They wanted me to learn about my faith and practice it, but I never ever felt comfortable with it, regardless of how it was presented to me. I can't say that it was "hog wash", but it was boring and silly to me. The stories I learned at church school were more like fairy tales. I knew that fairy tales aren't true. Why should I "buy into" these concepts?

Alice chimed in, "Let's talk about church briefly then call it a day, Okay, Maria?" I nodded that of course it is OK. She went on, "first of all, a church is merely a venue where people go to practice their faith or religion. It is called a "House of God", a "Temple", a Sanctuary", a "Cathedral", all meaning the same thing basically. They are places where people go to worship God. Maria, there are many, many religions. They are countless. And, each has its own beliefs, its own customs, and its own group of followers. But, the common denominator is that each, for the most part is worshiping the same God. So, you are not sure about what you are learning principally because you are smart enough to weigh in your own mind whether or not it all makes sense to you. In many cases, it is obvious that it doesn't. Your church school teaches you what is in the bible. They are not fairy tales, but they are more like parables. But, most important, it is what your Mom and your Dad want you to learn. They want you to be faithful to the same Lord with whom they were acquainted as they grew up. Maria, that is natural and perfectly fine. But, since you are smart, as you grow older, I suggest that you continue to study as you are now. But, always stay open minded. Try to understand why others worship in different ways. Try to understand why people practice different religious customs. Some even go on to become ministers, priests, rabbis and such. Then, as you learn about these different faiths, make your own judgments."

"Alice", I said. "Frankie from church told me that I think like a Jew".

"Why would he say that, Maria? He must have a reason".

"Well, we were talking about Jesus and I told him that I did not understand what "Virgin birth" meant. So, Frankie enlightened me about sex, at least as much as he knew about it. Having heard all of that, I questioned how Jesus could have been born if his parents didn't have sex. He then told me that I talk like a Jew and in fact, the Jews killed Jesus."

Alice nodded as though she had heard this argument before. "Maria, remember what I said. Nobody is necessarily right and nobody is necessarily wrong when you talk about religion. It is all about what you choose to believe and the methods that you use in order to worship. There are so many varied opinions. Frankie has grasped that which he has learned from his parents and from church and he has embraced these concepts as his ideals. That is fine. He too will learn more as he grows. But, don't "buy into anything" with which you are not comfortable. And, it is okay to keep your thoughts to yourself. Do not lie in the process, but you don't have to reveal all that you believe. When you are old enough and are sure that you are fully aware of what you believe in, it is okay to share it. In some cases, you will be rejected for what you believe, but think back to what I said earlier. You will garner respect for having a mind of your own."

I felt like I really knew what Alice was saying. I really didn't want to be force-fed anything in life, but I didn't mind getting a little direction along the way. I felt a small sense of confidence after listening. Alice stood up, looked at me, smiled, and turned and walked away. I wanted so badly to follow her, but I knew that wasn't what she wanted. She wanted to remain enigmatic for some reason. I turned and started walking towards home. I broke into a trot, and eventually a run. I felt like something had changed in me. I wanted to know so much more. I craved it. My life was changing very quickly. I was not sure that I could keep up with the change, but it was going to be fun to try.

The next few days were very frustrating for me. I came down with the flu bug or something like that. I pretended not to be sick as I wanted to go to school and, more importantly see Alice. Did she wonder what happened to me? Maybe she wasn't in the park either. But, I was petrified that I would not see my friend again, especially when I was so eager to learn from her. In a moment's time, she had become my mentor.

Sunday arrived and I was feeling much better. I told Mom and Dad that I just didn't feel like going to church that day. Of course, Mom blew a gasket. "Young lady, what do you mean you're not going?" She looked very concerned. "You will not stay in this house alone. And, neither your Dad nor I will stay away from church just because you do not want to go. Sweetie, there is nothing more important in our lives than going to church. You know that." Before she even had a chance to get the last word out, my thoughts shifted to my last conversation with Alice. Alice had spoken of prioritizing life and here I was already manipulating my Mom because I was now aware of priorities. I sat and thought without saying a word. Then I heard Mom say "Well??". I decided to offer a compromise. "Look Mom, I will go, but I would really like to sit with you and Dad in the service than go to church study." Mom frowned, thought for a minute (or two), and said "What?" As if she didn't hear me the first time around, I modified my delivery. "Mom, I'll go to church with you and Dad, but I am not going to church study." Mom was terribly confused by this change of events. "Maria dear, how will you learn about God, Jesus, and his Disciples if you do not attend church school?" Oh boy, here it comes. I knew I had to get it off my chest, but should I take the high road or the low road? I was conflicted at the age of twelve. The low road would have had me respond by telling

Mom that I could give a flying crap about Jesus and his Disciples. But, of course, I took the high road. "Mom, here's where I am coming from. I do not like the course of study. It is boring and I find Frankie annoying. I would just like to be with you and Dad. Please understand. It is not about going to church, it's about family, us". Well, holy shit, Mom fell for it hook, line and sinker. So, on Sunday I did not attend church study. I sat with Mom and Dad, yawned, half-listened to the minister, thought about Alice, and kept watching Mickey Mouse move the hands on my wristwatch so I could finally get the hell out of there. The minister was tossing out some crap about righteousness. This coming from a man who was almost forced to leave the church for reasons that were never explained to me. But, I know the reasons were not good.

On the way home from church Dad asked me what "that" was all about. I asked, "What was what all about?" He said "You know exactly what I am talking about young lady! You sat there squirming the entire time, paying no attention to the minister, kept looking at your wristwatch, and it was downright embarrassing". I asked why they were embarrassed. Dad's predictable response was "How are others there going to perceive us if our daughter cannot behave like an adult in church?" Okay, I was getting infuriated. "Dad, I am NOT an adult and that shit is boring." It appears that what I had just told Dad didn't go down very well because he stopped the car, pulled over, turned around and looked me in the eye. His face turned as red as Sally Murphy's uglier than crap Christmas sweater, and told me that my remark had just landed me an extended stint in my room. If he only knew how excited I was about THAT news, he would have grown even more furious.

For the next several weeks nothing changed, and finally Mom and Dad hoisted the white flag and reluctantly dropped me off at Aunt Sarah's house before church. I would wait there for them to return and pick me up when church was over. Aunt Sarah, by the way, was agnostic and though Mom and Dad constantly badgered her about being a heathen, she had many good qualities, so the tradeoff tilted in the direction of trusting me with Aunt Sarah. If Mom and Dad knew about the cigarettes that Aunt Sarah smoked, I surely would not have been going there. They didn't seem to come out of regular cigarette packages, they had no label on them, and they smelled a bit weird to me. And, Aunt Sarah would smoke one, head to the fridge, open the door and just stare at whatever was inside of it, almost as if something tasty was about to jump out straight into her mouth. Thinking back, I wonder why Aunt Sarah wasn't reluctant to smoke that crap in front of me. Maybe she was trying to tempt me to join in on the fun, but surely she must have more sense than that. I was only twelve for crap sake. Thank GOD I never tried that stuff. I can't imagine having lived a life being hungry and horny all of the time. Well, maybe horny is okay, but hungry, no way. I can imagine having grown up looking like my second grade school teacher, Miss Mason. One would have thought they might have used a forklift to get her into the classroom. She was "Miss" Mason for a reason. And, it wasn't because she ever "missed" a meal.

I know that I digress here more than I should, but all of these events drum up memories of life back then.

Well, I was feeling better, the Sunday church episode was one day behind me, so off to school I went. I was impatient for the day to end as I so wanted to see Alice again. The clock ticked ever so slowly that day. Finally, the day was over and I raced out the school door. I literally ran to the park. When I arrived, Alice was there waiting for me, magazine in hand.

"Alice, Alice, I was so worried you would not be here. I was sick last week and I had no way to let you know."

"No need to worry, Maria. I am here. I am sorry that you were ill. Are you okay now?"

"I'm fine Alice. It was the flu bug or something. Mom says that kids in school always pick up the bug from each other. So, maybe that's what happened. She is afraid that I will also get lice. I didn't even know what lice are until Linda Price went home crying one day. She was scratching away like a dog with fleas and of course Billy Stemmons blurted out in class "Linda's got the lice, watch out, Linda's got the lice. They a gonna bite you if you don't watch out. Linda's got the lice." Well, Linda was not entirely sure what lice were, but was getting the idea real quick. She bolted for the door and nearly tripped over my desk on the way out. But, before she made it over to the door, she headed straightaway for Billy's desk. Billy looked quite confused at that point and yelled, "Watchya gonna do, lice-head? Watchya gonna do?" The teacher that day was a substitute. She didn't even know everyone's name. So she screamed, "stop it everybody, stop it!" The class was howling as Linda grabbed Billy and rubbed her head against his like she was scouring a pot. Billy freaked out and threw her to the floor. Well, fortunately, Linda was not hurt by that maneuver, so she was able to get up and continue out the door. Billy wasn't in school the next few days, so everyone pretty much guessed that Linda's little post-scratching episode was effective on her attacker. Sorry, but I just reminded myself of that incident".

Chuckling a bit, Alice told me not to worry, that I'll probably remember that and other episodes similar to it for my entire life. And, she added, "I hope it is a long life".

Alice suggested that we really hadn't talked about my friends. I was reluctant to tell her that I really didn't gravitate to anyone in particular, and because of that, I was usually left out of everything. At that age, kids would have their own little groups which were commonly known as "cliques". I never felt like I belonged to any of them. There must have been something about me that suggested to others that, "no, we don't need Maria hanging around with us". I, of course, could not put my finger on it, but it was probably because I was quite ordinary in their eyes. "Ordinary" never got you friends. "Unique" did. I just couldn't grasp what unique had to do with wearing tight sweaters stuffed with tissue around the breast area, or wearing lipstick and eye shadow. Oh, and you'd better believe that all that makeup shit came off before they left for home. No, I was "plain Jane". So, I revealed all of this to Alice. She absorbed all of what I was saying and asked what I thought I needed to do in order to be accepted. My response was, "I am not sure, but I want to be accepted". Then, when I least expected it, Alice looked at me and said, "why?"

"Why "what" Alice?"

"Why do you feel the need to be accepted?"

"That's a good question, Alice. I haven't thought about it. But, I don't want to be a loner"

Alice paused, took a deep breath, turned and looked me in the eye. Then she began, "you never have to be a loner, Maria. And, there is no reason why you must feel that you have to be accepted. For what reason, do you feel that acceptance by relatives and peers is important?" I had no answer for that. "What you want to be, Maria, is respected". How do you get there? Well, most children your age don't get it. The ones that do are the people you will want to respect in return. It is an easy process that most people do not know how to employ. It all starts with treating people the way you want to be treated. Some will find it annoying that you are not catering to their needs and wants, but their needs and wants are superficial. You can be way ahead of "the game", Maria, and it is a simple process."

By now I was eager to know what it was that I needed to do in order to gain respect. I didn't know how to nudge Alice into becoming forthright with me. But, I was getting impatient to hear her. What she had already said to me made a lot of sense and I was ready for the next step.

"Maria", she continued, "I can't tell you how I know these things, but I too had a good teacher. My teacher was my own experience, my life's journey, if you will. So, please think about this. You want to be respected for who you are, not necessarily for "what" you are. Don't go around all of your life trying to please others. Have them be pleased just by knowing that you are there. Make a presence about yourself without making a nuisance of yourself. In school and the playground, start your greeting with a smile and follow it by a short, sweet statement. The statement can be as simple as, "hi, how are you today?" In the lunch room, walk up to any table at which you would like to sit and say, "good afternoon, may I join you?" Sometimes they will say "sure", but be prepared to be ignored. If they ignore you, that's fine, just finish your lunch, stand up, smile, and tell them thank you for letting me join you. Simple enough." This might confuse them, but it's okay."

I thought about this and it wasn't a bad idea. I asked Alice, "Does this apply to both girls and boys? I ask you this because the girls and the boys rarely sit together, especially brothers and sisters. Boys are embarrassed to sit with girls and girls feel that they are too "special" to have boys at their table." I recalled that I had briefly mentioned this issue to her in the past. It must have been important enough to me that I would raise it again.

Alice immediately jumped in and said "sit anywhere that makes you happy. It takes time for people to realize the nature of others. Don't worry about other children trying to figure you out. At that age, the depths of emotions are shallow. But the glass has begun to fill. You don't need to remember that or know what it means. Just remember that character development takes a long time. Do you think that Abraham Lincoln, at the age of 12, knew that one day he would become President of the United States? Of course he didn't. But, in a tough time in American history, he thought things out. He was smart enough to perceive what was going on around him and his character developed along the way. He generated the respect of a nation that had been torn apart by war, hatred, misunderstanding, and the desire for peace and unity. You may not want to become President, though it is not a bad idea, but you do want to be respected. Never forget that."

"I do so understand, Alice".

"Maria, there are safeguards that allow you to gain the honor of mutual respect. One of the first is to always "act" and not "react". Protect yourself when necessary, but not in a reactionary way."

I told Alice that I wasn't sure what she meant by that. I needed an example.

"Okay, Maria, if someone does you wrong in your eyes, don't immediately come back saying or doing something that you will regret later on. Don't react. Wait, think about what had happened, and carefully plan your next action, if you are going to take action at all. Some things are just not worth arguing over. Don't be afraid to say "I am sorry, but to me, it is not worth having an argument about this". It really works. If a boxer goes into the boxing ring with his gloves and boxing trunks on and starts jumping around, hooting and hollering with bravado, then nobody shows up, then who looks stupid?"

I said, "the boxer?"

"Yes", said Alice, "exactly". So, Maria, think about this every time you have an issue that you believe has an immediate impact on you, large or small, serious or frivolous, or anything. Be yourself, be kind, and don't intentionally hurt anyone. It will go a long way."

Alice went on, "Now I must go, Maria". I hope to see you again soon.

My heart was pounding. "Alice, I can't wait to see you again."

I learned not to panic if I didn't see Alice for a few or even several days. She would not leave me without saying goodbye. I came to know that about her. I was beginning to believe that she needed me, for no apparent reason, as much as I needed her. So, I didn't panic. But the brief interlude without Alice included an "episode" at school wherein I had to employ the use of my new outlooks on life. One day, for lunch, I decided to walk over to a table of boys, a few of whom I already knew. I asked them if I might sit down and join them which was close to being unheard of at school. They looked around at each other as if this was the preliminary stage of the plague, and finally one of them said, "okay, yah, okay". So, I sat down, pulled out my lunch pail, and started to eat. None of these boys even wanted to look up at me. And, they were completely silent. What possibly could have been worse than to have "ordinary girl" sit down with them at lunch time? Nearing the end of my consumption phase, I pulled out the orange and offered it to Peter Gold, sitting to my right. My thought process was: "Let his hands stink of orange all day". His thought process was: "She's flirting with me". Well, I am sorry to share this with you Peter, but not in your lifetime. But, that's not how boys think. I got up and left and politely said "thank you for allowing me to join you for lunch". They didn't even have the courtesy to respond. And, I am quite sure that Peter Gold took one hell of a ribbing after I left. Well, as it turns out, Peter was not going to leave this "non-interlude" interlude alone. The very next day, I was sitting in class minding my own business. Little did I know that someone (I was sure it was Peter) had sneaked a walkie-talkie into my book bag. These gadgets resembled CB radios and people could talk to one another by tuning into a channel, then pressing down on a button. Peter was not in that class, but he was close enough to have the signal reach my book bag. And, all of a sudden I hear, "Oh Mariiiiiaaaaa"". I was thinking what in the hell was that? And, where did it come from? Then, a little bit louder, "Oh, Mariiiiiiiaaaaaa". I was thinking, what the hell? Then, as the child he really was, he blurted out, for the entire class to hear, "Oh Maria, you make me want to pee-ya". Okay, I told myself, don't react. Take a deep breath Maria, hold it, and then blow it out. I reached down into my bag, found the object and pressed the on/off switch to the "off" position. Of course, everyone in the class had turned their attention to me, and thankfully there weren't any lewd comments. I needed to heed the advice of Alice and think this one out. The day went by and mid-afternoon, I headed for my locker. There was a note taped to my locker. It read, "I need my walkie-talkie back. I hoped you liked the joke. Ha ha!, Peter Gold". "Okay", I wanted to respond, but he was not there, "I thought your joke was moronic, you cretin asshole". But, no, I kept my cool. I quickly scribed a note and pasted it to his locker. It said, "Sure, meet me outside the front of the building after school".

Right after school, Peter was waiting patiently for me outside the front door. There were some kids milling around. He walked over to me smiling. "Hi, Maria". I responded, "Hi, Peter". As predicted, he said, "Can I (not May I) have my walkie-talkie back now?" I, of course replied "Oh sure, Peter", and as I pulled it out of my book bag, I accidentally (on purpose) dropped it on the ground. "Oops", I said. Peter looked down at it, a bit annoyed and just as he went to grab it, I bashed the heel of my shoe on it several times until it had been smashed to smithereens. Peter was in shock, not able to believe his eyes. He looked at me and said, "That was my father's, Maria!! What am I going to tell him now??." I immediately said. "You should have thought about that before you embarrassed the crap out of me. Tell your daddy what you did before you start pointing the finger at me, you little crap ball". The next thing that happened was amazing. I heard cheers all around me. It was obvious that others had taken in this exchange and before I knew it, they were all cheering for me, boys and girls alike. That's when I knew that respect was heading my way. I was so happy with myself; I wanted to cry with joy.

Just when I thought the Peter Gold episode was behind me, the very next day there was a note in the form of a paper airplane taped to my locker. A paper airplane?? Really??!! So, of course I couldn't wait to see what this creative shit-for-brains had to say. It read, "My father is very angry with you for destroying his walkie-talkie. He plans to call your father." Okay, I found this to be quite amusing, so I decided to respond. Alice had told me not to "get in the ring", so I just considered this some pre-fight weigh-in banter. I found a very large piece of drawing paper in the art room and wrote on it: "Hey, turd-nose, your "7-freaking-47" landed on my locker today. How creative! So, your dad wants to call my dad? How cool! Maybe they can have boys' night out. Here's our number: 499-555-8574." I signed it "Maria, who makes you want to Pee-ya". Of course I mounted it right on the front of his locker. Well, needless to say, his dad never called and Peter Gold never spoke to me again. I wanted to think that he met his match. I'll never know what happened to him, but I do not think that he'll be telling his grandchildren this saga.

Things were a little different at home. Mom and Dad could sense that I was developing a sense of independence. They were a little bewildered with the changes but I was careful to always be polite and loving. If I disagreed with them, I would tell them politely and go on my merry way. If they decided to press an issue that they knew I would oppose, I would seek a compromise or just let it go. I had once heard that there are many battles in life, but the main objective was to win the war. I was never at odds to the extent that I would consider myself in a war, but I did seek objectives or an end result in many cases. I learned just from being around Alice that happiness is the best goal.

A few more days passed and I found Alice in the park. I would not ask her where she had been as she would object to my questioning her. I, at times, felt like I was walking on eggshells when I was with her. I just did not want to say or do anything at all that would cause her to abandon me. There was some unspoken element of mystery about our friendship. But, for some reason, she wanted to be there for me. I could sense it. I wanted to honor anything that she desired from me, though she never asked for anything. When she taught me about respect, I truly believed she was seeking that from me. And, trust me; by the ground that I stand on, she had garnered all the respect in the world from me.

One afternoon, after school, I found Alice sitting on the bench, magazine in hand, staring at the sky. I greeted her and she kept staring upwards. I asked if I was disturbing her and she replied, "not at all". She asked me to sit down, which I promptly did. Then she asked, "Maria, if you could tell me one common denominator that all of the world could say was a mutual interest and a potential bond between people of all cultures, what would it be?" Wow! I would have had to think long and hard about that one. And, I was not really sure what "denominator" meant, but I thought about the context of the use of the word in her question and I figured it out. Finally, after a few moments of silence, I responded with "the desire for world peace?" "No", she said. That's a dream, but it is a great answer. Think again, Maria, there is something that exists today amongst all cultures." I dwelled on this and finally blurted out "LOVE!". That's it! Right Alice?" Alice told me that it too was a great answer, but it was also a dream, especially from those that do love. She told me that there is a lot of love in the world and that there was an inordinate amount of hatred. "What a great thing it would be", said she, "if the world could come together and decide that we can coexist, we can love one another, we can dream of a life that is safe without hatred."

I asked, "what is it then, Alice?" I just don't know. Her answer surprised me.

"Maria, the greatest common denominator of all cultures is music".

I sat there a bit stunned. I like music but I wasn't aware that everybody else did also. So, I questioned her about that.

"Maria, not everybody loves music, but every culture embraces it. There are many, many instruments in the world, some identifiable only with certain cultures. Voices are instruments also. And, of course, there are many types of music. You know of many of the ones that you and/

or your family have been exposed to, such as classical, popular, rock and roll, opera, show tunes, jazz, blues, etc. People have different tastes. Some like certain genres of music and do not like others. If you heard music of another country for the first time, you might not like it, but that's because it is different. But, the people of that particular culture probably love it. My point is that in every culture, every country, there is a need for and a love of music in some form or another."

"Why then, Alice, do you bring this to my attention? I know something about music and I enjoy it, but I am not an expert about it."

"Maria", chuckling, "no, no, nobody expects you to be an expert about music and nobody would expect you to like one form over another, but having a musical "foundation" is something that will give you strength going forward."

"What kind of strength, Alice?"

"Remember what I said, Maria. Music is a common denominator. It makes for great conversation, it is entertaining, it is self-indulgent, it can soothe you when you are blue, and it creates exhilaration in life. The Arts in general have for centuries provided the world with great artists, great entertainers, great films and their actors, wonderful music and visual arts. And, anyone can enjoy it, rich or poor, intelligent or not, young or old. It doesn't matter; it's just something that I personally believe you should embrace. And, you do not have to be a professional of any type to listen, play, or understand music and The Arts. It is there for you to enjoy on any level that you so choose."

I thought about this for a while and asked Alice to tell me what her favorite music might be. She answered by telling me that she appreciated every type of music but limited her listening to a certain few. She did not, however, reveal what it was. Perhaps she didn't want to sway me into believing that I should follow her fondness for a certain type of music, that I should make those decisions on my own.

That very same night, at home at the dinner table, I asked Mom and Dad if they would buy me a piano. Dumbfounded, they just looked at one another, and then looked back at me in surprise. "Where did that come from?" asked Mom. "Well, I said, I have music class at school and

I just think that the piano is a nice instrument". Mom looked at Dad again and Dad said nothing.

"Maria, I don't think so", said Mom. "Annie Leighton's parents bought her a piano and it was expensive indeed, about $1000. Annie took one lesson and her bottom never touched that piano bench again".

It didn't take me long to respond to that. "Mom, I am NOT Annie Leighton! If you buy me a piano, I will play it. You can "take that to the bank" as Dad says". And, Annie Leighton's bottom is so big, by the way, that it probably didn't even fit on the bench."

"Enough of that young lady! Your Dad and I will discuss it and we will let you know."

Well, it didn't take long for them to decide because on the following Saturday morning, a delivery truck showed up with an upright piano. Yes, it was used, but it was in tune and that was all that I needed. My goal was to be able to learn a tune and someday play it for Alice. What greater gift than that? My piano teacher was Miss Blake. I had asked the band director at school to recommend someone, and Miss Blake was his first choice. She had been a student of his and had gone on to become a locally famous piano player and singer. I say "locally famous" because her gigs were mostly local. Miss Blake could play anything and was soon a star at church, local clubs, private parties, and sat in on concert events. She was "over the top" sweet but firm. That was exactly what I needed. In just a few short weeks, I was playing some old classics with very basic music, but at least the tunes were recognizable. I did not share this endeavor with Alice at all because I planned to surprise her someday. I didn't know how I would pull that off, but it was something that I wanted to do.

Music did become a part of my life and I never regretted having taken it upon me to learn all there was to know about it. I even sang. But, more on that later.

As the weeks passed, Alice would continue to share her ideology with me. Where did this all come from? Why and how did she become so knowledgeable about life? And, with all that she knew, why was her life destined to have her sitting on a park bench with a magazine in hand, talking to a little girl? I just did not get it.

At dinner one night, I asked Mom and Dad if I could have a friend over for dinner. Mom answered for both of them, and said "Sure honey, who is it?" I answered that it was my friend Alice. So Mom, in her curiosity said, "Okay honey, but we never heard about Alice before. Is she a classmate?"

"No, Mom, she's just a friend, but she is so very nice".

"Okay, sweetie, ask her to come over Friday night. I will make a roast"

"Thanks, Mom!"

I was ecstatic that Mom and Dad would allow me to invite Alice. I now had two hurdles to clear. The first was to hope that Alice would be at the park, and the second was to convince her to come to my house for dinner. She was so very private. I was worried that I couldn't get her to come, but I was going to give it my best effort.

The first hurdle was cleared quite easily. Alice was sitting on the bench when I arrived at the park. She greeted me and asked if all was well. I didn't hesitate to jump right in and ask her to come to my house for dinner on Friday night. She told me that no, she couldn't do that. My work was cut out for me. I didn't ask why, but I employed the use of some of Alice's principles in order to convince her to come.

"Alice", I said. "You have taught me much over the past several weeks. Even if I only retain only a small percentage of what I have learned from you, I know that I will grow up to be a good person. I can think of no way to repay you for the precious gift that you have given me. But, to me, the best way to say thank you for what you have meant to me is to honor you by inviting you to my home. There is no selfish need on my part other than to make you a part of my family, just for one evening. You are already a part of me, Alice, because you will remain in my heart for as long as I live. But, for my parents to understand me and why I have changed, and why I now do the things that I do, they need to see my "unlikely mentor", the one person outside of my circle of family and friends who has influenced me most in my life. So, I ask you please to reconsider, please just this once".

I knew straight away that I had pulled that speech right out of my very bottom. The words just fell out of my mouth as if someone else had been speaking them. Alice didn't answer me. I waited. She didn't even move a muscle. Then, all of a sudden, she said "I will see you at your home on Friday evening. I will be here tomorrow, Maria, so please write down on a piece of paper your address and the time that you would like me to be there."

I was in heaven. I couldn't believe my ears. I had convinced Alice to come to my home. The last hurdle was cleared.

"But", she went on, "I don't want to embarrass anyone, but I do not like to talk about my past or why I am here. There is no problem chatting about common niceties, but I just want you to know and remember me from what we have shared here. Is that Okay?"

"Alice, that is perfectly okay". But, may I ask you one question only? I promise it will be my last and it isn't anything that I would ever discuss with anyone other than you, ever. It is something I, as your friend would like to know. It will actually help me to know."

"What is it, Maria?"

"Alice, someday I want to meet the "man of my dreams". My parents seem to be happy, but I am not entirely sure of it. When I am old enough to have a boyfriend, or even a husband, I want to be sure that I have made the right decision. I have heard of so many of the other kids parents getting divorced. Mary Platt's parents even had fist fights. Yakk! What type of person punches a woman?! And when the judge told them that he approved the divorce, idiot Mr. Platt actually tried to punch the judge. So, Mr. Platt spent a few weeks in the slammer and is still a nut job. I don't want any of that, ever. But, that aside, my question is; have you ever had someone special in your life, someone that you could not stand to be away from?"

"That's a heavy question, Maria, but I will answer you and then we will be done."

"Yes, Maria", there was someone very close to me. I didn't go looking for him; he just arrived at my doorstep one day, figuratively speaking, of course". He turned out to be one of the most wonderful persons I ever met, not just a great man, but an overall great person. He is gone now, and I am not going to talk about it, but I will tell you what I learned from it all."

"Okay, Alice, I will listen and not speak."

"First and foremost, remember that love does not come easy. It is not about how they look or what they can or cannot do for you. Love does precede relationships, but love takes time. It is a learning experience. If someone tells you they love you on the first date or soon thereafter, it isn't true. Love is a construction site where the materials are trust, caring, giving, devotion, mutual respect, and lots of compassion. The tools are actions that prove that these materials can endure the life of the relationship. Relationships are built over periods of time. The most important element of the relationship is the strength of the mutual love. And, believe me, Maria, it is always a work in progress. There are signs that you will learn that will teach you whether your partner is fully committed to you and vice versa. I will not list these for you, but always be aware. You are smart, you will know. You will have some bad experiences. Everybody does. But, because you are who you are, you will know when you have met the "man of your dreams". So think about this. Never ever act without full consideration of what you are about to do, especially in relationships. This is also true of your day to day life. Again, never act without investigating whether your needs go along with your desires. When it is decision time, weigh your options. Make a list if you have to. What are the good things, and what are the bad things? On one side of the list is are your advantages and the other side are your disadvantages. Then, look at the list and decide which list is longer. It's as simple as that. And, if there are disadvantages, don't immediately walk away. Perhaps some of these disadvantages can be repaired. If they are irreparable, it is time to move on. You have heard the expression that "it is better to have tried and failed than not to have tried at all". Well, I don't subscribe to that 100%. You have no need to fail. If you take every precaution, do your homework so to speak, do your due diligence about every aspect about what you are about to do, you should never fail. Maria, I think I know that you will be successful in all that you do in life, both personally and professionally. I will pray for that. For now, I must go. I will see you tomorrow with your information about Friday night."

I didn't know what to say. Alice had said what she wanted to; she picked up her magazine, and just walked off. I learned nothing about her life with a man, but I did know more about what I should expect.

Alice was in the park waiting for me the very next day. I handed her an envelope containing my address and told her to be there at 6:30 PM. I was so excited; I could have pooped my pants. But, in some way I was nervous. I wanted to surprise Mom and Dad about my guest and not tell them who was coming, but at the same time I wanted to forewarn them not to unload a butt-load of questions on Alice. But, knowing Alice as well as I thought I did, I was sure Alice could handle herself just fine. And she did.

I was peering out the window from 6:15 on waiting impatiently for Alice. And, at 6:30 PM sharp, a taxi pulled up in front of our house and Alice got out. In her hands was one of the largest and most beautiful bouquets of flowers I had ever seen. Alice turned and waved the taxi to leave, so that meant that she was confident that she had arrived at the right place. When she arrived at the front door, I decided to stay in my room so that Alice could meet Mom and Dad first. As Mom opened the front door, I heard Alice say, "Hello, I am Alice, Maria's friend". Unfortunately I could not see the look on Mom's face, but I am sure it was a look of surprise.

Mom said, "Well, oh well, it is nice to meet you, Alice. Please come right in. Oh, and these flowers, they are so beautiful. Thank you so very much, Alice. I am sure Maria will be down here soon. I will call her. Maria, oh Maria, Alice is here".

I barreled down the stairs and gave Alice a big hug. The look on Mom's face was in the order of "what the hell?"

I will not share the entire dialogue with you, but I will say that the evening went well. Dad offered Alice some wine, but she declined. Alice loved the meal and the company. She so appropriately ducked every question about herself. Alice talked about me more than I was prepared for, and it was all good. We talked about school, dad's job, our family, and even Aunt Sarah, the pothead. Of course Mom and Dad did not refer to her as a pothead because they had no idea about that. If they ever did find out, I would have found myself right back in church school, the very last place I wanted to be. Alice and Mom talked about the garden, decorating, and everything else that they might have had mutual interest.

Finally, after dessert, Mom's famous cherry cobbler, I told everyone that I had a surprise. Dad asked "what is that, sweetheart?" I told everybody to just stay put. I got up sauntered into the family room, sat at the bench behind my upright piano, and played "Claire de Lune". I had practiced this for hours on end when Mom and Dad were not around until I had it down perfect. And, the delivery went well. I got up, walked back into the dining room and everybody was just sitting there, stunned. I looked at Alice and a detected a tear running down her cheek. Alice politely excused herself and walked to the powder room. She came out five minutes later smiling.

"That was beautiful", said Alice. Mom and Dad just looked at me. Mom finally said "I had no idea". Dad said, "Me neither". "It'll get even better", I said. My heart was rich with pride, but more importantly, I had just delivered a gift to Alice, one that she never expected. It was also a statement to Mom and Dad that I had planned to stand behind my word. It was probably one of the greatest nights of my life.

Alice told us that she had asked the taxi to come by at 9:00 PM, so it was time for her to leave. We said our farewells and Alice left. After she was gone, not unexpectedly, Mom and Dad pummeled me with questions. "Who was she? How did we meet? What does she do?", and so on and so forth. I merely said that I had met her in the park and we had become friends. The mystery continued.

Life went on for me as usual. School didn't get any easier but I knew that kids were gravitating towards me. I had somehow made a difference and this was their way of letting me know. I was invited to lunch tables, after-school parties, sporting events, music shows, and other similar events. It felt good. What felt even better was that the inviters were kids from all different groups, some of which I didn't even knew were aware of who I was. School was becoming fun for me, and that, coupled with my music, made me a very happy girl.

The sad news was that I no longer saw Alice in the park. I never knew that our dinner invite would be the last time I ever saw her. I was heartbroken, but, at the same time, I understood. She was like a miracle that came out of nowhere and what a wonderful miracle indeed.

Well, the miracle eventually continued. We were sitting at the dinner table a few weeks after Alice had joined us. I'll never forget that night. Mom, Dad, and I had just sat down to eat. Mom said, "Oh, Maria dear, an envelope came for you today in the mail". I asked her who it was from. She told me that she didn't know as there was no return address and of course she would not open it. As curious as I was, I went to the living room to grab it. Returning to the dinner table, I opened it. Inside was Alice's *"Life Magazine"* with a smaller sealed envelope attached to it. Mom looked at the cover and said, "I wonder who sent that". I knew right away.

"It's an old one" said Mom, "and look, that's a picture of Gloria Weatherly on the cover". Under the photo of Gloria Weatherly was a caption that read, "Starlet again beset with tragedy". I took the magazine out of Mom's hands and quickly opened it to the story about Gloria Weatherly.

Alice was Gloria Weatherly. I couldn't believe my eyes. Mom and Dad couldn't believe it either. She was so so beautiful when she was young. Mom knew all about her. Gloria had won an Academy Award as "Best Actress" for the film, "The Treasure of Love". She was on top of the world. She was one of the great actresses of her time and was destined for continued stardom. But, almost exactly two months from the day she won the award, her husband, James Blanchard, was killed in a private airplane accident while on a business trip with a colleague. Gloria never recovered fully from the loss as this was her "knight in shining armor", the "match made in heaven". She always boasted publicly how much she loved James, and then, in a moment, he was gone. The *Life Magazine* article was about another tragedy in Gloria's life, the loss of her 17 year-old daughter to a rare form of leukemia. Mom knew that after this had happened, Gloria went into hiding and was rarely ever seen again. Her career was over, and if you asked her, so was life as she knew it.

This entire picture was amazing to me. I had been mentored by one of the great actresses of all time and didn't even know it. She had been to my house for dinner.

It was time to read what Alice (Gloria) had written. I slowly opened the envelope, pulled out the letter and began to read.

To my dearest Maria,

The mystery is now gone and you now know who I am. When I came here, I never knew that I would meet someone like you. I must start by apologizing for the secrecy, but I am sure you will understand why I did not let you in on my story. It is a depressing tale and you must go through life upbeat. I struggle every single day to stay positive in a world that came crashing down on me many years ago. Some events, of which you are now aware, changed my life forever. Meeting you, Maria, added so much for me, I can't even begin to tell you. You reassured me that I could still be loved, even by a stranger, a little 12-year old girl no less. And Maria, I fell in love with you as well. Yes, little girl, I love you, and always will.

We will no longer be in touch but I know that my wishes about your successes in life will come true. You are so very unique, and you aren't even aware of it. Just stand behind the principles you believe in, treat others with the dignity that they would expect, and you will be treated accordingly.

I am not sure what I would do differently if I had another chance to start over. I thought that I was on the right track, but fate had other answers for me. But, I did learn from what I lived, and what I loved, and that's why I wanted to share those things with you.

> *Maria, you have won a place in my heart forever. Be the person you want to be and always fight for your rights and for your loved ones.*
>
> *With all my love,*
> *Gloria*

Now, it is thirty years later, and I still have Gloria's letter. I cry my eyes out every time I read it. Mom called me after Gloria passed away several years ago. She had seen it in a newspaper story, and it was a very brief obituary. Mom sent me a copy of it, and I still have that. Had I written her obituary, I would have said that "while Gloria suffered through some personal life-changing tragedies, she had made a huge impact on one little girl's life."

My life has been wonderful. It took me a while to find my "knight in shining armor", but I did and I have been married for 20 happy years. He is the best of the best. I have two beautiful young daughters and of course their names are Alice and Gloria. I went on to become a Psychotherapist, and have counseled young adults for several years now. My music interests are varied, but broad. I still play the piano daily and have learned the flute, the guitar, and also sing on occasion. Music has been an important part of my life. I have countless friends and have been blessed by their presence in my life. But, I know deep inside that I'll never ever have a better friend than I had in Alice.

THE END

ON THE TRACKS

A NOVELLA

BY

Stuart R Schwartz

Timothy

The first summer after high school graduation can never be easy, especially if one has no idea what the future may bring. There were options, but I chose to procrastinate, much to the dismay of my stepdad, Ernie. I often lie awake in my room pondering why Mom may have married this creature. Have you ever known anyone to be unhappy all the time? Maybe his boss at the Post Office treated him with disdain. I don't know. Is that what people do? Do they take their work troubles home with them, then cast misery on their families? Well, I did not consider Ernie family. We had a mutual tolerance, but the lifespan of mine was running out of time.

It was mid-July, and as I continued to evaluate my options without a job or a plan, I sat and ate a muffin. That was my breakfast, along with a cold glass of milk. Ernie was the first to enter the kitchen that morning. No "hello Tim", just "Hey!, didn't I tell you not to fuck with the temperature dial in the fridge?" "I like my milk cold, Ernie". "Well, punk, you aren't the one paying the electric bills around here. Get a fucking job rather than to sit on your arse all day". "I will work, Ernie, I need time to decide what I want to do". "Well, time is up punk, start working or you're out, O.U.T., out!" "I don't like to be called a "punk", Ernie and who are you to tell me what to do?" Maybe I should have retracted that last quip, but it was out, lying right there on the table ready for him to just pick it up and run with it. But, just at that moment, Mom entered the room. A save, and a good one.

Mom tried not to look at me. Was she also upset with me? Why is she turning her face from me? I stood up to confront her and that is when I saw it. A good-sized shiner had emerged right below her left eye. Her top lip was swollen, and a flash of dried blood sat above her upper lip. There was a bruise just below her cheekbone. This was no painted-on high school mascot; it was the residual effects of a beating. "Mom, what in hell happened?" "Oh, Timmy, don't worry, I had a little accident with the car last night, but it will be fine". At least she called me by my real name, and this was no car accident. I looked Ernie straight into his eyes, but I wasn't talking to him. I was talking to Mother as I stared him down. "What KIND of accident, Mom?" "Why are you looking at me, punk?" "Mom, I want to know what happened." "She told you kid, isn't that enough?"

Mom had taken good care of Dad until the day he died. She was kind and tolerant. Even when Dad knew that smoking cigarettes and anything else he could fit in his mouth would someday lead to a shortened end, Mom was right by his side. Dad appreciated Mom, loved her. He loved the crap out of her. And, she loved him back. But, this guy? What in the hell was she thinking? Did she have a momentary lapse of reason? But, there she stood, at the kitchen counter, bruised from a beating, with the look of shame in her eyes. Did she really believe that this came as a result of something that SHE did wrong? What is the psychology behind taking a beating? She is standing at the kitchen counter slicing bread. For a flashing moment, my mind drifted to the ugly sport of bullfighting where the matador reaches for his muleta to bring finality to the event. I hated the thought that this happens, and I have always believed it to be cruel. But, for this flashing moment, I wanted Mom to seize this "sword" and drive it into the back of my stepfather. Of course, it did not happen.

"Why are you looking at me, Punk?"

"No reason."

"What, what? You thinking I beat her or something?"

"You said it, Ernie, not me."

"Why, I should take you out back and give YOU a beating just for what you are thinking."

"Go ahead you lowly piece of shit. Beat me too. Have at it!"

Ernie's face flared up a deep red, as deep a red as a newly painted barn. He stood up and appeared to be approaching me. Mom immediately jumped in. "That's enough, you two. It's OK Timmy, he didn't beat me." Then the tears came in droves. I immediately headed for Mom and gave her a huge hug.

"Leave her alone, punk, she'll be just fine".

"This is my Mother you asshole, and if you come near me or her, you will regret it for the remainder of your life, which, if there is a God, will be shortened post-haste."

Ernie had heard enough. He grabbed the chair and came after me. Mom jumped between us and was immediately tossed to the floor. The only thought going through my mind at that moment was to get the hell out of there before he caught me. Who knows how badly he would have beaten me??!! But, I wasn't going to stick around to find out. So, I ran. I ran fast. I'm a good athlete. Ernie is a turd-load. He was determined and as his adrenalin kicked in, he screamed. "I'll catch you, you faggot, and when I do, you will suffer. Suffer, punk!! Suffer!!" "You won't catch me, you ass-dragon". I ran and I was not inclined to stop until I knew I was safe from this beast. It was ten blocks from home before I turned around to see if he was still in pursuit. He was not. I just prayed that Mom was safe from him after this altercation. Something had to be done.

I waited an hour and found my way over to the Post Office. I wanted to just be sure Ernie's truck was there before I headed back home. It was there. But, I wasn't quite sure that I wanted to be in the same house again knowing that he also resided there. Mom's and my temple became his temple. The Kingdom of Ernie. Ernie, the wife-beating brute, King of the Fuck-offs." I found my way over to my friend Mary's house. I needed to go someplace that was safe from this creep. Ernie didn't know about my friendship with Mary, but he knew of my other friends. I knew Mary would be home as she too was uncertain about her next move. She opened the door to see a perspiring, ragged Tim, recognizable, but yet harried. "What's going on, Timmy?"

"Mary, I need for you to do me a favor".

"Come in, Timmy". Mary was dressed in tight jeans with holes appropriately placed throughout, as if it was by design, and I am sure it was. She wore a T-shirt that said "Rutgers University" on it. I remember her telling me that it is where her Dad went to school. Though Mary and I never had any type of relationship greater than good friends, she liked to tease me. It didn't stop on that particular day either as she swayed her bottom from left to right and back again as she led me to the family room. We sat on opposite sides of the sofa. "What's up?"

"Mary, would you call my Mom? Ask her to drive over here. The sooner, the better".

"What's going on, Timmy?"

"I can't go home right now Mary. I got into it with Ernie this morning."

"You two have been at odds for a while."

"Ever since he moved in."

Mary rose and picked up the phone. She waited for an answer. I eyeballed her natural curls. Finally, "Oh, Hi, Mrs. Stevens, this is Mary, Timmy's friend."

"Timmy is not home now, Mary".

"I know, Mrs. Stevens. He is here with me."

"Is he OK?"

"Yes, yes, he is fine. But he wants you to come over here and speak with him. He wanted me to call for some reason, but he is okay".

"I can't leave the house now, Mary. Please put Timmy on the phone".

Mary didn't have to say anything. She simply nodded her head and with a swish of her beautiful golden satin locks, she summoned me over to the phone. I obliged.

"Hey, Mom."

"Timmy, I don't want anyone to see me with these bruises. I don't want anyone to get the wrong idea."

"Wrong idea Mom? Maybe the public should know what is going on. The police, Mom, the police."

"No, no, Timmy. The repercussions would be very bad. I will take care of this. Don't you worry." Look, I will meet you at Green Brook Park in 20 minutes. I'll park by the fountain. We can talk then."

"Okay Mom, I'll be there."

"Wait, Tim, can you make it an hour? I have something important I need to do first." Don't worry, it is OK."

"Sure Mom, I'll stay here at Mary's for a little while. I don't feel safe anywhere else."

Mom showed up exactly an hour later. The bruise on her face had already turned the color of a faded rose and her lip was blue. When she looked at me, the look in her eyes reflected more than a bruise. They were full of emotion, perhaps a combination of fright, sadness, and perhaps some element of disdain. Having placed myself in the front seat, I leaned over and gave her a hug. She immediately burst into tears. I felt the emotion welling up inside of me and my eyes began to water. I felt a sting and perhaps knew that I would not be seeing Mom for quite some time. That bastard! Why?

"Timmy, I'll be fine. But, for a short time, it might not be wise for you to return home. I have no idea why he acts this way, especially towards you. I know you will find this hard to believe, but there are times when he can be a loving, caring man. I think that is why I stay. Deep inside, he is troubled. He wasn't like this when I married him. Something inside must have "snapped; I just don't know. I am finding that I cannot control what is going on. I recently suggested that he get some help. He jumped on me for that and told me that I was the one who needed help. I can forgive him for what he did most recently but, as you know, I cannot allow this to go on. I am so afraid of going to the police, Timmy. It would put his job in jeopardy, he might take it out on me, and you have always been in his sights as a potential scapegoat."

"Mom, Mom. I am scared as hell for you. I can take care of myself, but you have to live in the same house as that creep. Yes, you are right. I do find it hard to believe that he can be caring. He is a vicious animal, Mom. He is a wolf in a man's disguise, but he never impressed me as being a man. Look what the hell he did to you. And, you take this? Real men don't do this to women. If you are scared, then get out."

"Maybe eventually I will, but for now, I must stay. Timmy, this will be hard, but for your own safety and peace of mind, I want you to go to Ohio and stay with my sister, your Aunt Evelyn, for a while. I will call her, and she will be fine with that. In the back seat is your duffle bag. There are enough things in there to get you through the next few months. I will take you to the bus station now. There is a bus that heads to Cincinnati and it leaves in about an hour. And, Timmy, I am giving you this envelope. In it is two thousand dollars. I have been stashing a little bit each week from the money that Ernie gives me for groceries.

Please use it. Don't allow Aunt Evelyn to pay for everything. And, don't worry, I have more money hidden away."

"Mom, don't call Aunt Evelyn. If we are going to do this, I don't want anyone, especially that turdball, to know where I am. If he asks, tell him I ran away from home. Don't send me anything. In the few hours I have left here, I will go back to Mary's. I will ask her to be the source of communication between us. Mary is dependable, mature beyond her years, and she is my best friend. I know we are only teenagers, Mom, but Mary and I love one another. And, no, it's not THAT kind of love. It is just a mutual admiration that has developed over the years. She can be trusted Mom and "postal pop" knows nothing of her. So, Mary will call Aunt Evelyn and I'll have her call you when I arrive there. There's one more thing Mom. I do not think it would be wise for the communication between you and Mary to be by phone, email, or any other traceable means. I will tell her to meet you at a specific time each week, perhaps in the "Big King Supermarket" parking lot. That would be safe. You can meet her when the prick is at work."

"Timmy, go now. This is very hard for me. I love you, son, and I am so sorry that all of this has happened. I know that you will make good decisions going forward. You've got a good head on your shoulders."

I opened the door and quickly looked back. Mom was not looking at me but it was quite evident that the tears were rolling out of her eyes. "Mom, I love you too, and don't worry, I will be just fine. Don't forget Mom, whatever happens, I will be fine. And you must strive for that too."

Mary understood clearly what I wanted from her. What a great friend! She took me to the bus station and I bought a ticket to Cincinnati. The envelope with the cash had Aunt Evelyn's address and phone number on it, so I knew where I needed to go. I hadn't seen Aunt Evelyn in a few years, so I hoped that she would remember me. I just remember that she had a nice husband and I couldn't even remember his name. I also remember two little kids, a boy and a girl, and I didn't remember their names either. The bus left and I had two seats to myself. I guessed that Cincinnati wasn't the most popular of destinations. The bus did make stops along the way, so perhaps more folks would get on. It didn't matter; I had my music, and the opportunity to see a new landscape, a little bit more of America.

I knew a little about praying. Dad didn't go to church, and Mom went sporadically. I would go to Catholic Mass sometimes with my friends on Sunday morning so that we could get a quick getaway after church to head to the New Jersey shore. I didn't understand what was going on in the mass, but eventually, I did learn how to pray. So, as the big Greyhound bus bumped, turned, and rolled through the Pennsylvania countryside, I quietly recited "Oh Heavenly Father". The prayers were short, but frequent. They usually involved Mom and my quest for guidance. Let's just see if He is listening, and if so, if I had enough credibility to have Him act on my prayers. I was careful to pray only for "needs", not for "wants". I was taught that "wants" related more to materialistic desires and "needs" were what kept us alive and well. I "needed" Mom to be happy and healthy.

Sleep didn't come easy on the bus. My mind raced through scenario after scenario and touched on every imaginable subject as it churned including Mom, the beast, Mary, my future, and the notion of living with Aunt Evelyn in her roost. But, eventually, fatigue reared its welcome head and off I went into bus-dreamland. I still had two seats to myself, so I tried to do the one-across-two deal, but it wasn't going to work. It might have worked 4 years earlier, but somehow, I blossomed into a three-seat-across rider. I didn't awaken until the bus pulled off the road in Youngstown, Ohio. Nothing I saw out the window impressed me, but the bus needed fuel, the driver needed to change hands with another driver, and it was a good time for people to use the rest room, including me. The bus driver made an announcement that we would be 20 minutes at the Youngstown Bus Station, so if we needed rest rooms, etc., we were welcome to have at it. Alongside the bus station was a small strip mall. Still half asleep, I staggered over to the strip mall as I had spotted a convenience store. I sorely needed a Coke.

The Coke went down in the most refreshing manner I could remember. There must be something about riding in a bus that prefaces an appreciation for the finer things in life, things as simple as an ice-cold Coke, and perhaps a bag of chips. The strip mall included about six stores including a nail salon with a bunch of Asians working in it, a laundry, and of all things, a sport and bait shop. My curiosity overcame me, so I popped into the sport shop. Live bait ... hmmmm ... there must be a lake or river nearby. Halfway to the back, there was a large section of camping equipment. An attendant, seemingly the only other employed person in the store besides the front desk clerk, was back there helping a customer. They were wrapping up their conversation and the clerk asked if he could help me. I asked him why they sold bait, that I hadn't seen any water anywhere around. I, of course, didn't tell him that I was out cold until the bus stopped. He could tell that I was not a local and explained that the Mahoning River was close by and in parts of it, there was some great fishing.

"And what about all of the camping gear?"

"Well son, there are campgrounds around, but a lot of folks like to walk up and down parts of the river and look for good spots to fish. The fish bite early in the morning, so they camp out and wait for the rooster to crow."

Flash! Bam! Wow! In a mere instant, my adrenalin began to pump. In a nano-second, I had made the decision that Aunt Evelyn would not be seeing her nephew Timothy Beckett quite yet.

"Sir, I'm on that bus over there, and I will not be continuing. If I run over there and get my duffel bag, will you wait for me so that I can purchase some gear? You can look at my duffel and see what size I will need. You can start picking out some things including a tent and sleeping bag."

"Sure, son. Are you certain that is what you want to do?"

"I have never been more certain."

By the time I returned to the store, the clerk had pulled out a tent, sleeping bag, collapsible fishing pole, fishing lures, and a large backpack.

"This should be enough to get you started, but we will have to see if you can fit all of your things into the backpack. You may need something larger. I am also going to provide you with a convenient tool. It attaches to the backpack and will serve as a shovel, a hammer for the tent pole, and other handy-dandy uses".

"Where's the river?"

"I will also give you a map, son. In fact, I pass one of the small tributaries on the way home. If you can stand by for 45 minutes or so, I'll give you a lift down there. Have you ever camped before?"

I laughed. "I was a Cub Scout. We camped, but I do not remember much. I think I can start a fire though."

The store clerk laughed out loud. "Well, don't go burning our pretty countryside out of existence."

"I'll be careful."

I went out to the bus and told the driver that I would not be continuing. He looked at me and did not say a word. Perhaps I had matured to the point where I looked halfway responsible. Plus, I know there was a glimmer in my eye. Glimmers evoke happiness. He could see that I was beyond thrilled to extricate myself from the box on wheels. And, if he knew what I was up to, he might have been a tad envious. While I waited for the store clerk, I looked around the store a bit more carefully. I could feel the rush. I knew that I had to call Mary. I'm sure Mom left enough credit in my cellular to make the calls, so off I went. There was a strong signal, well yah, a Bus Station … Duh. I called Mary.

"Where are you, Timmy?"

"Mary, I can't say, but I hopped off the bus. You will have to tell Mom and she will ask you to call Aunt Evelyn. Listen Mary, and listen carefully. I will be just fine. I know this. Everyone must trust me, but there is something I have to do, and I know how I am going to do it. There is no danger. Please say you believe me."

"Of course I believe you and I believe IN you, Timmy. Why can't you tell me?"

"Mary, I just cannot. But, let's just say that I am on a "Huckleberry Finnesque" adventure. I never even had dreams of doing something like this. But, when it hit me, I knew. Mary, besides Mom, I love you more than anyone in the world. You have been my soulmate from early on and it will never change. I am telling you this because I want you to know that I would never do anything to hurt Mom, you, and of course myself."

"I know you, Timmy. I will do as you say, but promise me you will update me."

"The only reason I can imagine being out of touch for a while is if my cellular runs out of charge or credits. But, don't' worry ... it is all cool. Bye for now, Mary."

The clerk finished what he was doing and walked over to me. "Ready, son?" "Yes, sir." "The name's Ted." "I'm Timothy." "Ok Timothy, let's get your adventure on the road."

We rode for about 6 miles and Ted pulled off onto a dirt road. The road extended for about another half mile and that is when Ted pulled off to the side and stopped the truck.

"The river is about 200 yards to the right, Tim. May I call you Tim?" "Yes, sir." "Ted." "Yes, Ted." Well, walk down there and start heading south. There's a compass attached to the handy-dandy tool you purchased. Walk about a mile and set up camp there. Don't wait until it gets dark, because you've got a lot of figurin'out to do. Once you're set up, get an early sleep and you'll be up early enough to catch a fish or two."

"Thanks, Ted."

"Oh, and one more thing, Tim. Don't get scared. Fright will tarnish your plans. If you need food, or anything, follow your instincts. Always head west on your compass, and listen very carefully for sounds. You know; cars, trucks, people. Got it?"

"I got it, Ted. Thanks so very much and have a nice evening."

"You bet, Tim."

The river was calm. Little ripples playfully spoiled the calm and here and there a frog, fish, turtle, or other water being would cause a slight stir. It was very quiet out there and I needed to get a move on. I'm not sure why but I didn't feel totally uncomfortable with the area where Ted dropped me off. I guess it was because Ted considered it habitable. I wanted to be where nobody else might show up. I stayed on the west banks of the river tributary as it would have been a mess trying to get across. After walking for about a mile, I could tell that dusk was not too far off, so I began my search for my campsite, my temporary home away from home. To the right, there was a small clearing at the base of an aged oak tree. When I reached the tree, civilization slapped me right across the face as there was a heart carved on the tree with initials in it. The tree had grown considerably since the initials were placed there. But that would not deter me; here is where my campsite would be located.

Unpacking my new gear was less complicated than I expected. The most pleasant of surprises came when I found a wrapped brown paper package in the middle of it all. Upon opening it, I realized right away that there is goodness in this world. Ted had added an assortment of canned provisions for me. And, of course, one of my handy-dandy tool accessories was a can opener. Life could not be any better than this. I wondered if Huck Finn had a can opener. Admittedly, the can of sardines did confuse me at first. Was this food? Or bait? But, my good senses told me that if a fish could eat it, well then, so could I. Not counting the fish that I was planning to catch, I had enough food to get me through a few days. The water bottle, attached to the back pack was full, but I would ration it. I was sure there were other sources.

My first night away came quickly and though I had slept on the bus, I was tired and quite frankly, I could not wait to try out my new living quarters. And I'll be damned if it wasn't wonderfully comfortable. The thought of living like this provided my first erection since I saw Debra Plante bending over in class, intentionally revealing her prematurely developed massive breasts, which in my young mind created a dalliance. The arousal was short-lived when I pondered the thought of other creatures also living in my new surroundings. With a little luck, all of these creatures would be smaller than me. But sleep came quickly. And so did dawn.

My breakfast consisted of a nutritional fiber-something-or-other bar that Ted had included in the package. There were a bunch of them. Tasty? No! But I am sure it provided some healthy balance to what I was prepared to consume in the wilds of Ohio. The only weapon I had was a fishing pole and the small carving knife which was also attached to the handy-dandy tool. Hats off to the guy or gal who invented this contraption. My guess is that the person had never set foot in the wild, and it was probably made in China. Do people camp out like this in China? I don't think so. Let's face it, there is no place out here to plug in a rice cooker. The thought was not meant to be at all culturally racist, but I have read that rice is their principle means of subsistence. And, would you really like to know why these thoughts have come to mind? Well, I don't really know.

The fishing pole was assembled quite easily. Two pieces plugged into one another with a spinning reel. I picked out a lure that might look tempting to a fish. It was a baby frog made of rubber with a hook in it. This is what fools fish? What a pity! I could probably dig up some worms with my shovel, but why bother when all I had to do was strap a rubber frog to the end of my line. Down to the water I went, turning constantly so that I would not forget where my livelihood was stationed. The first few casts generated nothing. I tried again but reeled the froggie in a lot slower than before. Again nothing. After the fifth cast, I almost quit. I gave it one more try, and HOLY SMOKEY!, a fish hit the frog. I wasn't sure what to do, so I reeled it in quickly and found nothing on the end of the line. But, I knew that "Mr. Fish" was after my frog, so I cast out once again in the same direction. Sure enough, I felt a little tug at the end of the line in the very same spot as before. A slight jerk of the rod, and WHAMMO!, I had me a fish. And, a beauty of a fish it was. I reeled it in and recognized almost immediately how unhappy this fish was to find out that it had been tricked. The fish didn't scream or make any sounds, but I thought I had detected a "you bastard!" as I was pulling it in. The fish was a trout. Unable to gauge the weight of it, I could tell that anything greater than 10 inches long was a "keeper", which is exactly what I did. I wrapped a towel around my catch and plunged the carving knife into its head. I must say that I found this maneuver somewhat discomforting, but when I realized that Native Americans, the real founders of our regional inhabitancy, subsisted that way, all guilt disappeared.

The summer temperatures were warm enough at night that I did not need to build a fire. I was not much of a fan of sushi, so I had to figure out a way to cook my catch. My handy-dandy tool did not include a microwave, so the challenge was upon me. I gathered a bunch of rocks, large and small and made a make-shift oven, campfire style. Twigs and some larger scraps of wood would become my fuel. I washed some smaller rocks to sit on top of the pile. Those would become the cooking pedestal for my fish. It all worked out exactly as planned and my trout became the tastiest "homemade" morsel that had ever reached my palate. I was full, happy, proud, and felt completely liberated from civilization as I had known it. I was Daniel Freaking Boone.

I did not move for two more days. I was worried that Mary and Mom would become concerned but there was no cellular signal out in the wilds of Ohio, and I didn't want to run the battery down. There was no sign of animal life around me other than a few squirrels and birds. This was perfectly fine with me. I would have enjoyed some company. I drank some river water, but not before boiling it on my stone cooktop. Survival seems to include some natural instincts. It reminds me of a movie I once saw, but I cannot remember the name of it. I could get used to it.

After the two days at my little post, my pioneering spirit awakened in me, so off I went down the river heading south per my compass. I must have walked for 6 hours and I knew that I was still miles away from anything urban or suburban. No sounds to speak of. The closest reminder of the life that I once knew was the exhaust trails from jets in the sky. On that third day, or was it the fourth?, uh oh, I was losing track of time. Clouds rolled in and I realized I was in for a soaking. It was time to seek shelter. With one full episode of tent assemblage behind me, the task became easy, and my home was up and ready for habitancy in no time. Is this how Gypsys lived? Am I a gypsy? A nomad? A pioneer? What will my legacy become? My grandchildren will be proud to share the tales of Grandpa Timothy, American explorer extraordinaire.

The tent was set up just in time before the rains came. This wasn't your ordinary New Jersey afternoon shower. This was a torrential downpour. My first inclination was to protect all of my "stuff" from getting drenched. Some of it would survive a soaking, others of which would not. It must have rained for 6 hours, heavily, with no let up. I could see that small pools of water were creeping into my home, so I took measures to stop it along the way. Finally, the wind calmed, the rains stopped, and early evening greeted me with a ray of sunshine and a cool, crisp summer air. I found it to be extremely refreshing. I slept very well that night and I awakened to a strong desire to continue my "journey with no end". What would today bring? A new unknown adventure is the most exhilarating experience one could ever imagine.

Having packed and my burden attached to all my sides, my journey continued. A few miles down the riverbank, I began to hear a muffled rumble. What could be causing this unfamiliar commotion? I needed to know, so I headed in the direction of the sounds. I didn't have to walk more than 500 yards to find, in the middle of this Ohio wilderness, a railroad track. The rumbling grew louder and before I could digest what I was about to witness, the train was upon me. It was a freight train. I stood there in awe as it came closer and suddenly, the train engineer engaged the loudest train whistle I had ever heard. I had to believe he was whistling at me and as the locomotive was almost beside me, I could barely see its' engineer looking my way with a smile and a wave. Perhaps it was as exciting for him to see this pioneer out in the wilderness as it was for me to see him. I smiled and waved and chalked this little experience up to another new and exciting interlude in the life of Timothy Beckett.

As I watched the massive line of freight cars roll by, it seemed that it began to move slower and slower. What was happening here? Suddenly the train was at a full stop. Was there something blocking the tracks ahead? Maybe a damsel in distress tied across the tracks? AC/DC's "Thunderstruck" suddenly came to mind. Then speaking of minds, my mind was telling me that the "Big Kahuna" in the locomotive was inviting me to hop on. The thought was a combination of a dream and a desire so, feeling that I had nothing to lose, I walked down the tracks alongside this behemoth until I found a freight car that seemed vacant. It didn't take me long to toss all of my belongings inside and pull myself aboard. This was better than the movies. I even wondered if this was somehow being filmed. A vagabond kid roaming about to discover himself. Certainly not a new story line for a film, but it was MY film, and I was going to star in it whether anyone cared or not.

The box car in which I was now the sole inhabitant was empty, save a few wood pallets piled up in the corner. It smelled of fruit, maybe oranges, and the tangy aroma was far better than I could have imagined for these surroundings. I hadn't bathed in a few days, the river having been my wash tub. So, with the fresh fruit aroma, I was able to stand myself for a while longer. The locomotive idled for another twenty minutes, and once again, we were rolling. There was nothing exotic about this train; no circus animals, no toxic chemicals that I knew of, just "stuff" that needed to be moved around. My compass told me that we were heading south, an area of the country that I had never explored. My heart raced with excitement. I ate some of my provisions, drank some water, clipped on my ear buds, and enjoyed the ride. My car must have been one of the newer models as it was short of bumps and bruises and the ride was remarkably smooth for something that rolled along steel tracks.

Eventually I slept. I was jarred awake a few times during the night and eventually the hint of sun shone through the open door to the car. We were once again out in the country. It was evident that the ride took us through a valley as I saw mountains on the eastern horizon. The splendor of these mammoth hills rivaled nothing I had ever seen before. They were beautiful and I couldn't imagine anything that I had ever seen matching the grandeur and magnificence of these hills, not even Debra Plante's breasts. We began to slow down, and I then realized that we were pulling into a habitable city. The exhilaration of being somewhere new was refreshing. I didn't want to disembark in the middle of a city, so I stuck with it for a while. Two hours later, we were once again rolling to a stop. I looked out and saw fields of pine and pure nature, nothing more. I knew that this is where I had to be. I tossed my gear out of the car and jumped down to the tracks. There was not much around but there were signs that I was not the first human to set foot in these parts. Footpaths were revealed in the woods, possibly worn through by hikers. A soda pop can littered the side of one path, and to me this was a huge breach of nature. Damn the person who did this! Virgin explorers like me are appalled by such sights. I equated it with a poorly placed tattoo on a beautiful virgin. But, opinions are opinions so who am I to judge? A Greater Power will punish this desecrator of nature. I decided to stay close to the tracks just in case I was mentally and physically in need of another ride. I imagined a life on the tracks. The life of a hobo. How bad could that life be, especially if they know of no other? Are material matters of any interest to a hobo? And did the hobo care one way or another? My guess was …"Nope!" Had anyone ever done a study of the life span of a hobo? And do hobos care how long they live? I had a lot of research to do if and when I ever decided to return to society as I once knew it. I had to laugh to myself for being even remotely introspective about what I was now doing. Perhaps introspection of one's life should be limited only to monthly updates. Four days in a kid's life are merely a "blip".

It was probably time to reach out for Mary. I flipped on my cellular phone. The good news was that there was still a lot of charge in the battery. You have correctly guessed the bad news. No signal. The very good news about that phenomenon was that I was nowhere near a cellular tower. Thus, my life as an explorer continued without interruption. I was in a far-off remote land, living in nature, still far enough away from the civilized world to be comfortable in my own shoes. Far enough away from the Ernies of the world to know that I could not be harmed. I had garnered a sense of power I had never experienced before. But now, it was time to set up my minicamp. The railroad tracks were to be my escape route if I needed it.

It was night, I was restless, and sleep did not come as easily as before. Something was a-brewing. There was an air of discomfort. Oh, please Lord, I am not equipped for surprises. My soul picked up the distant rumble of an oncoming train before my senses deciphered what was going on. The sound was coming from the south. I emerged from my tent-temple, stood up on the solid turf before me, and awaited the arrival of the train. It must have been moving very slowly as the distance away never seemed to shorten. Eventually it was closer, and yes, it moved at a snail's pace. And then, just like my ride that picked me up in Ohio, it stopped just in front of me as if I had summonsed it to do so. I looked up and down the tracks and saw no sign of life. I didn't even get a glimpse of the rail engineer in the locomotive. This was the mystery train, the monumental night intruder, the delivery wagon for the world's wants and needs.

This huge bearer of freight just stood still. Maybe trains sleep too. I looked to the right and a figure was approaching, walking along the tracks. It was heading my way. I froze. Who? What? It came closer and I recognized the slow pace of a male. As he came closer, a shiver traveled up my spine. The feeling was not that of fear, but that of intrusion. This was Tim's world now. As he drew closer, I noticed he was wearing an orange jump suit. Was this a trainman's uniform? Perhaps he was just checking the train, the rails, or merely taking a walk in the night. Suddenly, he was directly before me. I stood frozen in my own tracks.

He spoke first. "Hello, young fellow". I saw numbers on his jumpsuit. It was a prison uniform. Oh shit! Is this a convict? Am I doomed? Is this the part in the movie where the kid shits his pants?

"Hello sir ... out for an evening stroll?"

"I just came off of that train. It wasn't too comfortable for me."

He seemed less threatening than when he first approached. "Uhm, is that a prison uniform?"

"It is. I just got out."

"Did you "get" out, or did you get "out"?"

"Well, let's just say that the system slipped, so I took advantage."

"My name is Tim, what's yours?" He paused, and finally he said, "John, John Smith." My first thought was oh sure. Yah, that's his name. But I didn't question him. I needed this man to be my friend, not my foe. "Listen John, if you would like, I have extra clothes, plenty of them in my backpack. I am not sure if you will fit in them, but you are welcome to try."

"I'll make it fit. Got a shovel?"

"Yah, I do."

"Good, we're going to bury the clown outfit. What are you doing out here, kid?"

"I ran away from home."

"Heard that story before. Tell me more."

"Not now unless I have to. I have a little extra food. Are you hungry, John?"

"I am hungry, but I am easy to please."

"John, where are we?"

"Well kid, the prison was in Georgia. I have been on the train for about six hours. I am guessing we are somewhere in East Tennessee. About four miles south of here, we passed through a town. It wasn't large, but I did see the sign at the station. I did not catch the name of the town, but I did see "Tennessee" following it."

"Let me get you something to eat. It won't be gourmet. You can stay with me. It will be tight in the tent, but we can manage."

"Why are you helping me, kid? I am an escaped convict."

"I guess I am helping you because I am a wee bit concerned about self-preservation and it isn't a bad idea to have a new friend on the road, or should I say "on the tracks"?"

It was not easy getting used to two occupants in the small tent. It might have made for a humorous episode of "Strange Bedfellows" if there was such a reality show. But fatigue reigns supreme and when you're tired, the circumstances become adaptable. The morning air was cool and crisp for a summer day. We decided that one of us would head to the town that John spoke of and pick up some provisions. He wanted food and cigarettes. I wanted food and a Coke, or two.

"John, if I go, how do I know that you and all of my belongings will still be here when I return? You are a criminal and I am just a kid."

"Thanks for the reminder, kid. Look, I have no reason to bolt. I am far from home, and I have no money. So, I will stay, but it might be a good idea to move away from the tracks, perhaps to a place where they cannot track me down."

We decided to pick up camp and move closer to town. We decided that we would stay away from the tracks, but far enough from any highway so as not to be noticed. We were about one-half mile away from the town that John had seen from the train. We set up camp in the woods, purposely away from any potential unexpected visitors. I figured out a way to find our location on my way back from town without getting lost. The compass was also my guide.

The trip to town was fine. I didn't have to actually get into town as there was a convenience store on the outskirts. I passed a sign that said, "Welcome to Greeneville, Tennessee, Population 15,250". That seemed quite sizeable to me. I purchased enough goodies to cover us for a week, but not too much that I could not carry it for the half mile back to our site.

This was also a good time to call Mary. The signal on my phone was strong. I stepped behind the convenience store and pressed her name on my phone. She answered immediately.

"Timmy, where in the HELL are you? Everybody is worried sick about you!"

"Everybody?"

"Well, just your Mom and me".

"Mary, I am fine. In fact, I am great. I am in Tennessee."

"WHAT??!! Tennessee??!!"

"Calm down, quiet yourself. I am OK. I have everything I need, and I am safe. Just let Mom know that all is well, and I will try to report in more often. The first several days on the road were tough and I couldn't communicate, but all is great. That's all you need to know. How is Mom?"

"Other than worried sick about you, she seems to be OK."

"Look, Mary, meet Mom, tell her I am fine. I'll be in touch. And tell her I love her, OK?"

"I will."

"And I love you too, Mary."

"Thanks, Timmy, you know I love you too, crazy boy."

"Bye, Mary."

John was happy to see me, especially when he saw the carton of

Marlboros. That little gift set me back some, but I needed this guy as my friend, not my foe.

We ate some of our provisions and drank Cokes. John smoked. We decided not to build a fire so as not to draw attention to ourselves. We sat outside the tent. It was eerily quiet, with only the chirping of crickets and the sound of cars and trucks in the distance. I decided to break the silence.

"John, may I ask what you were in for?"

"Well kid, if you really must know, it was murder."

Jezzuz! I am dining with a murderer. "Oh really? How long have you been in there?"

"Twelve years."

"And, how long before you would get out?"

"If I behaved myself, I would have been up for parole in twelve more years. This little episode might make it a bit longer."

"Why? Do you plan on getting caught?"

"Actually no. I am planning on turning myself back in."

"Uhmmmmm, then why did you leave in the first place?"

"They made it too convenient for me to leave. I needed a break. Can we change the subject?"

"Sure, was just curious … but when would you turn yourself in?"

"When I am ready."

We stayed there for two long days before we decided to pick up and move closer to the Smokey Mountains. Hardly a word was exchanged between us for those two days, but my curiosity about this man was ramped up considerably. The trek up to the mountain was laborious, but we made it. Once we got closer, I spotted a sign for a campsite. There were some images under the sign indicating that there was electricity, water, and toilet facilities. The light bulb in my brain transitioned from dim to bright in a few seconds.

"John, I think we should go to the campsite. And before you protest, here's why. If someone comes across us in the wilderness, they may think we are running or hiding from something. If we go to a campsite, we can stay to ourselves. If anyone asks, we are uncle and nephew out for a camping trip together."

"Pretty good logic, kid. But, if we do that, I will keep a low profile."

We walked up to the campsite. There was a tiny office and a young woman was inside. I told her I needed a site for a few days. She told me that it would be five dollars per night and that would include all the basic services. If I wanted anything extra, it would have been more. Pioneers don't need menus of services, so I declined. I paid for a full week in advance as required and we found a spot away from the central area.

When I checked in, I noticed a beer dispensing machine and a Coke machine near the office. I had the suspicion that John would like some beer, so I shoved ten bucks in the machine and scored five beers. I bought some Cokes also. John welcomed the stash. We sat outside the tent and made small talk about nothing in particular. I even had a beer and it went down magnificently. It was time to sleep, so we crawled into our little tent.

John had been relatively quiet all night, so I was surprised to hear him utter the words …"My name isn't John."

"Could have fooled me."

"And I am not a murderer."

"That's comforting."

"You have been a good travel companion to me, kid, and you have helped me even when you were totally unaware of who and what I am. So, I thought it would be good for you to know a little bit more about me. Perhaps you will be more comfortable after what I tell you. And to be honest, I would like to know more about you and where you are and want to be in life."

"That's fine. You first?"

"Tim, my name is George Pernetti. I am from Brooklyn, New York and was sentenced to thirty years for murder. My escape was a fluke. After all those years of being a "model prisoner", the door was open for me, so I ran through it. I plan to go back. You see, they used to allow me to go out in the yard and do my workouts whenever the cell doors were open. The warden, the guards, and everyone associated with the prison seemed to like me. Well, they were doing some work on the barbed wire mesh you see atop the tall fences and walls. There really is no way out. There was a gate through which the workers would come and go. They were checked each time they passed through the gate. Well, someone left the gate slightly ajar; they didn't know I was in the yard, so I walked through it. It likely took another hour or so before they figured out that I was gone. Someone must have taken a lot of flak about it."

"What about the murder charge?"

"Well, that story is a little longer. Ready to hear it, or are you sleepy?"

"I'm a bit sleepy from the beer as I rarely drink it, but now I am eager to know."

"Okay then. Growing up in Brooklyn, I had a best friend who will go unnamed. He has become a cop in New York City. At an early age, we both had an obsession for guns. He always wanted to be a cop, so guns were important to him. I liked them solely for the sport, but I wanted to be a businessman like the ones I would see walking up and down Wall Street when I went into the City. When we were a little older, we would go to a Police Athletic League sponsored gun range where we would shoot pistols. I became an expert at shooting and even competed. My friend was also quite good, but he could never outshoot me. Getting bored?"

"No, no, please continue."

"I am going to make a long story short here. We both did very well in school. I was from a tightly knit Italian family and school was important, especially if we had immigrant parents, which I did. I ended up getting a scholarship to Columbia University and majored in Economics. I did well there, and I loved learning. On weekends, I went to a technical school and took classes in electrical engineering. To the surprise of everyone, I became degreed in both. I earned my Bachelors in Economics at Columbia and a Certificate as a Master Electrician from the Tech School. Well, I had a bunch of Italian friends who all seemed to be from good families. Their parents seemed to have money and I was both proud and envious of them. One day, just before I started my hunt for a job, one of the kids, again to go unnamed, approached me and asked if I could do a wiring job for them. I was excited to have some work. I was told that I was to wire someone's car so that when they started it up, a siren would go off and a loud bang would come out of the back from a "noise box". They wanted to scare the crap out of the driver. This was to be a "lesson" to the driver for fooling around with someone else's girlfriend. It made perfect sense to me. You probably already figured out that the "noise box" was a bomb and there was no siren. Tim, the blast was heard for a mile in every direction, and they could barely find enough pieces of this guy to have a proper funeral. I was crushed. What had I done? I was used for the purpose of a vendetta. Two days later, another fellow who I only knew peripherally handed me an envelope. In it was fifteen thousand dollars in cash and a note "for your troubles".

"Holy shit, George!!"

"Yeah, so I took the money as I wouldn't have known to whom it should be returned. The "bad guys", we will call them that, learned of my electrical expertise and my handiwork with a gun. It didn't take long to figure out that I could make a shit-load of money at an early age. It is what impressed me. Material "stuff" was my food, my passion, my desire. I was young, and stupid. So, I did another "job", and then another, and another, and before I knew it, I was known as a "professional hit man". It was my avocation. I was the best until I got caught. The other guys set it all up. All I had to do was pull the trigger. So, at the ripe young age of twenty-four, I already had two hundred fifty thousand dollars stashed away."

"Crap, George, how did you get caught?"

"It was my mistake kid. Since I had so much money, I went out and bought a pair of "special edition" Nike shoes. I was always careful about leaving tracks, footprints, fingerprints, and all of the smart things a professional killer would do. I had a hit in Staten Island. It was a two-bit crook who had intruded on a large gang's territory. I walked up the driveway from behind some bushes when he pulled his car up. I was careful not to walk in the grass or dirt where the footprints could be found. Well, this guy saw me in his rear mirror before he pulled into the garage and immediately backed up as if to run me over. I ran like hell and left enough footprints all over that even an amateur Sherlock Holmes could find. But my job was not done, so like a fool, I headed back to his place. He was hiding behind the house and when he heard me panting from running, he came out firing. Fortunately, this guy could not hit the side of a barn if he was leaning on it. So, I fired back and only needed one shot to take him out. I left the scene, but my tracks were all over the place. I didn't even think about it, but since I was a suspect in other hits, they came after me and found my shoes. A perfect match."

"Was there a trial?"

"Oh yes. But I wouldn't give up the names of my employers. The judge knows how we work, so they let me off with just 30 years."

"Why are you going to turn yourself back in? You said you were going to go back."

"I need to serve my time and not be on the run. When I get out, I want to be clean and have a decent life with a job if anyone will hire me. It would be nice to have a family. I truly believe that the prison will know that they were partially to blame for my departure and if I continue to be a good inmate, I could gain parole before too long."

"Well, it all makes sense to me, George."

"What about you, kid?"

I told George my entire story that same night. Butt-snuff Ernie, Mom, my late Dad, Mary, my indecisions about life, leaving the bus, and everything he might have wanted to know. George seemed appalled when I told him about Ernie beating my mom.

"Tim, I am not sure I understand the part about your step-father beating your mom".

"I don't understand it either, and I suspected it was happening. I could hear her whimpering on several occasions. He is just a bully and probably the unhappiest person in the world. The bruises really upset me, and he was always taking things out on me too. I had to get out of there, George."

"I understand. What's your mom's name?"

"Wendy, Wendy Stevens. She took Ernie's last name, but I would not. Besides, he made no effort to adopt me, thank the Lord."

We chatted some more, and I slept well that night. I was glad that we really got to know one another, and I felt very comfortable knowing George.

The following night, a young couple walked past our tent as we sat outside of it drinking beer and munching on sandwiches. They stopped and said "hello'. Before answering, I looked over at George as if to ask if it was okay to speak with them. George nodded his head slightly as if to say, "sure, no problem". I acknowledged them. They were in their early twenties, and I guessed that they were boyfriend and girlfriend. The girl asked our names. I answered quickly.

"I am Tim and this is my Uncle John. We go camping together on occasion."

"Well, I am Claudette, and this is my twin brother Claude. We are from "over the hill" so to speak, from North Carolina, Charlotte."

My immediate thought is that some moron named their twins Claude and Claudette? No wonder some kids turn on their parents. They invited us to join them for some beer and chips, and much to my surprise George jumped in and said "fine". He must not have thought that these kids were any type of threat to him. The evening was quite fun. They were nice people and full of giggles. Claude likes to play campfire games, so he decided that we should each name our favorite movie and talk about the best scene. Claudette liked the final scene of "Breakfast at Tiffany's" when George Peppard delivers his guilt speech to Audrey Hepburn. I liked the scene in "Alien" when the creature crawls out of the victim's chest, Claude liked the scene in "Rocky" where Sylvester Stallone runs through the city and climbs the steps. And George surprised the crap out of me when he talked about a scene from "Goodfellas" where two of the gangsters kill off everyone in a robbery. I nearly shit, and Claude is yelling, "yeah, yeah, I remember that."

Over breakfast the following morning, George springs his plans to leave me and head back to New York for a while before he turns himself in. He wants to visit some of his family. I told him I understood. But, he had some words for me prior to his departure, words that I will never forget.

"Kid, I must go. It was through God's grace that I met you. You're a great kid, and I am sorry about what you went through. But, good things happen to good people. Your Dad is gone, and you really don't have anyone close to mentor you. But, if I may, I'd like to give you some advice."

I told George that I of course would welcome anything that he had to offer.

"Tim, you are quite young, barely out of high school. I learned from a major mistake. I succumbed to temptation. I made a ton of money because I wanted "stuff". I did some very bad things. I stole people's lives for money. I cannot turn this around. If I were to do it over again, it would be much different. My suggestion is that you get your ass into the military. Yes, the Armed Forces. Try to get into a branch where danger is not at your doorstep. It's only a few years of your life, but the beauty of it is that when you get out, the military pays for your college. Work your ass off in college and don't be deterred by nonsensical temptations. You know what they are, so I don't have to tell you. I wish I had the chances and challenges that lie ahead for you. And one last thing. Try to remember me so that perhaps our paths will cross one day."

"Of course, I can never forget you, George. If you are really leaving, would you do me a favor?"

"Sure, as long as I am able."

"I am going to that office up there and will get some paper and an envelope. I will write a brief letter to Mom before you leave. When you get to New York, will you drop it in the mail for me?"

"Sure will!"

"Thanks, George! And, though I know you haven't asked, I am giving you two hundred dollars for the bus ride back to New York." It would not be smart to get on a plane or train at this point, but the buses usually travel through the night, so you should be safe."

It almost appeared that George's eye welled up with a few tears, but he hastily concealed it from me. It would be hard to say goodbye, but it was inevitable.

"You are a special kid, Tim. Get the letter written and I will be leaving later today."

I handed George the money and the letter for Mom and watched him walk away towards the road. The tears rolled out of my eyes. In just a few short days, I came to admire this criminal, this victim, this inhumane pillar of humanity. George was exceptional. I would pray every night for him and mention him in the same prayers that I say for Mom. But, for now, it was time to get back to pioneering and move on with my life.

George

It was hard saying goodbye to the kid, but I knew it was time to move on. I just hoped that he would be fine going forward but he seemed quite tough and mature for his age. Fortunately, there was a bus from Greeneville, Tennessee to New York City. I had to change once in Washington, D.C. which did not make me too happy, but I would deal with it when the time came. The good news was that there were no questions asked and I had my ticket in hand.

The bus rambled along the Interstate at a fair enough speed, but, for my liking, it was not fast enough. I was eager to remove myself from this tin can with all its odors, its noises, and the overall feeling that I was trapped. I had committed a few phone numbers to memory while I was calling from prison, so I would reach out to my close friend Tommy while we stopped in D.C. I managed to sleep and hoped that I could finally replace these clothes that the kid gave me with something more suitable. But his generosity was surely appreciated.

We arrived in Washington, D.C. and were supposed to be there for forty-five minutes before we were shuttled off to another bus for the ride up Route 95 and the New Jersey Turnpike. I never liked those two highways, but I liked them now because they were the way back home, even if the stay was only temporary.

I called Tommy. Damn, will he be surprised. He answered with a "Yeah?" I am sure I awakened him. Softly speaking, I said "Tommy, its George".

"Holy Christ, George! I heard you split the can! Where in hell are you?"

"Quiet, Tommy! Look, I can't talk long, and I won't tell you where I am now, but I'm heading for the City and I need a few favors."

"Sure, sure, anything George".

"Look, Tommy, call my sister Patty. Tell her I need some things, but I cannot go there because the authorities will certainly case her place. She knows where I have some money. I need a business suit, a nice one and all the trimmings, Tommy. I'll need about thirty thousand in cash. Tell Patty I will return what I don't use. Rent me a car in your name, I'll reimburse you. Get me a "piece", but I have no plans to use it. I just want it for protection, that's all. I need some shirts and slacks. I am now about the same size as you, Tommy, so just buy something that will fit you. Get me a hotel room somewhere out in Long Island, or even on the New Jersey side, again in your name. I do not want to stay in the City. Are you following all this?"

"Yes, yes, I'm writing it all down."

"I also want you to run a tag identification and vehicle type for an Ernest Stevens in Coleville, New Jersey. He goes by "Ernie", but I am sure his name is likely Ernest. Oh, oh and one last thing. Remember my friend Rick, the cop?"

"Yes, I sure do."

"Good, get me his number, but do not call him. I'll do that."

"What??!! Why??"

"Not important, just do it".

"Ok, gotchya George. Great to hear from you and I am glad you are OK."

We arrived in the city about noon that same day. The bus ride had sucked, but I made it. I bought a ball cap with some of Tim's money that I had left over. It would shadow my face while I moved around. I again called Tommy.

"Tommy, it's me again, George."

"Look, George, I already have most of the things you asked for. Your sister Patty was in shock, needless to say. She wants to see you. The suit will be ready later today and I will pick it up with the other clothes in a few hours. The "piece" was the easiest thing to get ... ha ha ... and there's plenty of shells to go with it. It's a 9MM. I got a silencer for it, but those things are not that effective as you know. I have a room in my name at the Hilton is Secaucus, New Jersey. I'll be there at 5:00 PM. There is a bus from Manhattan for you to take. Do not get there before me. I will get the room and you can come in later. Wear a hat because those places have cameras all over the freaking place."

"Tommy, thanks! Take Patty with you. But, let her know that the visit must be short and sweet. I appreciate everything and will see you later. How will I know your room?"

"Meet me in the lobby at 5:15 PM, no earlier, no later. Patty will wait in the room. I will have the rental car which I will leave for you. Patty and I will take the bus back to the City."

It was so good to see my old pal Tommy, and my sister Patty. All went well as I had planned. Tommy took care of every detail including a beautiful room service spread. It was a good job by Hilton, so I am sure they must get some dignitaries staying there, excluding me of course. By 10:00 PM, I was exhausted. Tommy and Patty needed to get back to the city, so we said our farewells, and off they went. I slept like a baby and my room service breakfast hit the spot just as well as dinner had the night before.

I dressed in the Armani suit, fresh with a nice patterned blue and gold tie, French cuffs, cufflinks, and the entire shooting match. Please excuse the expression. I looked dandy, just like a Brooklyn lawyer. It was a far cry from my orange, prison-issued jump suit. Tommy had done a stellar job.

The ride out to Tim's hometown took about an hour. I had taken the address off of the envelope I was to mail to his mom. It was going to be my pleasure to hand-deliver it myself. As I pulled into town, I could tell that it must have been a nice place to have grown up. A sweet middle-class community with neatly trimmed lawns, freshly painted fences here and there, houses with wrap-around porches, and kids on scooters. I pulled up in front of 2990 Bricklee Street and saw the name "Stevens" on the mailbox. I parked out front and strolled up to the front porch. I rang the doorbell and knocked on the door simultaneously.

An attractive woman in her early 50's I was guessing answered the door.

"Yes, may I help you?"

"Yes, ma'am, my name is John Smith, and I am here to deliver a letter from your son, Tim." She looked skeptical and did not invite me in. On closer inspection, I noticed a bruise over her right eyebrow.

"How do you know Tim? Do you mind if I ask?"

"No, no, that's fine ma'am. I was recently on a business trip to Tennessee. I met a few young folks in a restaurant and we made small talk. One of them was Tim. When he heard I was from these parts, he asked if I would mail this letter to you when I returned. I figured that you were close enough that I would hand deliver it."

"May I see the letter?"

"Of course, Ms. Stevens, it is yours."

"Why yes, that's Tim's handwriting. Would you like to come in for a cup of coffee, Mr. Smith?'

"Sure, but I am unable to stay too long."

"Please sit down Mr. Smith and make yourself comfy. I'll get some coffee brewing."

I sat and waited as Tim's Mom made the coffee and brought it out with some muffins.

"This looks great, ma'am, so thanks."

"Oh, it is nothing. How did Tim look?'

"He looked fine and quite happy. I do not believe that you have any reason to be concerned. He is a good kid and will be fine."

"What type of business are you in that you were in Tennessee, Mr. Smith? I knew that Timmy was there through a mutual source."

"Oh, yes, well, uhmmm, I am in the pest control business. I head up sales and we are expanding to other States. I do not do any of the pest eliminations any longer myself, but we have technicians all over the east coast. I sort of graduated to the new position; you see."

"Yes, yes, I see."

"Ms. Stevens. I noticed that you have a bruise over your eye. Did you have some type of fall or something like that? Just curious."

"Oh, that … yes, something fell out of the freezer and when I went to pick it up off of the floor, I accidentally banged my head on the refrigerator door."

"I see. It looks like a nasty bruise. Forgive my question."

"It's quite alright. I am just so clumsy you see."

"Well, I must be going, and I am sure you are eager to read Tim's letter, so I'll be on my way."

"Thank you so much for stopping by, Mr. Smith. I so appreciate it, and I am sure Timmy does as well."

"It was my pleasure, Ms. Stevens."

I could tell that she was standing by the door watching me from the time I left the house until I entered the car. When I turned around, she was standing at the door waving. I nodded, smiled, started the ignition, and pulled away. I decided to drive around town and other neighborhoods until the time the post office closed its doors. At the end of the day, I drove to the back of the post office. I spotted Ernie's pickup truck almost immediately and parked beside it. I did not spot any security cameras. Though it was still daylight, I parked close enough to Ernie's truck that I could somewhat conceal myself. There were several other cars in the lot, so mine would not be too conspicuous. Someone had pulled out of the spot directly adjacent to Ernie's truck, so I was in luck.

Ten minutes passed when the puke bomb in all his glory finally emerged from behind the post office. I knew instantly that this was my guy. He made his way to his truck and saw me fiddling with the door to my rental car as he was unlocking and entering his truck. I nodded and smiled. He just looked at me emotionless. Just as he slid behind the wheel, I opened the passenger side of his truck and hopped in.

"Who the fuck are you and what the hell are you doing in my truck? Get the fuck out!"

"Oh hi, Ernie, I'm George, George Pernetti."

"Who are you and how the hell do you know my name? I said get the fuck out!"

"Ernie, Ernie, calm yourself down now. Look, just start up this beast and let's go for a short ride. And, Ernie, forget that I told you my name, OK? Deal? Why? Because I prefer that nobody knows that we are having this conversation. And the consequences for discussing this outside of our little forum here are not very good. Capish?"

"I am taking you nowhere, you piece of shit."

Though I hated to do it, I pulled out the 9mm and gave the old boy a whack across the right wrist.

"Son of a bitch!! OWWWW, you Mother Fucker!!"

"Now, now, Ernie. That is no way to treat a guest. Now, let's get on the road or that little bruise you just incurred will look like a pimple on an elephant's ass compared to what is coming next."

"You're not a guest, asshole! Get the fuck out before I call the police."

"Call the police, Ernie. I'll wait."

As Ernie reached for his cellular, the trusty 9MM came down on his other wrist.

"Bastard!!!!!!!"

"Ernie, start driving and drive straight and slow. If you make any mistakes, the pain will be insurmountable."

Ernie smartened up quickly and off we went. It was a half mile down the road when I spotted a sign for a State Park.

"Pull into the park, Ernie. Keep driving until I tell you to stop."

Not surprisingly, Ernie obeyed this time. We rode through a section of the park and near the back there was a marshy area. There were no other cars here, so I assumed it would be a good place for us to have a chat. I told Ernie to pull over and he obliged.

"Now Ernie, get out of the truck and walk over to that bench next to the tree. No tricks, Ernie. I hate tricks."

I asked Ernie to sit down on the bench. I rested myself on the other end.

"I think that we should have a nice friendly chat, Ernie, What do YOU think?"

"Why should I talk to you at all? What do you want from me?"

"Say Ernie, ever ride on a bus for a long distance? Let me tell you, it is very tiring, and it makes me quite irritated. And, since I recently had to do that, I feel irritated right now."

"Yeah?, well I am sorry to hear that."

"Ernie, do you have any kids?"

"I have a useless step-son. The little lazy-ass ran away from home not too long ago."

"Hmmmm ... wonder why he did that?"

"He did that because I called him out for being a good-for-nothing."

"Oh, I see. Do you miss him?"

"Not really."

"Ernie, have you ever beaten your wife?"

"Of course not, you prick. Why are you asking me that?"

"Well Ernie, I get the impression that you are telling me a little fib right now."

"The answer is no, I do not beat my wife."

I had the 9MM aimed at his knee through my pants. Though I hated to ruin the beautiful Armani suit, I let a round fly right into his knee. The sound of the bone shattering disturbed me some, but not as much as his screams.

"Ernie, listen up. When you lie to me, bad things happen. Now no more screaming or I will stop the screaming in a manner that you will truly not enjoy. So, I will ask again, did you ever beat your wife?"

"I did ... owwwwww ..."

"Why Ernie? Why would you beat her?"

"She's lazy, you prick, she won't work. She saps my paltry paycheck and watches soap operas."

"Wow, Ernie. How unappreciative of her. So, who then raises the boy, washes your laundry, cleans your house, makes all the meals, goes shopping, minds the yard and garden, cleans the cars, makes the beds, and other various household chores?"

Ernie didn't answer that question. So, I posed another question.

"Okay, Ernie, you told me you beat her. How many times did you beat your wife, Ernie?"

"Once ... this pain is awful!!!!!"

"Uh oh, I think I detected another fib, Ernie."

"Once prick".

Bam!!!! The 9MM sounded off again and there went the other knee into pieces. Ernie screamed again even after I told him not to and dropped to the ground.

"Ernie, HOW MANY TIMES??" I was shouting now.

"I don't know."

Well, I had enough of this coward and though I had never intended to create another widow and had even made a vow to God that I would not, this one would be a blessing to many people, probably more people than we could have accounted for. And hopefully God would forgive me. So, the third discharge from my piece entered his right eye and struck his brain, silencing him immediately. I found my way into the woods before anyone could find him, and more importantly, find me. It was a long walk back to the post office. I had waited for sunset before I reclaimed my rental car from the parking lot. I soon headed back to the Hilton.

My suit was ruined, but it would soon be in the trash with my shoes and anything else that I had on that day. My days of carelessness were behind me. I slept well knowing that I have removed some stress from a few people's lives. I am sure there was going to be some related anxiety, but I could not worry about that. The creep needed to be eliminated.

The next morning, I called my childhood friend, Rick, the cop. He was off duty, so he was able to pick up my call on his cellular.

"George??! Jezzuzz!!! They told me down at the station that you "flew the coop". Of course, they wanted to know if I knew anything about it."

"Yes, Rick, the prison handed the escape to me on a silver platter."

"You really shouldn't be calling me, George. I don't want to be in the middle of this."

"I am calling you for a reason, Rick."

"Oh really, what would that be?"

"I am turning myself in and I want you to be the one to arrest me. I want you to tell the authorities that I had planned to turn myself in, but that I wanted you to be the conduit."

"I can do that, George. When are you coming down?"

"Rick, I need a few days with my family and a few friends. I will stay out of trouble, Rick, don't worry. I want to remain clean."

"Okay, George. Then, we didn't have this conversation. Come to the station Monday morning. I will take care of it from there."

"I will see you there on Monday, old pal."

"Good luck, George."

I was at the police station first thing Monday morning and Rick was there awaiting my arrival. He had to act surprised to see me, but I was okay with that. It did not take long to process me and return me to the authorities. They decided to send me to Pennsylvania where I could be watched more closely. After a meeting of prison officials and some of the local prosecutors who put me there in the first place, it was decided that this incident would not affect my record. The Georgia prison took some of the blame, admonished me for "walking out", and cited the fact that I had been on great behavior my entire time there, a "model prisoner".

Timothy

I stayed at the campsite for four more days after George had left. Claude and Claudette from North Carolina became my temporary soul mates if there is such a thing. We hiked, exchanged stories, played games, drank beer, and talked about the cultures from which we came. This trip was an annual event for them, and they were in their third year.

They didn't wander too far from home but picked nice spots to visit. Their Dad was the Dean of a small college in North Carolina, so they encouraged me to apply there.

After four days passed, I packed up and decided to head back to town. Claude and Claudette had a car parked outside of the campgrounds, so they gave me a lift into Greeneville. I had to decide my next move in a hurry, but I knew that either home or Aunt Evelyn's would not be one of them. I reached town and sat on a bench in front of a laundromat. It was time to call Mary once again.

Mary must keep her phone close by as once again she picked up on the first ring.

"Timmy!!"

"Hi, Mary."

"Timmy, I have some awful news for you."

My heart stopped when I heard this, and I wondered immediately if Mom was okay. What had the son-of-a-bitch done to her now?

"Timmy, Ernie is dead."

"What??!!" I couldn't believe my ears. He must have had a coronary or something. "What happened, Mary?"

"He was shot, Timmy. They found him in the State Park, a bullet in what was left of his brain."

"Holy shit! Do they know who did it?"

"No, in fact the Police Chief had a press conference and said that they could not identify a motive. Nothing was missing from Ernie. His money, wristwatch, everything was intact. There were no fingerprints or anything on the scene. And Timmy, get this, he was shot in each knee first, both of which were totally destroyed, and his wrists were banged up too."

Nobody had any earthly idea who might have done this except me.

"Is Mom okay, Mary?"

"I spoke to her just this morning, Timmy. Yes, she's quite upset, but she will be fine. She told me about something very unusual that happened though."

"What was that, Mary?"

"Some businessman stopped by her house. He said he met you while on a business trip. You had given him a letter to mail to your mom, but he told her he was in the area, so he stopped by."

"Did he say his name?"

"Yah, I think he told her that he was Mr. Smith and that he was in the extermination business."

I wanted to laugh out loud, but I restrained myself. I was so thrilled that George more than kept up his end of the bargain. I just responded by saying, "Oh yeah, that guy."

"Timmy, they are going to have a service for Ernie. You had better head back home."

"I might head back home, Mary, but it won't be to attend a service for that pile of horse shit."

"Whatever, Timmy, but everybody wants to see you, especially Mom and me."

"I'll see what I can do, Mary. I've got to go. I'll catch up with you soon."

My thinking cap firmly in place, it was time to make decisions. I loved my freedom and my life on the tracks. What would happen if I were to leave it now? But George may have been right. I should get on with it. Maybe I should enter the military, see the world.

I asked a passerby where the train station was, and I headed in that direction. I was not inclined to ride in a bus again and there was plenty of money left for the trip. The train for New Jersey would leave me in Newark, and I could take a bus home from there. I purchased the ticket and off I went. Trains have a different sound and feel than a bus. Clickety clack, clickety clack became my theme song and my ability to add lyrics to those enchanting sounds made the trip back home a lot easier.

When Mom opened the door, she beamed with delight. My adventure was behind me for the time being anyway, so it was nice to see her again. It is hard for me to describe the kind of love that I felt for her, but my love was amplified by knowing what she had gone through. Mom didn't flinch when I told her that I would not be attending Ernie's service. She simply nodded as if to say "I understand". On the day of the service, Mary came by the house and sat with me. We did not speak of Ernie but she wanted to know about my little adventure. I told her a lot about it, but left out some of the most important parts, as you surely can understand.

Mom returned from the service with a few friends. Mary and I had gathered some food and beverages for the attendees which were quite sparse. There was not a lot of love lost on this disgrace to mankind.

In the next few days, some unexpected and unusual events took place. The day after the service, a flower delivery truck pulled up in front of the house. The driver emerged with the largest bouquet of flowers I had ever seen. The colors were bright and vivid. There was a thick, tightly sealed envelope attached to it with the words "For Wendy Stevens" on the front of the envelope. Mom opened it and found, much to her surprise, five thousand dollars in cash and a note that said, "Here's a little something to defray the costs of the funeral and to help you get on with your life". It was signed "A friend". Mom was shocked to say the least. Ernie had a small life insurance policy and some social security benefits heading her way, so I was comfortable that she would get on just fine.

The very next day, Mom and I were sitting on the front porch when a drab, blue four-door sedan pulled up in front of the house. There was some type of seal on the door. A man in uniform climbed out with a briefcase. Mom and I just sat looking curiously at this uniformed gentleman as he approached the front porch.

"Hello, I am Sergeant Jeffrey Rawlins, United States Air Force. I am looking for Timothy Beckett."

"I am Timothy Beckett."

He shook my hand. "Nice to meet you, son."

"The pleasure is mine."

"Mr. Beckett, we received an anonymous call suggesting that you are interested in joining the United States Air Force."

"Well, I don't know what to say." Mom turned her head and simply stared at me.

"Well, Mr. Beckett, the caller had nothing but high praise for you and asked that we offer you the opportunity to serve with us. He asked that we provide you with the most favorable program available. So, we will have a look at your high school grades and issue you some tests to take. If all goes well, you will go into our service/study program. If, after two years, you have succeeded in achieving the results we seek, you will become a candidate for the US Air Force Academy in Colorado Springs. How does this all sound to you?'

"Where do I sign?" My new life was about to begin.

Just when I thought that all of the craziness of the past several weeks was behind me, the very next day, Bill Phelan from our local Ford dealer pulled up in a shiny new red Ford Mustang convertible. What the hell? Behind him was one of the dealership yard cars with a driver waiting for Bill. Bill did not say a word. He merely climbed out of the Mustang, waved, turned around and rode off with the other driver. I stood up and glared at this prize sitting in our driveway. I slowly approached the car and just gawked. On the front driver's seat was an envelope. Inside were a set of keys and a note: "You will need a way to get around for the next few years. Don't get on buses. They can become very irritating. Good luck and serve your country well."

Young men can cry if they want, and I did plenty of that. I was on my way and for once in my life; my direction became vividly apparent to me.

Ten years later

"Good Sunday afternoon, ladies and gentlemen. From the flight deck, this is First Officer Timothy Beckett. I would like to take this opportunity to welcome all of you to Trans Global Airlines Flight 495 enroute to San Diego. We are now cruising at 36,000 feet and we should experience a smooth flight all the way into our destination. We do ask, however, that you keep your seat

belt fastened when you are not moving about the cabin. Also, as most of you know, today is Mother's Day, so we wish all of you Mothers on board a very happy and healthy Mother's Day. If I might add, we have a very special guest on board today. My Mother is with us today and you will know who she is as one of our crew members is delivering flowers to her at this very moment. She is accompanied by my beautiful wife Mary, also celebrating this special day, and our four-year old son, Georgie. Thank you for flying with us, and always remember folks ... it is okay to be a dreamer ... they often come true."

THE END

LAMBIE

A NOVELLA

BY

Stuart R Schwartz

All of this nonsense started a long time ago. I was four years old. I really do not remember much about the beginnings of my relationship with Lambie, so my mom has helped remind me. It's a story that needs to be told. It's a story that includes so many emotional factors including, but not limited to intrigue, mystery, love, surprise, laughing, crying, and heartbreak. Now, as I transition to my young adult years, I can share the details of my relationship with Lambie.

At the age of four, I really did not have many friends with whom to cavort. Yes, there were cousins, but either I did not like them, or they lived quite far away. I couldn't sleep very well and was known to toss and turn through the night. Mom was at wits end not knowing how to satisfy my interpersonal needs, the absence of interludes with others, and my erratic sleep patterns. So, Mom made the trek into town and stopped at Barney's toy store. By the way, there was no relationship between this toy store and the despicable dinosaur. Mom had hardly entered the store when she spotted Lambie. He had no name when she saw him but was appropriately named upon her return home. Lambie was a white stuffed lamb as you might have guessed. He bore a red ribbon around his neck. He was small and not "built to scale" as they say. So, perhaps Lambie was six inches wide, six inches tall, and six inches long. He was equipped with all the appendages that one would expect to see on a lamb. No, there was no penis or testicles, but kids weren't supposed to see that on a stuffed animal anyway. There would have just been too many questions to answer.

Lambie went everywhere that I went. We did sleep together and for some strange reason, and much to my mom's delight, there was a calming effect on me, and I slept motionless throughout the night. Lambie was under the covers with me, and we slept face to face. Lambie did not snore or move at all during the night.

As the years passed, Lambie and I became somewhat dependent on one another. Wherever I went, he went, and vice versa. Car trips included Lambie at my side. He was my companion, my hero, my soulmate, my protector. He made me feel invincible. Nobody around me was going to mess with me because my little white lamb was there to protect me. And Lambie knew that I would be there for him anytime he needed me.

It wasn't until I was seven years old before I realized that Lambie could talk. Please bear with me as I am fully aware that it sounds incredulous, but it is true. It must have been ten o'clock PM and after a full day of running around the yard, playing on swings, bar-b-que, and other activities, I was totally exhausted. So, I crawled into bed and climbed under the covers. I was close to the middle of the small single bed and just nodding out when I heard, "move over". My eyes opened as wide as saucers, and I lifted my head hurriedly and looked around. Lambie was staring right at me. He looked me in the eye and said, "It's me, move over". How does one respond to a stuffed animal? It just was not possible. But, pretending to be aware of a talking lamb, I moved over. The next thing I knew was that he was right there at my side, all stretched out. I had officially lost my mind at the age of seven.

I decided not to tell Mom about the talking lamb as she would proceed to do one of three things; a) ignore me, b) take Lambie away from me, or c) make an appointment with a therapist. None of those options seemed suitable to me so I decided to keep this little episode to myself. Lambie wasn't about to compromise his relationship with me by starting a conversation with Mom, let alone anyone, so I simply let it go.

Everything was fine for a while until one morning when I headed downstairs for breakfast. I was preparing to go to school when I heard, "you're taking me with you". This didn't come in the form of a question. I was being told what I needed to do. So, in my sheepishly thin and quiet voice, I responded, "Taking you where?" "To school". "Nope". "Yup". Lambie seemed quite adamant, so I stuffed him in my book bag and negotiated the stairs towards the kitchen with book bag and its new occupant in tow. After breakfast, I wandered out to the school bus stop. It was a warm, slightly humid morning and I was uncomfortable in my wool pants and long-sleeved cotton shirt. I was alone at the bus stop.

"Get me out of here. It's hot. I cannot take it. I have wool on."

"You're not getting out. Everybody will laugh at you."

"People don't laugh at animals."

"The people you are talking about are kids. They laugh at other kids who carry around stuffed animals that talk".

"I won't talk".

"Still, boys carry baseball gloves, not stuffed lambs."

"I will shit in your book bag."

"What are you going to shit? Stuffing?"

"I will baaaa in the classroom. Explain that, silly Billy".

"Try it and you are history".

I felt that Lambie's proclamations were only a threat, and I would not let this creature get the upper hand on me. So, in the book bag he stayed. I did not hear a peep from him and made it through the day without incident. That very night, I went to bed at the normal time, about nine o'clock PM. Every time I was about to nod off, I heard, "baaaaaa". The freaking lamb had decided to not allow me to sleep.

"What is wrong with you?"

"Nothing."

"Then, what is all this baaaaing when I am trying to sleep?"

"I need you."

"Well, I need you too. I need you to shut the hell up."

"Are you going to let me out of the book bag?"

"Since you're not going to school with me again, I don't care where you are."

"Oh, I'm going."

"Oh, you're not."

"I am".

"What will you do if I don't take you?"

"Keep you awake … … forever."

"I will take you to the shelter. You weren't my idea in the first place."

The following silence was deafening. I felt bad. Here was a stuffed creature carefully stitched to make my life better and I was dissing him. I thought about how I should handle this and decided I would rise above any potential abuse from my school friends and adhere to Lambie's desires. It was obvious that Lambie needed me, and I wasn't showing my appreciation of his affection. Our lives were about to change. The following day after a night of "baaaaa", I advised Lambie that he could leave the book bag, but he must remain silent.

"Lambie, if you even mutter one word, back in the bag you go".

"I don't talk to strangers".

"That's good because there will be some abuse from kids".

Little did I know what kind of abuse I was in for. Never underestimate the rudeness of second graders when there is a reason to insult, bully, and chastise other kids. I wasn't aware of the psychology behind this type of behavior at the time, but I have some good ideas today why kids act and react the way they do. Manners aren't high on the list of dinner table topics when you are seven years old.

The bus ride to school the next morning was relatively uneventful. Lambie sat on my lap. He was immobile and did not murmur a word. He looked straight ahead and acted as any other stuffed animal might have acted given the opportunity. Was this some sort of game he was playing? Or was he just trying to behave to keep on my good side? All went well until class began. Miss Thomas walked up and down the aisles handing out an assignment. When she reached me, she spotted Lambie on my lap.

"Billy Buttons, what is that on your lap?"

"A stuffed animal?"

"Well, yes, I noticed that it is a stuffed animal Billy, but what is it doing on your lap?"

"Oh, uhmmm, well, I found it in the playground and I was just hoping that I can find the real owner."

"How about I put it up in the front of the class and perhaps the REAL owner will spot it."

"That sounds good, Miss Thomas."

As she reached for Lambie, I could hear him say "there is absolutely no way I am going anywhere other than right where I am sitting now." Miraculously, I think, Miss Thomas did not hear this outburst.

"Uhm, Miss Thomas, I think I decided to keep this thing here because I may know who it belongs to."

"THING??!!!, THING??!!"

"SHUT UP!!"

"What was that, Billy Buttons?"

"I wasn't talking to you, Miss Thomas."

"Then to whom were you talking, Billy?"

"To myself, I was talking to myself."

"Okay then, hold on to the bear and try not to allow it to become a distraction."

"BEAR??!! BEAR??!!"

"Shut up, I said."

"Billy Buttons?"

"Sorry, Miss Thomas, I must be hearing things."

That night it was time for a heart to heart with Lambie. This short-lived relationship was about to change, like it or not.

"Lambie, I will take you to school, but there are new rules."

"I hate rules."

"Well, you will like these or off to the shelter you go." I was wondering how long I could use the shelter as a deterrent, but I would try it until Lambie figured out I was "crying wolf".

"Oh no, not the shelter."

"Okay then, here's the rules: Rule number one: You will stay in the book bag, or you don't go to school. Rule number two: You do not speak at all, not to me, not to the teacher, not to anyone. Rule number three: If I get into any trouble whatsoever on your account, you are lamb history. Is this understood?"

Lambie sighed a soft baaaaaa, and merely whispered "yes". That was enough to make me happy.

The next day in school was going quite well until I realized that when I stuffed (excuse the expression) Lambie into my book bag, a portion of his head was sticking out of the cover flap. And how (you ask) did I discover this? Well, about five minutes into class, Mary Mildieu was sitting right behind me and let out with a soft "baaaaaa" of her own. Others looked around and before I knew it, there were a few more "baaaaaas". It caught on like wildfire and within seconds, the entire class was going "baaaaaa, baaaaaa, baaaaaa" as if we were in a herd of stray sheep. I looked down behind me and saw Lambie's head.

"Crap, crap, crap!" And of course, Miss Thomas jumped into the fray.

"Class, class!! What is going here?"

Her walk down my aisle seemed to last a lifetime. It appeared as if she was approaching in slow motion. I was scared. And I thought I actually heard an "oh shit" emerge from the book bag. She stopped at my desk and just stared at me. The class had quieted down.

"Billy Buttons, you will have to leave the bear at home from now on."

"Lamb."

"What?"

"Lamb, it's a lamb, Miss Thomas."

"Billy, I don't particularly care if it is a flying monkey. I want it out of here. Do you understand?"

"Yes, I understand."

I didn't want to hurt Lambie, but we needed to take some preventative measures. I could just picture myself going through life being haunted by my relationship with a stuffed lamb. Looking back, I can't imagine that a kid at the age of seven could think that far ahead, but just a few episodes convinced me that some action needed to be taken. So, the very same evening of the mass "baaaaaing" event, we had a talk.

"Lambie, you must think about what is happening to me because of you and what you want me to do. The kids will rip me apart."

"Why?"

"Why? Because second-grade boys do not carry stuffed animals around with them. They carry baseball gloves."

"What should I do then?"

"You should be a stay-at-home lamb. We can be best friends right here at home."

"I will miss you."

"Lambie, I am not going away anywhere. I will always come home to you."

"Okay, I will try it for a few days."

"Lambie, you have to do this forever until we die."

"That is not fair."

"I have homework now, Lambie. We will go to sleep soon and everything will be okay. I promise."

The next day in school was worse than I could have ever expected. Kids would walk past my desk and put their fingers at the top of my book bag and peer in. I would yell "hey!", but it only incited the kids to harass me more. Miss Thomas looked at me and raised one eyebrow as if to say "what is your little surprise today, Billy Buttons?" And the "baaaaa's" kept coming. I had finally had enough. I got up, walked out the door and headed to the principal's office. I was going to call home to have Mom pick me up. Miss Thomas would have nothing of this. "Where do you think you are going, Billy Buttons?"

"I am going home."

"No, you are not."

"I do not like the way everyone is treating me."

"Well, if you behave, nobody will treat you badly."

"I am always behaved. Goodbye."

I went to the principal's office on my own and walked right in, past the secretary, and right into Mr. Pokem's office. I was surprised when Mr. Pokem didn't admonish me for barging in like that.

"How may I help you, son?"

"Please call my mom. I am going home. I need a ride."

"What seems to be the problem, son?"

"My name is Billy and I am being taunted by the kids in the class. And Miss Thomas has not helped me."

"Why would they do that, Billy?"

"Please call my Mom, Mr. Pokem. The number is 383.555.2299."

"Well, you haven't answered my question, Billy."

"I don't know why they pick on me."

"There must be a reason."

"I have a friend with me in class and they don't like it."

"What type of a friend?"

"A lamb."

Mr. Totem made the monstrous mistake of giggling. This never ends. How could my life be ruined by a lamb? I got up without saying a word and headed for the door. I would walk home as it was not that far. Mom was waiting at the front door. It appears that someone from the school had called ahead and warned her of my departure.

"Billy, why did you leave the school?"

"Why, Mom? Because my life is ruined because of that stupid lamb."

"How could that be?"

"It could be because kids my age don't carry stuffed animals to school."

"Leave it home."

How could I explain that the damage had already been done and there was no turning it around? I agreed to go back to school the next day and subject myself to the abuse. Things began to return to normal, but I knew it would never be the same. There were the occasional "baaaaa's", a few "mooooo's" and even some "oinks". But I stood tall and let it pass. Lambie seemed okay with staying at home but refused to leave my side regardless of where I was, except for school. I sensed that he knew why he was banned.

Six years passed and I turned thirteen without any fanfare. Lambie was still a major part of my life. Everywhere I went, he tagged along. I resigned myself to the fact that he was a great friend to me and that I would take some abuse. School was still out for him, but one morning he managed to find his way into my book bag. After all those years, Lambie became sick and tired of being at home all day with nothing to see, hear, or do. I carried a backpack while I attended Junior High School and Lambie sneaked into the side pocket. I should have noticed the bulge when I left home, but since I always leave just moments before the school bus arrives, I did not notice that he had squirmed his way in there.

By the time I had reached eighth grade, I still did not have any interest in girls. But that didn't mean that they had no interest in me. Janet Hamett was sending me notes regularly and discreetly bumped into me when she walked past me. I was supposed to take a hint, but I let it pass. She was very cute, but I almost felt like I would be betraying Lambie if I became too close to her or any other girl for that matter. Lord only knows how he would have punished me. So, I lived in lamb guilt through those Junior High School years. The day Lambie sneaked into my backpack was the same day that Janet Hamett had decided that I was going to be her object of affection. Worse things could happen, and they did. You see, Janet stopped by my desk and did the usual bump on the arm. But this time she stopped. I looked up and saw luscious blue eyes peering down into mine and the cutest smile framed by sweet dimples. This was the first time ever in my life that I felt a stir in my loins. Oh God! I was in love. Janet did not say a word. So, I mustered up all of the bravery that lied within and started the conversation.

"Hi, Janet."

"Billy, do you have a girlfriend?"

"Wow, no. But why do you ask?"

"Because, Billy, I have wanted to be your girlfriend for the longest time."

I couldn't say anything. I was stunned. And, just when I least expected, Lambie pushed his little lamb head out the top of the backpack pocket. I saw it happen before Janet did, and without thinking said, "Get back in there!"

With a twist of her beautiful head, Janet responds, "Get back in where, Billy?"

"I wasn't talking to you, Janet."

"Then who" … … … and just as she was getting ready to spill the rest of her sentence, she spots Lambie.

"Oh how cute, Billy. Is it yours?"

"Uhmmmm, no. No, no. I found it in the front of the school and picked it up."

"LIAR!"

"Shut up, Lambie!" It finally dawned on me that I was the only one who could hear Lambie. But everyone could hear me. I didn't get it, but I would deal with it.

Janet looked at Lambie, looked back at me, then back at Lambie.

"Billy, who do you think might own it?"

"Oh, I don't know."

"May I have it, Billy? It looks so cute."

I knew that would not work at all.

"I was thinking about giving it to my mom if I did not find the owner. She likes stuffed animals."

"That is so sweet, Billy."

"Yah, I try to help Mom out with fun things now and then."

"YOU ARE A LIAR".

"Quiet, Lambie!"

"Billy, are you talking to the lamb?"

"No Janet, but I need to get back to what I was doing."

"Billy, do you want to meet me Saturday at my house? My parents will be home, but we can play games in my playroom. They love when I have company."

"Sure, Janet, I will be there mid-morning."

"Great! See you then, Billy."

Saturday arrived and I prepared to head over to Janet's house. Love was in the air. Lambie was sitting up in the bed watching my every move. I glanced over at him on occasion, but not a word was exchanged between us. Just as I was about to grab the doorknob, Lambie spoke up loud and clear.

"You're taking me."

"Ohhhhhh nooooooo, I am NOT taking you."

"You always take me."

"I USED to always take you."

"You have to take me."

"I don't have to do anything."

"If you don't take me, I will create chaos in your life."

"You already have, Lambie. But, I must go now. I don't want to be late."

"You told her "Mid-morning", you have a window of opportunity."

"Lambie, you are not going and that is final!"

Just then I heard something that I never dreamed could come from that little stuffed creature. It was the loudest lamb scream I have ever heard. It was a shriek. Thank God nobody else could hear him but me.

"Lambie, okay, here's the deal. I will take you, but I will discreetly park you somewhere in or around the front of their house. I will go inside without you. Maybe I can prop you up so that you can watch me through the window. Deal?"

"Okay, but I think we can work on a strategy."

"What kind of a strategy is that, Lambie?"

"Okay, you get her to fall in love with you, and then once she knows how wonderful you are, there would be nothing that would stand between us."

"Us?"

"Well, you and I are forever until we die."

I thought about this statement and realized that some greater power had made choices for me. Off we went to the Hamett residence. When I arrived, I quickly perused the house and decided to place Lambie in a bush by a window at the side of the house.

"Why here?"

"Because I do not want to take the chance that you will be seen."

"Okay, but don't be long."

Janet opened the door within seconds after I rang the doorbell. She must have been standing at the door waiting. I was escorted into the kitchen where both her mom and dad were sitting drinking coffee. Both acknowledged that they had heard a lot about me, but I could not imagine what they knew. I hardly even knew Janet. Mrs. Hamett offered us apple juice and freshly baked cookies. Of course, we obliged. After exchanging some pleasantries, we retreated to the playroom. Mr. Hamett winked and said, "now you kids behave in there."

"Oh Daddy, don't be silly."

Oh sure! As soon as we passed through the bedroom door, Janet grabbed my hand and led me over to the TV. She asked me to sit as she tuned into one of her favorite teenage morning shows. I sat there staring at the TV as Janet returned and sat down beside me. She placed her hand in mine, looked into my eyes, smiled and turned her attention to the TV.

When I placed Lambie outside a window, I never imagined that it was the window to the playroom. We sat for fifteen minutes without exchanging a word. Then, out of the blue, Janet leaned over and kissed my cheek. What happened next was appalling. I heard a tapping, scratching at the window. It sounded like a tree or bush branch, and it didn't stop immediately. Janet and I looked over at the window simultaneously. I saw Lambie's head drop out of sight, but Janet evidently did not.

"Did you hear that, Billy?"

"Yeah, it sounds like the wind may have picked up and moved a branch against the window."

"Oh, maybe, but I never heard that before."

"I'm sure that's what it was, Janet."

"Oh, okay."

Janet got up to change the station. I immediately looked toward the window and saw Lambie's face pressed against it staring straight at me. I immediately shook my head "no". He returned the horizontal head shake. I gave him the "angry squint" and he slowly lowered his head back below the windowsill. This wasn't working. I immediately set my sights on developing a new strategy. At noon, Mrs. Hamett yelled through the door. "Hey, would you kids like some lunch?" It was hard for Janet to respond quickly as her lips were on mine and her tongue was finding its way down to my tonsils. The muffled "jusshh a minutz Mooom" didn't quite register with Mrs. Hamett. "Can you kids hear me over the TV?" Janet quickly released me from her lip lock to say, "in a minute Mom, we are on the way."

Lambie was frantically scraping away at the window throughout all of this and any element of a libido lift that might have occurred within me was quickly vanquished. Janet decided to return her lips to the upright and locked position and as she moved in for this particular wrestling hold, she peered at the window.

"Christ, Oh my God!"

"What, Janet, what?"

"I must be hallucinating."

"Drugs are bad for teenagers."

"No, I mean, I mean that I thought I saw your stuffed lamb's head lowering itself down from a position where it might have been looking through the window."

I REALLY had to think quickly here. "Oh, that, ha!, ha!, ha!. Yeah, I brought it along as a good luck charm and it seems to be working, wink, wink."

"Billy, the head moved."

"Oh yeah, maybe I stuck it on one of the branches that is moving from the wind."

"There's no wind, Billy."

"Can't explain it then."

"Do you take this thing everywhere you go?"

"Oh, no, no, no, just when I have a whim."

"Well, can you please not have a whim the next time we have a date?"

"Does that mean that we are going to have another date?"

"Of course, it is, Billy Buttons."

"Okay, I'll leave him behind."

After lunch at the Hamett's, I retrieved Lambie and went home. It was time for a drastic measure. Mom greeted me at the door. By the way, in case you were wondering, I only mention Mom. There is no dad. He left when I was two. Neither Mom nor I ever heard from him again. Mom doesn't even think that she is divorced, and he might even be dead. So, there is no dad.

"Did you have fun, Billy?"

"Yes Mom, it was fun. Mom, do we still have that pet crate from when "Nick, the Cat" was alive?

"Yes, in the garage."

"I am going to borrow it, okay?"

"For what?"

"A science project."

The decision to stick Lambie in the pet crate was a tough one. It was a brash, difficult maneuver that would create some bad blood. I set up the crate in a comfortable corner of my room. In it I placed a fluffy towel, some small toys that remained from my childhood, and a bowl of water. I have absolutely no clue why I put water in there, but my mind set was to simulate the existence of a real life pet. I picked up Lambie and brought him to the crate. The protests commenced even before I opened the door.

"You're not putting me in there."

"I am."

"Why? I have been well behaved."

"You have not."

"I meet a girl and you tried to trash the deal before I even went into it."

"I was just curious."

"In you go."

The whining and baaaaing and other strange sounds lasted for a few hours. I couldn't stand to hear it and just stayed in the kitchen. It was likely as torturesome for me as it was for Lambie. When it was time to go to bed, I allowed Lambie to leave the crate and climb into the bed with me. Nobody spoke. Though it was Sunday, I decided to stick Lambie back into the crate just so he could get used to it while I was at school. That didn't go well either. At the end of the day when it was time to prepare for bed, I checked the crate. It had been eerily quiet in my room all day, and I thought it was an indication that things were going well. But when I finally checked on him, he was flat on his back with all four legs pointing upwards. He did not move, nor did he make a sound. I called out for him, and even reached in and shook him. Nothing. I had killed Lambie. Grown boys usually don't cry, but I wailed. I had committed murder and there was no legitimate excuse for it. My options were limited. I could either hide him in a closet or perhaps cremate him in the fireplace. A backyard burial was also an option. Mom wouldn't understand options two and three, so in the closet he went. I put him on the top shelf in the same position I found him ... all fours pointing upwards.

Monday in school was a tough day. I could not concentrate. I had inadvertently killed my best friend. Between classes, Janet approached me.

"You look solemn today, Billy Buttons."

"I had a tough weekend."

"Even the part at my house?"

"That was the highlight."

"What went wrong?"

"I shouldn't share this with you Janet, but I killed Lambie."

"Excuse me?"

"You know, the lamb that looked through the window?"

"Your good luck charm?"

"Yup."

"What do you mean you killed him?"

"I locked him in a crate because he misbehaved and he died in there." After I dropped this little bit of news on her, I felt that it was the right thing to do. I mean anyone who would kiss me the way she did, driving her tongue onto my esophagus, would understand anything that I shared, but noooooo.

"Billy, you're surely joking."

"Nope, he's dead."

"No, I don't mean that. You're joking if you want me to believe that the lamb ever existed in the first place."

How was I to explain this? I sure as hell couldn't tell the girl that might someday be my wife, the girl who exchanged saliva with me that I had a talking, living lamb in the form of a stuffed animal. But honesty is the best policy so I let it fly.

"Janet, he did live. He has been my best friend and companion for eight years. He was my soul mate, and now he is gone."

"Billy, do you know what a shrink is?"

"No."

"Well, I suggest you find out. Then pay one a visit. I must go now."

That was the last time Janet would speak with me. I can't say I blame her. But I did what I thought was right. I had just hoped that she did not share this little tidbit of news with everyone else in the school.

The very same day that I was dumped by my one-date girlfriend, I strolled home slowly from school. I was a depressed young fellow, not even a teenager. Janet had broken my kissing virginity and dumped me, and my Lambie was dead. I was an official loser. I walked into the house, bypassed the kitchen and went to my bedroom. My first inclination was to go to the closet and look at the still, sorrowful figure that was once my Lambie. I opened the closet door, looked up, and only saw a bare shelf. I quickly turned and there he was in all his little lamb glory, sitting on my bed.

"I thought you were dead."

"Playing dead."

"You little prick!"

"I needed to get out of that crate. You were punishing me for no reason."

"I had a reason, but ya know what? I'm not going to discuss it."

"Have I been a burden on you?"

"You have, but let's try to make this work. Lambie, you are my best friend. You sleep beside me every night. When I am sick, you are there for me. Mom still tucks you in with me. How can I walk away from this? I will think about this for a few days, and we will move on someway, somehow."

I decided that night that I would allow Lambie to accompany me whenever and wherever. The first year of this interlude was highly episodic. I was scorned, spurned, and ridiculed. I took every bit of it. One day, in my freshman year of high school, I was confronted by four bullies while on my way home. The pushing and shoving started immediately.

"Where's the bear?"

"It's a lamb."

"Where's the lamb?"

"Not telling."

Then one of the bullies, Nick McCrick, ripped the book bag off my shoulder. He went through it like a race car leaving the pits on race day. Nick took Lambie out of the bag, tossed the bag to the ground and ran off with Lambie. I heard Lambie scream for help, but there was nothing I could do. Ryland Yarick must have seen all of this happening and approached me.

"You OK, Billy?"

"Not really. They stole my lamb."

"Wait here."

I watched Ryland race down the street. He was a big guy and a star football player. Why was he helping me? I guess I'll find out. In the distance I could see Ryland catch up with the high strutting perpetrators. An argument ensued and to my surprise, Ryland picked up one of the bullies, hoisted him up in the air, and slammed him into a bush alongside the sidewalk. Ryland was yelling at the bully on the ground. The bully was pointing in the direction of a patch of trees about ten yards behind them. Ryland walked back towards me, stopped at the patch of trees, and slowly walked back towards me. In his hand was my Lambie.

"Billy, why do you carry this around with you?"

"Why are you helping me?"

"I've seen you in church with your mom on occasion, so that's how I know you. And why did I help you? I don't like to see kids outnumbered, especially by bullies. I may not be finished with them. I would do that for anyone."

"I'm sorry you had to get involved, Ryland."

"Oh, it's OK, but you didn't answer my question. Why do you carry a stuffed animal around? You're only asking for trouble. How old are you? Thirteen? Kids your age don't carry stuffed animals."

"I'm thirteen, soon to be fourteen. It's a long story, but Lambie is a good luck token for me, always has been, always will."

"It has a name?"

"Yes, Lambie."

"Look Billy, you're a nice kid, but as long as you keep flashing your lamb around, you're asking for trouble, and I am not always going to be around to help you."

"What should I do?"

"Let me give you a suggestion. You need to earn respect. Respect isn't just handed out to everyone. You have to earn it. And it ain't easy."

"How did you earn respect, Ryland?"

"Billy, when I was five years old, my parents insisted that I become a piano player. Not just a casual player who goes to recitals occasionally. They wanted me to be like my uncle Ted, a well-known concert pianist. So, the lessons began. It consumed my entire life. It was eat, sleep, and live for the piano. I played and practiced at least six hours per day."

"Wow!"

"Yah, and I was tall but skinny. I ate regularly, but I think the stress of having to be the best at the piano kept me from getting heavier or stronger. Then, I would play recitals in school. All the kids knew me as "Ryland, the piano dude." Kids are tough, Billy. I am not sure if it was out of jealousy or envy, but any chance they could attack me verbally, and yes, physically, it happened. I was a piano nerd. It started when I was still young and carried on for a few years. I would go home crying and all my parents could say was "just ignore them". Well, that's easier said than done."

"So, what did you do?"

"I started running. When I wasn't eating, sleeping, or of course playing the piano, I ran. Everywhere!"

"And that helped?"

"A little. At least I could run away from my attackers. Ha Ha! But, if they caught me, it was the same thing all over again. Then one day, after school, I was about ten, a few bullies saw me and decided to have some fun with me. I started running but two of them were older than me and they caught up with me a few blocks away. I could hear them screaming "Where's your piano, fag?" "Don't you play outside like normal kids?" Then the kicking began. My legs, my ribs, everywhere. When I went down, one of the kids stepped on my left hand and said, "play with these, queerboy" and then they ran like hell. My hand wasn't badly injured, just bruised, but the humiliation hurt more than my body."

"This is sad, Ryland."

"At the time, I was devastated. I went home, went straight to my room and cried. I must have cried all night. The next day I saw two of my attackers in school. They smirked and laughed at me. Enough was enough. After school that day, I decided that the piano was no longer going to be my priority. I was going to become faster and stronger. The exercise regimen began that day."

"What is regimen, Ryland?"

"It's a plan or a routine."

"So, what happened?"

"I started running even more often. I took my allowance money that I had saved and bought a set of weights. I asked my parents to sign me up for taekwondo classes. They objected of course because it had nothing to do with the piano, but when I told them that I would quit piano, they lightened up and sent me to classes. In just a short time I was becoming faster, quicker with my hands and body, and stronger. I began to eat more and started growing. And Billy, with all of that, I still played the piano."

"And now you have "earned" respect."

"Well, I hope so. But like I said, it wasn't easy. And guess what! You can pull it off too. You want to carry that stuffed lamb around? Then do what you need to do, and the lamb will be an afterthought."

"May I ask you a question, Ryland?"

"Sure."

"Can you help me get on the right track?"

"What do you mean, Billy?"

"I want to earn respect. I can't do this alone. I need help, your help if you are willing. I can pay you."

"You don't have to pay me, Billy. Look, meet me at eight o'clock on Saturday morning at the school track. We'll talk about it and maybe do a little workout. You can bring the lamb if you want."

"I'll be there."

Saturday morning couldn't come quickly enough. I felt gratitude towards Ryland for agreeing to take me on like this. But I knew I needed to do something. I picked up Lambie from the bed and told him we were going out for a while. He appeared to be grateful.

"Where are we going?"

"We are going to re-start my life."

"Am I included in your plans for this restart?"

"You are if you behave yourself. You may be left alone for parts of it, but you will be with me."

Ryland was old enough to drive a car, so he was standing alongside his car when I pulled up on my bike.

"Good morning, Ryland."

"Hey Billy, ready to get started?"

"Sure am. Say, can I leave Lambie locked in your car? I don't want him stolen from my bike."

"Oh boy, well, yah, you can leave it."

"Fine, let's go."

The workout was far more than I would have expected the first day. After three hours of running, exercise in the gym, some light weight-lifting, I was totally exhausted. I knew that I could not quit. Ryland was doing me a huge favor and I could not let him down.

"How ya feeling, sport?"

"Good, Ryland, thanks."

"Okay then, see you every morning at seven o'clock AM."

"What?"

"That's right, we will do this every day of the week before school and on Saturday mornings. You get Sundays off."

"I don't want to take up all of your time."

"You're not. I work out each day anyway. It will be good to have a partner. Before too long, you'll be in great shape."

"I see. Okay then, see you on Monday." I retrieved Lambie from Ryland's car, mounted the bike, and headed home.

"That wasn't so bad, was it, Lambie?"

"Nope."

"Get used to it, the new "me" is right around the corner."

"Why are you doing this?"

"I'm doing it for you, Lambie."

"Well, that's a lie, you're doing it for you."

"Let's just say that I am doing it for both of us."

The next several months were grueling. Ryland was intent on restoring what little self-confidence I had. But, day by day, I felt myself getting bigger, stronger, and faster. It seemed like my body had potential that I knew nothing about until the day I began the workouts. It felt good. Ryland had become a friend, a mentor. One Saturday morning, I had the best workout ever. I lifted more weights than I had in the past, my speed had increased dramatically, and I was growing like a fortified beanstalk. After the session, Ryland approached me by my bike.

"Say Billy, do you know my sister Tina?"

"No, can't say that I do."

"Well, just between us boys, she asks about you all of the time. She's one year behind you at school."

"I'd like to meet her."

"It just so happens that my parents have asked if you would like to stop by for dinner this evening."

"Give me a time, and I'll be there."

"Six thirty"

"See you then!"

I carefully prepared for the dinner at the Yarick's house. If Ryland's younger sister Tina was really interested in me, I was going to make the best of it. It would be the first interlude with a girl since Janet Hamett blew me off. I pulled out my "Sunday best" outfit and carefully shined my shoes. I even took the change out of my pocket so that there would be no jingling. My stash of chewing gum fit perfectly in a sub-pocket, and I was ready to go.

"Where are you going?"

"None of your business, Lambie."

"I need to know."

"You do not need to know."

"Baaaaaaaa, Baaaaaaaa!!!"

"Okay, okay, I am going to Ryland's house for dinner."

"I'm going too."

"You're not."

"I am."

"Ryland wants me to meet his sister. This is the first opportunity with a girl since you chased Janet Hamett away."

"I did nothing of the kind."

"Yah, you did, and it won't happen again."

"If I mess this up, you can crate me again."

"Really, Lambie??!! Do you really think that I am stupid enough to buy into that little game?"

"You can crate me."

"Okay listen, you can go, but just one minor, teeny-weeny, itsy-bitsy incident and you will be buried alive in the backyard. Get it?"

"You wouldn't."

"Oh yes, there's where you are wrong, I will!"

I decided to grab a large safety pin and pin Lambie to my belt loop. Lambie wouldn't complain as he seemed to have no nervous system. Pain was not a factor here. The only pain he seemed to feel was the emotional variety, and if all went well, this would not be a factor this evening.

I was greeted at the door, first by Ryland, and then his mom and dad who were standing behind Ryland. Tina Yarick was last in line standing about five feet behind everyone else. My first glimpse of Tina revealed that she was H.O.T. hot! We exchanged niceties and everyone convened to the family room where Mrs. Yarick served up some soft drinks and some mini-hors d'eouvres. Of course the first item of conversation was the little stuffed lamb pinned to my pants pocket. Mrs. Yarick was the first of the Yaricks to say anything.

"Uhmm Billy, what's that at your side?"

"Well, I know it seems gay, but it is my good luck charm, my little lamb." That was my first mistake as I knew not if there were any gays in the Yarick family tree. But I seemed to have gotten away with it. Then Tina's first words entered the conversation.

"Billy, do you take it everywhere you go?"

Lambie had promised to behave, but I guess he couldn't resist jumping in. "Tell them my name."

"Well, I don't take him everywhere. But his name is Lambie." The prolonged silence was loud and hurt my eardrums.

Then Tina chimed in, "Lambie?!"

"Uhmm, yah."

"Cute." Was she serious or was she patronizing me in a facetious manner?" It wouldn't take long to find out.

Everyone convened at the dinner table. The salad was wonderful. I had never seen such a beautiful display of interesting lettuce, shaped carrots, bell peppers, some type of cheese, and even some nuts. The dressing was tart and sweet at the same time and I hoped that Mrs. Yarick would share the recipe. How nice it might have been if Mom could replicate this delicacy. It was then time for the entrée. Mrs. Yarick entered the kitchen and return with a very prideful smile on her face with a covered platter in her hands. The platter was set on the table.

"Billy, I hope you will enjoy my rosemary-crusted leg of lamb."

This was the beginning of the end.

"Arrggggghhhhhh!!!!, Baaaaaaaaa!!!!, Ughhhhh!!!! Leg of LAMB????!!!!!"

"Oh Jezzzuzzzz, please shut up now." Okay, this was an immediate lesson in how not to be reactionary.

Mrs. Yarick did not take well to my outburst.

"Excuse me, Billy?"

"Oh sorry, that wasn't meant for you."

Then of course Tina had to pipe in, "Then who was it for, Billy."

"For Lambie."

Tina merely leaned forward and looked me straight in the eye, "You talk to your lamb?"

"Well, yes."

Ryland saw this coming and merely leaned back and didn't say a word. Mr. Yarick was also discreet by removing himself from the exchange. Tina stood up, turned to everyone at the table and said, "I'm sorry, I am no longer hungry. I am returning to my room. Thank you for coming, Billy." My evening was once again ruined, and the remainder of the evening had me fighting off every symptom of anxiety until the minute I left.

Once again, there was silence during the return trip home. The "Yarick Debacle" would rest in my mind for weeks to come. When we returned home, I unfastened Lambie and put him on the bed. He was the first one to speak.

"That wasn't my fault."

"Oh really? Then who's fault was it? If you hadn't been there, my evening would not have been trashed."

"You didn't have to respond to my feelings of total disgust when the lady unveiled the leg of lamb. Nobody else could hear me."

"I could hear you, you little four-legged pile of lamb shit."

"That's quite harsh."

"It won't happen again, Lambie."

"Why? Gonna bury me in the yard?"

"Yes, I am. You are going underground."

"Can I at least have a casket?"

"You are totally crazy!"

"I want a casket. I refuse to rot in the ground with bugs and worms crawling all over me."

"You will not have a casket, no flowers, no headstone, no nothing. You will be nothing more than a string of memories for me, some good and others quite bad."

"Sniffle, baaa, ohhhhh."

"Do not lay your pathetic remorse on me now. You were warned. I am done with you. It was nice while it lasted."

Digging the hole in the corner of the yard was easy. Since Lambie was so small, the hole didn't need to be that deep and the ground was somewhat soft. This task, as sad as it might be, was going to be easy. My tortured life was about to be over and I would soon start anew. The hole was deep enough now and wide enough. I laid the shovel down, walked upstairs and grabbed Lambie. I fought off tears and sorrow as I carried him downstairs. The death penalty is harsh but I could not lose perspective that I was dealing with a stuffed animal. God would forgive me. Be strong, Billy Buttons, be strong and do what you have to do. I placed Lambie in the hole and he did not fight it. He was resigned to the fact that the end was in sight. I looked down at him as he lay on his back. All four legs were pointing straight up.

"May I say something before you cover me with dirt?"

"I prefer that we did not talk, but I guess I should allow you the decency to say something."

"Well Billy, I know that I deserve this. I will not fight your decision to lay me to rest. But anything that happened between us happened because I love you. This relationship was awkward from the start because there aren't many instances of talking stuffed animals. But, I do have emotions and I don't know why. God acts in unusual ways sometimes. You gave me a chance to be right for you, but the fact that you were all I had led me to act in ways that were not pleasing to you. I ask that you forgive me for this. Please do not forget me, Billy. Please know that I will die here with a smile and a happy heart. You gave me everything I needed while I was around and there's nothing that could have pleased me more. Goodbye, my Billy."

These parting statements tore me apart, but I had to do what I set out to do. No, I wouldn't forget Lambie as he did have a favorable impact on my life. Those who knew about our relationship would hopefully understand and spare their comments. Hopefully, with time, most would forget this part of my life and I could go on living normally like most other teenagers. I covered the gravesite and returned to my room. Sleep would not come easily but I anticipated that the hurt would go away with time.

Two days passed and I found myself missing Lambie. Mom and I were eating breakfast and she could tell that I was extremely quiet for the past few days. Mom never really discussed my relationship with Lambie, but in my heart I knew that she knew. My cereal was softening in the bowl of milk and her coffee was getting cold when the phone rang. Mom picked it up after the fourth ring. She had a habit of letting the phone ring a few times before picking up. It was our neighbor, Mrs. Ganetta.

"Hello?"

"Mrs. Buttons?"

"Yes."

"Oh hi, it's your neighbor, Greta Ganetta."

"Hi, Greta, it's Betty here."

"Betty, our Golden Retriever, Jake, escaped a few hours ago. We have searched the neighborhood, called the police, and we are devastated over the thought that he won't come home. I am now calling all of the neighbors just in case you might have seen him."

"No, we haven't seen Jake, but if we do, I'll bring him in and call you."

"Thanks! I appreciate anything you can do."

"Good luck in finding him."

"Thanks, bye."

Animals play such a large part in our lives and I could only imagine how badly Mrs. Ganetta felt over the possible loss of her beloved Jake. My animal interlude was different, and I had chosen my last act, but I pretended to feel that it was much different. I never understood how some people cannot love pets. It's an unconditional love and to not understand it is a very sad commentary. I have known people to make excuses for not having pets such as allergies, etc., but to me it was merely a case of having sparse emotions. My own emotions were completely shot, so before I could muster up the strength to head off to school and my session with Ryland, I climbed the stairs to my room and went inside to fetch my gym gear. I opened the shades to look down at Lambie's grave site. Shocked was the only response I could muster at what I first saw. The largest dog I had seen in a long time was busily digging up Lambie's grave. Son of a bitch! Literally! Old Jake was feverishly digging while dirt was being flung in every direction. He was on a mission. I yelled down the stairs.

"Mom, Mom call Mrs. Ganetta."

"What??!!"

"Call Mrs. Ganetta. Her dog is in our yard, digging away. I'll get him."

"Okay, okay."

By the time I reached the yard, Jake had uncovered his prize and he was running around with Lambie in his mouth. The chase was on. As soon as Jake figured out that I wanted back what was rightfully mine, he took off, Lambie in tow. I could spot Lambie hanging out of his mouth, motionless. As soon as I got close to Jake, he would take off again. He ran into another neighbor's yard. I pretended not to be chasing him again and tricked him into taking a rest. Jake lay down in the front of a house two doors down, wrapped his left leg across Lambie's belly with the other paw across his head. He began to pull at one of Lambie's legs. This attempted mutilation was unbearable to watch. Quickly thinking, I sprinted back to my own house, opened the refrigerator and pulled out a piece of leftover steak. Tonight's dinner was going to a better cause. I left the house and Jake was still working on his destruction mission. I slowly approached with steak in hand. Jake's keen sense of smell revealed a fresher, tastier treat. As I approached, Jake was trying to decide between the steak or Lambie, or both. I cautiously held out the steak. Jake had decided that he would outmaneuver me. This was not his first rodeo. He had an iron grip on Lambie and would not let go. I would have to act fast. Just as I came within a foot of Jake's mouth, he lunged for the steak. In a nano-second, I grabbed Lambie and the dismembered leg in one fell swoop and ran like hell. Victory!

Mom fought the idea of taking Lambie to the veterinarian. "Billy, it's a STUFFED animal, not a real-life lamb. And you're missing school!" But I pressed her hard, so she humored me and relented. Off to Dr. Wilson we went. Mom must have called ahead while I was getting ready because we were met with a high degree of cordiality.

"Let's see what you have here, son."

"A dog ripped him apart. But he had died beforehand. It's a long story."

"I see, Billy."

"Can you help him, Dr. Wilson?"

"I think so. Just leave the lamb here for a few days. We will do our best."

"His name is Lambie."

"Okay, sure son. We'll see you in a few days."

I caught Mom winking at Dr. Wilson. I can imagine how stupid this all looked and sounded, but I feel like I owed it to Lambie to do this. It was simply the right thing to do.

I saw Ryland the next morning.

"I'm sorry about what came down the other night, Billy."

"It was all my fault."

"Well, you do have a situation. I understand it, but you'll have to admit, it is quite different. But you chose to live it, so you'll have to ride with it the best way you are able."

"I took some measures to end it, Ryland, but it backfired. I don't even want to get into it, but things have changed."

"Oh?"

"I'll explain later. Let's work out."

I waited the two days per Dr. Wilson and had Mom take me over to the veterinarian office. The receptionist greeted me with a smile. "Dr. Wilson will see you soon." I waited patiently as I saw other folks going in and out with their dogs and cats. There was even a rabbit. Not surprisingly, none of them were stuffed. It was near the end of the day, and it appeared that Dr. Wilson waited until all his other patients were seen before we went in.

"Hello Billy, and Mrs. Buttons."

"How's Lambie?"

"Well, Lambie is all patched up and ready to go home. He'll need some rest." The receptionist carried Lambie in and handed him to me. He was motionless. But he was very clean and it appeared that he had never suffered as a result of a canine attack. I decided not to blame Jake as that's what dogs do. They fetch and destroy. Lambie was his prize that day, and I cheated him out of his romp with Lambie lodged between his fangs. I had tricked Jake into relinquishing his prize so I hoped that he would not hold it against me forever. Golden Retrievers are a gentle breed, so my fears were minimal.

Life for me went on as usual for the next several weeks. There was no sign of life from Lambie. I would park him alongside of me each night when I retired to the bed. Every morning he awakened in the same position, his four little legs pointing upwards, lying in the same position as where I had placed him the night before. Ryland and I continued our vigorous workouts. I was in shape now. Sophomore year was coming up and Ryland convinced me that I was ready for football. The summer passed and still no movement or words from Lambie. School was starting back up in a few days, so I was preparing myself for yet another year of education and now sports. The night before the first day of school, I plopped myself down in bed and closed my eyes.

"Move over."

"Holy shit!! Who said that?"

"I did. Are you going to continue to hog the entire bed?"

I could recognize that voice anywhere and without the slightest hesitation, the tears began to roll out of my eyes.

"Lambie, are you okay?"

"Of course, I am. Are you going to move over or not?"

"Sure, yes, sure." I wanted to ask Lambie if he had remembered anything, but why stir it up. I decided to treat him as I did before. But somehow he knew. The next several days proved to me that he knew that his lesson had been learned. There were no requests to follow me anywhere and I had no need to have him at my side. Well, not for the time being anyway.

Football went better than I had expected. Even Ryland was surprised by my progress. As a sophomore, I was a starting running back on the team. The first game against a relatively weak opponent became a rude awakening for me. I was not ready to be a starter. I fumbled the ball twice, ran in the wrong direction once, and stayed on the field when I was supposed to leave, thereby drawing a penalty from the referee. We eked out a win, but it was far from pretty. The coach did not hesitate to pull me aside after the game.

"What happened out there today. Billy?"

"Not sure, Coach Curtis. I thought I did okay in practice. Maybe nerves?"

"I counted on you Billy, but you let me down. I won't start you for the next game. The opponent is a bit stronger, and I can't take any chances."

"I'll try harder, Coach, but I understand why I have been demoted."

"Okay Billy, keep working. It's a long season."

I tried hard not to feel gloomy about my performance. Ryland tried to console me and suggested we focus on a few key maneuvers that plagued me on the field. Then Ryland suggested something that I would not have thought about had he not raised the issue.

"Billy, this is going to sound crazy to you, but."

"Go on, nothing in my life can appear crazy at this point."

"That lamb, the one that sort of got you into a little trouble at my house?"

"A little trouble?"

"Well, you mentioned that it is a good luck charm of sorts."

"Of sorts."

"Bring it to the game."

"Oh, no, no, no, no."

"How can it hurt, Billy?"

"Oh, you have seen how it can hurt, Ryland."

"I'm telling you. Bring it. Listen, it is no secret that many athletes have good luck charms, traditions, and superstitions. One baseball player wears the same socks for every game without washing them. He wears them until they rot. Others carry rabbit feet in their pockets. Some have mascots. It's endless. I'm telling you, just try it."

That evening after dinner, I sat Lambie down to discuss the mascot option. I call it an option because the other option was to remain planted in my room. He seemed to understand the rules. I decided to give it a try. The next step was to discuss this with the team. I decided to do it after practice the following day. Coach Curtis usually had a team meeting after each practice, and I asked him to give me an opportunity to speak to the team. I told him that it would be brief. He complied with my request.

"Look guys. Coach Curtis gave me a chance to start last week, and I flubbed it up. The team counted on me and I did everything other than prove that I was qualified to be a starter. There's something that you guys don't know about me. Get ready because it will seem very silly. But here goes. I have a good luck charm in the form of a stuffed animal. Okay, I hear your giggles and snorts, but I am quite serious. I would never have considered bringing this up, but my friend, Ryland, knows about it and suggested I bring him to the game. Please bear with me. For me, this little stuffed lamb has a personality. It's unusual to say the least, I know. But I ask you to just accept what I am and what I do, and I promise that I will not let you down again."

The room was quiet. The Captain, Brad Baker blurted out, "sounds cool to me." Others joined in. Matt Mason said "hey, if it keeps us winning, I'm game." Similar comments followed without dissent, so Lambie was on his way to watch high school football.

The following Saturday, I dressed for the game and brought Lambie out to the field with me. The team manager who is responsible for equipment, water, etc. agreed to keep an eye on Lambie. I sat Lambie on the bench right next to the water buckets. Peter Panzer, a Junior, started in my place. He was playing an average game and we quickly fell behind 13-0. The opponent was tough. In the last play of the first quarter, Peter Panzer came limping off the field. I could hear him tell Coach Curtis that he had turned his ankle. Coach Curtis looked up and down the bench.

"Buttons, you'll play in Peter's spot until he works the kinks out of his ankle."

"Yes sir, coach."

I went into the game to start the second quarter. We had the ball on our own 18-yard line. Our quarterback handed the ball off to me and I was hit almost immediately by an opponent. The ball popped straight up into the air and landed directly in the hands of one of the opponent's defensive linemen who just sprinted into the end zone. We were now down 20-0. I was devastated. I headed for the bench and tried my best to avoid Coach Curtis. Lambie was propped up at the end of the bench, so I shuffled over to him and sat down. I looked at Lambie.

"I saw that, Billy."

"Yah, sorry you had to witness it."

"What happened?"

"I don't know. I think I lack the confidence. Look, nobody is even looking at me or talking to me. I am doomed."

"No, you have confidence Billy. Look at what you have done for me. You knew that you would be harassed and scorned for taking me along with you, but you did it anyway. Why? Because you were willing to make sacrifices to make me happy. Now it is time to think about yourself and the value you bring to the team. Tell yourself that you will grip that ball and hang on to it, and when you do, you will carry that ball to wherever the ball needs to go. You would do that for me, now do it for your team."

"But Coach Curtis will never put me back in the game."

"Look, walk over to Coach Curtis. Tell him that you are sorry for dropping the ball and let him know that you are confident that you can recover from that. I will watch every move and I will be your good luck charm."

"Okay, I will."

Coach Curtis was surprisingly receptive to my plea. He told me that our chances of beating this team were slim and since there was nobody else he could put into the game at that position, he would give me one last chance.

"Just get in there and do your best, Billy. You have the size, the speed, and the power. The only element of your being that I have not seen is your heart. Football is a mental and emotional game too. You have the physical ability, but without heart, you can never succeed."

I went back in the game. Down 20-0, we were on our own 36-yard line. The quarterback called us into the huddle and called the play. I was to run between the right guard and right tackle, then look for daylight. The ball was snapped and I grabbed it from the quarterback. The guard and tackle had opened a nice little hole for me, so I dashed right through it, cut right, avoided an oncoming linebacker, headed for the sideline and ran past the cornerback and safety. They simply could not catch me. It was a 64-yard touchdown run and everyone, save the opposing team and their supporters went wild. We went for a two-point extra point try and made it. The score was now 20-8. I ran off the field and everyone patted my head, back, butt, and shoulder pads. I brought life to the team. I looked for Lambie and he was just sitting there looking straight ahead. I took a seat beside him and had some trouble wiping the smile off of my face.

"Nice going, Billy."

"I'm not done yet, Lambie."

"That's right, you're not."

We held the other team in check, and it was our turn to get the ball again. Coach Curtis nodded to me, so I ran onto the field. Using two passes, the first two downs yielded only four yards. It was now third down and six yards to go. The quarterback called my play again. "Do this again for us, Billy." He took the snap and handed me the ball. But, this time, the hole did not open. The opponents had seen this play coming. I bounced off the linemen, spun around to my left, and ran laterally. I spotted a bit of daylight up field, so I pivoted on my left foot and took off towards the goal line. The free safety had a good angle to catch me, but I turned on the jets and sprinted past him. I scored, we made the extra point, and we were now down 20-15. I ran off the field, headed straight for Lambie, grabbed him, and hoisted him into the air. The team now had an official mascot, and nothing was going to stop us now. It became a long afternoon for our opponent. I had gained 220 yards, scored three touchdowns, and we went on to win 36-27. The scene in the post-game locker room was celebratory. Team captain, Brad Baker snatched Lambie out of my hands, hoisted him in the air and began to chant "Lambie, Lambie, Lambie." The team followed and the entire locker room resonated with the chant of my little friend's name. By the following week, there was a banner across the top of the entrance to the locker room. It only exhibited one name, "LAMBIE".

The season was magical. We went undefeated, I had a banner year, and Lambie became our little hero. We won the District and State Championship and ranked very high amongst high school football teams nationally. At the end of the season, I was approached by college recruiters from at least four major universities. I was only a sophomore. Mom would appreciate that she didn't have to pay for college if I kept up the good work on the ball field. And Lambie? Yes, Lambie was our hero, our temporary mascot. I planned to take Lambie to college with me and he would be my soulmate, my hero.

The next two years of high school went quickly. I continued working out. Ryland had joined the military, so I was on my own. But I had the routine down quite well. Lambie was at my side throughout and he was always on his best behavior. Lambie became popular at school and in some instances, he was allowed to do overnight stays at the homes of just a select few. Lambie never spoke to anyone, and I began to wonder whether he was really talking to me throughout or if it was just my imagination. Maybe someday I would know.

My college selection process was made easy by the fact that I wanted to live close to home to keep Mom happy. Plus, they offered me a full scholarship if I played football. State University was an entirely new experience. This was not high school, and the football players were bigger and faster. I needed to prove myself. Lambie shared my dorm room with me and my roommate, a technology nerd named Clyde McBride. Clyde didn't see anything at all wrong with having a stuffed animal. I was careful not to speak to Lambie in Clyde's presence. I didn't necessarily feel that I was "treading on thin ice" with Clyde's acceptance of Lambie. I just didn't want to lose Clyde as a roommate because of him thinking that he was accidentally placed in a mental ward. Lambie took it all in and really didn't have much to say. This was a new experience for Lambie as he had never really been away from home before. But Lambie was aging. His coat was greying, and his stiches were coming apart. Some of his coat was thinning and under closer examination, this phenomenon revealed itself to me as mirroring human aging behavior. Humans go to cosmetic surgeons when their appearance changes.

What do I do with Lambie? I knew that Mom would have the answer, so I brought Lambie home from college and asked Mom to rejuvenate him as best she could. In that short weeks' time, I met a freshman girl in my European history class. Clara O'Hara and I hit it off immediately. She had been sitting beside me when I noticed her long, curly, golden locks. Her profile was elegant, and her natural eyelashes were long with an upward curl. Her full lips were painted a bright crimson red and her skin appeared as soft and delicate as a baby's bottom. I had to get to know her. I was never good with pickup lines, so I had to muster up a way to approach her. In class that day, we discussed how the Communist occupation of some Eastern European nations affected how people practiced religion. She had seemed very attentive during this lecture, so I used this as my lead line.

"Hi, uhmm, I am Billy Buttons and I've got a question related to our coursework for you."

"Hello, Billy Buttons. I am Clara O'Hara." Her smile and immediate response were infectious, and it led me to believe that she was as interested in me as I may have been in her.

"Okay, what's the question?"

"Well, when the Communists insisted that there is no God in certain Eastern European countries, we learned today that many of the residents practiced their religions at home or privately in small groups. What became of the beautiful churches and temples that existed long before the Communists ever arrived?" I really wanted to know the answer to this.

"It appears that the churches and temples became forbidden ground. They were probably dismantled in a few instances, but I expect that for the most part they were preserved and maintained by the government. The Communists likely thought of these as historical sites, monuments to a culture that once existed."

From that conversation, in just a few short days, my relationship with Clara O'Hara blossomed into a mini love affair. We spent every waking moment together. We met for breakfast, lunch, and impromptu dinners. We talked about our classes, our families, and anything that would draw upon our mutual interests. Football was not interesting to Clara, but I planned to make it that way. I already knew that football was going to capitalize my time, so if I could get her interested in it just minimally, our relationship would survive. I was careful not to mention Lambie as he was back home becoming rejuvenated, but sooner or later she would have to meet him. It had been a few weeks since I had brought Lambie back home. I called Mom and she told me that Lambie was still under repair and that he would be ready for me to pick him up in just a few short days. I had missed him more than I should admit, but the separation from Clara would be difficult too. But I needed to retrieve my best friend and I was eager to see his new look. So, I planned to head home the following weekend. Clara understood.

"I'm heading home this weekend, Clara. But I just wanted you to know that I will miss you. But there are things to do, and I hadn't seen my Mom in a while."

"Oh, no problem, Billy, I've been putting off some important things also and this will give me a chance to catch up. It has indeed been a whirlwind between us."

"It has, and a great one at that."

The bus ride home from school on the following Friday afternoon seemed to take forever. I had made the decision not to have a car on campus. I did not need the expense of a car and I really hadn't planned to drive anywhere anyway. I finally arrived home, said "hi" to Mom and headed straight to my room. Mom had propped up Lambie on my bed and at first glance, I could hardly recognize him. He was staring straight at me. I almost detected a smile on his little lamb face. He was as clean as a whistle, tightened up like a diva with a facelift, and had a robust hearty look about him.

"Well?"

"Well, well, well."

"That's all you can say?"

"I, I, I am like flabbergasted. Are you my Lambie?"

"How many other talking lambs do you know?"

"Yeah, right, right. You look, well, you look … amazing!"

"You like?"

"Yes, I like. I missed you, Lambie."

"I missed you too, Billy."

"Look, I have to go spend a little time with Mom, but I'll be back in a while. Don't go anywhere."

"Oh right, I was planning on heading out for a Green Day concert."

"Cute, very cute. See you in a few."

It was great catching up with Mom. I thanked her for attending to Lambie for which she suggested that it was no problem at all; in fact, it was fun. We discussed school, my plans for football, Clara, and life in general. My Mom had an even temperament, no highs, and no lows. She extremely understood and I always recognized how lucky I was to have her as a mom. I would work to pay her back for all she had done for me, including the life-changing event on the day she brought Lambie home. The weekend went by without a hitch. When it was time for sleep, Lambie would cuddle up to me and never leave my side. I could tell just by his actions that he truly missed me. Very few words were exchanged other than a "good night". Monday morning came and I was eager to return to college. Lambie was safely stashed in my overnight bag.

Clara was happy to see me the afternoon of my return. The week was to be a busy one with classes, football, and everything else related to being in college. But we did make time to see one another. Coach didn't want anyone outside of our football circles to visit our practices, so Clara was somewhat disenchanted when she was turned away. Lambie stayed back in the room, but once it was game time, I was planning on having him on the bench with me. I had already cleared this with Coach, and it seemed that he had been previously advised of this little ritual. "Billy, if it helps us to win games, I don't care if you have a crocodile with you." I told him that a lamb was the extent of my animal associations.

Friday arrived and I planned to spend the evening with Clara. We would indulge in a casual dinner, perhaps pizza, and take in a local band at a nearby venue. From there, we would "play it by ear". The evening went well and neither of us was tired by the time the band finished. I wasn't sure how to make any provocative suggestions when right out of the blue Clara whispers, "your place or mine?" I wasn't sure how well I was prepared for what was to come, but I suggested that my roommate, Clyde, had left for a conference for the weekend. Clara thought that it would be a good idea to go to my room as she did have a roommate staying with her and that there were likely more interesting things to do in my room.

"Maybe you can tell me more about football, Billy. I never quite understood the game."

"Sure, no problem. I am not sure that I am that good at explaining, but I'll give it a try."

We arrived back at my room and Lambie was sitting up on my bed. He didn't have anything to say when Clara and I entered the room, and that was a good thing. We sat at the edge of the bed for a while and simply talked for thirty minutes. I showed Clara my high school annual, and she seemed to like what she saw. The football pictures particularly interested her. There was a photo of me on the bench with my friend, and team mascot Lambie, at my side.

"What's with the bear?"

Lambie of course heard her and spurted out, "BEAR??!!"

I knew that Clara could not hear him, so I failed to respond to him."

"Uhmm, actually, it's a lamb."

"Oh, a lamb, sorry."

"No problem, Clara. In fact, he's right behind you in the bed."

"Oh, how cute. Do you feel like lying down, Billy?"

"Yah, sure, let's lie down."

"Want to douse the lights?"

"Sure, I'll get them now."

We both put our heads on the pillows and Clara began to unbutton my shirt. Lambie was lodged between us and blocking the way thereby interfering with her mission to disrobe me. She proceeded to pick up Lambie and toss him across the room.

"Sorry, Billy, it was in the way."

Oh, no problem at all."

Then, out of the corner of the room, "WHAT DO YOU MEAN NO PROBLEM??!!"

My immediate inclination was to blurt out "oh shit!" But I kept quiet. That's when the howling commenced. It was awful. "BAAAAAAA, OWWWWWWW, AGGHHHHHHH"

"Okay, I have had enough of you."

"What's that, Billy?"

"Oh, sorry I wasn't talking to you, Clara?"

"Then who might you have been talking to? What did I do to break your mood?"

"Nothing, oh nothing at all. It's just that."

"Just what, Billy? I want to know."

"To be honest, sometimes I imagine that I hear Lambie saying something."

"Lambie? You call it Lambie? The mascot has a name?"

"Well, he is also my friend."

"Oh really! How nice. So why are we having a conversation with a stuffed animal when we are about to spend, or should I say, WERE about to spend our first night together?"

"I was just, well just trying to calm him down a little bit. He likes to stay in the bed with me whenever I am in the bed."

"Oh, how wonderful, Billy. I am soooooo sorry. Let me go pick up the little guy and return him to where he belongs."

Clara climbed out of the bed, walked to the corner of the room, picked up Lambie and tossed him back at me. She didn't appear very happy with me, and that fact became a lot clearer when she headed for the door and said "Look, Billy, I thought we had something special, but it is obvious that you have some growing up to do. Let me know when that happens. Perhaps I might still be around. Goodbye!"

I now had another failed relationship because of my life with Lambie.

"What was that all about, Billy?"

"You haven't figured it out?"

"Well, it was going to be her or me. Sorry you had to choose."

"SHE did the choosing, Lambie."
"Are you going to bury me again?"
"No."
"Are you upset with me?"
"No."
"Then what??"
"Look, just don't talk to me now. I need time to think about things."
"Okay."

The decision had to be made. What to do, what to do! First it was Janet Hamett, then Tina Yarick, and now Clara O'Hara. I could not allow the list to continue to grow. I finally decided that this may be God's way of telling me that I do not need women in my life right now. I decided that I would concentrate on my studies, play football, and enjoy college life. The hunt was over. And that is exactly what I did. I finished college with a 3.6 GPA, admirable enough, and was a third team All-American football player, and the team won the conference two out of my four years in college. I could not ask for anything more. I graduated and was congratulated by my friends, Mom, and most of my football pals. Even Clara O'Hara sauntered up to me and wished me well. Lambie was on his best behavior and was known pretty much throughout the campus. He had done it again by being the able mascot. The real mascot, a bulldog, was probably envious of Lambie's fame and tried to haul him off the bench on more than one occasion. I politely asked the bulldog's handler to keep from having that happen again. After graduation, I went to the big city for my first job, an intern at a well-known public relations firm. I found a decent apartment where I would have two roommates to make it more affordable. That's what recent college grads do, they team up for the sake of creating efficiencies. The job was working out quite well and I could not ask for a better start to my new life.

After the first month on the job, one of the Junior Executives was asked to take me on assignment with a new client. The executive was a rather thin, averaged-height brunette with a beautiful Irish face. I found out later that she was Italian. I could swear that she had some Irish blood in her, but she denied it. Her name was Mary Tamare (pronounced to-mar-ee) and she was two years older than me. The assignment included a visit to the client's home office. The client owned a chain of small taco stands and it was hauling in a LOT of money. They ran into problems when two customers became ill and filed a lawsuit contending that our client was using inferior ingredients. The client won the lawsuit because the claimants failed to prove that it was our client's food that caused them to become ill. But our client suffered from the bad publicity and needed a "shot in the arm". So, we had our public relations work cut out for us. The meetings went well. The only surprise was that a Chinese family owned the taco stands. My immediate thought was that they probably had tacos in China, but soon realized that the Chinese are quite enterprising and could figure out a way to make money selling practically anything.

Our meeting went well, and we finished earlier than anticipated. Mary suggested we grab a cup of coffee. The workday was nearing an end and I had no reason to go home yet, so I agreed to join her.

"You've got quite the resume, Billy Buttons."

"Not really, I've only been with the firm for a month."

"Well, I meant your graduation with honors from State U, and your football All-American achievements."

"I had some good reasons to apply myself, so I got lucky."

"It takes more than luck to do what you did."

"How did you know about those things, Mary?

"When my boss told me to take you along, I looked up your records in Human Resources so that I could know a little more about you."

"Aren't those things private?"

"Some of it is, but we are allowed to review some basics without crossing the line. These are things anyone would know. I don't know if you are a serial killer or a pedophile, so I'll just assume everything else is cool."

"No, I am none of those things thankfully."

"Do you have a girlfriend?"

"No. I haven't been looking."

"I see."

"What about you?"

"Me? A girlfriend?"

"You know what I mean."

"To be honest, I was engaged to my college sweetheart for a year, but we broke up six months ago. So, you won't have to ask, we were not compatible on many levels."

"Sorry to hear that."

"Oh, no, no, it's OK. It has worked out much better that way. Say Billy, are you doing anything later this evening?"

"I have no plans."

"The reason I ask is that AC/DC is in town and the last time I looked, there were plenty of lawn seats available. Come on, my treat!"

"You like AC/DC?"

"I love all of the hair bands from the 80's. But I believe AC/DC tops them all."

"Okay, you're on."

"Great, meet me in front of the Seven-Eleven at 7:00 PM. That'll give us plenty of time to get there and grab some seats."

"See you then."

The concert was great, especially when Mary grabbed my hand during "You Shook Me All Night Long". I liked this woman. She was charismatic and her energy radiated around me. The fact that she was older didn't trouble me and in fact, I thought perhaps I could learn from her. I wanted to get to know her better and I was prepared to make that happen. The only potential hurdle I would need to clear was, yes, you guessed it, my Lambie. I was sure that just like her predecessors, this might not end well. I can't say that I learned anything from my past experiences other than just take life as it comes. When it is right, it'll be right. The next several weeks saw Mary and me on some assignments together. We became a team and she provided good mentoring for me. We did spend ample off-duty time together but there was no indication that either of us might be interested romantically. I was guessing that the handholding at the AC/DC concert was just a one-time emotional lift for each of us. But Mary was growing on me. I liked everything about her. My strategy would be to get closer and work towards having Mary really care about me so if bedtime was to arrive, she wouldn't become a track star and run in the opposite direction. I knew it would take time, but I had time on my hands.

Two more months passed. I had just arrived back in the city from visiting Mom when I received a call from a local college friend who had to give up two tickets for a Tesla concert. He was leaving town on business and did not want to see them go to waste. Of course, I took the tickets and called Mary right away. She was so excited to hear this news that I could feel her heart pounding right through the phone. The concert was on a Saturday night and Mary picked me up in front of the Seven-Eleven, our designated meeting place. We had a blast. Tesla played all of their favorites and the beer flowed all evening. After the concert, Mary drove me back to the Seven-Eleven. I was about to disembark from the car when she surprised me.

"Don't I get a kiss goodnight?"

"Of course, you do, Mary."

"Then why do you have the door half-way open?"

"Oh, to get some fresh air."

"You're full of shit, Billy Buttons."

"Yah, I am."

The kissing was more passionate than I had ever expected. Mary's deep breathing alone told me how much she was enjoying my company. I could hear her whimper as we embraced. Oh, please dear Lord, do not allow this to end. And it didn't.

"Billy, let's get a room."

"Excuse me?"

"A room, Billy, a motel room."

"Oh, well, ok."

"Are you afraid of me, Billy?"

"Oh, no, of course not. It's just."

"Just what?"

"I need to go home first and pick up a few overnight things, you know, a toothbrush, change of clothes, etc."

"Okay, me too. I need to get some items also."

I would stuff Lambie into my overnight bag. If this was going to end poorly, it was going to happen this very night. No delays. I had learned my lessons.

Mary took me home and waited outside while I packed up some things. Both of my roommates were there, so it was a good thing I didn't drag Mary to my place. Lambie was safely stashed and did not ask me where we were going. He trusted me at this point. Mary drove off and stopped in front of her place. I waited patiently in the car while she grabbed her things. When she returned to the car, she tossed her overnight bag into the back seat right next to mine. Before she pulled out of the parking spot, she looked at me, pulled me close and locked her lips on mine. I was on my way to heaven and only one thing could stand in the way. I did not have any conversations with Lambie regarding his expected behavior; I simply wished that he would know that my level of tolerance was limited. This evening was what I would consider "a beginning". It was either the beginning of something wonderful, or the beginning of the end.

Mary pulled in front of the Holiday Inn Express. When I suggested that I would go into the office and pay up, she told me "Already done." She was way ahead of me. Our room was not fancy, but it had everything we would need, namely a bed.

"Don't put on any lights, Billy."

"Okay."

"It won't kill the mood because I brought some candles and a bottle of champagne."

Mary was far more prepared for this evening than I would have imagined. And I was far more receptive than she might have imagined. We sat on the edge of the bed drinking Brut Champagne from fluted glasses. Nothing ever tasted better to me. I could feel beads of perspiration forming on my forehead. Music came from a small device that Mary had also brought along. Cinderella was singing "Nobody's Fool" when I could feel Mary unbuttoning my oxford shirt. I reciprocated and we both chuckled at what was coming. I left Lambie in his bag, so luckily, he did not see any of this. All I needed now was for him to screw this up royally and I would be depressed for years to come.

We set down our glasses and continued the mutual disrobing process. Both of us were naked except for some random pieces of underwear which would eventually be removed. I was in my Fruit of the Looms shorts and she in her panties and ample bra. I was happy to see that the bra was more ample than the panties. My nerves were quite calm for the moment considering the circumstances and I was eager to get the show rolling. As my head began to descend in the direction of the pillow, Mary looked at me with a curious look on her face.

"Billy?"

"Yes."

"Well, I have a little ritual that I do before I get comfortable in bed."

"I am all ears."

"Well, I have to get up."

"Okay."

Mary climbed out of bed and walked over to her overnight bag. It was dark and I saw her reach in, but I did not see what she pulled out. She walked towards me and had both hands behind her back. Was I about to get spanked? Or maybe whipped? My curiosity was riding a very high wave.

"Billy, I hope this is not a deal breaker, and it may have contributed to my breakup with my fiancé, but it is something I must do."

Yup, I was going to be whipped, or tied up, or something kinky.

"Okay Mary. I am ready."

Mary bent down just slightly and with her right hand extended whatever was in her hand directly in front of me. At first glance I couldn't make out what it was until she spoke.

"Ta da!! Mary had a little lamb."

"HOLY SHIT!!! YOU ARE FREAKING KIDDING ME!!"

"Uh oh, did I blow it?"

"No, Mary, you did not blow it."

"This is a mind-bending state of affairs."

"Well, what then? Do you think I am a weirdo, Billy? Are you going to dump me over this?"

"I am speechless, Mary."

"Billy, my little Lambkin has been my companion for as long as I can remember. Sometimes I even talk to her. I'm sorry."

"Okay Mary, bear with me while I catch my breath. Lambkin?!"

"I will, I'm just …"

"No, no, wait, Mary. Okay, okay, sit down on the bed with your little Lambkin. I too have a little surprise."

"What is it, Billy?"

"Just wait there." I walked over to my overnight bag, and with one swift motion lifted Lambie out and walked back to the bed. "Meet Lambie."

"What??!!"

"Meet Lambie. He's my soul mate, and yes, I also talk to him at times."

Mary just sat there with her mouth hanging open. She too was obviously speechless. Without saying a word, we raised ourselves simultaneously, walked our little love cherubs over to a chair and sat them down side by side, facing one another. I thought that I heard a slight sigh from Lambie. There were definitely sounds coming from that part of the room. Who would have ever imagined??!! The evening produced the best sex anyone could want and produced a string of revelations, most of which you have likely figured out by now. Mary and I were to become a couple and Lambie had found his life partner as well. As bizarre as it was, there was nothing that would keep any of us from disbelieving the power of fate.

So, the story has a happy ending. Mom once told me that people are drawn together for some of the wildest reasons. This might have been the wildest on record. Lambie would talk to me again, but only when it was convenient for him. When he did talk, he always first told me that he was thankful for what I had done for him. He told me that he loved me more than he could ever love Lambkin. If he had a life, it seemed to have been fulfilled. For Mary, this string of events confirmed in her mind that God had a calling for her and it was to meet me. I could not disagree. This tale ends on a high note. Only the future will tell how it will carry on, but if I have read my stars correctly, it is something that would be cherished for many years to come.

THE END

SURVIVORS

A NOVELLA

BY

Stuart R Schwartz

Claire Mitchell looks out of the back patio window of the sprawling massive Mitchell estate in Saddle River, New Jersey. It is early June, blooming season had begun, and cadres of gardeners are busily planting, snipping, pruning, and performing all other chores related to keeping the grounds fresh-looking and Spring-like. One of the workers spots Claire and provides the "smiley wave" to which Claire waves back and mouths the words ..."hi, how are you?" The response is a thumbs up. Claire's kind demeanor is contagious and those around her always feel her sincerity.

Claire had decided to attend Bucknell University in Pennsylvania soon after her graduation from private school in New Jersey. Bucknell provided her with the opportunity to get away from home to a place where she would be somewhat unnoticed, but close enough to head home and visit on occasion. And, now, a recent graduate, as the age of 22, her time would be devoted to determining what she should do with her life. Dad, Charles Mitchell, had always suggested that Claire, as an only daughter might want to work for Mitchell Industries in New Jersey. He would promise to prime her for a strong position in the company upon his retirement. Working for this giant of a company and equally giant of a man would be an honor, but she was just not sure if that would suit her well. Claire wanted to experience life a bit first, but she did not want to be a burden on her family in any way. Living at home was fine for now, but going out and learning about new cultures, attitudes, lifestyles, and more were even more appealing to her.

Claire had only known about life growing up in a wealthy family and going to school. She knew there was much more out there, but how could she find it? There was so much she didn't know. Perhaps, she thought, she could work out an arrangement with Dad to work as an apprentice at Mitchell Industries, but, at the same time, have the ability to take ample time off to explore the world. It would be the best of both worlds. But, "would Dad agree?"

Mitchell Industries was one of the largest suppliers of surgical implements in North America and many parts of the world. It was based in New Jersey and privately held by Charles Mitchell. There were many times that larger, publicly-traded companies had offered to purchase Mitchell Industries, but Charles would hear nothing of it. This was his baby and he did not want any "hot shots" to come in and try to change the culture of the company and the way it did business. Charles' Grandfather, Herbert Mitchell, had started the small company 80 years earlier, working in a small rented space behind a grocery market in a semi-rural town in New Jersey. Herbert learned that surgery could be performed more efficiently and quickly if there were implements that were more user-friendly.

One of Herbert Mitchell's childhood friends was a noted surgeon. One day, while the two walked through a park on a bright, clear Sunday afternoon, Herbert's friend suggested that Herbert use his skills as a metal worker to create an implement that would make the surgeon's job easier. Until that date, Herbert limited his craft to building model airplanes, model cars, and making stick figures out of metal pipes and wires. He accurately and precisely built his models and figures. Herbert's idols were the Wright Brothers. They were an inspiration to Herbert and accordingly had a strong influence in his love of airplanes and making models of same.

Herbert quizzed his surgeon friend at length until the point when he completely understood the needs of the surgeon. The implements must meet certain standards of weight and size. The materials from which they were made had to be easily sterilized, but most important; they had to be convenient for the surgeon to comfortably hold for long periods of a time without fatigue. There was a lot of curiosity from those who knew Herbert when he walked around with a metal implement in his hand all day, moving his wrists at the same time. Though curiosity prevailed, Herbert would never reveal the "method to his madness". This was his secret only to be shared with his surgeon friend. Herbert knew the value of patents and if he could only develop something that could be useful and make life easier for surgeons, he was going to create it and patent it, and he did.

Herbert's achievements were not limited to only one device, but helped him to generate the incentive and skills to create more and more. Before long, there were several patents, more space in which to work, and even a full-time helper. The requests for Herbert's implements came rolling in as word spread. Before long, a semi-automated facility was developed that would allow Herbert to manufacture more devices, enabling him to fill more orders, more expeditiously. More workers were hired, an attorney was put to full-time use, and Mitchell Industries was created.

Herbert eventually married, had two sons, Charles and Frederick. Frederick died in a boating accident at a young age. The loss of a son was a terrible setback for Herbert. He and his wife, Alice, grieved for the remainder of their years. Charles had to do everything in his own power to create a balance in the family after the loss. He was old enough to understand the nature of the loss and continually consoled his parents. When Herbert had to leave the factory for a year after the loss of Frederick, Charles stepped in and did what he could to keep things going. Charles never had time to go to college and learn about business and industry, but his keen sense of perception enabled him to keep the ship afloat.

Herbert returned to work after one year, but the mourning never ended. His drive and enthusiasm had waned, but Charles learned more each day, and before long, at a young age of 25, Charles became the CEO of the largest supplier of precision surgical implements in the world. Charles averted anyone that questioned his ability and focused on nothing other than to fulfill his father's dream of creating this large, highly respected industry. There were requests for interviews from media of all types. Charles always declined, but cordially stated that he really had to continually sharpen his focus. These types of events detracted from what he needed to accomplish.

It was no secret that Charles was heavily pursued by female suitors. He was young, handsome, wealthy, and kind. Charles never knew the definition of "being a great catch", but he was wary that women may have pursued him for reasons less than honorable. For this reason, Charles avoided social circles and events that exposed him to anything other than his work and his personal interests. He knew that someday, if time allowed, he would open up and find someone who met his needs. There were many times when Charles would return home to his small house and feel lonely. He would cook up a light dinner, read a book or some journals, then retire to the bed early. Each day provided a new challenge for Charles, all of which were excitedly anticipated and accepted. Charles thrived on creating new business opportunities, keeping his employees happy, and making a favorable impact on the medical world.

Charles's only diversion was to keep fit by biking. He bought the fastest, most efficient two-wheeler on the market. Biking became a passion for him. In the evenings, rain or shine, Charles could be seen pedaling through the New Jersey countryside, only stopping for the occasional drink of water or temporary rest. There were neatly cut paths through certain areas of the State Park that were designated for bicyclists, runners, and the occasional walker. Most knew their place on the paths, so the chance of an accident was remote. There were several rest areas along the way, each with a portable potty and a water fountain. It was an ideal situation for someone whose sole recreation outside of work was bicycling.

On a brisk autumn evening, Charles was out on the paths. He wanted to finish before the sunset, so he was moving at a rapid pace. His energy level waning, it was time for a rest. As he pulled into one of the rest stops, he was surprised to see a sole bike leaning against a tree with no rider in sight. Before he even had a chance to look around, the door for the portable-potty swung open and out of it emerged a very fit woman. She appeared to be Charles's age or perhaps a few years younger. She introduced herself to Charles as Annette and told him how embarrassed she was about having been caught in this situation. Charles, in his soothing manner, suggested that everybody has body functions and it was not embarrassing at all. He went on to say that he hoped that she would wait while he relieved himself as well. With a chuckle, Annette complied. The interlude was the beginning of a long friendship which commenced as often as possible on the trails.

Charles and Annette became closer as time went by. It was difficult for Charles to get away from the business, but it didn't seem to matter to Annette who was also busy with her baking duties. In time, with some fear of losing Annette, Charles decided to take a long weekend and drive with Annette to a retreat in the rolling hills of West Virginia. Annette was excited about this getaway as well and hoped that Charles had decided that spending more time together would strengthen their relationship. Charles had other ideas, and on the Saturday evening of their stay in a little cottage in the rolling, lush hills of West Virginia, Charles asked Annette to marry him. Annette didn't hesitate to agree and it became the beginning of what was to become a very strong marriage and love affair.

Charles and Annette waited eight years before they decided it was time to add a member to the family. After several misses, Annette finally became pregnant and gave birth to a baby girl, Claire Marie Mitchell. As it worked out, Claire was to be an only child. Charles continued to work hard but he and Annette decided not to lose sight of the needs of a child growing up in their household. There were to be no full-time nannies and she would only attend the very best of schools. Claire was to be groomed as not only a successor to Mitchell Industries, but also an independent child who could go through life without having her hand held on a daily basis. Claire complied by doing well in school, making numerous friends, and having an open mind. She was well-liked by all of the family as well as the friends she made along the way. Upon Claire's graduation from Bucknell, she was offered the opportunity to go to graduate school at the University of her choice so that she could continue her studies in the field of Political Science. If she wanted, she could take a brief hiatus and do some traveling.

As Claire continued to look out the patio window, Lada Gaga's voice suddenly appeared singing "Bad Romance". Claire knew after the first bar that it was a call on her cellular. She glanced at the phone as if to determine whether she should answer it or not. Finally, just as soon as Lady Gaga was preparing to sing the line "I'm in a Bad Romance", she picked up. It was her Mom's sister, Susan, calling.

"Hi, Aunt Susan".

"How did you know it was me?"

"Caller ID, How is everything?"

"Well, I just wanted to know if you were picking up your folks at the airport. They arrive back from Paris today."

"Daddy usually has a driver pick them up. He thinks it is an imposition to have one of us deal with the airports."

"He's probably right, Claire. Well, let me know when they get in, or I am sure one of them will call me. I am eager to know how the trip went. How romantic!!! Paris! Some day!"

"Take me with you, Aunt Susan! It is one city I have always wanted to visit. I actually took up French in school because I always thought that just the name "Paris" was so enchanting."

"Well, we will both find out one day".

"Bye, Aunt Susan. Someone will be in touch later after they are home."

An hour passed as Claire had decided to stretch out on the sofa to do some reading. She was a big Stephen King fan and always grabbed his latest offerings. His stories seemed bizarre to Claire, but she enjoyed his sense of humor in every book, and practically every chapter. He seemed to have a keen way of making horror a 'tongue-in-cheek" adventure. As she read, Lady Gaga once again came to life on her cellular.

"I've got to change that ringtone."

"Claire, Claire, turn on the TV right now!"

"What? What, Aunt Susan?"

"Just turn it on, that's all. I will stay on the line."

Claire reaches for the remote and starts flicking through all of the local stations. They are all airing the same "Breaking News". It seems that JFK Airport tower has lost contact with Passionaire Flight 103 from Paris to New York City. Claire stays on one news channel.

"Airport authorities are trying to determine if this is merely a communication issue. There have been incidents like this in the past. The public is asked not to panic until more information comes in."

"Aunt Susan, are you there?"

"Yes"

"They say not to panic. What??? What time are they due in? What airline are they on? Oh my God!"

"I don't know, Claire. See if there is an itinerary around somewhere in the house."

"Hang on."

Claire knows that her parents usually leave her instructions and a list of flights and hotels. She rifles through some papers in the kitchen.

"Here it is, here it is."

"Still there?"

"Yes, what, what?"

"Let's see, Claymoire Hotel, something in Provence, okay … flights. Oh shit!!"

"What, Claire?"

"Passionaire flight number 103, arriving at 3:30 PM".

"I am coming over now, Claire. Ohhhhhh..!!!!!"

"I am here, Aunt Susan, come quickly".

Claire has not taken her eyes off of the TV screen since hanging up with Susan. Nothing has changed. There is no evidence of a crash, but communications are lost. Susan pulls up in front of the house and bangs on the door. Claire rushes to the door to open it, looks at Susan, with a frantic look on her face, and without saying a word, rushes back to the TV. Both stand there in front of the large screen without sitting. Neither has spoken a word.

"JFK authorities are now saying that the aircraft, Passionaire Flight 103, had lost contact with a check point near Newfoundland, Canada. It was supposed to be passing over Newfoundland about 12 minutes ago en route to its destination, JFK Airport in New York City. Stay tuned for more updates as they come in."

Claire and Susan simultaneously look at one another. Tears are streaming down Claire's face and Susan is simply frozen with fright with a very distressed look upon her face. "No, no, no, no, no" cries Claire.

"We have an update. This has just arrived at our news desk. It appears that Passionaire Flight 103 is indeed down in the Atlantic Ocean.

Canadian Air Force officials have determined that there are what appear to be pieces of an aircraft afloat at sea, approximately 65 miles off the shoreline. There is still no confirmation, but the immediate and sad unofficial word is that the sightings are of Passionaire Flight 103."

Claire grabs Susan and heads to the sofa. They both sit and squeeze one another, crying, sobbing outwardly. Lady Gaga begins her "Bad Romance" chant, but Claire is not of the mindset to answer. They sit for more than an hour without a word. Neither moves until there is a loud knock at the front door. The Saddle River Police are there represented by a male and a female officer. "May we come in?" Claire just waves them in and walks away. They retreat from the front door into the family room where they all sit just staring at one another.

"Ms. Mitchell, your father had asked that we notify you in the event of any emergency. His secretary had left a copy of your parents' itinerary at the Police Station. Unless there has been a change of flights, we are regretfully here to inform you that they are likely gone."

Claire sobs loudly. The woman police officer goes to the sofa where Claire is sitting and sits beside her. She takes her hand. Claire is sobbing uncontrollably.

"I am so sorry, Ms. Mitchell. I know there is nothing we can do or say to make you feel better about this. But, if you can think of anything, please give us a call. Here's a card with the number of the police station on it. Would you like us to mention this to any of your neighbors?"

"Please don't. I really don't know our neighbors that well."

"OK, that's fine Ms. Mitchell. Call us if you need us. We are there for you."

"Yes, thanks, thanks."

The officers leave. The male officer had nothing to say that entire time he sat there. He was either too dumbstruck to talk, or he plainly had nothing to say in this situation. Claire and Susan nudge up to one another and embrace.

"I need a drink and a tranquilizer, Aunt Susan."

"Double that."

"Come, let's go to the kitchen. There isn't much that we can do but pray that there is some hope. Some survivors. Or maybe it just didn't happen at all."

Susan merely looks at Claire with a "time to accept reality" look on her face. The two sit and drink wine, sobbing intermittingly. At 11:00 PM, Claire wakes up in a daze on the family room sofa. Still in a daze, she notices that Susan had left her a note on the coffee table. "Call me in the morning. I hope you can sleep. I am devastated." Claire, still foggy from the over-consumption looks around at the empty house and once again begins to sob. Drowning one's sorrows is temporary; the sorrows re-emerge and explode shards of emotion within her. Every type of emotion possible, save joyful ones, rage through Claire's mind. What next? Sleep evades Claire for the remainder of the night. She takes a shower, throws on a pair of workout clothes, and roams the house. Every sign of this cohesive family jumps out at her from every angle, from family portraits, to decorations, a coffee pot, an empty bedroom, a beautiful garden, and the feeling of love that always embraced every corner of this estate. A feeling of nausea rises from the depths of Claire's belly and she does everything to keep from getting sick and passing out. Lying awake all night is taken as a strange combination of a curse and a gift. The curse makes her focus on the tragedy while the gift enables her to remember all that they had together. This just can't seem to be happening. Numbness greets denial as Claire steps outside and looks over the gardens. It is eerily quiet, as if someone told the gardeners to stay away and pay their respects. Claire longs for the sounds of mowers, clippers, voices; but there is nothing other than the still of emptiness in the air.

The house land line phone had been ringing all morning. Claire had opted to not speak with anyone until she was ready. But, now it is once again ringing and it is mid-morning. Claire wanders over to the phone sitting on a table in the family room. She merely stares at it and after the first ring picks up. She opts not to say a word. "Claire? hello, Claire? Are you there? It's Victor Wells." Victor is the family attorney and good friend.

"I am here, Victor".

"Claire, oh Claire, we are so sorry."

Silence.

"Claire, I know you probably do not want to speak right now, but Veronica and I would like to stop by and see you this afternoon, but only if you are up to it".

"Come, Victor, any time".

"OK, Claire, we will be there at 2:00 PM. I am so sorry, Claire. I wish there was something we could do for you."

"Thank you. I will see you later."

At exactly 2:00 PM, Victor and Veronica are at the front door. Claire opens the door and lets them in. Both embrace Claire and they proceed to the patio.

"Sorry, I have nothing to offer the two of you to eat or drink."

Veronica leans towards Claire, "Don't even mention it. We are fine."

After several minutes of condoling conversation, Victor reaches into his pocket and pulls out a piece of paper and a pen. He obviously had prepared some notes.

"Claire, this devastating loss will be hard on all of us for a long time. But, we will get through it. I am the executor of the estate and I will keep you advised of every single action that takes place along the way. Besides the company, your Dad and Mom had many assets. You are the only dependent and sole survivor, so you, of course, are the sole benefactor. But, it will take weeks, maybe months, to sort it all out. I have planned a meeting with the company attorney, Fred Michaels, tomorrow. And, don't worry about a thing. Nothing will be decided about any of this without your consent."

"I know nothing about how all of this is handled, Victor, and the company?"

"I told you, don't worry, you are in good hands. Everybody will be working to make sure that all is taken care of in a manner that serves you, your parents, and the company best."

"Thank you Victor. It's all in your hands. Please don't think me rude, but I need to be alone again."

"No problem, Claire, we understand. We are leaving now but will stay in close touch."

It takes Claire a few days before she is ready to leave the house. She finally decides to hop into one of the cars and go to the store. Fortunately there was enough food to get her by for a few days. The solitude had done her well. She had figured out how to silence the phones and ignore the media. Sleep was at a premium, but she knew that her survival would have been paramount for her parents, so she would do her best to move on. Claire walks briskly through the local market with her workout clothes on, sunglasses firmly in place, and a baseball style cap on her head. When she arrives home, there is a tall gentleman walking up her driveway with a box in hand. He looks strangely familiar, so she stops the car and lets down the window.

"Hello, Ms. Mitchell".

"Hi."

"Oh, I am Anthony Donato. We live next door."

"Yes, yes, I know who you are. And, your wife is Suki, from Donsuki Salon in New York?"

"That would be us. Well, we heard about what had happened, so we decided to wait a few days. Suki made some of her famous Korean pancakes for you."

"That's quite sweet, Anthony."

"Well, it's the least we could do. Listen, Ms. Mitchell."

"Claire."

"Yes, Claire. Suki and I would like to have you join us for dinner this evening. Nothing fancy. We cook burgers and the like outside. We will have some wine and beer too."

Claire looks at Anthony for a moment without expression. "Sure, yes, OK, I will be there. What time?"

At 7:00 PM, Claire knocks on the Donato's front door. When the door opens, Suki, Anthony, two handsome twin boys and a beautiful young teenage girl are there to greet her.

"Hello everyone, I am Claire."

"Hi! I'm Suki."

"I'm Sean."

"I'm Jack."

"And, I'm Shannon."

"And Lucy lives outside."

"She lives outside??"

Sean explains, "Well, Lucy is our dog." Everybody chuckles.

"Well, this is overwhelming, thanks for the invite."

Anthony steps up. "We know what you must be going through, so we just wanted to be neighborly."

The evening was actually fun for Claire. There was plenty of food, lots of wine, and beautiful piano music offered up by Shannon and Jack. Claire managed the first smile of the week and it felt good. She almost did not want to go home. But, it was time to face reality again, so home she went.

The memorial service took place in a very large Methodist Church in Paramus, New Jersey. Every seat was filled and there were several people standing in the aisles and behind the pews. Hardly a sound could be heard. Audible sobbing and sniffling were apparent throughout the building. The two empty caskets in front of the stage was an eerie sight. The bodies had not been recovered, but the evident lack of signs of life created a resignation that they were gone. The robed minister strolled slowly to the pulpit as young altar assistants lit candles on each side of the pulpit and the stage. Claire, wearing a black knit dress and wearing sunglasses, is quietly seated in the front row. On her left is Aunt Susan and directly to her right is Victor Wells.

"When we enter the Ministry, we understand that part of what we do is to preside over services such as this one. It does not get easier, and in this case, it is one of the most difficult. If you look around, you can see the amount of love and caring that exists for Charles and Annette Mitchell. The magnitude of this loss is not limited to family and friends. It extends to our community, the business world, and all of those who knew how important this family was to all of us. So, today we honor their lives, and remember the most favorable impact that they both had on all of us. We pray, Lord, that they shall rest peacefully and that the memory of these two great figures in our community will be everlasting."

Victor Wells' office assistant had arranged for many people to mourn with Claire and others at the Mitchell Estate following the service. The home was filled with people. The gamut of emotions ranged from pure unsettling grief to pleasant smiles. The caterers brought enough food to serve the entire community. Claire wandered about and wished that this would be over soon. She quickly tired of hearing words of sympathy, answering questions about how she feels, and discussing her plans for the future. Some were crass enough to inquire about her plans for Mitchell Industries to which her standard, but polite, answer was "I do not know at this point, thank you." Victor approached Claire and asked her to step out to the patio with him for a moment, to which Claire pleasingly agreed.

"I have met with Mitchell Industries Corporate Counsel, Fred Michaels. He too is devastated. I am taking care of the probate work, and Fred has already begun research on the corporate structural needs. We would both like to meet with you tomorrow afternoon. Does that work for you?"

"That's fine, Victor, I will be here."

"Great then, we will be here tomorrow, and hopefully, by the time we leave, you will know which direction we will all agree to take. Oh, and Claire, please bear in mind that you will be asked to make some major life decisions. I will help you along the way, but the final word must come from you."

"Got it."

Fred Michaels, a short man wearing a fashionable suit and a bold power tie, arrived at the same time as Victor. Victor was dressed more casually, but had an air of confidence that left Claire feeling quite comfortable. She was unsure of Fred Michaels, but if Victor felt confident that he would represent the company and Claire well, then she was happy with him.

Victor seemed to be the one to lead the meeting and started by asking Fred if he had explored the options for the company. Fred seemed prepared and started.

"Claire, the company is well-run. Your Dad, Charles, was the Chairman of the Board. Through the years, your Dad carefully hand-picked people for each division of the company. He wanted to be certain that it could basically run smoothly on its' own. Your Dad, of course, did not predict his early demise, but it became quite obvious that he wanted the company to survive any potential "nicks" let's call it, and continue without any bumps or bruises. The issue becomes that of ownership. It is not a public company, it is privately held by your family, now you."

"What does that mean, Mr. Michaels?"

"Well, simply stated, you are the sole owner of Mitchell Industries."

"Mr. Michaels."

"Fred."

"OK, Fred. I just finished college. I majored in Political Science. I know as much about running a company as you know about roping cattle."

"Here's your options, Claire. You can take a seat on the Board and run the company, or you allow the Board of Directors to elect a new Board Chairman and hire consultants to oversee all operations. I personally believe that this option is absolutely, unequivocally workable."

"What are the other options?"

"The other options are to work out some type of hybrid of what I just mentioned or simply sell the company. I don't believe the sale of the company is the best option."

"Oh? And why is that?"

"Well, for a few reasons. I am not sure that the market value is the same as it has been without your Dad at the helm. And, there aren't too many suitors for this type of industry."

"Didn't another company offer to buy us a few years back?"

"Yes, good memory, Claire. It was Brandt Davidson, a medical equipment giant."

"Would they still be interested?"

"Perhaps, but honestly, with their knowledge that your Dad is gone,

I am afraid that the offering price might be less than the company value."

"Contact them, Fred. Tell them I am selling the company."

"Wow! That was a quick decision."

"I'll await their response."

"Are you sure you don't want to give this more thought, Claire. I mean …"

"No thought, I am selling. Victor, your turn."

Victor and Fred look at one another with raised eyebrows and an element of surprise. Victor is temporarily rendered speechless then politely asks Fred to leave as he wants to speak with Claire about personal finances. Fred obliges, offers his continued condolences, and quietly leaves.

"Claire, why would you sell the company? It would provide a nice residual stipend for you. And, the company will continue to run just fine."

"Surely you are kidding, Victor. Any amount of money generated from the sale of Mitchell Industries will be far greater than any stipend I will need to go forward."

"But, you are still a very young woman. Who knows what the future has in store?!"

"Discussion over."

"Okay, Claire, the will probate is in order. There is a waiting period and there will be taxes to pay, but I did a quick ballpark estimate of your Dad and Mom's net worth. Are you ready?"

"Go on, Victor."

"Well, between the home, life insurance, which they both had by the way, savings, mutual funds, other investments, the net worth is in the neighborhood of Five Hundred and Forty Million dollars."

"That's considerably more than I expected."

"Your Dad was a very clever and bright money manager, and he did it without any help from the outside. Look, I'll wait to hear back from Fred regarding Mitchell Industries and I will get back to you. In the meantime, if you need anything, just let me know."

"Thanks, Victor. I think I'll go for a walk right now."

The week that passed after the initial meetings was quiet, but productive for Claire. She had made up her mind that she cannot allow this tragedy to stop her from living. Life would be different without Mom and Dad, but it might be a good idea to continue their legacy, whatever that might be. Claire knew of the many philanthropic organizations with which they had both been involved. She dug through countless records, correspondence, and made several calls. She knew that there was a lot of work to be done. Getting started was her biggest hurdle. At the end of the week, Fred Michaels called for an appointment with Claire. Claire welcomed Fred and they adjourned to the patio. Sipping iced tea that Claire had prepared, they looked out into the garden where a sole worker was attending to the plantings.

"Are you going to be okay, Claire?"

"I think so, Fred. Only time will tell. I have prayed for strength. Let's just hope that the delivery truck shows up soon."

"Claire, the Board of Brandt Davidson has met. They continue to have high interest in the purchase of Mitchell Industries."

"And?"

"Well, they have come up with an offer."

"Yes?"

"They are offering $750 Million dollars, a straight cash deal."

"Didn't they make an offer when they had interest a few years ago?"

"Yes, they did. They had offered $900 Million then."

"What changed?"

"Well … …"

"Well, what Fred? Because my dad is no longer there?"

"Sadly, I think so Claire."

"Oh, really??!! Okay Fred, you can go back to them and tell them that I am offering a counter of $2 Billion."

"Oh, Claire. We can't …"

"Wait, can't or won't?"

"They will never go for that Claire. Let's be practical here. The $750 Million offer is at least four times EBITDA."

"Great, Fred, but I do not know what "ebudah" is, and quite frankly I don't care. $2 Billion."

"Claire, be reasonable, EBITDA are earnings before certain events take place such as interest, taxes, etc. I don't think I can go back to them with your counter offer."

"WHO are you working for here, Fred? Mitchell Industries or Brandt Davidson? If you are unwilling to take my offer to them, I will find someone that will."

"No, no, Claire, listen. Okay, okay, I will take the offer to them, and I will try to sell it, but please do not get your expectations too high."

"Call me with the results, Fred. I will eagerly await your call. For now, I have some things I must do."

"Thanks, Claire, I'll be back to you as soon as I know something."

For four days from the time that Fred departed, Claire was able to continue her research, do some walking, and think about her next steps. The phone had grown quieter as most began to realize that Claire just wanted to be left alone for the time being. The first caller on the fifth day was Fred himself.

"Claire, I have some answers for you, will you be home?"

"Yes, I will be here, Fred."

"See you in an hour."

Claire watched out the front window as Fred pulled up in his shiny black BMW sedan. He appeared to be shuffling some papers in the front seat, gathered them up, stuffed them into a briefcase and headed for the front door. Claire had swung the front door open before Fred had even reached the top step.

"Come in, Fred. Want some iced tea?"

"Sure. Meet on the patio?"

"You've got it."

Five minutes later they are both once again sipping iced tea. Claire decides to skip the pleasantries and get right down to business.

"What have we got, Fred?"

"I brought your counteroffer to the Brandt Davidson attorneys. I gave them two days to deliberate and decide. At first, they thought that you were "working them."

"What does that mean, Fred?"

"Never mind. Here's what they came up with. They will pay $1.35 Billion for Mitchell Industries, cash deal, no stock."

"I accept, with one condition. Closing must be in 30 days or less."

"Claire, I don't know …"

"There you go again, Fred. I am confident that you will facilitate a closing within 30 days."

"And, if they cannot do it?"

"Then, a $100,000 penalty for each day that passes the 30 day mark."

"Fair enough, Claire. I'll jump right on it."

Claire was well aware that she needed help managing this newly found wealth. She felt like she could manage. Her attitude was that it was just money, and if safely stored, she could draw on it for her needs. She was careful not to list her "wants" as what she wanted was not attainable with money. Peace, love, good health, tranquility, and a family were among the common things that most people want, but they do not sit on the shelves of department stores. Who could she trust to help her manage this pile of assets? Claire's Uncle David is a financial planner. Why not call him? But, Claire distinctly remembers her Dad telling her one day that one should never lend or borrow money from a relative. And, in fact, nobody should have any type of financial relationship with a relative. It would "only lead to problems", ones that were irrevocable or irreparable. So, Uncle David was out. She knew that he would call and would likely be insulted, but she decided to merely say, that "my finances are under control, but thanks anyway." While dwelling on this bittersweet dilemma, she decided to call upon her Finance professor from Bucknell University, Dr. Edward Goldblum.

"Good morning, Professor Goldblum, this is Claire Mitchell. Do you remember me?"

"Of course, I remember you, Claire, and yes, I have heard the tragic news. I am so sorry."

"I need your help with something if you will?"

"I will do anything for you that I am able, Claire."

"Professor Goldblum, I have come into a large amount of assets and I need some help managing them."

"Have you thought about hiring a Financial Planner, or as some of them call themselves, Asset Managers?"

"I don't want that, Professor Goldblum." I want someone young and smart, with a good head on his or her shoulders, and eager to help without stuffing their own pockets."

"I have an idea for you, Claire. I have a colleague who actually teaches Asset Management at Wharton Business School in Philadelphia. I am sure that he may know of a few students who might want to meet with you. With your permission, I will give him a call."

"Go right ahead. Let's start with three. We can meet at our family attorney's office here in New Jersey. I will pay their travel expenses for the meetings."

"Sounds great, Claire. I'll be in touch with you just as soon as I have some answers."

Within a few days Claire was sent a list of three names to contact. Victor's assistant set up the meetings and she was ready to begin the interview process. Victor offered to assist, but Claire felt like she knew what she was looking for. She asked Victor to sit in on the meetings, but she would make the choice.

The first candidate walked into the conference room where Claire and Victor sat waiting. He was tall, wore a neatly-tailored Brooks Brothers suit, his hair had been perfectly groomed, and his demeanor without even having said a word was one of extreme confidence. Claire had always observed body language in the past. Her Dad had told her that sometimes you can tell more about a person simply by the way they carry themselves. Claire pretty much knew what was coming as she began the questioning.

"Hi, I am Claire Mitchell, what's your name please?"

"I am Brett Forston, the third."

"The third?"

"Yes, of course my Dad and Grandfather were also named Brett."

"Yes, Ok then. Brett, do you know why you are here?"

"Well, I am told that you are seeking an experienced Asset Manager."

"Uhmm, that's not necessarily true. Experience was not in the equation. Plus, you just finished school, so where does the experience come from?'

"My family has known that asset management has been my passion, so I have been assisting the family in these financial matters."

"Your Mom and Dad?"

"Yes, and cousins, aunts, uncles, and such."

"I see. Well how do you think you can help me?"

"We can put together a plan that will maximize your returns and keep you liquid whenever you need it."

"Who is we?"

"Well, me of course, and any other professionals we need to consult with along the way. Oh, and you of course, Ms. Mitchell."

"Okay, Brett, that would be all for now. Thank you."

"That's it?"

"Yes, that's it, Brett. Thanks."

"When will I know what you have decided?"

"You can know right now. You are not hired. But thank you for coming in. Victor's associate will be sure that your expenses are taken care of. Have a nice day."

"Thank you."

At noon, the second candidate enters the conference room. This candidate, named William Cutler, mirrored Brett except that he wasn't as "experienced" as Brett. He had told Claire that he recently became engaged and was excited that he would have the chance to earn some income as they would need it for the marriage. Claire knew the commitments involved in preparing for a marriage and actually working on the new relationship. She wasn't prepared to share her business needs with some other woman's social needs. William was thanked and dismissed as well.

At 2:00 PM, candidate number three is shown into the conference room. He looked a bit disheveled, not as well-groomed as the prior two, but there appeared to be some effort made to pull himself together prior to the meeting. Not all of his hairs were in place and one side of his shirt collar was propped up and the other was not. This fellow's priorities were other than making first impressions. But, Claire observed that he had an innocent look about him.

"Hello, I am Claire. Sit down and make yourself comfortable. Your name please?"

"John. John Smith."

"Creative."

"Huh?"

"Never mind. John, do you know why you are here?"

"Yes."

"Well, tell me then."

"You are wealthy, you are single, and you need help organizing, tracking, and accounting for your assets."

"Close. Do you think you can help me?"

"I'm pretty sure."

"Pretty sure?"

"Well, I have never done this before. But if you tell me what you want, I can pull it off."

"John, are you in a relationship?"

"Are you allowed to ask me that?"

"Oh, oh, right, no, I guess I am not. Are you in a relationship?"

"No."

"Can you work under duress?"

"Sure."

"Why do you think so?"

"I have made it through six years of college with a constant badgering from my parents to succeed or else. The pressure was always on, even when I felt like I needed a rest. I endured that for six years to the point that I missed their haranguing when it was quiet."

"Okay, John, here's the rules. You tell me if you can live with them. If not, I want to know now. You must be honest, because if you are merely looking for a job, that isn't why you are here. You can do very well with me, but you must adhere to my needs. Get it?"

"Got it."

"Okay, John, for starters, the hours are 24 hours per day, seven days a week. If you need time off anytime, let me know and I will give it consideration."

Victor looks over at Claire with an incredulous look on his face. He shakes his head and prepares to hear more.

"John, you must report what is going on at all times. I hate surprises. If I call you with a request, I expect it to be fulfilled expeditiously. You never question what I do. Most important, if you are asked who you work for; do not reveal it to anyone. Not your mother, not your father, not your siblings, not your friends, not anybody. You can just say that you are working for a private equity firm and leave it at that. Got it so far?"

"Yes, I'm good."

"Great, John. How much money do you expect to make your first year out of Wharton?"

"Well, I don't really have expectations. But, I am told that starting salaries straight out of school start at about $65,000 – $80,000 per year."

"I see. Okay here's the deal. I will pay you $120,000 per year. I will rent an apartment for you near to where I live, and I will cover your related expenses. Do you have a car?"

"Yes."

"Good. Use your car. Keep track of your car expenses. Also, internet, phone, etc. Get a separate phone number to be used only for my business. If I call you and you are on the line, excuse yourself from whomever you are speaking, and take my call. Are we clear on everything?"

"Yes, Ms. Mitchell. When would you like me to start?"

"Tomorrow."

"Uhm, okay."

"What are you thinking, John Smith?"

"Honestly?"

"Honestly."

"I am thinking that you know what you want and will clear any barriers to make certain it happens. I also think that you put a lot of value on loyalty, honesty, and hard work. I think that I can be what you seek."

"Great then. I am looking forward to working with you!"

After three weeks, it became apparent to Claire that she needed a break from everything related to the tragedy. Her mind wandered constantly from where to start to how to continue to what's next? Phone calls, piles of mail, unexpected visitors, and the daily exposure to a life that was took its' toll on Claire's nerves. It was time to get away. But where? Mom had kept a large file of vacation destinations, so Claire took the initiative to pull out the file, spread all its' contents across the family room floor and start digging. Warm places, high places, adventurous places, spas, cities, countries, and it was endless. In the center of this array of travel destinations was a large map of the US. Across it, her mom had drawn a line from one end of the country to another using a highlighter. Stapled to the back of the map was a long note outlining a proposed car trip. She and Dad had planned a cross-country jaunt. How exciting! It did not take long for Claire to decide that was exactly what she was going to do. She would pack up enough clothes and other necessary travel items, hop into a car, and hit the highways.

The cars in the garage were only reminders of what was. Claire had had enough of reminders. She called Victor and asked that he and John Smith coordinate the sale of the vehicles. She did not want to see them again. They were to be moved to another location and liquidated. The one car that Claire had used herself, a two year old Honda, was not what she wanted to take on a road trip across the country. It was certainly reliable and could make the trip, but it did not fit into her plans. Claire decided to visit a few automobile dealerships in Paramus and make a decision there. The first place she pulled into was Towne Square BMW. Claire pulled up in front of the dealership. Dressed in a workout outfit, no makeup, hair pulled back, a pair of trainers on her feet, she walked in. It was early so there weren't any customers as yet. A tall, well dressed salesman in his early 40's approaches Claire.

"Good morning, miss, how may I help you?"

"Dunno, may I look around?"

"Sure, take a look. We have some very nice beauties sitting out here."

Claire finds her way over to a red BMW convertible with the top down. She walks around it a few times, the salesman hot on her heels.

"How fast does the top go up and down?"

"Quickly."

"And, how is the quality of the sound system?"

"You know that this car lists for $80,000."

"Uhm, I asked about the quality of the sound system. How did that question become answered with the price of the car?"

Just then, a well-dressed middle-aged couple enters the showroom and walk over to a BMW sedan near the front. The salesman tells Claire, "Excuse me", and saunters over to help the couple. Claire just looks up very surprised and decides to wait and see if he returns. After fifteen minutes, it was obvious that he was not coming back. Somewhat disappointed, Claire walks over to a line of offices. The largest office is on the end, and a gentleman in his fifties is sitting at a desk scratching some notes or numbers on a pad.

"Excuse me. Are you the manager?"

"Actually yes, I am. Tony Rialto. May I be of help to you?"

"Yes, you can. I was looking at a car, that red convertible over there. The salesman seemed to be quite interested in helping me until another customer walked through the door. I never saw him again."

"Well, maybe he thought you were just looking."

"What in the hell does that mean?"

"Well, you know. Maybe he thought you weren't serious about buying a car."

"How would he know THAT?"

"I am not sure."

"I wanted to buy that car and I am ready, but forget it. And please pass this message to your salesman. If it will fit, tell him to shove that convertible where the sun doesn't shine."

"Ouch."

"Sorry, but that's how I feel".

"I am sorry that you had this experience Ms … …"

"Mitchell, Claire Mitchell."

"Uh oh, oh shit, Claire Mitchell as in just lost your folks tragically?"

"That would be me."

"Ms. Mitchell, I am so sorry for what happened here. Allow me to walk you to your car. I really don't want you to leave with a bad taste in your mouth."

"No problem."

"Look, Ms. Mitchell, wait here for me for one minute. I promise I will be right back."

Out of the corner of her eye, Claire sees that Tony Rialto is chatting with the salesman who ditched her. The conversation seems to be a bit heated. The salesman's arms are spread out in the "why" position. The salesman leaves, grabs a jacket and heads out the door. As promised, the manager is back.

"Sorry, I had to take care of something."

"Did you fire him?"

"Yes."

"You didn't have to do that. I didn't expect …"

"Not at all, Ms. Mitchell. I don't care if a chipmunk came in here to buy a car. Once a customer is engaged, you stay with the customer. He should know that."

The two walk out the front door. Claire looks to her right and sees a large lot filled with cars.

"What are all of those cars?"

"That's our used car lot."

"Can we stroll over there a second? I want to look at something."

"Sure, your wish is my command."

"That red pickup truck over there, in front of the office. Who's is it?"

"I believe it just came in on a trade."

"May I see it?"

"Sure, anything that makes you happy."

The two walk over to the red pickup. It looks quite clean, appears to be well taken care of, and there is no body damage. The used car manager walks out and says "hello".

"How much for the pickup?"

"It just came in on a trade. $2000, and it is yours. It's a beauty, nice and clean."

"How much did you give the person on a trade?"

"Well, I am not sure."

Tony Rialto steps in and asks how much the trade-in value was. He could sense that Claire was interested and still agitated. He wanted to show her some good faith from the dealership.

"We gave the owner $1000 on the trade-in."

"Okay, I'll give you $1100."

"Well, we have to place a warranty on it, pay commissions, etc."

"Put a new set of tires on it, tune it up, detail it, and I'll give you $1500. You can deliver it to my house. I will provide you with the address."

Tony looks at the used car manager and says, "Tommy, do it."

Claire arrives home and calls John Smith.

"John, I have a new asset I want you to manage."

"Fine. What is it?"

"A pickup truck."

"Oh boy, how do I manage that asset?"

"Here's how, John Smith. You get it registered and insured. You install the license tags on it, and you have completed the management for now."

"OK, gotchya."

Claire has a few items to take care before her journey. She and John Smith will go through all of the assets, decide which should be liquid for her use when needed, and begin drawing a roadmap of where they should be invested. John is delightfully aware of most important investment opportunities, but Claire has suggested that he "go conservative" and not take much risk. There is enough capital available to generate a significant return without compromising the values of any of them. The next item of business is to prepare herself for the journey.

"Good morning, thank you for calling Donsuki Townhouse Salon, may I help you?"

"Yes, may I please speak with Suki?"

"May I ask who is calling?"

"Please let her know that Claire Mitchell is on the line."

"Sure, please hold for a moment. I will let Suki know that you are waiting."

"Thank you."

"Hi Claire! How are you?"

"Suki, I need a favor, please. May I make an appointment to have my hair done?"

"Claire, when would you like to come in?"

"Whenever it is convenient for you."

"Listen, how about I pick you up at your house at nine o'clock tomorrow morning. I'll just fit you in. That way, you can roam around Manhattan while I finish up, and I'll give you a ride home, okay?"

"Perfect! Listen Suki, I want you to change my look."

"Okayyyy?"

"I no longer want to look like the pretty little rich girl. I want a tomboy look, something different."

"Do you want some color streaks in it also a la Cyndi Lauper?"

"Hmmmm, let's see what kind of magic you can pull out of your little stylist hat."

"Great, see you at 9:00 in the morning."

Donsuki Townhouse Salon was a warm surprise. It is quietly nestled between other townhouses on the highly fashionable 62nd Street in Manhattan, between Central Park and Madison Avenue. There was an exciting buzz inside as stylists, assistants, manicurists, and others were busily preparing for the day. Some had already started on customers. The air was filled with a cheery aura as transformations were commencing. End results would yield a vibrant look for its customers. There would be much deserved emotional as well as financial rewards for its operators. It was obvious that the employees of the salon admired and respected their boss, to the extent that the room actually lit up when Suki walked in. There wasn't a soul who did not greet her with an exuberant "Hi, Suki!" as she passed through. It became quite obvious to Claire that this rare combination of talent and charisma contributed to Suki's huge success in her industry. Suki guided Claire through the maze of stylist chairs, wash basins, and busy staff and sat her in the throne that had housed many high-profile personalities over the years. Claire's excitement about what was about to take place temporarily erased any feelings of sorrow that surrounded her in recent days.

"Let's see. What should we do with you?!"

"Suki, my look is in your hands. No more pretty little rich girl. I am about to hit the road on a long car journey across the continent. I do not want to stand out in any way, shape, or form anywhere along the way. Nothing prissy, and nothing bizarre. Just an ordinary girl on a mission to see America."

"I think I can handle that. I'm not sure about how to fit you in with Kansas, Nebraska, and the other middle States, but, I will give it my best. Ready?"

Claire watched through the mirror as the swift, flashing scissors sheared through her hair. In a matter of minutes, Claire's locks were falling gracefully to the salon floor. The end product was a short cropped style with a varied degree of length here and there. If it was manageable at the salon, she would make it manageable on the road. Interestingly enough, the artist otherwise known as Suki, had created a masterpiece. Claire never realized that the "tomboy look" could be delivered with any degree of elegance, but it was. It was hard for Claire to hide her exuberance as she stood, danced around the chair and continually gazed into the mirror. This was exactly what she came for.

"Suki, I love, love, love it. And I love you. I will go downstairs and pay then spend some time walking through Central Park and window shopping."

"Claire, there will be no paying. Come back at 3:00 and we will head back home."

"You are amazing, and I'll see you later."

Claire returned to the salon in time for the departure for New Jersey. In her hand was a neatly wrapped package from the Henri Bendel department store.

"Suki, this is for you. Thank you so much."

"Oh Claire, you didn't have to do that, but it is so appreciated."

"The magic that you make cannot be rewarded with money alone. You would not accept my money, but I want you to accept my appreciation in some way. You awakened a dormant spirit within me, a spirit that disappeared several weeks ago. Your talent and inspiration alone have helped me realize this new beginning. Thank you so much."

The ride back to New Jersey was as enjoyable as the visit to the salon. Claire was in the presence of a brilliant modern day philosopher. There were many "Suki-isms" from which to draw on. The most important lesson was that money does not equate with class. "Smart people never say they are smart, and rich people never say they are rich." Class includes many elements that we learn through interaction and observation. "Be yourself, Claire, and always remember that frogs were once tadpoles too." Kindness, caring, and empathy are contagious. When you exhibit these types of emotions, the world is yours at your fingertips. "Use your resources to help those who are less fortunate for reasons beyond their control. You will create a legacy, one that will be honored for years to come."

One week later, the pickup was clean, running smoothly, and packed. The journey was about to begin. John Smith had been at the house helping Claire prepare for the trip in any way that he could. "Be safe, Claire, take your time, don't pick up any hitchhikers, and call frequently to let us know how it is going."

"Thank you, John Smith. Protect the "kingdom" and don't worry. I can be as tough a cookie as needed.

"Good bye, Claire."

Claire had decided that her first stop would be in her college town of Lewisburg, Pennsylvania, home of Bucknell University. She would walk the campus and try to catch up with some acquaintances. The ride through New Jersey was beautiful. She never understood why New Jersey took such a bashing from folks who really did not know the State. The rolling hills and clean landscape rivaled anywhere else that she had been. Cows, horses, country cottages, and little villages adorned the landscape. Someone had once told Claire that New Jersey had more horses per capita than any other State. It made sense to her as it was a small State, but yet many of the rural spreads had been carefully preserved over the years. The Delaware Water Gap was always a breathtaking sight. The historic Delaware River wound quietly through hills that had been undisturbed. The images of this wilderness within close proximity of cities and growth blazoned through Claire's mind. She pulled over to grasp the view and relish in the fact that this was what her journey was all about. To discover and rediscover would create memories and enhance her knowledge of the world outside of the New York/New Jersey complex.

The Pennsylvania countryside was no less spectacular than that of the western part of New Jersey. The pickup was running smoothly and didn't seem to be burning as much fuel as she anticipated. Claire turned off the radio for a while and put her mind to work, gently recapping the last several weeks. She did not want anything to stand in the way of this escape from New Jersey and her recent past. But, tragedy has a way of nicking the soul. The thought of her parents and the grief they must have experienced as the plane plummeted to the sea rung deep. She had a difficult time shaking this image. All of the distractions that she encountered or even created herself could not extinguish the thought of these two wonderful people having to experience panic like that. There is no cure for loss, but happy thoughts and new aspirations can relieve the magnitude of loss. She finally pulled into Lewisburg and not much had changed in the few months since she left. The only thing that had changed was that she was no longer a student. Her brief stay in Lewisburg would be like any local.

The Lewisburg Country Inn was as unassuming a motel as any

she had seen. Claire had driven past it while she was a student, but never thought of it as anything other than a place that family or alumni might stay when visiting the Bucknell campus. So, this alumnus was going to give it a shake. Her room was cozy and had a vintage color TV. Everything appeared to be clean, and that was one of two criteria. The other was that it needed to be safe, and that too was apparent. Now settled, it was time for a beer. Having driven for three hours and close to two hundred miles, the reward of a cold one felt well-deserved.

Vaughn Bar looked as good as any other hole-in-the wall pub that she had seen. Claire had miraculously never set foot in this one when she was a student, so the new experience would suit her well. A few tables were occupied but there was nobody at the bar, so Claire nestled up to the bar and pulled a stool up under her. The bartender, a husky fellow in his late thirties with an attempt at a beard strolled over to Claire.

"What'll it be, miss?"

"A draft."

"How old are you?"

"22"

"Prove it. A student?"

"Was"

"And now?"

"Just passing through. Here's my ID."

"Yup, twenty two, you're good. Will a Budweiser work?"

"Does it have alcohol in it?"

"Yup."

"It'll work. Got anything to eat here?"

"Oh, sorry miss, only bar snacks."

"What's that in the jar up there on the bar, the greenish stuff?"

"Ha! Those are pickled eggs."

"People actually eat them?"

"Some people love them; some come in here just for them."

"Yah, I'll pass."

"There's a pizza place down the street. They'll deliver here. It's actually pretty good pizza."

"I can't eat an entire pizza."

"Well, no problem then. Wally, one of my customers is here every night, about 15 minutes from now, and sits at the other end of the bar. He would be quite happy to help you demolish a pizza."

"Okay, order me a pizza with Italian sausage, mushrooms, and onions."

"Uh, oh, Wally doesn't like mushrooms."

"Really!"

"Just kidding, Wally will eat anything."

Both laugh, and fifteen minutes later, almost as if there was a timer sitting on the bar, in strolls Wally. The pizza was soon to follow. Claire guessed that Wally was in his mid-fifties and had a bright red face and shocks of grey hair steaming out from under a baseball cap. He looked down at Claire and seemed to be more focused on the pizza than Claire.

"Hey pal, want some pizza?"

"Why sure."

"Well, slide on down here then. I'm not going to serve you from here."

"Thanks. I am hungry, just got in from work."

"What do you usually eat when you come in here every night?"

"Just hope someone ordered a pizza."

Both laughed out loud at this little exchange. Wally was indeed quite hungry and ate the lion's share of the pizza. Claire didn't mind as she was only good for a few slices anyway.

"My name's Claire. And yours?"

"Wally."

"Right. What type of work do you do?"

"Well, I wash windows."

"Interesting, Wally. In houses?"

"Houses, stores, schools, everywhere and anywhere."

"No problem doing the higher windows?"

"Well, yah, it has become a problem of late. I have knee issues and can't get up the ladder. But, my customers are loyal, so they keep me on. One of these days, I'll bring on a helper to do the hard ones."

"No fear of anyone ditching you for the competition?"

"Nope, ain't no competition." More laughs.

"What about you missy? A student here?"

"Uhm, no actually. I was a student, but now I am just passing through."

"Is that your pickup out there?"

"Yes, it is."

"Nice looking ride. I can't really say that you look like the pickup type though."

"Oh really, what then is the "pickup type", Wally?"

"Uhmmm, well, can't really say, but I'd think you'd have a flannel shirt with a hole or two in it."

"That's called stereotyping, Wally. And it's a bit warm for flannel right now."

"Yeah, sorry."

"No problem. Hey, you have a business card? I may still have some friends here in Lewisburg who could use your service."

"Sure do. Here's the card and it's got my address and telephone number on it. Thanks."

"My pleasure, Wally."

"Think I'll head back to the motel. I'm a bit tired as I have been doing some driving. Nice to meet you, Wally."

"Same."

The long ride, the beer, and the pizza wore Claire out. But, little by little the intervals between stops will expand. There are things to see and do, people to meet, and new wonders to capture. Claire washes up for bed, grabs a book, climbs under the covers, and decides to make a call.

"Hello, this is John Smith, how may I help you?"

"Very nice, John Smith, but it's just me."

"How is the trip going?"

"Smoothly. Listen, have you ever seen one of those contraptions where a worker climbs into a bucket of some type, presses some buttons, and then gets levitated into the air?"

"Yah, they are called aerial lifts, or high lifts, or something like that. My uncle used to work for a roofing company and used one."

"Good, find one, it doesn't have to be new, buy it, and send it to the address I am about to give you."

"I'll work on it. Who do I say it is from when it is shipped?"

"Nobody. Just do it."

"Okey dokey."

John Smith knew better than to question his boss. If she wanted the lift, she had a good reason. He would jump right onto this mission first thing in the morning.

Claire was up bright and early the next morning, ready to continue her odyssey. She decides to stay on Route 80 as it will ultimately be the direct line to her destination, California. She will stop near Toledo, Ohio this evening as six hours on the second day is the longest stretch she wants to tackle this early in the trip. It becomes curious that Route 80 is also known at The Ohio Turnpike in most parts. The other curious observation is that there are many country and western radio stations throughout Ohio. Isn't that restricted to Southern States? She supposes not. Toledo doesn't appear to be an exciting place, but it is a good place to "call it a day". One of the highway signs lists some of the motels from which she could choose. A Red Roof Inn sounds good, principally because she likes their TV commercials. Good marketing. The Red Roof Inn was easy to find and there was a single room available at a very reasonable price. Once settled, hunger sets in and it is decision time. The pizza the night before and another fast food joint for lunch did not meet her dining standards. So, she heads for the Red Roof office to ask for a recommendation.

"Good evening!"

"Hello, miss."

"Are you the concierge?"

"You are funny, miss. In fact, I am. And for that matter, I am also the maintenance man, the housekeeping coordinator, and as you may have noted earlier, the reception and reservations clerk."

"Well, great then. I need you to recommend a nice, healthy place where I can enjoy an evening meal."

"Just down the road, one mile on your left is a Sizzler Buffet. It is a very popular spot with the locals."

"Got it, and thanks."

"Oh, miss. Tonight is "kids eat for free with one adult meal night", so it may be a bit busy.

"I can handle it."

The parking lot at the Sizzler was packed, and Claire's was not the only pickup truck. This was going to be her kind of place. Two Harley Davidson motorcycles were alongside the only parking spot she could find. To Claire, they were chromed Gods adorned with leather in various places. Dad had always warned Claire not to climb aboard one as they are terribly dangerous. But, the temptation was there and Dad never expected to pass on the way he did. So, where is the danger? She was sure she could identify their owners inside the restaurant. As she passed through the door, the first thing she noticed was that it was packed. So much for finding the bike owners. The "dining rule" at the Sizzler is that you grab a tray and head down the line, which is exactly what Claire did. The steaks were near the front of the line, followed by an assortment of condiments and some side dishes. The corn on the cob looked less appealing than most as these half-sticks of corn were floating in a pool of warm corny water. At the end of the line were desserts. This was going to be a culinary haul. Once paid, Claire would need to find a place to sit. This particular establishment took a lot of pride in serving a large amount of food to an equally large amount of curiously large people. They did not however plan well for seating as practically every table was full. Claire walked around the seating areas with a dismayed look on her face. All of this wonderful grub and no place to consume it. A family of three was seated at a table of four. The woman at the table, likely the mom, looked up at Claire.

"Miss, you are welcome to join us if you cannot find a seat."

"Oh, I don't want to crash your little party here."

"It's not crashing at all. Come join us."

The couple introduced themselves as May and Al Johnson, and their son, Ethan, was with them. May and Al were likely in their late thirties, and Ethan was probably about ten or eleven.

Claire introduced herself, thanked them, and sat down.

"Well, this sure is a popular spot."

May took over the conversation. "It's the only place of its sort around. Plus, tonight is kids eat free night." With Al out of work, eating out has become one of them luxuries, so this place fits our budget just perfectly. We enjoy it."

"Oh, I am sorry you are out of work, Al."

"Well, yeah, one of those things, I am guessing."

"If you don't mind Al, one of what things?"

"My company supplied certain parts for the auto businesses up there in Detroit city, but them foreign companies make them for less, so our plant was shut down."

"I suppose that's a trend now. I am so sorry to hear it."

"Somethin' will come up, I'm not scared."

"I am sure it will, I'm sure it will."

May nodded as Al spoke, and then chimed in, "it's been very hard on Ethan here. He's been a good boy, doing well in school and all, but his dream has collapsed."

"What dream is that, Ethan?"

"Well, I want to play baseball and be on a Little League team, but the uniforms are expensive, so Dad said that I will just have to wait until next year."

"One year is not a long time."

"I love baseball, Ms. Claire, so I am just happy to stay at home and watch the Tigers on the TV."

"As in the Detroit Tigers?"

"Yah, that's our team."

May felt like she needed to add something to the conversation. "Miss Claire, Ethan has Cystic Fibrosis. He does quite well with it, but we are trying to take advantage of some of the things he enjoys while he can still enjoy them, like going to the ballgame. But with Al not working, things are a bit more difficult, but we manage. God has a way of answering our prayers, so we always try to stay positive about all of this. And you, Ms. Claire, are you from around these parts?"

"Actually no. I am from New Jersey, just passing through."

"Oh, well enjoy the stay."

"Thanks, and Al, I know a bunch of people in various parts of the country. If I know of anything that might suit you workwise, I can let you know."

"Geez, that'd be great. Here, I'll write down our address and phone number on a piece of paper. Thanks, Ms. Claire. We'll let you enjoy the rest of your meal. Thanks for joining us."

"Thanks for having me."

As Claire prepares to leave the Sizzler, she hunts around for the bikers, but they are nowhere to be found. In fact, the bikes are gone from the spot alongside her pickup. She wonders why she never heard them pull out. They can be demonstratively loud. Back in the hotel room, she undresses, takes a very welcome shower, climbs into bed, and then calls John Smith.

"Hello, John Smith."

"Hello, Claire."

"Got a pen?"

"Yup."

"Okay, I need you to arrange some things."

"Handing out some more gifts?"

"John, are you forgetting the rules? Never question me."

"Whoops, sorry. Shoot."

"Send a check to Ethan Johnson in the amount of Five Hundred dollars. I'll give you the address. On the check memo write "For baseball uniform and related supplies". Call the Detroit Tigers ticket office and arrange three season tickets for The Johnsons, include the directive in the envelope. Also, arrange a gift certificate for Sizzlers restaurant in Toledo in the amount of $500. Get it all out as soon as possible. And, most important, find out whom the best Pulmonologist Is in New York

City, preferably one who has treated Cystic Fibrosis patients. Make an appointment for Ethan Johnson, fly the family of three to New York and put them up in a decent hotel. It doesn't have to be the best, just close to the doctor's office. Got it?"

"The seats?"

"Seats?"

"Yes, where would you like the seats to be for the baseball tickets?"

"Oh, someplace in the mid-priced range will work."

"I'm all over it. Nice gift, Claire."

"They gave me a seat in a restaurant."

"Oh, yah? Now it all makes sense to me."

"Funny, John Smith, I will call you tomorrow."

"Okay, safe travels."

After a good night's sleep, Claire felt highly refreshed. Pulling her map out of her backpack, she considered making this a "progress day" where she would eat up several miles before stopping. She had nothing against Illinois and Indiana; she merely wanted to get closer to her west coast destination. Her objective for the day was to get to Omaha, Nebraska. In the back of her mind, a great mid-western steak could be very appealing. The thought of this meaty slab of perfection, with juices flowing from every part, sided by a giant baked potato enabled her to press on. She was ready, the pick-up was gassed up, and off they rolled. It was pretty much a straight shot to Omaha. There were a few stops along the way for food and potty. A feeling of euphoria lingered for a long part of the trip, enhanced by more country music, of which Claire was becoming used to. For the first time during the journey, she focused on lyrics. "You were a great catch then, but a poor catch now"; "I thought my life was complete until I met you"; "In my body there's a man, but in my heart there's a boy." Yes, these were sappy, but amusing and, to some extent, endearing. The highway sign that read "Omaha – 12 miles" made Claire's heart pound. A tiny bit of spittle trickled down her outer right lip as she thought of her sizzling steak, hopefully unlike the "Sizzler's steak" being placed before her. How charming to think of this romantic interlude between a meal and herself. Claire hated clichés for some reason, but "isn't this what life is all about" immediately came to mind.

At the "six-miles-to-Omaha" sign Claire pulled into a truck stop/filling station. It was time for the pickup to get fueled and ready for the next day. She would worry about where she would stay later, sometime after the interlude with a side of beef. As she stood by the pump fueling the pickup, she spotted a tall, rather handsome man heading her way. He wore nicely cut jeans and a sporty Ralph Lauren shirt. Looking around, she could see that he was coming from the area where all the big-rig trucks were parked and heading to the restaurant/shop area. They made eye contact as he was passing. Claire nodded a "hello", and he said "hi there".

"Nice little 4-wheeler you've got there."

"It gets me around."

"New Jersey tags, you've been on the road."

"Very observant."

"Out of boredom, we truckers observe such things."

"If you are so bored, why do you drive a truck?"

"Because it is in my blood, it is what I enjoy most in life."

"Most?"

"Well, maybe not "most", but it is a passion. I'm Hank, real name's Henry."

Claire wasn't entirely sure she wanted to divulge her real name to a trucker, so she replied, "Yah, I'm Norma."

"As in Norma Jean?"

"No, but that would have been a good idea. As in Norma Hope. Norma Hope Smith."

"Well, are you ready for this? My full name is Henry Thoreau."

"Impressive."

"Well, my father was from Quebec, immigrated to the Boston area, not unlike the original Henry David Thoreau, so they thought it would be cute to name me after him. You'll see that there is a striking resemblance, except I did not go to Harvard."

"You're funny! Say, listen, Henry, do you know these parts very well?"

"Sure do, I am through here quite often."

"Okay then, can you suggest a great steak restaurant for me? I have been craving a big juicy prime steak all day long."

"I know just the place, Norma. It is probably the finest restaurant in Omaha. Say, if you will allow me to treat you, I'll take you there. No strings, just a good meal among new friends."

"I agree. Let's do it. Do I have to ride in your big rig back there?"

"Do you mind taking your pick-up? I can show you the way."

"You're on."

The ride into the city was about six miles just as the sign said. On the way, Claire became curious about how Hank knew of this place.

"How did you know about this restaurant, Hank?"

"It's legendary. I don't get out here very often. It's hard to maneuver a rig in the city, let alone park it. So, I either call a taxi or get one of the trucker sluts to take me."

"Trucker sluts?"

"You have probably heard, or may be interested in knowing that there is a breed of woman that hangs out by the truck stops looking for a one-night stand."

"Oh my! And you participate in this?"

"Oh, no, no, no. I don't need that type of aggravation. They are there for one reason and one reason only."

"Money?"

"You've got it. But, since they will do anything for money, I pay them to give me a ride into the city. I take a taxi back."

"And you never pay them for other more intimate favors?"

"Never have, never will."

The meal was everything that Claire had hoped for. Two glasses of a good California wine complemented the meal beautifully. Claire felt slightly light-headed and became a bit more talkative. Earlier, she had refrained from saying a word as she relished the best steak she had ever had.

"Why did you decide to become a trucker, Hank?"

"The truth?"

"Yep, the truth."

"When I was a kid growing up in Massachusetts, I always watched as the big trucks would pull into town. Sometimes I would ride my bike to the outskirts of town, sit on a hill, and just watch the trucks rumble by. I decided maybe when I was twelve years old that someday I wanted to be a trucker and drive big rigs around the country. My parents thought it was a joke, and a pipe dream. But, I always knew that it was what I wanted to do. I felt like I needed to be a good student in order to win the respect from my parents, especially on this issue, so I eventually graduated as Salutatorian of my high school class. Everyone in my family and most of my friends thought I would go on to college like my Mom and Dad did. By the way, Dad was a lawyer and Mom is still working as a history teacher. But, no, I went straight to driving school so that I could live my passion."

"Amazing. Any regrets?"

"None. I have a friend in Boston, Norma. He's a black guy who I always admired. We played sports together and he finished in the top ten of my class also. He stayed close to home and attended Tufts University. Heard of it?"

"Of course."

"Well, my friend and I stayed in touch. A few years ago, he called and asked how life was going. I knew that he was a high-ranking executive at a large investment house in New York City. I told him that I could not be happier. I am working and earning money doing what I dreamed of doing. And guess what his response was."

"He envied you?"

"Exactly, Norma. He told me that he was quite well off, had a beautiful wife and family, but could not say that on a day to day basis that he was at all happy. He told me something that I will never forget."

"And, that was?"

"Norma, he said that if he had to do it all over again, he would follow his dreams and make a living doing what he enjoyed most in life.

He did not want to look back and say that he made all this money, but was never happy."

"What do you think he wanted to be or do, Hank?"

"I really do not know, but sitting in an office all day after a one and a half hour commute, barely seeing his family, and taking limited vacations was not his dream."

"It makes a lot of sense to me."

"What about love, Hank? Is it okay to ask you that?"

"It's personal, Norma, but love has eluded me. Doing what I do requires me to make sacrifices. I was married when I was only twenty years old. It lasted one year, almost to the day. It was my fault, but my love for the highway was in so many ways more intense than my love for her. I'm thirty-one now, and I guess that if I can make enough money and slow down a bit, I can find love again."

"Hank, you are still very young, I am sure it can happen."

"We shall see, we shall see. What about you, Norma? Have you found love?"

"No, no Hank. I am still young, only twenty-two. I have had a few boyfriends in the past, but nothing serious enough to have called it love. So, it is time to change the subject, right? In fact, it is probably time to get you back to your truck."

"Cool, let's go."

The ride back to the truck depot was quiet. Claire felt a bit buzzed.

"Hey Hank, may I see your rig?"

"Sure, it's right over there."

"Is it yours?"

"It's 100% mine, note is paid off and I am a debt-free driver, and they are few and far between."

The two stroll over to Henry's rig. To Claire's surprise, it is indeed a beautiful sight. She could tell how meticulous Hank is by how clean he kept it. There was custom paint on parts of the cab, and most other parts were chrome or neatly kept steel.

"Wow, I never imagined. May I see the inside?"

"Sure, climb up and follow me."

The inside of the cab was as immaculate as the outside. On the dashboard sat a small framed photo of an older couple.

"Your parents?"

"Yup."

"Nice. Where do you sleep?"

Hank reached up and slid a panel across. Behind it was a decent sized mattress and pillows.

"This must be heaven for you, Hank."

"It is."

"Where do you shower, clean up, etc.?"

"These truck stops are nicely equipped. They have showers, toothbrushes, toothpaste, etc. They sell them quite cheaply and they seem to be happy if we just buy their fuel. See, they compete for our fuel dollars. Where are you staying tonight, Norma?"

"Ha, I don't even know yet."

"Well, if you can trust me, you can sleep up in the cab with me."

"Hank, I do not trust you at all, but okay, I think I will. But it has been a long day and I need a shower."

"Let's go over to the depot and get you cleaned up. Then we can come back here. See what kind of guy I am, saving you a hotel bill?"

"You are quite kind, Hank."

The two cleaned and showered acquaintances climb into the cab of the truck. Claire wore a pair of shorts and a T-shirt she had retrieved from the pickup. Hank had on a pair of jeans and a Cummings Diesel T-shirt. Despite the cramped quarters, Claire adjusted quickly. There were two sleeping areas, the one below had an almost full-sized bed, and above it was a bunk.

"Don't think it forward of me, Henry Thoreau, but may I sleep alongside of you?"

"Do you snore?"

"How would I know that? I just hate bunk beds, unless you want to sleep up there, but I don't want to extract you from your environment. Plus, I am so tired from the long drive, nothing could happen anyway."

"Fine with me, Norma. Say, want a glass of wine before you retire?

I have a small carafe that I replenish every so often. It is in a carton, but I believe it is last year's vintage."

"Funny! Do you have wine glasses?"

"Paper cups?"

"Perfect."

The wine wasn't as bad as Claire had expected, and the chocolate chip cookies went well with the vintage, Chateau d' Walmart. Both tired, they climbed into the bed side by side. It took approximately 20 seconds for Claire to be completely unconscious. Hank was careful not to move much in the cramped quarters, but he could tell that Claire was as comfortable as a lady bug on a fern. Hank eventually fell asleep and awakened once during the night, only to find Claire's arm draped across his chest. The sun eventually rose and flashes of light found their way into the cab despite the assortment of room-darkening curtains.

Claire was the first to speak. "What time is it?"

"Oh, about 6:00 AM."

"Wow, I slept quite well. Did I snore?"

"Dunno, I was out too."

"You didn't try anything with me, Henry Thoreau."

"You didn't either, Norma Smith. I was just wanting to show you respect."

"Will you respect me in the morning?"

"What?"

"I think it's a line from a country and western song."

"I see, and yes, I think I would respect you anytime."

"What if I wanted some intimacy, Hank?"

"You can't always get what you want. And, I don't think it was a country and western song where that came from."

"Well, one of things that my Dad always preached was the difference between "wants" and "needs." But, in a case like this, I may have wanted it because I needed it. Does that make sense?"

"It does now."

"So, now that we have cleared the air of that Hank, let's grab some breakfast."

"The truck stop has an awesome breakfast. I know of some truckers that stop here just for the breakfast. And there's a place up the road with cheaper fuel, but a crap breakfast."

"Then let's have at it, trucker boy."

Breakfast was as good as Hank had described it, if not better. Claire had always thought that an egg was an egg, but nooooooo, these were made with love and compassion for the consumer. The toast was marvelous and the coffee was as fresh and bold as any Claire had ever had.

"Norma, where's your next stop?"

"Not sure, Hank. What do you think? I would like to limit my daily excursions to ten hours."

"I have an idea for you if you are up to it."

"Go on."

"Try to make it out Interstate 80 to Rock Springs, Wyoming. It is a little more than half way to Reno, Nevada. There's a clean nice Super 8 Motel in Rock Springs. They have a café attached to it where you can eat. The next day, drive out to Reno, Nevada. I have a load that I'll drop in Cheyenne, Wyoming. From there, I'll meet you in Reno at the truck stop. Do you like fish?"

"I enjoy a good piece of fish, yes."

"Okay, Norma, there's a restaurant in one of the casino hotels in Reno. They serve fresh Lake Trout from Lake Tahoe daily. You haven't had a piece of fish like this anywhere. I am willing to bet money on it."

"Hmmm, let me think about it, Yes!"

"OK, I will write down the name of the truck stop and mile marker. I'll meet you there sometime around 6:00 PM two days from now. Oh, and be careful about speeding in Utah. They're tough, especially on truckers."

"But, I'm not a trucker."

Hank gives a head nod towards Claire's pickup.

"Oh, guess I am a trucker of sorts."

The next two days were long for Claire. Just open highway without many attractions, at least none that she was interested in seeing. Hank had raised her excitement level to new heights with his mention of Reno, and Claire was determined to get there. Something about this man was alluring, but she could not put her finger on it. He was intelligent, attractive, and fun, but more than that, he was charming and had class. But, there was some unknown factor beyond all of that, and Claire was destined to know what it was. She would no longer stereotype or classify truck drivers, or anyone else for that matter. Claire dwelled on the story of Hank's friend who worked on Wall Street but could never say that he was happy. The conversation was eye-opening, and Claire believed that the quest for wealth as opposed to the quest for happiness could ultimately be destructive. Somewhere between Omaha, Nebraska and Reno, Nevada, Claire had made the decision to just go with the flow. She would allow fate to be her guide for the future. Planning is good for weddings and babies, but not personal growth. Oh, she knew what measures she would have to take to stay healthy, save falling out of the sky in a metal tube, so she would focus on being a healthy, alert woman. If frivolity became part of the equation, so be it, provided she could keep such antics under close personal supervision.

In the afternoon of the second day after Omaha, the 25 mile sign for Reno appeared before her. To Claire, the Gates of Heaven were before her, and she was about to open them and step in. What could be better than to spend a day of bliss with a fine gentleman? She pulled into the truck stop an hour earlier than planned. There was no sign of Hank's rig, but she hadn't expected him to appear until later. This was a good time to catch up on a light snack and get a shower. The shower facilities at this truck stop were even nicer than the last one. These places do not spare anything to keep these guys and gals happy. The women's showers and vanity areas were serviced by a full-time attendant. The attendant looked at Claire admiringly and asked if there was anything that she could do to make her visit comfortable. Claire immediately realized that a trucker's life was something far, far beyond anything she had imagined. Her immediate thought was to ditch the pickup and ride around the universe with Hank and his rig. Her Bucknell education in Political Science might not come in handy along the way, but it couldn't hurt.

At 5:45 PM, Hank's rig pulled into the truck stop. Claire watched as he maneuvered the rig into a parking spot for 18-wheelers to the right of where she was parked. Claire locked her pick-up and headed for the lot where Hank had parked. Hank watched as she approached the rig, climbed out, and greeted Claire with a powerful hug. The chills ran through Claire like a herd of wild horses in pursuit of an elusive field of fresh grass.

"Well, you made it, Norma."

"A piece of cake. I'm even showered and gassed up. Good to see you, trucker man."

"You too. I thought a lot about you along the way, my friend. Look, let's head over to the depot. I'll clean up, and then we can head into Reno. Are you ready for that?"

"Was Sitting Bull ready for George Custer?"

"Gotchya!"

"By the way Norma, do you have a dress?"

"I have a summer dress, why?"

"The place we are going to is a bit up-scale. It is one step above jeans and a T-shirt."

"Are you going to wear a dress, Hank?"

"Well, since I gave up wearing dresses a few years ago, I suppose I'll just wear a pair of slacks and a polo shirt."

"I won't embarrass you, Hank. Get on with it."

After an hour passed, Claire and Hank were in Claire's pickup heading for Reno. Claire watched in awe as they passed by some beautiful resort properties, and eventually pulled into the Eleganza Hotel. The sign read, "Welcome to the Eleganza, Reno's Five-star, Resort Casino-Hotel". They pulled into the valet lot. As they emerged from the pick-up, an attendant approached them.

"Welcome to the Eleganza. Will you two be checking in?"

Claire paused for a moment, then, "we don't know yet."

The attendant smiled and gave them a ticket for the pick-up.

"Your truck will be in safe keeping. Have a nice evening at the Eleganza."

The restaurant was indeed elegant. It was ornate with beige walls with gold trim. There were cherubs posted in carefully designated visual areas and a harpist in the corner. The servers were dressed in tuxedos and the dinnerware and silverware were of the finest quality.

"Hank, really?! A harpist?!"

"Look, Norma, I just eat here, I do not contract the entertainment."

"Holy crap, Hank, how often do you eat here?"

"Once, just once."

"You have only eaten here once?"

"Uhm, yah."

"Was your date as cute as me?"

"Norma, nobody is as cute as you."

"You are avoiding my question."

"Are you already jealous that I was here with someone else?"

"No, no, just wondering."

"Well, if it makes you feel better, I was here alone. I saw this place in one of our guidebooks, and since I love fresh trout, I decided to give it a try."

A server approached their table.

"Good evening folks, and welcome to the Eleganza. May I start you off with a glass of wine?"

Hank stares at Claire for a moment. "Yes, please bring us a bottle of Cakebread Chardonnay, the three year old vintage please."

Claire just looks at Hank in a gaze of wonderment.

"You know your wines, Hank?"

"Well, my specialty is the box wines of recent vintage, but when I go out, I like to treat myself, and now you, of course, to something decent. May I order for you when he returns?"

"Sure. I trust you implicitly."

"When we first met, you told me that you do not trust me at all."

"Well, when we slept together in very tight quarters the first night and you didn't even so much as give me a peck on the forehead to say goodnight, I figured that either you are gay, or you were a gentleman that I could trust."

"Oh, and which of those categories have you decided that I fall into?"

"The jury is still out."

The server returns to the table with the wine, an iced bucket, and two dinner menus. He goes through all of the wine pouring machinations and tells them he will be right back to take their order.

"Don't be right back. We already know what we want."

"Okay then, sir, I am ready when you are."

"We will both have the caprese salad, followed by the Lake Trout sautéed in butter with chives, a side of asparagus, and some well-done French fries. And for dessert, we will both have the soufflé, one vanilla and the other chocolate.

"I am sorry sir, but we do not have French fries on the menu."

"Okay then, would you mind asking the chef if they can be prepared? I am happy to pay extra for them. I had them here before and they were the best."

"Yes, we did have them and they were good, but the chef decided to take them off of the menu."

"Please ask, okay?"

"Sure sir, no problem."

Claire fidgets with her napkin and looks at Hank with a very serious look on her face.

"Hank, that is a pretty fancy meal. Are you sure you want to spend that kind of money?'

"Ha! What else will I do with the money? It is my pleasure, believe me."

"May I help pay for it?"

"Norma, you're not even working yet, I can't ask you to do that. Plus, it isn't about the money at all. It is something that I enjoy and I want you to enjoy it with me, so it is worth every penny."

The meal and the wine were more superb than Claire's greatest expectations. Each smiled with every bite and the soufflé was the coup d'état. The evening could not have begun any better.

"Hank, what next?"

"Let's see. Do you gamble?"

"I like to gamble a little but I really don't know any more than merely dropping a chip on a number in roulette. How about you?"

"Well, I am not what you would consider a gambler, but I know how to play all of the games."

"How would you know that?"

"It's called "truckers killing time on the internet". I play the games for fun. No money changes hands."

"Okay, I have an idea, Hank. I will do the gambling and put up the money. You stand behind me and tell me what to do. If I win, we split the pot. If I lose, it's my loss."

"Norma, I cannot let you do that."

"Yes, you can and we will win. Excuse me for a moment or two, Hank. I need to use the potty."

"I'll be right here, Norma, no worries."

In the ladies room, Claire slips into one of the stalls. She immediately opens her purse and begins counting the money that she had brought on the trip. Just to be safe, she had stashed twenty thousand dollars in one hundred dollar bills. She had hardly used any of it and decided that this night would be a one-of-a-kind night. She pledged to herself that gambling would not become a ritual in her life and that some of this money would go towards having some fun with Hank.

"I'm back, thanks for waiting."

"What do you want to play, Norma?"

"Your choice, I'm a novice."

"Okay, let's look for a blackjack table. I'm good at that. Let's walk around and see if we can find a five-dollar table. But, they are hard to come by in these fancy places."

"I don't know what you mean, Hank."

"Oh, sorry. Tables are designated by the minimum bet per hand. So a five-dollar table is the least expensive. So, let's walk around the tables and see if we can find one."

The casino was massive, and it was crowded with people of all sorts. Some were dressed "to the nines" while others appeared to have cashed in their last paycheck just to indulge in their habit. There were yells, screeches, hoorahs, and sighs from every corner. The cling clang jingle of noisy slot machines filled the air. Hank became more and more distressed as they walked around.

"Norma, I can't seem to find a table for us, not even a ten-dollar table, sorry."

"I see a table over there. It says blackjack above it and there are only three people sitting there."

"Norma, it's a one-hundred dollar table, a little out of our range."

"Wait, Hank, if I bet one hundred dollars and win, how much will I have?"

"Two hundred dollars. But, if you lose, you will be out one hundred."

"Let's go for it."

"Are you sure?"

"I am sure as a tight-rope walker under the big top."

"Oh, that makes me feel secure. Okay, let's go."

The two walk over to the blackjack table. Claire sits down, reaches into her purse, and pulls out one of the one-hundred dollar bills.

"Mister dealer, one chip please."

"One?"

"Yep."

The dealer tosses the chip her way and she places it on the circle in front of her. She turns to Hank.

"Are you ready, trucker man?"

"Sure."

The dealer deals the cards and Claire is dealt a Queen and a nine for a total of nineteen. The dealer shows a five of hearts.

"What do I do Hank?"

"Nothing, just sit back and watch."

When everybody is finished with their bets, the dealer flips over his down card revealing a nine of spades, for a total of fourteen. The dealer looks around and pulls another card from the deck. It is the Jack of Diamonds.

"Ha, ha Norma. The dealer busted. You win."

"See Hank, I now have two hundred."

Without having to pull another one-hundred dollar bill out of her purse, Claire stays even for the next ten minutes. Then, her luck changes, and she goes on a mini-winning streak including two blackjacks. Her winnings are now about one thousand dollars.

"Norma, maybe it is time to quit?"

"I love this, Hank. Just a few hands more."

"Okay, go for it."

Claire pushes all ten chips into the circle.

"Norma, no, no, no. What are you doing?"

"Trust me Hank, I feel lucky."

With all the chips in the circle, Claire draws a queen and a ten, for twenty. She turns and smiles at Hank. The dealer is showing a ten, and finishes distributing the cards. Much to everyone's dismay, the dealer turns over an ace for a blackjack.

"Norma, you have lost your winnings. Why don't we call it a night?"

"Wait, I don't give up easy, Hank."

Claire reaches into her purse and pulls out ten one-hundred dollar bills. Hank just stares with a look of horror and amazement at what he sees. Claire shoves all ten bills into the circle. The next two hands are winners. With a bit of a hot streak, Claire amasses fifteen thousand dollars in winnings.

"Okay, Hank, I am ready now."

Hank is just silent, still trying to absorb what he had just witnessed. Just as they are preparing to leave, Claire is approached by a gentleman in a suit. Claire had noticed him behind the gambling tables throughout the evening. This man is very sharply dressed and walks with an air of authority.

"Excuse me miss, are you by any chance guests of the hotel?"

"Well, no."

"If you are so inclined, the Eleganza would enjoy offering you a suite for the remainder of your stay."

Claire and Hank look at one another. Hank is nodding his head vertically and vigorously.

"Yes, sure, yes. That is very nice."

"If you will follow me, I will arrange a suite for you. Do enjoy your stay and we are happy to have you as guests at the Eleganza."

The magnetic card key slipped into the door of a top floor suite. On the door, it said "The Prince Charles Suite". Hank wondered if the real Prince Charles had really stayed there. The two walked in and their jaws dropped open. A huge king-sized bed, okay maybe a prince-sized bed, sat in the middle of the room. To the right of the bed was an open bathroom with a large whirlpool tub with two robes lying across the front. The living area was large enough to throw a SuperBowl party for family and friends. On the dressing table sat a wine bucket with a bottle of Dom Perignon champagne and an assortment of strawberries.

"This is living, Hank."

"I have a question, Norma."

"Have at it, trucker man."

"Yah, look, are you a drug dealer?"

"Excuse me??!! Do I appear to be a drug dealer to you?"

"Well, no, you don't have to be a user to be a dealer."

"I am NOT a drug dealer and I take that as an insult."

"Yeah, well not every twenty-two year old girl just out of college can dip into her purse and randomly pull out hundred-dollar bills either."

"So, stereotypically speaking then, you have surmised that since I am able to do that, I am a drug dealer?"

"What then? Did you hit the lottery?"

"Yep, that's it, Henry Thoreau. I am a lottery winner."

"No shit?"

"Actually no, I didn't hit the lottery."

"What then?"

"Why is this so important to you?"

"It's not important, Norma. You just took me by surprise."

"Graduation gift."

"Graduation gift?"

"That's what I said. The pick-up was my idea."

"So, you almost blew your graduation gift at the blackjack table?"

"I would have saved some of it, don't worry about that. Get the champagne open."

"Yes, ma'am, coming right up."

The chilled, bubbly champagne was the best that either had ever had. The strawberries were ripe but not soft. There was a CD player in the corner of the room where Claire had found a Barry White CD. She knew almost immediately that she would find some intimate music to play. Someone had thought this out just perfectly. The intent, she was sure, was to entice the guest into more night stays, and Claire was slowly gravitating towards the lure. She was also gravitating towards the enormous bed, the same bed that she fantasized about back in Omaha.

"Hank?"

"Yes?"

"Hankie need a spankie?"

"What?"

"Hank, let's crawl into the bed. I am unable to drink any more. The music has put me in a mood of sorts."

The two climb into the bed and face each other, each smiling that oh so recognizable devious smile.

"Henry?"

"Yes, Norma?"

"May I undress you?"

"Be gentle."

Claire starts with his shirt and slowly pulls it over Hank's head.

"Put your arms up dear." Hank obliges.

"Ooooohhhhh, nice, no tattoos."

"Keep looking."

"Later."

Claire moves down to Hank's pants and unfastens his belt. Beneath the belt is a button. It is a bit of a struggle for Claire to unbutton the pants, but gets it done. The zipper fly goes down as easily, almost as if it was lubricated for the experience. She then squirms down almost to the foot of the bed, and drags Hank's pants down past his knees, then his ankles, and eventually they end up in a heap at the foot of the bed. She then looks all over Hank's body as if she is on a search mission.

"Roll over."

"What are you looking for?"

"Tattoos."

"Sorry, none. Needles are not my friend."

"Roll back over on your back." Hank once again obliges.

"And now, the unveiling."

Claire grabs Hank's boxer shorts and tugs them down taking the same path as she did when she removed his pants. The boxers end up on the floor on top of his pants.

"Oh, what have we here? Hi little guy."

"Little?"

"Just an expression, Henry Thoreau. No worries."

Claire gently strokes Hank's penis and feels a bit of a twitch. The levitation has begun and this is no magic trick.

"Hank?"

"Yes dear?"

"Does it have a name?"

"Does what have a name?"

"You know what I am talking about. Did you name it?"

"Of course not."

"Come on, Hankster, all men name their private parts. Don't lie to me."

Speaking in a very soft muffled tone, "Mister Winkie."

"What? Say again?"

A little bit louder and clearer than before, "Mister Winkie".

"You named it MISTER WINKIE? Ha!!! That's a riot."

"Thanks for breaking the mood, Norma."

"And these luscious spheres right below Mister Winkie, these beautiful nuggets of love?"

"The Boys".

"What?"

"You heard me, "Mister Winkie and the Boys."

"Oh My God!!! That is so awesome."

Claire lies directly beside Hank and looks into his eyes. With both arms now wrapped around hum, she draws him closer.

"Uhm, Norma, I am at a bit of a disadvantage here."

"And what might that be?"

"I am here completely "nakie" and you are almost completely dressed."

"Oh, oh, now you expect me to do all of the work?"

"What ever happened to equal opportunity? Women's Suffrage? This isn't the 1920's, you know."

Hank lifts himself up to his knees and begins the task of disrobing Claire. When he lifts her shirt off, he sees a magnificent pair of breasts snuggled under a soft fabric bra. There is an ample amount of cleavage, but not so much that they would be extraordinarily large. He tosses the shirt on the floor near his clothes.

"Keep them separate, Hank. We don't want to get out clothes mixed up do we?"

"You sure have a way of altering the mood, dear."

"Keep working, trucker man."

Hank slips off Claire's slacks and carefully folds them and lies them next to the bed. He resumes his position by her side. Her bra and a pair of panties that resemble a couple of threads with a gauze pad attached to them are all that is left.

"Are you finished?"

"Almost."

Reaching behind Claire, Hank unsnaps her bra and in one swift motion has it off and placed on the floor next to the bed. As he draws her close, he reaches down and slips off her panties. The two of them now lie naked face to face. With his hands wrapped around Claire's head, his fingers through her short-cropped hair, he brings her face to his and kisses her on the lips. He senses that Claire is responding well to his advance as she begins to breathe a bit more heavily. Their nude bodies are close enough now that nothing would fit between them. The feeling of Claire's breasts pressing against his chest arouses him to an even greater extent. The touching, the feeling, the digital familiarization of each other's bodies excite them both even more.

"I want you now, Hank. Oh, I want you now."

Hank nudges Claire over onto her back and gently spreads her legs apart. Her receptive response allows him to move her freely. Hank rolls over the top of Claire in a most delicate motion so as not to hurt her as he scrambles into position. He looks down at her soft pink breasts and becomes even more aroused than before. As Hank enters her, she squeaks a small pleasurable sound, one only common to the act that has now begun. The gentleness of the movements seems as if this ritual had been masterminded only for them a long time ago. Both moan with pleasure as the love making continues. The missionary position is the only method that they try as it seems to be well-suited for this interlude.

"I am ready, Norma."

"Me too, oh me too."

And, as if there was a timer alongside the bed, they both let out a relatively loud audible moan just as they reach the height of their ecstasy simultaneously.

"Oh My God, Hank! Oh My God!"

It is now over but their positions do not change. Finally, Hank removes himself and rolls over onto his back.

"That was unbelievable, Norma."

"Claire."

"What?"

"Claire, my name is Claire."

"What? I don't get it."

"My name is not Norma. It is Claire."

"Then why?"

"Hank, do you always give out your real name in a one-night stand?"

"This wasn't a one-night stand."

"It was in Omaha."

"But nothing happened there."

"Guess the "gay theory" is out the window."

"What?"

"Never mind. I'm tired, Hank, want to sleep?"

"After a whirlpool bath?"

"Great idea."

Claire and Hank head to the tub. Claire turns on the faucets and regulates the temperature of the water flowing into it. Once filled, they climb in. Hank reaches behind him and presses the button for the agitating water flow. It is soothing and relaxing. Neither wants to leave. After twenty minutes of numbing jet action, they agree to stand and towel off. In the bed, they remain naked with Hank lying on his back and Claire snuggled up to him, her arm draped over Hank's chest. Both fall asleep almost immediately. They awaken exactly at 7:30 AM, look at each other, smile and resume where they had left off the night before. The sex is equally, if not more satisfying. They experiment with a few new positions, and once again climax simultaneously as if there was some virtual finish line to cross. They decided to use the breakfast "hot line" and ordered breakfast to the room. It was no disappointment. It was time to make some decisions about the day ahead.

"Hank, this has been magical, but it is time for me to move on to my next stop."

"Which is where?"

"I am guessing San Francisco would work. What about you?"

"I'm, picking up a load in Seattle, but I'll get there a bit early. Care to join me?"

"No, Hank, but let's promise to stay in close touch. Does that work for you?"

"It does for me, if it does for you, Norma, I mean Claire."

"Hank, "Parting is such sweet sorrow"."

"Yes, it has been no less than magical."

"We will meet again. I can assure you of that."

"I have heard that before, Claire."

"No, no, trust me on this one. We WILL meet again."

"I will hold you to that."

Claire calls for the pickup at the valet station and provides Hank a lift to the truck stop.

"I'll miss you, Mr. Winkie, and the Boys".

"We will all miss you, Claire. Safe travels and here's my card with all of my contact information."

"Give me an extra, just in case."

"Sure, here ya go."

Claire and Hank part ways and they are both on the road again. San Francisco is only about four hours from Reno, so that's where Claire will go. Before she leaves the truck stop, Claire calls John Smith.

"John?"

"Good morning, Claire."

"John, sorry I have been out of touch, but the trip has been interesting."

"You'll have to tell me about it when you return."

"That's a deal, but not all of it."

"That would be fine."

"How is everything going, John Smith?"

"All is well. I have been spending a lot of time going through your assets. And, wow, I have my work cut out for me."

"Don't feel pressured John, it'll get done."

"Well, it is not so much the pressure as it is trying to get organized. I just need to see what you have and then make some decisions. You probably don't want two billion dollars sitting in a bank account. We need to move it around sooner than later. I am not worried about the banks for the short term, but you know the old adage about having all of your eggs in one basket."

"I do, but we will be okay, right?"

"Yes, it will be just fine, at least for now."

"Listen, John, I need a favor."

"Okay."

"Check to see if there is a Four Seasons Hotel in San Francisco. If there is, make a reservation for me there, say for two nights. If I need to stay longer, I'll work it out."

"Miss Mitchell, may I ask you a question? And, please, please do not take this the wrong way. But, am I also your personal assistant?"

"Well, John Smith, let's look at it this way. You are my asset manager, and I am one of the assets you are managing."

"Ha! It is actually fine with me. I am already enjoying working with you."

"Keep it that way, John Smith. Send me a message about the hotel. I will be there in four or five hours."

"Will do, and safe travels."

"Thanks, John, goodbye."

Claire's arrival at the San Francisco Four Seasons was met by a curious eye by the valet. Claire supposed that they do not see many young women pulling up in pick-up trucks and checking in.

"May I get your luggage for you, ma'am?"

"No, I've got it. I travel light, but thanks."

"Enjoy your stay at the Four Seasons."

"Thanks!"

The room at the Four Seasons was on a mid-level floor. The view of the city was more than acceptable. It was simply decorated, but extremely elegant. The place has class. All of the amenities were in the room, but were tucked away very discreetly. Whoever designed this place was genius. Claire would maximize her stay. She sat at the desk and fiddled with the Wi-Fi connection, eventually getting it to work. Stopping what she was doing, she began reflecting on her trip from coast to coast. There was satisfaction in knowing that the trip served several purposes. She was able to put her mourning on a lower shelf, at least for the time being. Her destiny had been placed in the hands of God, and some very nice things happened along the way. Meeting Hank and having been able to help out a few people in need created rewards that would have been unequalled had she sat at home in Saddle River. Her purpose in life may not yet have been defined, but she was getting the idea of what it might be going forward. The ride was not over by any stretch. After a brief nap, Claire began feeling hungry and headed down to the concierge desk for some dining ideas.

"Good evening, how may I help you?"

"I'm hungry and need a recommendation."

"The Four Seasons is very proud of our fine dining, so we always suggest that you simply stay here and enjoy a great meal."

"No offense, but I seek something a lot more casual. I'll try it tomorrow. But, for now, some soup and a sandwich would work just fine."

"Would you like to know what I do in those circumstances?"

"I guess you are going to tell me anyway whether I want to hear it or not."

"That's funny. But, seriously, and very personally, may I ask you a quick question?"

"Do you like to read?"

"Yes, I love to read, but I prefer to eat right now."

"The reason I ask, is that there is a wonderful, quiet café at the foot of the hill. It is a bit of a walk, but it is worth it. Their food is wonderful, inexpensive, and it is a "Libro café". You can pull a book off the shelf, read it, buy or borrow it if you want to keep it, and enjoy a nice meal. And, they play some great background music. I go there often myself."

"Okay, what the name of the place?"

"It's called "The Murph Libro Café"; here's how to find it."

"Thanks, I believe I will."

The "Murph" seemed to be a small café from the outside, but as Claire stepped through the door, it seemed to be much larger. She was greeted by a young woman with menus in her hand as Claire entered.

"Here to eat?"

"Perhaps."

"Here's a menu. Take a seat anywhere; someone will be with you in a minute."

"Thanks."

The walls were all books on shelves stacked up to an average eye level. There were categories listed on the shelves. Claire chose to sit at a small table in front of the "fiction" section. On the table was a list containing "Rules of the House". There was also a small menu listing drinks, none of which seemed to contain alcohol. At this point, Claire did not need alcohol. Claire perused the menu and identified just what she was seeking, a bowl of seafood chowder and a ham and cheese Panini. A young server with a smile that took up most of the lower part of her face approached Claire's table.

"Something to drink?"

"Sure, a medium latte machiato please. I already know what I want to eat also."

"Great, let me know and I'll get it started for you."

"I'll start with the seafood chowder."

"Awesome, my personal favorite."

Claire often wondered why a server's personal favorite would have the same appeal to the customer, but she decided to humor this young girl.

"Well, I guess that makes it worth trying then. And, I will also have the ham and cheese Panini."

"Oh wow! You picked my two personal favorites off of the menu."

Claire struggled to keep from rolling her eyes. "Thanks, I'll be right here."

While awaiting her meal, Claire stood and began trolling through the books on the shelves. There were so many to choose from, but it was made easy by the fact that they were listed alphabetically by author. Claire's trip across the nation did not include any reading. By the end of each day, she was quite tired from driving. Books on tape never excited her, so music was her driving companion. But, perhaps on the way back, she would indulge in some literary offering. She stood on her tippy toes to see the top shelf and bent down to see what treasures were below.

"Need a recommendation?"

A fellow in what appeared to be his early twenties was sitting two tables away sipping on a soft drink with book in hand. He had been completely indulged in his book and had not noticed Claire until she stood up and started going through this vast library.

"Sure, yes, what do you think?"

"Have you ever read "A Confederacy of Dunces" by John Kennedy Toole?"

"No, never heard of it."

"Well, it's a great novel. The author, Toole, had committed suicide sometime around 1969. Eleven years later, his mother found the manuscript, brought it to another author whose name escapes me at this moment. The other author thought the book to be so well written that he had it published. It won a Pulitzer Prize a year later. I know where it is on the shelf if you are interested."

"Yes, yes, I am very interested."

"The plot is unusual, but you will enjoy the story. It is genius if you ask me. Oh, and by the way, I am Cliff Ford, like the car."

"My name is Claire."

"Pleased to meet you, Claire."

Claire reads the foreword of "A Confederacy of Dunces". The foreword was written by Walker Percy, and from what she sees, she knows that this will be an enjoyable read.

"Cliff, would you want to take a break and chat?"

"Sure, I'm just killing some time here."

"Come on over to my table. Want something to eat?"

"No, it's fine. I had a sandwich earlier, but I am happy to watch you eat."

Cliff slides over to Claire's table and puts his book down.

"I'm usually not that forward, but I have never been out here and thought you could give me some insight, assuming of course that you are from the area."

"Well, actually, I am from the other side of the Bay, the town is called Concord. I take the train in and usually come here to Murph's to read and chill."

"Nothing going on in Concord?"

"Not really. I am a bit unhappy with my living situation right now, so I come here. I'm not working yet, so this is a good break for me."

Claire's seafood chowder arrives and looks quite appealing.

"Look, Claire, I'll slide back over to my table so that you can eat in peace."

"No, it's okay Cliff. Please feel free to stay. I can eat and talk at the same time. It's a trick I learned in college."

"Nice trick. Was just trying to be polite."

"So, what's so bad about the living situation?"

"Are you sure you really want to hear my story, Claire? You don't' even know me."

"What better way to get to know you?"

"Well, it's a bit complicated, but you can eat while I enlighten you with my recent and not so happy life."

"I am all ears."

"Okay, I am from a working class family. My Dad was a carpenter and my Mom was an assistant in a bridal shop."

"Was?"

"More on that later."

"But, both worked quite hard, and they were doing it all for my little brother and me. I did well in school, so they wanted me to have a great education. My dream was to go to the University of California at Berkeley, but I knew it was expensive. But, I was able to get a partial scholarship and Mom and Dad took most of their savings to get me through. I majored in Business and really made an effort to do well, and I did."

"Sounds good so far."

"Yeah, well, I just recently graduated and went home for the summer so that I could take some time to decide what I would do next. After a few weeks, I decided to go on to graduate school and get an MBA, also at Berkeley, Haas School of Business. I was able to pick up a few odd jobs after school, one of which was to help Dad with his carpentry. Mom and Dad seemed quite happy that I wanted to continue with my education but they were concerned about how they would pay for it.

So, I went out and was able to set up a student loan for my MBA. I did receive a partial grant, so the loan was not for that much. Am I boring you yet, Claire?"

"No, no, please continue. I'm enjoying my soup and hearing your story."

"Okay, so with that decision behind me, I continued some work and looked forward to starting on my MBA. At the same time, I was having some issues with guilt. I saw how hard Mom and Dad worked, mostly on behalf of my brother and me. They received very little in return. That's why I decided to encourage them to take a trip. They had barely ever been out of California, let alone a vacation. I knew that they couldn't afford it, so I asked my Uncle Steven, a very successful pharmacist to help pay for it. He was more than happy to help out. So, with the help of my Uncle, along with a small amount of savings that I had, we surprised my parents with a nine-day trip to France."

Immediately Claire thought to herself, oh, no,no,no no, no. She had an unsettling premonition of what was coming.

"Well, my parents left for the trip and were supposed to return ten days later. Here's the tough part. You may have heard about this, but on the way back from Paris, their plane went down in the ocean, somewhere outside of Canada."

Claire nearly choked on the soup she had just consumed. She looked straight into Cliff's eyes and was dead silent for what seemed to be an hour. It was only for a few seconds.

"Oh, yes, I did hear about that. I am so sorry, Cliff."

"Well, yeah, it was the worst thing I could ever imagine. You just can't imagine what it is like to lose your parents that way, Claire. I still have nightmares every night."

"I can only imagine, Cliff."

"So, not to bore you much longer."

"You are definitely not boring me."

"Okay, so my Uncle, the pharmacist, and my Aunt Helen took my twelve-year old brother and me in to live with them. They are nice enough people, but it is not home. Every day, just from being around them, I am reminded about this tragedy in my life. So, now, I kill time here at Murph's, read, walk a lot, and have pretty much given up my desire to go to Grad School. I need to find new meaning in my life until I can continue. Did I ruin your day, Claire?"

"Uhm, no, not at all. Cliff, I am going to finish my lunch and buy this book then I must go. But, would you like to meet me for a beer this evening?"

"Sure, if it is no bother to you."

"I wouldn't have asked you if it was going to be a bother. See, I don't know anyone around here or my way around, so I thought it would be nice to hang out. I'm staying at a place down the road, so just tell me where to go, and we will meet, okay?"

"On the next block over, there's a hole-in-the wall pub called "Jerry K". You'll find it if you just follow this street for one more block."

"See you there at 7:00 PM, does that work?"

"See you then, Claire."

On the walk back to the Four Seasons, the tears begin to roll out of Claire's eyes. What were the chances of meeting someone in the same situation as hers? To lose a set of parents on the very same flight surely puts a stamp on the fact that it is a small world. Cliff has seemed like a very nice fellow with no new direction in sight.

Jerry K's was just as Cliff had suggested; a hole in the wall. But, the atmosphere was quite appealing and Claire knew that she would enjoy having a few brews with her new friend. Cliff showed up at exactly 7:00 PM.

"What did you do with the remainder of your day, Cliff?"

"There's a theatre that shows old films every day. They keep changing them up. I am a fan of Marlon Brando. They were showing "On the Waterfront" today. What an amazing flick! Have you ever seen it?"

"Sure have, loved Eva Marie Saint."

"Ready for a beer?"

"Sure, Claire, and thanks for hanging out with me."

The evening at Jerry K's was fun. Cliff had no desire to reflect on the loss of his parents and Claire was not going to let on that she knew as much about it as Cliff. The music in the background was a mixed bag. Cliff was an interesting guy who fought for everything he had. His drive to succeed was not only designed to propel himself into the business world, but to thank his parents for standing behind him all along the way. It was getting late and Cliff did not want to miss the last train back to the East Bay. Claire was also quite tired.

"May I walk you back to where you are staying, Claire?"

"No, no Cliff, it's just down the road, and I'd like to just head back alone if that's okay."

"Oh, sure Claire, no problem."

"But Cliff, I do have a favor to ask of you."

"Okay."

"What are you doing tomorrow?"

"Ha, same old, same old."

"Well, I have always wanted to see Napa Valley and take a wine tour. Would that interest you?"

"Sure! I haven't been out there in a few years, and I pretty much know my way around. Do you have a car?"

"I have a pick-up."

"How about if I pick you up right here at 10:00 AM tomorrow morning?"

"Perfect. I will be here, no worries."

"See you then, good night."

"Good night, Claire."

Napa Valley was everything Claire had hoped for and more. The rolling hills lush with vine after vine of some of the world's most cherished grapes. Each vintner strived for perfection from that which they grew. It took a perfect combination of sun, irrigation, and varietal grapes on vines grown for the result they had sought from year to year. Claire knew that there was more to this than simply growing the grapes, harvesting them, pressing them and drinking. These people were artists whose canvas was the palate of their prospective consumers. They worked long and hard to place a masterpiece before their admirers, one that would give them pride in their crops and their work. Some had created legacies that would be passed on for decades to come, ones whose reputation had grown from the quality of their labors. This is what wine is all about. Claire and Cliff visited five wineries, all of different styles and reputations. Some were what Claire would classify as "boutique wineries" and others as the mega-wineries whose quality was of a high standard despite their size. By 4:00 PM, Claire was feeling a bit "buzzed". There had been wines to sample and the numbing sneaked up on her quietly. Cliff was alert and happy to drive the pick-up back to San Francisco. On the way back, Claire napped for thirty minutes and was awakened by a sudden stop.

"What was that, Cliff?"

"Sorry about that, Claire. A skunk found itself crossing the road and I needed to stop suddenly to avoid it. That would have been a stinky interlude had I hit it. But it scrambled to safety in the brush back there."

"Well then thank goodness for that."

"I'm glad we're getting back a bit early, Claire. I am concerned about my little brother, so I plan to take him to a movie tonight."

"Will he be alright?"

"I think so. The plane crash left a mark on him. He was extremely close to my parents. The aunt and uncle are okay, but he has been terribly depressed. He won't eat much, won't meet up with friends, and just sits around all day staring at a television that he may not even be paying attention to. So, I try to give him as much extra time as possible."

"That's quite sweet of you, Cliff."

"Well, I just care about him."

"I have an idea for you, Cliff. Why don't you just drop me off at Jerry K's and just take the pick-up home. I won't be needing it for a few days and this way you can get home quicker and have a change of scenery with your ride."

"Oh, it's okay, Claire, I couldn't."

"Yes, you could, Cliff. Just do it. We can catch up tomorrow sometime."

"Are you sure?"

"I am as sure as I have ever been."

Claire and Cliff pull up to Jerry K's. Claire opens her door and pops out. She walks around to the driver's side. Cliff waits patiently before leaving.

"Do you have something with your phone number on it?"

"No, Claire, I am sorry."

"No problem. Reach into the glove box. There are a few pieces of paper and a pen. Give me your phone number, and write down mine."

They exchange numbers. Claire steps up on the running board of the pickup and gives Cliff a small kiss on the cheek.

"Thanks for everything, Cliff. Look after your brother. He needs you, and, Cliff."

"Yes?"

"It's all going to be okay going forward."

"Well, thanks Claire. I hope you are right."

"Somehow I just know."

Back at the Four Seasons Hotel, Claire collapsed on the bed. She reflected on the day and the various twists and turns in her life in the last several weeks. There was something that she knew she needed to do and her mind was gravitating in the direction of making something happen, something that would reward her with a sense of accomplishment. But, her success would have to be gained by helping others. Monetary rewards were of little or no interest to Claire. She could live her life in any way she so desired without having to worry about how she would support herself. How could she turn this tragedy into an opportunity? She would grab a salad in the hotel restaurant, return to her room, and make a series of phone calls. Victor Wells answered the call on the first ring.

"Claire! How the hell are you?"

"I'm great, Victor. I am in San Francisco, so I am sorry that I am calling late."

"It's not late, and I am happy to hear from you."

"Listen, Victor, I have made some major decisions and you are the first person with whom I am sharing."

"I am listening."

"Victor, have you ever set up a not-for profit Foundation?"

"Can't say that I have, but it should not be difficult. Why?"

"Okay, I will make this short and sweet. Contact John Smith in the morning. You have his number. All of this will be strictly confidential. I do want to call it The Mitchell Foundation, but please keep my name quiet for now. There is no need for anyone to know that I am involved until they either figure it out or I tell them."

"Okay, continue."

"Victor, this Foundation will be used to help children and other survivors of parents who were lost tragically, not unlike my parents. We will provide aid to these people in the way of moral support, counseling, educational grants, stipends to keep them going until they find their way, etc. Are you following me?"

"Claire, it is a huge undertaking."

"I know. Look, find an office, perhaps large enough to staff ten somewhere in the Parsippany or Roseland areas of New Jersey. It is central and close to major highways. Rent the space in your personal name until the Foundation is off the ground. You will be reimbursed. Still there?"

"I am here."

"Good, call Fred Michaels and get me the name of the recruiting firm that our company used to use. They were good. I need to call them. Get me the number of one of the generalists. Let John Smith know that I will capitalize the Foundation with twenty million dollars for starters. That should get it going. After that, if we can show some results, we will seek grants from major industries."

"How do you know about all of this, Claire?"

"I lived with a very intelligent, benevolent business man for the first twenty-one years of my life. I am sure I left some things out here, Victor, but you have enough to get the ball rolling."

"Claire, I give you a lot of credit for what you are doing. I'll jump on it first thing in the morning."

"Okay, Victor, I am not sure when I will be back, but it will be within a week or so. Call me any time and I will check with you along the way. Deal?"

"Deal!"

The next call went to Hank Thoreau.

"Claire, where in the hell are you?"

"I am still in San Francisco, Hank. See, I told you that you would hear from me."

"What's up?"

"Hank, when are you heading back East?"

"I was going to spend another day up here in Seattle. I looked for a load, and there were some available, but not to places I wanted to go right now. So, I'll go back empty."

"Really? Well, then may I ask you a big favor?"

"Okay."

"Take me along on the trip?"

"That's not a favor, Claire. It would be an honor and we can have some fun along the way."

"How awesome! I can't think of anything more exciting than to ride across the country with you in the rig."

"What about your pick-up, Claire?"

"I'm gonna sell it and I have found someone who will sell it for me. He just doesn't know it yet. Ha Ha!"

"Okay, listen, why don't you fly up to Seattle tomorrow afternoon. I'll pick up the cost of the plane ticket so that you don't have to worry about the expense. I'll meet you at a truck stop just east of the city. I'll call you with the name of it in the morning. Take a taxi from the airport as it isn't that far. We'll spend the night in Seattle and leave the next morning."

"Perfect! I can't wait to see you again."

"Me too!"

The excitement of taking the cross-country trip in the 18-wheeler with Hank, coupled with the idea that this Foundation was going to be a hit, kept Claire from garnering much sleep. It was still a bit early, but it was time to call Cliff.

"Hello, Cliff?"

"Claire?"

"Yes, it is me."

"Wow, when can we meet? I need to return your truck. It's a sweet ride by the way."

"Look, Cliff, something has come up back East and I must return. I need a favor, and I'll make it worth your while."

"Is everything okay?"

"Oh yes, all is good, but I need to get back. Here's the deal, Cliff. Sell the truck and I will split the proceeds fifty-fifty with you."

"That's hardly fair."

"Okay then, you can keep sixty percent and give me forty percent."

"I didn't mean unfair that way. You are offering me too much to sell the truck."

"Cliff, you're doing me a huge favor, the truck is only worth a few thousand dollars. So, let's make it a deal."

"Okay, Claire, it's a deal, but keep me in touch and let me know what is going on with you."

"I will be sure to stay in touch, Cliff. Bye for now."

Just as promised, Victor had sent the name and phone number of the human resources recruiting firm. Claire was eager to get this going and decided to get it done before flying to Seattle to meet Hank.

"Good morning and thank you for calling Wilson recruiting."

"Yes, good morning. May I please speak with Natalia Novakova?"

"Sure, one moment please."

"Hello, this is Natalia."

"Hi Natalia, I am Claire Mitchell."

"Oh yes, Claire. I was expecting your call. We are so sorry about your loss, Claire. And, you can call me "Nat", less syllables."

"Thank Nat, yes, it has been rough, but we must move on."

"Mr. Wells called and said that you have an assignment for us?"

"Yes Nat. I will tell you all about my needs. But first, this may be difficult, but I want my name kept out of this until it is time. If anyone asks, you can tell them that you are doing search work for a Foundation.

It will be called The Mitchell Foundation, but as far as you and your firm are concerned, I must keep a very low profile. I do not want this to get out."

"I hear you, Claire. Victor Wells had told me the same thing, so nobody in the firm here knows about this but me. When I speak to candidates, they will only know that it is some charitable Foundation."

"Perfect, Nat. Are you ready? Get ready to take some copious notes, because the assignment is a bit lengthy. In a minute, you'll see how I can help you out here, but I need you to work quickly. I am happy to pay a bonus if you can put together the team in less than two weeks."

"Wow, Miss Mitchell, that's a tough assignment. But, I will devote all of my time to it, and a bonus will not be necessary."

"Okay, here we go. First of all, here's a little information for you. This Foundation is designed to help young people, say up to the age of twenty-five to move on with their lives after tragedy has separated them from their parents."

"Oh yes, Miss Mitchell. I see where you are coming from."

"Good, then for starters I need a research person, someone who will identify those who need help. This research person should have an assistant. Plan to pay twenty to fifty percent more than they are making now for a good solid person. Next, I need an accountant, preferably a young start-up with at least two years' experience. Again, offer him or her a salary necessary to get a good one on board. I am leaving this up to you. Are you still with me?"

"Absolutely."

"Good. The accountant will be working with my personal asset manager, John Smith. John will be keeping an eye on all of the Foundation's fiscal affairs and will report to me along the way. Next, I need a personal assistant. I prefer a young woman with a college degree. She must be strong-minded and aware of the fact that this is not a nine-to-five job. She can be called upon at any time. But, make the salary commensurate with the job."

"Do you want to interview any of these people, Miss Mitchell?"

"Nope. You do the hiring. If they aren't working out, they will be asked to leave. Please feel free to tell them that so there will be no hard feelings. Remember, I do not want to be exposed to this team until I am ready, okay?"

"Sure, that's fine."

"Now, I need an Operations Manager and I have already picked someone out. His name is Cliff Ford, like the car. I will send you his contact information following our chat. Offer Cliff a handsome salary as he will be relocating from the West Coast. Also, let him know that he will have a company car, so there is no need to drive out east. The Foundation will pay his airfare and related expenses. Still hanging in there, Nat?"

"I am right there with you."

"Last, this may be a tough one, but I need a Logistics Manager. The assignments may require that we be in certain places. We will be delivering supplies, setting up apartments in some places, and maybe even moving some food around. I have identified a gentleman named Henry Thoreau. Yes, I know. He's not the original. He calls himself "Hank". You can tell him that the American Truckers Association gave you his name on a referral basis. He is a trucker, Nat, but he's intelligent and a good man. He may not want to give up his trucking, so be prepared to tell him that the Foundation will allow him to do some of his own hauling on a select basis. But, he will be needed to fulfill the Foundation's needs first. Find out how much he pockets each year and double it."

"Wow, he must be a good one."

"Yes, so that's it. Each will be afforded all of the benefits common to a company's offering. We will work out the details of that later, but assure them that the benefits will be as good, if not better, than any other company."

"I can start on this right away, Miss Mitchell."

"That's what I was hoping to hear. I will call you in a few days for a progress report."

"Thank you for thinking about us, Miss Mitchell. Sadly, we lost a lot of business when your company was sold, so this is a nice "shot in the arm" for us.

"No problem, Nat. I know that you did great work for Dad's company. That's why I called. Bye for now."

The flight to Seattle was uneventful and Claire was able to catch a thirty-minute nap on board. It rejuvenated her. The thought of the eighteen-wheeler trip with Hank made her heart pound. This was going to be the "last hurrah" before the real work began. And, though he was totally unaware of it, Hank would become an integral part of it too. That was assuming of course that Nat could get him on board. Nat sounded quite confident on the phone, so Claire had her hopes high. Hank was exactly where he said he would be at the truck stop. As Claire approached him, he pressed a handful of beautiful flowers out before him. This man had a heart and he was ready to share it with his new friend. Hugs and sweet kisses behind them, they called a taxi and headed for the city for some clam chowder and Alaskan King Crabs. Hank insisted on picking up the tab for dinner and Claire did not argue. She knew that someday, some way, she would make it up to him. They opted to stay in downtown Seattle with an early morning taxi back to the truck stop. Claire's exhaustion caught up with her at the least appropriate time, but she knew that this too would be made up to this star of a man. The eighteen-wheeler pulled out of the truck stop at 8:00 AM the next morning. Claire felt settled in almost immediately.

"Want to hear some music?"

"Whatchya got, trucker man?"

"I've got satellite radio, so you can pick anything you like."

"Oh really? How about some opera?"

"Well, almost anything you like."

"Where's your culture, trucker man?"

"My culture was stranded on an island somewhere, never to be seen again. But, seriously, if that's what you want to hear, have at it."

"Okay, I am going to look for some of the hair bands on here. Maybe a little Tesla or Cinderella, or AC/DC?"

"Now we're talking."

The trip was progressing just as Claire thought it might. Good music, some decent meals, fun jokes, and a view of the country that

Claire had not seen. Hank chose to drive across Interstate 90 rather than Interstate 80 so that Claire could see some parts of the country that she had never seen before. On the third day, just outside of Sioux Falls, South Dakota, Hank's cellular rang. His ring tone sounded like a well-preserved fart.

"Are you going to pick up that fart, Hank?"

"It's not a fart, it's actually a trumpet."

"Well, someone has been feeding the trumpet some beans. You might think about changing it."

"I don't recognize the number. The area code is 908."

"I think it is New Jersey, Hank."

"I don't know anyone in New Jersey, so I am not picking up. It could be a solicitation. I'll let it go to my messages."

"Suit yourself."

An hour later, Hank played back his messages.

"Hello, Mr. Thoreau, my name is Natalia Novakova from Wilson Recruiters. Please call me back at 908.555.3745 at your earliest convenience. It is important that I speak with you."

"Must be someone looking for a reference or something."

"Are you going to call back?"

"Well, I may as well see what it is about, so yes."

Hank's cellular is attached to the dashboard of the truck and has a speaker. He calls back and Natalia answers almost immediately. Claire is excited that she will get to hear both sides of the conversation.

"Hello, I am Hank Thoreau and I have a message that you called."

"Oh yes, thank you for calling back, Mr. Thoreau."

"Call me Hank."

"Hank, you were referred to us by another member of the trucker's association."

"Who?"

"He asked that he remain anonymous, but he did speak very highly of you."

"Okay."

"Hank, we have an opportunity for you that you may find very interesting."

"I already have a job. In fact, I work for myself and am doing just fine."

"Well, this job may allow you to continue doing that while you make extra money helping this firm."

Claire squirms in her seat as she is listening. She hopes that Nat doesn't blow it.

"I'll listen but I can't say that I will be interested."

"Hank, there is a new Foundation that has just been formed. It is one that helps young people that have had some recent tragedy. There is a need for a logistics manager, someone who can supervise the shipment of materials, food, and other items necessary for the support of the benefactors."

"It's not my bailiwick."

"We believe that you would adjust quite easily. May I ask you what your annual income is, Hank?"

"Look, I really don't know you, so I am not inclined to give you that information."

"I am sorry. My name is Natalia Novakova and you can call me Nat."

"Okay, Nat, I will not give you that kind of information."

"I completely understand, Hank, but the Foundation is prepared to make a very lucrative offer including many benefits including complete healthcare and travel expenses."

"Thank you, Nat, but I will not be interested. Thank you for calling. Please do not think of me as rude, but I must be going now. I am driving and I need to pay close attention to the road."

Hank disengages the call and begins to whistle as if he was totally unaffected by the call.

"What was that all about, Hank?"

"You heard it, Claire."

"I know it's none of my business, but maybe you should consider it."

"Why?"

"Well, maybe the money is excellent."

"I make enough money."

"Yes, but if you don't have to worry about benefits, perhaps it is easier to plan."

"I don't know."

"Hank, may I ask you a personal question?"

"And, if I don't feel like answering it?"

"Then don't, but have you ever thought about having a partner and maybe even a family some day?"

"I think of it once in a while."

"Do you think you'll find a woman who can deal with your being on the road all of the time?"

"Maybe."

"Maybe not, Hank. Face reality, any quality woman is going to say "sayonara pal" when you are never there for her."

"What are you saying, Claire?"

"I am saying that it might not be a bad idea to hear them out."

"But, what if I end up working for some creep?"

"Creeps don't run Foundations, Hank; sweet, benevolent people do."

"Yah, maybe you're right. I'll think about it for a few days before I call the woman back."

"That makes sense. Minimally, try to learn more about the job. Then, it will be easier to make a decision."

The trip out Interstate 90 was great. Sleeping at truck stops became routine for Claire and she almost wanted to admit to Hank that she enjoyed it. But, even a suggestion that she was happy doing that might lead him to walk away from the opportunity at the Foundation, assuming he bites on the chance. There was work to do, and now that she had decided to move forward with the Foundation, she was not about to allow anything to stand in her way. Cruising along, Hanks suggests a route change to Claire.

"Claire, it might add a day to the trip, but how about we take the northern route and once out of Cleveland, head north through Buffalo and Syracuse, New York before heading south towards New Jersey."

"Can we decide over lunch?"

"Sure, there's a truck stop about 20 miles east of here. I know their food is good."

The truck stop was somewhere between Chicago and Cleveland. Both were hungry and welcomed the opportunity to pull off the road. As they entered the truck stop, an official greeter was stationed at the point where the trucks pull in. Dressed in a bright red aristocratic style outfit and a giant smile, the greeter waved them towards a slot to park the eighteen-wheeler. The restaurant was staffed by servers in similar outfits and Claire wondered if this was the norm, or was something special going on that day.

"Interesting outfits, Hank. What's going on here today?"

"Oh, nothing special. These truck stops compete for business, especially when there are a greater number of them in any given area, so they each do something to be different and to leave an impression. By the way, they have the best Reuben sandwich I have ever had anywhere."

"Count me in on that, and add a Coke."

The food is delivered, and after the first bite, Claire's eyes open wide and she produces a huge smile which Hank takes as a patronage of this wonderful delicacy.

"Hank, what will you do once we are back?"

"I'll hunt down a load and take off again."

"You won't take any time off?"

"This is time off for me, Claire. I'm not carrying a load and we are taking longer to get back."

"That's your idea of time off? I mean, how about a few days in the country, or see some films, or take in a concert somewhere. Do you ever do that?"

"I once went to an AC/DC concert, Claire."

"Oh great, Hank, when was that, fifteen years ago?"

"Maybe."

"Look, it's none of my business, but I overheard the conversation you had with the recruiter. What an awesome idea to be able to continue doing this, but supplement it with a steady income and some time to yourself? And, from the way it looks, it might be in New Jersey. That would give us the chance to hang out now and then."

"Well, I don't know."

"Hank, do you not like me?"

"What?"

"Me, Hank, do you not like me?"

"Of course I do."

"Then why are you rejecting the chance to stay close, even if we are just friends? Is this why you never have been in a serious relationship?"

"That's a bit of a low blow."

"It absolutely is not a low blow, Hank. It is a vote of confidence from a new friend, someone who thinks that you are a special kind of guy. Do yourself a favor and at least hear this woman out."

"Okay, Claire, perhaps you're right, I'll call her from the cab after we are finished eating."

"Just listen to what she has to say. You don't have to do it. Look at it as an exploratory mission."

The two finish their lunch and head back to the rig. Hank cranks it up and waits for the cool air to escape from the series of vents. He picks up his cellular and presses in the number from which Nat had called.

"Thank you for calling the Wilson Company. How may I direct your call?"

"Nat, uhmm, forgot her last name. Sorry."

"Novakova, you would like to speak with Natalia Novakova I assume."

"Yes, that's it."

"Hold one moment please."

"Hello, this is Nat."

"Nat, this is Hank Thoreau, you called the other day and we chatted. It was about a Foundation."

"Thanks so much for calling back, Hank. Do you have some questions for me?"

"Just a few. First, where is the company located?"

"The Foundation has just leased space in a beautiful office park in Roseland, New Jersey, near Interstate 80."

Claire raises her eyebrows and smiles approvingly as she did not even know this little piece of information.

"Okay, would it be possible for me to meet with the owner or founder?"

"Hank, the founder is not going to be available to meet until the team is assembled. And, we are almost complete. But, the Foundation's attorney has been taking these meetings and he is highly capable and can answer any question you might have."

Again Claire smiles and quietly nods with approval when she hears this news. Victor and Nat have been going at this full tilt.

"Okay, you mentioned salary. About how much are we talking here?"

"It will be somewhere in the range of six figures depending on our mutual needs."

"Wow, okay, when can I come in?"

"Tomorrow?"

"Too soon. How about three days from now? I am on the road and will not be available sooner than that."

"That's fine; I will send you the address where we can meet via a text message just as soon as we hang up."

"Great, see you then. Goodbye."

"Claire, any thoughts about this?"

"Hank, I can't speak for anyone but myself, but I think it is definitely worth the meeting."

One and one half days later, Hank's eighteen-wheeler is rolling south on the New York Thruway. A sign for "New Jersey State Line – 15 miles" comes into view.

"This has been a great experience, Hank. I cannot thank you enough."

"It has been great for me also, Claire. I so enjoyed it."

"The first town you will come to is Mahwah, New Jersey. Please let me off there, perhaps at the grocery store."

"How will you get home?"

"I'll call a taxi, no problem."

"I am happy to take you home Claire if they will allow my rig on the city streets."

"No, it's okay Hank. I am a bit embarrassed about where I live."

"Claire, Claire, lots of people live modestly. No need to be embarrassed at all."

"No it's okay, Hank. I prefer to find my way home by myself, but thanks!"

"Oh, and by the way, I don't even know your last name."

"It's not important. Someday I will tell you when the time is right. For now, just know me as Claire."

"As you like it."

The big rig rumbles across the New Jersey State Line. Within a mile on the right there lies a sizeable "L-shaped" strip mall with a grocery store as an anchor. Hank pulls in and stops in the outer side of the parking lot.

"Hank, let's stay in touch, okay?"

"Yes, for sure, for sure. I will stay here for a while but get home safely and I will hopefully see you again soon."

"Sure, trucker man, and let me know what happens with that Foundation offer."

"Will do! Bye!"

"Au revoir."

An hour later, Claire was home again at the estate in Saddle River. The first call she made was to John Smith. He was happy to hear that she had returned and asked if she could meet to go over finances. Begging a day to rest, they agreed to meet two days later. The next call was to Victor Wells.

"Claire, are you back?"

"Yes, and it was good to get away, and at the same time it is good to be back. How is everything going?"

"Well, the office space is rented, your recruiter has been busily assembling the team, and we all missed you."

"That's sweet, Victor." How long before you believe the team will be in place?"

"I'd say two weeks at most."

"Good. Set up a meeting at the new offices for two weeks from today. It will be a first team meeting. You can preside over the meeting but I would like to be introduced."

"I can do that."

"And, Victor, please remember that my name is not announced until which time I do it myself after you open the staff meeting. I know a few of the candidates, so I prefer to surprise them rather than let them know up front. I don't want to give them any reason to decline."

"Gotchya!"

"Okay, keep me posted.

The day before the staff meeting, Victor calls Claire to advise her that the staff has been hired, the meeting is set for 9:30 AM, and that he would like to introduce her at 10:00 AM. Claire agrees. Claire becomes quite nervous about how certain of the staff will respond to her being there, specifically Hank and Cliff. Did she make a mistake about not having revealed herself, or was this the correct move considering the way she had met them? She would soon know.

At 9:30 AM, the next day, Victor enters the conference room of the Foundation office in Roseland.

"Good morning, everyone."

All respond with a "good morning."

"As some of you already know, I am Victor Wells, attorney for The Mitchell Foundation. I will start by thanking you all for becoming part of the team, and we expect that great things will happen under your watch. In a short while, I will be calling the Founder and CEO in to meet with you also. But first, something about The Foundation. Our Founder was a victim of a tragedy that tore the family apart. As a result, this person became quite wealthy and is actually a billionaire."

The staff all looks around at each other with eyebrows raised and curious looks on their faces.

"This tragedy led the Founder to believe that there are many others out there who have suffered the same consequences. These are mostly children with no recourse in life, nobody to turn to, no money to keep their lives on track, and worst of all, crushed dreams and aspirations. Our founder believes that, once identified, these people should be able to carry on with their lives with help from the outside, specifically from our Foundation. We will be seeking grants and contributions from major industry, but, in the meantime, our Founder has agreed to set no limits on the amount of money that should be spent on restoring the lives of the victims and survivors of such tragedies. Each of you will play an integral role in helping to restore lives and making dreams come true."

All seem to nod their heads in agreement with this charge.

"I have purposely not asked you to introduce yourselves as yet. I am aware that you are all meeting one another for the first time, so I thought it would be a good idea to make these introductions in the presence of our CEO and Founder."

Victor steps aside and picks up the conference room phone.

"We are ready for you, Miss Mitchell, please come in."

The door to the conference room swings open, and dressed in a very fashionable, beige colored business suit, in walks Claire. The silence when she walks through the door is deafening. Most do not know what to make of this entrance, especially Cliff and Hank. When it finally sinks in several second later, Hank is the first to say anything.

"Holy freaking shit!!"

From Cliff, "Oh My GOD!!!"

Everybody is looking at Hank and Cliff and Claire merely stands up front with a slight smile on her face.

From Hank, "JEEEEZZZZUUUZZZZZ!!!"

From Cliff, "Really???!!!"

"Good morning everyone and thanks for being here. My name is Claire Mitchell. I am sorry for the surprise, Cliff and Hank, but I just thought it would be better this way. And yes, Cliff, it is a small world. I was in shock when you told me how you lost your dear parents. You were on the other side of the country and who might have known that something cosmic created this meeting of two people who lost their parents in the same tragic plane accident."

Cliff slaps his own forehead at this point.

"And Hank, you became a true friend to me. Your kind heart and your generosity helped me in my recovery process and I knew almost immediately that you were providing me the inspiration for what I had to do. That being said, Hank, I believe we can create a legacy here and I want you to be a part of it."

Hank is just staring at Claire and discreetly wipes a tear from his eye. It is a very emotional moment for him.

"I will ask each of you now to share your name and your title here at the Foundation. You will all become familiar with one another and work always as a team. There are no outsiders here. A team is a group that works together for a specific goal. Please do not lose sight of that."

One by one, the group goes around the room and states their name and for what position they were hired.

"Briefly, we will rely on our research people to identify those who will need our help. You will do this by reading media reports and any other means necessary. In a short amount of time, we will be identified by the outside for what we do and we will have cases referred to us without having to search for them. We will meet regularly like this and each person in this room will participate. The last thing I will repeat is that you must never lose sight of your mission. If you run into obstacles, with my help, and the help of others, you will clear these obstacles. I have nothing more to say right now. So, thank you, welcome aboard, and let's make The Mitchell Foundation an institution upon which many needy lives will rely upon to help chase their forgotten dreams."

Claire exits the room but is not inclined to meet anyone personally at that point. This meeting and events that led to it were a huge drain on her emotions and she needs time to gather her thoughts, put on her CEO hat, and make things happen.

The following months included some rousing success stories, new friendships, a growing bond between the Mitchell Foundation team, and an overall feeling of short-term accomplishment with knowledge that the best was yet to come. Each member of the team worked to perfection for every detail. Each person further expanded their roles with new challenges. As the Foundation grew, new team members were hired and Claire knew that they would soon need more office space. It was a great problem to have.

After a year, Claire's assistant took a call that would lead to a huge and beneficial exposure for The Mitchell Foundation.

"Hello, is this The Mitchell Foundation"

"Yes, how may I help you?"

"My name is Karen and I am the Producer of the Wendy Duncan show in Los Angeles."

"Oh my!"

"Yes, is Miss Claire Mitchell available to speak?"

"She is. Give me a moment and I will get her on the phone."

"Hello, this is Claire."

"Claire, Wendy Duncan has asked me to reach out for you. She has heard about the incredible work you have been doing and asked that I invite you to do a segment on her nationally syndicated talk show."

"You're kidding!"

"Not at all. In fact, we have slotted a thirty-minute segment on the second Wednesday from today. Are you available? All of your expenses will be paid by the show."

"Yes, I am available. Thanks! Let me put my assistant back on the phone and you can work out all of the details with her, and thanks again!"

The Wendy Duncan Show is one of the highest rated afternoon talk and entertainment shows on television. Claire has no idea how they hand-picked her and why, but she wasn't going to take the time to figure that out. Her next call was to Suki.

"Thank you for calling Donsuki Townhouse Salon. How may I help you?"

"This is Clare Mitchell calling for Suki."

"Just a moment please."

"Hello, Claire!"

"Suki, I needed the hugest favor ever and I will make it well worth your while."

"Let me know what that is, Claire."

"Would you take a trip to Los Angeles with me in two weeks?"

"Oh wow! What's the occasion?"

"I've been asked to appear on the Wendy Duncan Show and I am paranoid about being able to get my hair to cooperate."

"Claire, does Rodeo Drive fit into the equation?"

"Great minds think alike, Suki."

"Of course I will go."

"Awesome, so I will have my assistant set up the flights, etc."

"I am so excited about this, Claire. See you soon!"

The studio for Wendy Duncan's Show was a lot smaller than it appeared on television. Claire was quite nervous, but a tequila shot in her hotel room helped to calm her nerves. Suki had coiffed her hair to perfection. Her suit was fashionable but conservative. This would be her moment. As she waited in the green room, Claire could hear Wendy Duncan going to a commercial break. "Next up, a woman who experienced family tragedy and emerged from it to make life easier for so many others. We will be right back."

It was now time and Claire was ready. Wendy Duncan introduced Claire and asked her to sit down beside her. The cameras rolled and Claire was ready. If this was going to be part of her mission, then a little case of the nerves would not stop her from flying the Foundation's banner.

"Claire, we heard about your Foundation from a local family here in Los Angeles. We have questions for you and will field some questions from our audience, but first, what inspired you to do this?"

"Wendy, the shock waves that ran through my body when I heard that my parents lost their lives in the Passionaire tragedy devastated me. For days to follow, I lost hope about being able to continue with a normal life. I was fortunate enough to be left enough financial resources to live on for the remainder of my life, but I realized right away that money would not bring me happiness. Money would not reunite our family. I took a road trip alone, and while on this little odyssey, I met some wonderful people, some much less fortunate than I. I even met a fellow about my age way out here on the west coast who lost his parents the same day as I lost mine, on the same flight. I knew right away that there had to be hope for people like me and the fellow I just mentioned. My resources were strong enough that I could be that person who could form a team designed to help others in similar situations."

"Your story is a bold one, a story that so many of us really do not think about unless we are personally affected. So, we all thank you."

There is loud applause from the studio audience. Even Wendy Duncan rises from her chair, looks at Claire, and applauds with them. The applause subsides and Wendy once again sits.

"Claire, we have a little surprise for you today. We have located some of the people whose lives you have changed and we have asked each of them to come out here and tell their story. First up, come out here Lewis."

"Hello, my name is Lewis Harper. I am 19 years old and live in Cincinnati, Ohio. My parents were killed six months ago when they were driving home from a dinner show and were hit by a drunk driver. I am an only child and had planned to go to college. There was a limited amount of money and a house with a big mortgage, all of which was terribly overwhelming for me. The Mitchell Foundation learned of my situation, came to my aid with an interest-free student loan with great terms, relief on the mortgage until the house is sold, and a great grief therapist. I have nothing but great things to say about Miss Mitchell and the things her Foundation are doing."

"Hello, I am Marissa Turner. I am ten years old. Mommy and Daddy were in a fire in our house. My brother and I climbed out the back window, but Mommy and Daddy died from the smoke. We were taken to a place for children with no families because we have no relatives. The Mitchell people came to our rescue. They placed my brother and me in a foster home with very nice people. We can now be normal like we were before, but I miss my Mommy and Daddy so much."

"I am Thomas Gladding from Mobile, Alabama. I am twenty-two years old and was robbed of my parents eight months ago when they were victims of

a carjacking and murdered. They were honest, hard-working people who spent most of their lives trying to set the stage for a great life for me. To this day, I am grieving, but The Mitchell Foundation came to my aid almost on day one after the deaths of my parents. I now have a new job, have been seeing a wonderful therapist regularly, and am able to make ends meet. Without The Mitchell Foundation, I would have been lost. I could not have ever imagined such a favorable impact on my life following the deaths of my family."

Claire Mitchell and her Foundation have made life easier for so many people. In the years to come, their impact will be felt nationally, and perhaps someday globally. Many large corporations have jumped into the mix with very large grants and annual stipends. These include auto manufacturers, food companies, the IT industry and so much more. This is just the beginning of a legacy that will live forever. There are many more chapters in the future for Claire and the Foundation, many stories to be told, and many broken hearts to be mended.

THE END

PYRAMID

A NOVELLA

BY

Stuart R Schwartz

Colonia, Illinois is a small upscale suburb of Chicago. It is close enough to Chicago thereby allowing its residents to travel to the big city to enjoy the food and culture that it has to offer. But this little untarnished community can also sustain itself as a mini cultural center. And, besides offering so much in the way of family entertainment, it is also the home of great restaurants of practically any ethnicity. Colonia is also the home to top level executives, entrepreneurs, wealthy ballplayers, and some entertainers. The neighborhoods almost mirror those that would have been imagined in Stepford with manicured lawns, lush landscaping, squeaky clean streets, and tight law enforcement. There is hardly any criminal activity in Colonia since the bad guys and gals are keenly aware of the multitude of law enforcement officials that roam the neighborhoods with great frequency. But living in Colonia comes with a price. Its taxes are high, the home costs are far greater than other suburban communities, and local services are pricey.

Orchard Street is a quiet tree-lined little boulevard with large homes built in the early 1970's. The homes have been well kept and exude the feeling of wealth, success, and personal dignity. The mix of residents on Orchard Street include some old money empty nesters, a blend of working couples in high level occupations, and a few traditional four to five member households with at least one high earning head of household. The neighbors on Orchard Street keep to themselves for the most part. But the Williams's and the Schultz's are close friends. They live five houses apart on the same side of the street. Morton Williams is a successful attorney and a partner in a boutique Chicago law firm, Gladstone, Morris and Williams. Ralph Schultz owns his own private accounting practice in Colonia and specializes in providing investment counseling to high-net-worth individuals. Morton Williams's wife, Toni and Ralph Schultz's wife Dawn are best of friends and always find something interesting to do together. Neither Toni nor Dawn work outside of their daily house-related details. The Willams's and the Schultz's had met one evening while walking their dogs. Both couples had been out for an evening stroll down Orchard Street, the William's with their Poodle "Frisky", and the Schultz's with their boxer "Mako". Frisky and

Mako, much to the amusement of the couples, became friends immediately. The "sniff-fest" commenced while both couples stood by and watched the festivities. Of course, they struck up a conversation which transitioned into the Williams's visiting the Schultz's home to cap off the evening with a glass of fine wine and some late snacks. It was to become a beautiful, lasting friendship.

The friendship grew as the two couples began to realize that they had much in common. Both couples enjoyed films, concerts, and an evening together where they could enjoy a dinner or snack, always accompanied by a bottle or two of great wine. Morton Williams considered himself a wine connoisseur and he was quite good at selecting wines that would be favorably received by all parties. Morton and Ralph had plenty of stories to share. They had somewhat parallel lives growing up and there were many similarities and common stories regarding their respective businesses. The wives would enjoy catching up on local gossip, shopping ideas, new shops, and great places to have lunch. The lunches would always last well into the afternoon and wine was usually in the equation. One afternoon while Toni and Dawn were having lunch, Dawn's sister Susan called from Chicago. Dawn picked up her cell phone.

"Hi Sis!"

"Hi Dawn."

"What's cookin'?"

"Hey, can you get over to Arlington Thursday night? Say, about 7:00 PM?"

"Not sure. Why?"

"Well, one of the girls at work got me interested in this network marketing deal. It's quite slick, Dawn. The products are unbelievable. But I can't tell you about it now. You'll have to come see to understand.

"Can I think about this, sis? I don't know what Ralph has planned if anything. Can I call you back in a few?"

"Sure, I'll wait for your call. Try to make it. You're not going to believe this."

"Okay, I'll call you."

"Sorry, Toni, it was my sister Susan. She's got some kind of network marketing dealie she wants me to check out Thursday night. I don't really have to check with Ralph, but I didn't want to say "yes" right away."

"What are you thinking, Dawn? Gonna go?"

"I don't know, maybe. Susan has needed some breaks. I guess I could spare two hours of my week to help her out if it means anything to her. I don't like those sorts of things, but I suppose I could humor her and go. Arlington isn't that far anyway. Wanna go too?"

"Well, sure; why not? It's something different. What do we tell the hubbys?"

"Oh shit, Toni, I don't know. Let's just tell them that my sister Susan has invited us to meet for dinner. They don't need to know any more than that."

"Yah, that's true, let's do it."

"Okay, I'll call Susan and let her know."

The three women met in the lobby of the Arlington Centre Hotel & Suites at 7:00 PM on Thursday as planned. People of all ages were milling about awaiting the doors to open to the conference center. Susan seemed quite excited that Dawn and Toni had agreed to attend. Susan barked out her preliminary instructions.

"When the doors open, I want us all to get as close to the front as possible. You are not going to believe what you see and hear tonight."

With a roll of the eyes, Dawn suggested that she was sure she would not believe it.

"Come on, Sis, be open-minded. This IS life changing if I have ever seen it."

Dawn suggested that a martini might be life changing for her now. Toni was quiet throughout the initial meeting and seemed ready to hear what all the hoopla was about. The doors opened promptly at 7:00 PM and there was a mad rush for the purpose of positioning. Susan pushed her way through the door grabbing Dawn's hand in the process. She pulled Dawn along the aisle heading for the front of the auditorium with Toni in tow close behind.

"Susan, I DON'T want to sit in the front row. Conspicuous is not on my list of privacy strategies."

"Okay, okay, third row, here we go." Susan stumbled her way down the third row of chairs, never letting go of Dawn's hand. Toni was a few steps behind them eyeing her friends' attempt to get preferred seating. Eventually they were all seated directly in the middle while everyone else was busily positioning themselves.

"Susan, what is this all about?"

"I'm not going to give it away, Sis. You'll just have to wait for the presenters. I will tell you that I was completely blown away and my life is nothing like it was in the past. I feel renewed."

"Exactly how many presenters are there?"

"Enough. Just be quiet and be prepared to listen. Oh, and listen carefully as some of it is a little complicated."

"Complicated?"

"Yeah, you'll see, I had trouble understanding all of it at first."

"What can be complicated, Sis? You buy cream, or soap, or detergent, or jewelry, or water filters, take it home, use it, and tell your friends about it. That's complicated?"

"Okay, it's obvious you don't get it, Dawn. So please just listen."

The lights in the room were dimmed and everyone became very quiet. There were some soft rumblings from the audience followed by the occasional "shhhh". A heavy burgundy curtain separated the crowd from what was hiding on the stage. As the lights continued to dim, the curtains began to draw open thereby eliciting a cheer from the audience. Toni had a very surprised look on her face when she panned the audience and saw people begin to rise, stand on their feet, and chant "Panetal, Panetal, Panetal". The chant continued and grew to high decibel proportions when a very slick and distinguished looking gentleman walked out onto the stage with a microphone in his hands. That's when all hell broke loose and the pandemonium began. This enigmatic matinee idol stood there in all of his glory sucking in every sound from the raucous crowd. He was tall, extremely well-dressed, dignified, and his smile was what appeared to be a plasticized stay-in-place manufactured grin. After a significant amount of waving, bowing to the crowd, winking, and acknowledging several individuals, he did the "sit and calm down motion" with both his hands. His arms outstretched before him, he lowered them to a forty-five degree angle and back up again. People began to sit and all eyes were on the presenter. This man was a born showman and possessed all the body language necessary for inciting a rally riot. As the crowd quietly roared with anticipation, he murmured his first words.

"*Good evening Arlington, Illinois.*"

Once again the crowd erupted and began its chant, "Panetal, Panetal, Panetal". Susan was one of the revelers and didn't quiet down until most of the others had.

"*Let's start by asking our Silver, Gold, and Platinum Leaders to stand.*"

Around the three-quarters filled auditorium, people began to rise. They were young, middle-aged, and some even appeared to be seniors. They might have come from all walks of life. There seemed to be an equal number of men and women of all races and creeds.

"*Let's hear a round of applause for our leaders!*"

Again, the crowd erupted, and annoyingly enough began their Panetal chant. After thirty seconds, the speaker smiled widely and held his arm out as if to say, "yes, yes, we are ready". The crowd quieted.

"*For those of you who do not know me, I am Fred James. Thank you all for being here. And, thanks to our leaders who may now sit. I would like to know how many of you are newcomers to Panetal. Please raise your hands.*"

Several hands went up. Dawn and Toni didn't raise their hands immediately. Susan looked over at them nodding her head affirmatively. Dawn and Toni glanced at one another and sheepishly raised their hands.

"*Well, it looks like we have a great turnout of first-time visitors tonight. Thanks to all of you for coming out. I believe that you are going to be pleasantly surprised with what you see and hear this evening. Tonight, is yet another "pre-launch" function for all of you here tonight. And, if you don't know what "pre-launch" means, then you are going to be extremely happy to learn that only a very few, yes, a select few individuals will become Panetal Associates at* the ground floor level. And guess what! There is no better place to be than on the ground floor when the sky is the limit."

Fred James was again interrupted by an eruption of applauds and hollers. If adrenalin had an odor, it would be a highly fragrant room. Fred and his constituents were beaming. The scene was reminiscent of the tent that housed Neil Diamond's "Brother Love's Traveling Salvation Show." "Pack up your babies and grab your old ladies 'cause everyone knows, everyone goes to Brother Love's show". Fred waited patiently for the crowd to settle down.

"Our first presenter tonight is someone who many of you already know. And, if you do not know her, you soon will. Here to tell you all about the magnificent Panetal product line is none other than our own Director of Marketing, Jane Worley!!! Come on out here, Jane."

From behind a curtain at the side of the stage emerges Jane. To a huge round of applause and the accompanying hollers and whistles, Jane saunters out to the center of the stage. Dressed in a beige taffeta dress and elegant mid-sized heels, Jane is the picture of success. Her smile radiates throughout the room. Jane places herself in the middle of the stage. Fred James smiles, politely bows to her, hands her the microphone and heads off stage, waving goodbye to the crowd. Dawn whispers something inaudible to Toni and Susan looks on at the exchange. Susan provides the "what's going on?" look and Dawn politely shakes her head horizontally, as in "oh, nothing." Susan leans over towards Dawn and tries to speak in a loud whisper.

"Sis, wait until you hear about these products. Jane Worley is the Goddess of Panetal. She has added four times the number of associates than any other leader."

"I'll take it all in."

Toni remains silent throughout the exchange and merely looks over at the two conversing. The audience has simmered down, and Jane begins her presentation. A large screen behind her is lowered and upon it appears the Panetal name, its' logo, and photos of some products.

"It certainly is exciting to be here with all of you today. Many of you know me, but for those that do not, I am Jane Worley, a proud Platinum Associate of

Panetal. My success with Panetal has little to do with my work, because with products like these, the results come easy. In a nutshell, when a new, unique, blockbuster product hits the market with no availability on a retail shelf, people will literally swarm to get their hands on it. And that's what happened with Panetal. Almost from the very day it was introduced, I started making calls to my friends and family only to tell them this exciting news. Within a few weeks, I could not keep up with the calls that were coming in to my home and cellular phone, and that was without having to make any of my own calls. Yes folks, the only word that I can think of to describe what we offer is "revolutionary". Panetal products are guaranteed to reverse the aging process, and it has been proven. Unlike many of the so-called aging process products, Panetal has been researched and approved by one of the most highly respected dermatologists in the country, Dr. Jerry Graham. On the screen behind me, you are about to see several "before and after" photos of Panetal users, and these results came after only one month of application."

A relatively large screen drops behind Jane, the image of the Panetal logo disappears and the first of several before and after shots appear. There are a multitude of "oohs" and "ahhs" from the audience as each image appears on the screen. Toni decides to comment on what she sees and leans over to Dawn and Susan so that both can hear.

"They've got a decent photoshop technician working for them."

Susan seems somewhat affronted, "No, Toni, don't be so skeptical. Ha! You'll know when you try these products."

"Look, Susan, I am perfectly happy with the way I look now without rubbing anything but cold cream on my face."

"Yes, well not everybody is as lucky as you are, Toni. Look, that's not the most important part. What IS important is that it has helped many people and we can make a LOT of money helping those who will enjoy looking younger. Just wait until you see the earning potential."

"When do we see that?"

"In just a few minutes; be patient, please."

"As you can see from these photos of actual users of Panetal products, they all look much younger and more vibrant. Blemishes are gone, age lines have disappeared, and their skin and pores are much healthier looking after just a *few weeks application. Dr. Jerry Graham used this on his patients and when he saw the quick results, he decided that he would recommend it to all of his patients, young and old. The inventors of the formula then partnered with Dr. Graham to produce what might be considered the biggest breakthrough in skincare history."*

"I'm getting it, Sis, when do we get to the meat of this deal?"

"Can you PLEASE be patient?! It's coming up."

"And now, a little surprise for each of you. Before you arrived this evening, we placed a package under each seat. These are for you to take home with you. In it is a brochure that explains the wonderful benefits of the Panetal products. A sample of the Panetal miracle skin cream is there for you also. And you will see a descriptive brochure about how you can make more money than you would have ever imagined by being a Panetal associate. But, please don't pull it out now because next up to tell you all about the financial benefits of being a Panetal associate is our President, Fred James."

Fred James glides towards Jane who is still standing in the middle of the stage. They provide one another with a "half-hug"; Jane hands the microphone to Fred and walks off the stage. She never takes her eyes off of the audience as she leaves and issues a royalesque hand wave which continues until she disappears behind the curtain.

"Hello again, my friends. As you arrived this evening, you may have seen a spanking new Cadillac sitting in the circular drive under the portico of the hotel entrance. Well, do you know who that belongs to? I'll tell you." As he points to folks sitting in the audience, he begins, *"it belongs to you, and you, and you, and you and you. Yes, this is the car that our lucky hardworking leaders will drive away once they reach Executive Platinum level. This is no pipe dream, folks. This level is definitely attainable. And, I might add, some of you are already very, very close, and ... ... we are still at pre-launch. Look at this chart behind me. You will see that it represents different levels of achievement. Everybody, without exception starts down here as a junior associate. Many of you will advance to these mid-levels and a precious few will eventually become Executive Platinum Leaders and it won't take much time at all to get there."*

Dawn appears to have become restless. Toni remains quiet and merely sits and watches, listens.

"Susan, how much longer will this be?"

"I have never seen you so disinterested in anything."

"Sis, I don't think this is for me. I don't need creams and I don't want a Cadillac."

"Dawn, look. It is going to be good for me. You can do as little as help me along with this. Just listen to what he has to say. It's almost over."

"Okay, but I'll give it twenty more minutes."

"That's fine."

"The last speaker of the evening is our good friend and Director of Sales, Bob Winfred. Bob will explain the specifics of how you can make enough money to change your lifestyle almost overnight. Thank you for your time. Don't forget that our first major Panetal Conference will be held right here in Chicago in just a few short months. We will see you all again soon. Come on out here, Bob."

A less enthusiastic round of applauds greets Bob Winfred. Bob accepts the microphone from Fred and begins.

"Behind me is a graphic that will enlighten you as to how Panetal will change your life. Just follow along as I speak, and of course I am available at any time by phone or email to answer your questions."

"Oh sure he is."

"Dawn!!!"

As Bob spoke, the audience listened with keen intent. There were many furrowed brows indicating that many were either confused or just didn't get it. There were an equal number of raised eyebrows and half-smiles, these usually offered by the knowing group of attendees. It appeared that the best way to make money is to convince others to participate. He explained that there is a "start-up fee" which includes some samples and a personalized web site. The deal became more confusing when Bob explained the trickle up revenue flow, different levels of participation and achievement, and commissions and fees. The screen behind Bob became dark, then all of a sudden lit up with a graphic that only showed a check in the amount of $20,000. At the top of the check were the words "MONTHLY INCOME". Bob went on to explain that some people have virtually made millions of dollars in similar network marketing efforts and there is no reason why this would be any different.

"Thank you for listening, and here once again is our President, Fred James."

Again, the applause became increasingly louder as Fred held up his hands as if to say, thanks.

"We hope you enjoyed tonight and let's keep churning, digging, and having fun making you financially independent. For you newcomers, stay in close touch with your leaders and you won't be disappointed. Good night."

Susan said her farewells at the door. She asked both Dawn and Toni to think about what they had heard and to let her know how they wanted to proceed. Both politely agreed to let her know and headed to their car. The ride back to Colonia was without traffic giving the two friends little time to discuss the evening's events and other social matters while on the way back to Orchard Street. Dawn spoke to Toni in an apologetic manner.

"I could have told Susan what I thought at the door."

"And what would that have been?"

"Hogwash, Toni, it's hogwash."

"I liked it, Dawn."

"What?"

"I said I liked it."

"What could you have likes about it, Toni? Every one of those people including the ones in the audience gave me the creepy crawlies."

"Think about it, Dawn. Everybody can make money at this if they work at it. Sure, the original investors will do well, but they have opened up this opportunity for so many others. And just look at the products. If they do work, would you want to be on the outside looking in while some others are getting rich off of it?"

"Well, I dunno, Toni. Let me think about it."

"What's there to think about?"

"I am just not sure, but it is true that I would like to help my sister Susan."

"Look, Dawn, give me Susan's contact information. I will call or write to her. I'll coordinate this thing. You just agree to participate."

"Okay, I'll trust you on this."

"Dawn, the worst thing that can happen is that it sucks, and we are each out Five Hundred Dollars."

"Toni! Five Hundred Dollars?! Five Hundred Dollars?! Do you know how many pairs of shoes that buys in Neiman Marcus??!!

"One?"

"Ha ha! Very funny!"

"Okay, call Susan and let me know what we need to do."

The large Panetal packages arrived simultaneously at the Williams's and Schultz's homes. Toni was quick to get on the phone to tell Dawn that her package had arrived.

"Dawn, the Panetal stuff arrived today. There sure is a lot of products here."

"Yes, mine arrived also, Toni. What are we supposed to do now?"

"Well, there's a meeting with a small group tomorrow night. Let's ask a lot of questions and get the ball going."

"What will you tell Morton?"

"I'll just tell him that it is a "girl's night out". He won't care. We do this all the time for other reasons. There's never been a question."

"Okay, I'll call Susan and let her know we will be there."

The meeting the following night was highly informative. Little was mentioned about actually selling the product. The most important element seemed to be the process of recruiting. Both Toni and Dawn were provided with their own Panetal web sites and a booklet which suggested many ways to recruit new associates. The last half of the booklet was devoted to outlining the structure of the levels and how to achieve the next higher level. A new title was associated with each level including the ultimate prize level, the Platinum Star Executive.

"Dawn, we can do this. We can attain the top level."

"How do you suggest we get there?"

"I think I have a system in mind."

"Shoot."

"Later."

"Why not now?"

"It's my brainstorm, I don't want to share it with anyone else, and I don't want you sharing it either. We will be partners in this. Nieman Marcus, here we come."

"Toni, don't be spending any money until the checks clear. And, what's with this $39.95 per month we must pay? That doesn't seem right."

"Dawn, listen, that's an administrative fee. You heard them. No problem with that, it'll be chump change once we get rolling."

"If you say so."

"Look, come over to the house tomorrow morning. Just wait until Ralph has left for his office. If Morton is also gone, the coast will be clear for us to get going."

"Okay, see you in the morning."

Dawn showed up at the Williams's armed with a box of donuts.

"Got some coffee a brewin', Toni?"

"The pot is on the counter, ready to go. Thanks for the donuts, but that'll be another hour on the treadmill for the next four days."

"Toni, are you really serious about this Panetal thing?"

"As serious as a heart attack."

"Okay then, what's your plan?"

"Ready?"

"Yup."

"Remember when your sister Susan mentioned that people peruse the internet for ways to make money?"

"Yah."

"Well, where do they look?"

"Dunno."

"Think about it, Dawn. They go to job sites, or they go to Craigslist."

"Craigslist. Don't tell me you don't know Craigslist!"

"Of course, I do, but I thought it was just for people that wanted to buy and sell stuff."

"That too. Look, I'll log on and show you. Come over here."

"Oh, I didn't know they had so many options."

"Well, they do. Okay, do you see this section that says "jobs"?"

"Yup."

"Do you see where it says, "sales and business development"?"

"Yes."

"That's where we place the ad. But we aren't going to do it until we experiment with a few friends first."

"Like who?"

"Like anybody, Dawn. Work with me here."

"I can call Mary Thompson down the street."

"That's a start, but I am guessing for each ten you call, you might get one. Here's what we are going to do. Let's each make a list of all the people we know who might even be remotely interested. I'll write a script; we'll call them and get them to one of the meetings like the one we went to with Susan."

"Okay, I need to do it from home because I have a lot of names on my laptop."

"Perfect, so do I. Look, do this. Go home, start making a list of contacts, then come back over. I'll be doing the same thing while you're gone, and we'll make some calls together when you return."

"Got it."

While Dawn was gone, Toni wrote a script for phone calls and a Craigslist ad. She was ready to roll and make a business out of this opportunity. Dawn returned later in the afternoon with a printout of at least seventy-five names. In the center of the kitchen table, Toni has already set up two laptop computers, laid out paper and pencil and had a tabletop land line available. This enterprise was ready for big time.

"Okay, Dawn, here's the script. I will read it to you. Try to listen carefully, but I'll have it sitting here in case you need to refer to it. But, it'll come naturally after a few calls. Why not read it aloud once so you can get used to what we should say. If you feel like it needs to be modified, I am open to that. And, depending on who you call, you can ad lib also."

"Got it. Ready?"

"Ready."

Hello, Myrtle, this is Dawn calling. How are you? (wait for response).

"Really, Toni??!! Myrtle??!!"

"For Cripes sake, it's a made-up name, just continue reading it, Dawn."

Myrtle, I'm calling because my friend Toni/Dawn and I have become involved with a wonderful money-making opportunity. This is not just another of those network marketing programs. This one is for a product that will "knock your socks off", really.

"Knock your socks off, Toni??!!"

"C'mon Dawn, just keep reading."

Myrtle, we're having a little get-together at Colonia Country Club on Saturday morning, and we'd like to tell you more. We'll have coffee, pastries, and some nice chitter chatter. Can you make it? (wait for response). We will tell you all about what we are doing. There is absolutely no obligation to join us for this great opportunity, but we think really like what you'll hear. And we will only take an hour of your time.

"Who's paying for the goodies at the country club, Toni?"

"We are, continue."

Thanks for taking the time to chat today, Myrtle. We are excited to see you at Colonia Country Club this Saturday at 10:00 AM. I promise that you will not be disappointed with what you see and hear.

Colonia Country Club is an older club serving the upscale Colonia community. There are some strict rules for membership which were adopted to keep out "undesirables". The country club's unwritten definition of "undesirables" was limited merely to people who they desired not to have as members. This phenomenon was a major turnoff to Dawn Schultz so she hoped that the selected venue would not be a turnoff for prospective Panetal associates. Toni assured Dawn that the lure of anything free would overshadow anyone's trepidation about pulling their car up to the Colonia Country Club's valet circle. And Toni was correct. The meeting on Saturday drew twenty-two people including three couples. It would have been difficult to advise their friends not to bring their spouses. The club management was happy to provide a small conference room to their valued members. Toni and Dawn were regulars for lunch, so of course they qualified.

The meeting went extremely well. Dawn had invited her sister Susan to assist in the presentation. Susan was considered a strong associate not just because she had been able to recruit new associates, but because she knew the product line, and she could sell. By the end of the morning, twelve people had signed on to be associates with Panetal. There were six thousand dollars in checks in hand of which Dawn and Toni would receive a share. They were all smiles when they left the room. Susan walked out to the car with them.

"Oh my God, you two are amazing."

Toni had felt encouraged about the result and was the first one to respond, "Well, everything was in place for us to make this happen. This is merely the beginning."

During the ride back home, Toni and Dawn were still "on a high" reflecting on their success at the country club.

"Toni, when do we tell the husbands what we are doing?"

"Anytime, Dawn."

"How do you think they'll respond?"

"Don't care."

"You don't care, Toni? You don't care? What if they think we have lost our marbles?"

"Take Ralph to the bedroom."

"What??!!"

"Take him to the bedroom. Give him a good one, Dawn. Then, just before he rolls off, provide a little speech for him."

"What kind of speech would that be, Toni?"

"Oh, Ralph sweetie, don't go yet. Let's wallow in the bliss that we just created."

"Surely you're joking, Toni. We haven't had sessions like that in a while."

"Then start."

"Toni, I can't just, well you know."

"Can't? Or won't? In the middle of the session, head south. He'll feel guilty leaving the room when it is all said and done. Then you lay it on him. That way, he will just go along for the ride, so to speak."

"So, are you saying to do the "oral thing"?"

"Look, Dawn, do whatever comes naturally but soften him up ... excuse the expression ... before you lay it on him. Got it?"

"Yah, I got it. So, what's our next step?"

"I'm thinking that Monday we start the Craigslist thing."

"Do you think it will work?"

"Of course, I do. Does a clock have two hands?"

"What?"

"Never mind. Yes, it will work."

Dawn and Toni both chose the following day, Sunday to let their husbands know what they were doing. Toni decided to broach the subject over breakfast.

"How's the eggs, Morton? The way you like them?"

"Perfect."

"Want more coffee?"

"No, I'm good."

"Morton, I'm working on a project."

"Nice, what?"

"Well, I'm helping Dawn's sister Susan out with something she's doing. You remember Susan, right?"

"Yup, flake."

"What?"

"A flake, Toni, Susan's a flake."

"Well, she is going to become a little money-making machine flake. And why do you judge?"

"Well, perhaps I judge because Dawn is always asking Ralph to send her a check; I should buy a locksmith business for the number of times she loses her keys; she can't keep a job because she doesn't like working for anyone; and she dresses like a "hookaire"."

"A "hookaire", Morton? How do you know how a "hookaire" dresses?"

"I'm just guessing, Toni. So, what are you helping her with?"

"It's a network marketing deal and this one is a good one."

"Oh, I'll bet it's a doozy."

"You don't know, Morton. You just don't get it. I can make extra money with this. And I can even win a Cadillac if I work at it hard enough."

"A Cadillac Toni??!!" For God's sake, you have a Lexus Coupe sitting in the garage."

"It's not a Cadillac Morton, and I didn't earn it, I just deserved it."

"You DESERVED it? For what? For being the best shopper on the street?"

"Lighten up, Morton. I have always wanted to do something like this, and I am going to show you and the rest of the universe how it is done."

"Toni, look, the only ones that make money doing this are the ones who start it. Let me guess, you get paid to recruit people."

"Of course, we do."

"In my experience, honey, these are called pyramid schemes. They border on being illegal."

"Oh please, Morton, they had a lawyer verify that it is strictly legal."

"Oh, for crap sake, Toni. I am a lawyer and I can make a bank robbery look legal."

"I have had enough of your bullshit, Morton. I am doing it and there's nothing you can do or say to stop me."

"Oh really? What does Ralph have to say about Dawn's participation?"

"He loves the idea."

"Oh is that right? I'll get on the phone right now and talk to Ralph about it."

"You will do nothing of the sort, Morton."

"Then he doesn't know. Why do you lie about things?"

"It's not a lie; I just know he'll be on board with it. He loves Dawn so much that he would go along with anything she wants to do."

"So, now you're saying that I don't love you."

"I am not saying that, Morton. And, in fact, I am not saying anything more, period! Finish your breakfast so I can do the dishes and get back to work on this."

"Fine, I'm going out for a little golf then."

"Be my guest, Morton. Have a "bogus" on me."

"Bogey, honey and we do not want them. We want pars, birdies, and eagles."

"Whatever, Morton."

Meanwhile, over at the Schultz residence, Dawn's enlightenment of Ralph is far less tedious. Dawn was busy studying Toni's script for Craigslist. Ralph was reading the Chicago Tribune Sunday edition.

"Whatchya doing, honey?"

"Oh, just studying something, Ralph."

"Studying?"

"Yes, want to know about it?"

"Sure, sweetie."

"Put the paper down and I'll tell you."

"It's down."

"Toni and I are in business together."

"Oh really!"

"My sister Susan is involved in a marketing program for a miracle skin cream and asked us to join in."

"Okay."

"Okay? That's it?"

"Well, my "Okay" was more in the form of a question."

"Well, we think we can make some money doing this, and it will be fun along the way."

"If it will keep you busy honey and you enjoy what you're doing, I am guessing it is worth a shot."

"Is Morton on board with this?"

"I'm guessing so. We already had a meeting and signed up several new associates. I think it is going to be quite good."

"Well, good luck with it, sweetie. Keep me posted on how it goes."

"I will, Ralph. Thanks for understanding."

"Any time."

Monday morning had Dawn and Toni posting ads on Craigslist seeking entrepreneurs. Carefully worded, the ad proclaimed that associates could potentially make thousands of dollars working from their homes. It suggested that prospects respond via an email and that someone would contact them. The emails came pouring in enabling Toni and Dawn to spend several hours on the phone responding. Their strategy was to set up meetings at a Starbucks. They felt that everyone they called surely knew about Starbucks and since there was one on every corner, it would make for a good rendezvous spot.

The meetings went well and the largest hurdle was to convince prospective associates to divvy up five hundred dollars. Some balked and some seemed eager to join the fray. After a few meetings, the girls were able to tighten up their presentation and make it even more appealing. The meetings continued, new associates were signing up each week, and a decent number of products were sold. At the end of the first month, Toni left the house to check the mail. When she returned to the house, she opened the envelope from Panetal and in it was a check in the amount of Fourteen Hundred Fifty Dollars. She immediately picked up her phone and called Dawn.

"Dawn, have you checked your mail today?"

"No, why."

"We received our first check. I am sure we were each sent one. Are you ready?"

"I am."

"Fourteen Hundred Fifty Dollars."

"Holy crapolie!"

"Yah, and that was just our first month. I told you this was going to work."

"Toni, I'm hooked. It's fun and we haven't even sold any product yet."

"Oh, we will, we will. I am eager for Morton to get home as I will rub this check in his face. He was such the skeptic."

"Let me know how it goes."

"Okay, I'll call you later."

That evening, both Toni and Dawn flaunted their prizes in front of their husbands. The reactions were quite similar. Morton Williams conceded that Toni was having fun and making a little money on the side. Ralph Schultz was also appreciative of the fact that Dawn could keep busy doing something more productive than shopping and visiting vanity venues all day. The following day, Morton called Ralph in his office to see if he was available to meet for their ritualistic lunch. They tried to get together at least once every few weeks. The topics of conversation were usually centered on sports, politics, and the state of the economy, not necessarily in that order. Ralph obliged and suggested that they visit his favorite lunch spot, an Italian restaurant called "Barney's". Neither Morton nor Ralph could ever figure out how an Italian would be named Barney, and if that actually was his name, why he would use it for his restaurant. But the food was quite good and reasonably priced. On this day, the conversation did not begin with "what an asshole Senator Clumbie is"; it was all about the "girls" and their venture.

"Morton, what do you think of this gig that the girls got involved in? It was Dawn's sister Susan that initiated their interest ya know."

"Hmmm, well actually, Ralph, I think it is okay. Everyone needs some type of passion, and it keeps them out of trouble."

"Mort, do you know much about these network marketing deals? I was actually involved doing some accounting with one several years ago."

"To be honest, I don't know a lot, but I think they are scams for the most part."

"Well, yes, but not necessarily all of them."

"Aren't they like Pyramid schemes, Ralph?"

"Well, for sure most are. To me, the authentic ones are the ones where the focus is on the products; you know, like Mary Kay, Avon, Amway, etc. But the ones that put all the focus on recruiting others are to me like pyramid schemes. I am afraid that's what the girls are in the middle of right now, a pyramid scheme. I haven't seen or heard of them trying to sell any of that crap. All they do all day is recruit others who will recruit others who will recruit others. So, the ones making the big buckaroos are the ones who started the whole thing in the first place. A large percentage of the profits trickle up into their pockets. And the pockets are large. These guys are nothing less than hucksters, but they make a nice little fortune selling promises and horseshit products. And the same people keep showing up with new deals. It's a racket, and a good one at that. I am just surprised that the Feds don't slam them, but somehow, they know how to work around that. Actually, Mort, my job as an accountant is to study and know the tax laws, and once passed, to find ways to skirt them or should I say "comply within the bounds". That's what these guys do. They avoid Ponzi and other illegal schemes by hiring people like us to keep them "holy". But, if the girls aren't vulnerable, I'm good with this shit."

"I completely understand, Ralph, I do. What does it take to start one of these deals?"

"What are you suggesting, Mort?"

"Just wondering."

"Mort, it takes a butt-load of money to get one of these off of the ground."

"Can it make money?"

"If it is done right, and there are some huge "ifs", it can make a fortune."

As the weeks passed, Dawn and Toni's Panetal business grew by leaps and bounds. Their "team" ranked very high nationally and each was beginning to rack in some large bucks. The national Panetal convention in Las Vegas was just weeks away. They had both decided to go and invite Morton and Ralph to go along with them. Toni broke the news to Morton at dinner.

"Honey, Dawn and I want to go to Las Vegas for the Panetal National Meeting. Do you think that you and Ralph would want to join us?"

"I seriously doubt it, but I have no problem at all with you and Dawn heading out there. I can't speak for Ralph."

"But Morton, if you and Ralph came to Las Vegas, you wouldn't have to participate in our meeting. In fact, we wouldn't want you to."

"Uhmmm, Toni, there's no fear of having us wanting to join you for that."

"Just think, Morton, you and Ralph can play golf or gamble, or do your guy thing while we work."

"Work?"

"Yes, Morton, work! This is no Space Trek convention where they dress up like space people and run around fake-lasering folks."

"Well, okay, I heard the strip clubs are quite good out there."

"Go to a strip club, Morton and the laser becomes a Taser. Your nuts will be screaming for a medic."

"Let me speak with Ralph, honey. If he is willing, then I'll go."

The convention center at the Las Vegas Hilton was enormous. Panetal had a designated area and it was full for the first group meeting. Toni and Dawn had invited Morton and Ralph to join the festivities as observers. Reluctantly they agreed to go but only if they could stand on the sidelines thereby allowing them to bolt out of there when they had seen and heard enough. The room was buzzing with people from all over the country. Some wore shirts with the Panetal yellow and grey colors with the logo emblazoned on their chests. Others had Panetal ball caps and banners citing where they hailed from. On stage, a curtain had been pulled in order to expose a large white background with a projected image of the Panetal logo with one podium square in the middle. A lone spotlight shone on the podium. Suddenly the lights slowly dimmed, and that mere manipulation of the lights threw the crown into a frenzy. Something big was about to happen. Toni and Dawn were lost in the crowd. Morton and Ralph stood behind the last seats along a wall. As the hooting and hollering grew louder, Morton and Ralph turned their heads to look at one another, both with the curious frown embodied on their faces. Out from behind the curtains slowly emerged Fred James, the "Billy Graham of Panetal". The hollering became screams and the goings-on in the room were reminiscent of a Pentecostal Revival meeting. The only thing that seemed to be missing was folks rolling down the aisles, screaming "hallelujah!" It took a good five minutes for the room to quiet down as Fred James tried to quiet the crowd in his "thespian-esque" manner. When it appeared that he would be able to begin his rant, Fred leaned up to the microphone.

"Thank you! Thank you! Thank you all for being here this evening. I want everyone in the room raise your arms, look up towards the sky and thank God for the enlightenment that he hath bestowed upon you. You, my friends, are the pioneers of a new era in network marketing, the birth of greatness, the commencement of newfound riches, the arrival of Panetal."

Once again pandemonium broke out among the crowd. At this point Morton looked straight at Ralph, leaned over and began to whisper in his ear.

"Can you believe the girls have bought into this bullshit?"

"Not really, Mort, but I say we bolt and find a place to have a stiff one. This cluster fuck will be going on for a few hours at least."

"There's a bar with some lounge entertainment inside the hotel. Let's pound a few there and wait it out."

"I'm all in, Mort."

The lounge show in the Las Vegas Hilton featured a beautiful black blues singer, accompanied by a pianist, a guitarist, a bass player and a sax. The music and the voice were mixed with precision and the volume was at a level that allowed Morton and Ralph to chat without yelling at one another.

"Ralph, I have been thinking about the conversation we had at "Barneys" about these pyramid deals. And what I witnessed tonight cements my opinion."

"And what might that be?"

"We need to do one. You and I, Ralph. We need to be the founders of one of these suckers."

"It's not as easy as you might think, Mort, and it takes a lot of cashola."

"I know, I know, but I think I have the gist of what we need to do. At least hear me out and let me know what you think."

"Okay."

"Ralph, you are a great accountant and you know a LOT of people. Build a model and then let's figure out how to get it funded."

"What's the product, Mort?"

"I don't know, and for now, I don't care." Don't you see how these schemes work? You said it yourself Ralph. Some hot shots build these companies, these pyramid models, and they worry about what they will surround it with later. We will find a product that will knock everyone's socks off, don't worry, but first and foremost, we build the model, the very model that will make us a fortune. And from what I can tell, we need to sink big bucks into it and get some super sharp people behind us."

"Mort, you know that I do a lot of financial planning for some "high net worth" individuals. If it looks right, perhaps I can get some behind us."

"I like what I hear. Ralph, if we should even think about doing this, the girls must not know. Period!"

"I'm all over that, Mort."

"Let's head over to Barneys after we get back and discuss it further. We may have something here."

Morton and Ralph saw little of their wives for the remaining two days in Las Vegas. The Panetal meeting provided an opportunity for the men to see a bit more of Las Vegas. Neither Morton nor Ralph was big on gambling, but the sights were fun and the restaurants were as good as any they had experienced in the past. Both were eager to return to Colonia. They had much to do.

The meeting at Barneys took place on the Wednesday after the return trip from Las Vegas. It was unusually quiet that day and it gave Morton and Ralph a chance to chat without having to raise their voices. Both ordered the fish special, a Tilapia cooked Alfredo style with garlic.

"Damn, Ralph, this place is tops. I never get tired of eating here."

"Barney does it right, that's for sure. Glad it isn't too busy today so we can talk."

"Okay, have you given this more thought, Ralph?"

"I have, and I even started building a model."

"Shit, you're way ahead of the game."

"But Morton, there is something that we must bear in mind here.

If we do this, we MUST try and comply with the FTC. I looked at some of their diatribes on multi-level marketing programs including opinions written by and for the FTC. In most of the programs, 99% of the participants lose money. None of the MLM's will disclose this. The founders do not lose money unless it all comes apart before it picks up any momentum. So, there is some risk. Some are great, and with ample effort, people can make money. So, even though we come up with a strong model, the product will have to be saleable."

"Gotchya."

"Morton, you've seen it and heard it, what do we need to do to get it going?"

"Let's get the model tested somehow. Maybe you know a fellow accountant who has specialized in this. Once it passes muster, I think we should find a product. And, I have no clue what that product should or could be."

"It has to be something that will sell, not some supplement or skin cream. It's all crap. Perhaps a "Herbalife type deal" or Mary Kay, or something like that. We must come up with something that people aren't really "wanting", something they "need"."

"Let's think about it for a few days and get together again next week, same time, Okay?"

"You've got it!"

Upon their return from Las Vegas, Toni and Dawn stepped up their campaign to find new recruits. They parked themselves in a local Starbucks where they were graciously allowed to spend the day meeting with new prospects. When they had a larger group of prospective associates, they would rent a small conference room at a Holiday Inn. The list grew and as their binary lines grew, more money would come in. They felt that they had found their potential goldmine, and nothing could stop them now.

Morton Williams couldn't sleep. He was actually excited about the prospects of getting a network marketing deal up and running. Having tossed and turned for an hour, he gently slipped out of bed, not to awaken Toni. Descending the stairs to the first floor, he decided to have a "middle of the night snack". One peek into the refrigerator revealed that Toni had been too busy to have gone grocery shopping. He didn't see that as a problem, as there were other consumption avenues to be explored. Morton headed to the "snack cabinet" but, at first glance, didn't see anything that suited his fancy. A package of Fig Newtons had been sitting in the same place for several months without having been touched, and for all that he was concerned, it would continue to go untouched. A quick peek at the Fig Newtons expiration date told Morton that his estimate of them being a few months old was undershot by almost two years. A glance upwards revealed the tea bin. He slid it down and just for the hell of it, pushed each little box aside from one another. Toni had stashed several varieties and the one that read "Sleepytime" immediately drew Morton's interest. Within minutes, the teapot was whistling, and Morton was ready to resume sleep, hopefully with this little snack. Fishing around for something to munch on with his tea, he uncovered a jar of peanuts hiding far back in the cabinet, along the wall. Not many peanuts were missing from the jar, and they did not expire for another year, so his immediate thought was that Toni was hiding this little delicacy from him. With a smile, he opened the jar, poured a handful in a napkin and began to munch. Just as the first few had been consumed, the teapot whistled and it was time to brew his tea. There would be no sugar in the tea for Morton as that might have been a part of the problem that had kept him awake. Having consumed the tea and the peanuts, Morton returned to the bed, quietly slipping under the covers. Toni was still out like a marquis sign after midnight. Morton gently leaned his head back on to the pillow and within two minutes, he was unconscious. Morton arrived in his office freshened and chipper and immediately called Ralph.

"Ralph, lunch at Barney's at noon."

"I already have a lunch appointment, Mort. Let me see if I can move it around."

"That'd be great."

"Look, if you don't hear from me, I'll be there, Okay?"

"Got it."

Morton, eager to meet Ralph was at Barney's fifteen minutes early. By 12:15 PM, he was nervous that Ralph would be a no-show. Just as he was prepared to pick up his phone and call, Ralph breezed through the front door.

"I was getting nervous that you wouldn't show."

"Sorry, Mort, I had another appointment and I had to do some maneuvering to change it, but I am here."

"Ralph, sit down."

"Whatchya got?"

"I have a product."

"No shit!"

"Yup! Ready?"

"Been ready."

"Tea."

"Tea!"

"Yes, you heard me, Ralph, tea!"

"What the fuck??!!"

"Listen, Ralph, I had an epiphany last night. I got up because I couldn't sleep. I moseyed on down to the kitchen and pulled out Toni's tea bin. I found one that said "Sleepytime" and drank it. Before I knew it Ralph, I was out like a light. Bammo, gone! Totally crashed!"

"But, Mort, tea? Who needs tea?"

"Who, Ralph? Who? Everybody! Ralph, there's tea for everything and everybody. There's tea for sleeping, there's tea for anxiety and stress, ones for virility, teas for fat people, skinny people, weak people, strong people, tea for stomach issues, teas for skin disorders. I can go on and on and on. There's fucking tea for anything. You can probably rub it on your ass if you have hemorrhoids."

"You rub it on your ass, Mort."

"Seriously, Ralph, this can work."

"I think there's a MLM for coffee, Mort."

"Maybe, but it ain't tea."

"Okay, Mort, how does this tea differ from all the ones you can get in the grocery store?"

"I thought about that, Ralph. Ours has secret, proprietary ingredients. Those store brands do not."

"What secret ingredients?"

"Hell if I know, but we will think of some."

"Oh my God, Mort, you can't just dream up secret ingredients."

"WE are not. But Doctor Blanketyblank and his or her team of nutritional scientists will."

"Doctor Blanketyblank??!! Where do we find this person?"

"We will find this doctor. We will pay this doctor well to attest to the authenticity of our claims. We will be the Kings of "Tealation"!"

"Tealation?"

"That's our name, right there."

"Holy shit, Mort. I need time to think about this."

"One thing to think about, Ralph; I checked prices of teas and they ain't cheap. People are already paying out the ass for it, so our prices will fit the model and there will be no surprises. We will be competitive and we'll still be true to the model. Everyone gets paid."

"Okay, Mort, I have one last question. Who will make these teas?"

"I have no idea, but I am guessing we find someone that is already making it, someplace cheap like India and we pay them to make the Tealation private label brand for us."

"You've thought of everything, Mort."

"Not everything, but I truly believe we are on our way."

"Look, Mort, I need to get back, so I'm leaving. Let's meet again tomorrow after work for a beer. Tell the girls we have some kind of professional meeting. Let's brainstorm this some more."

"Good, see you tomorrow evening."

Morton returned to his office and set aside the work he had been doing for some clients in order that he could be prepared for the following day meeting with Ralph. He made several calls, researched the Internet, and even had his assistant make bogus inquiries to existing MLM participants and companies. Some were naïve enough to offer up information that in Morton's mind should have remained proprietary. But, as far as he was concerned, if they wanted to spill the beans, he would hold the bucket to receive them. He made a mental note to address confidentiality in employee briefings. If the FTC were to take a close look at Tealation, the result of the inquiries must be lily white, and as pure as a virgin in a flower garden. Morton arranged with Ralph to meet at the bar in Barney's Restaurant. It worked out great as the girls had a Panetal meeting with some new prospects the same evening. Ralph was there before Morton this time and was nursing a Captain Morgan and Coke when Morton walked in.

"How can you drink that shit?"

"You never know, Mort, until you try it."

"I'll pass."

"Want to get a table?"

"I'm not hungry yet, Ralph. Let's sit and one of those high-tops over here. I have some notes to go over with you anyway."

"Been doing your homework, Mort?"

"Well, if we are going to make this thing work, we need to be on top of the details.

The two friends adjourned to a table and Morton pulled out his notes. A server arrived and filled their drink orders, another Captain and Coke for Ralph, and a draft Budweiser for Morton.

"Okay, Ralph, we have a lot to go over, and I am sure I left some things out, but are you ready for what I have now?"

"Sure, let it fly, Mort."

"Okay, here we go. For starters, we need a motivational speaker as our CEO. He needs to be quick on his feet, above average intelligence, and look and dress like Bob Barker, or at least a younger version of Bob. We can train him on what we are doing. Next, the products. We need to find a company that will make any type of tea and package it for us. Now that reminds me that we need a graphic artist to design the logo, packaging, and all of that related stuff. Following?"

"So far, I am."

"Okay, Ralph, we need a doctor or Ph.D. Nutritionist who will attest to this shit. Or maybe even both. We need actors also."

"Actors?"

"Absolutely, Ralph. We need actors who can pretend to be users of the products and give testimonials. They will have to limp, cry on cue, laugh, frown, and follow a script that we will prepare."

"Holy shit!"

"There's more, Ralph!"

"We need collateral material for handouts. We need a web designer. Every Tealation Associate will have their own web page. They will be able to track their income, use it for solicitations, and anything, yes anything related to this venture."

"Wow, Mort! You have been busy!"

"Most of all we need money. So, here's your part. I'll give you price points for the products, an estimate of monthly charges to Associates for the web site and their participation, and the upfront buy-in fees. You need to slip these into the model so that we can determine what our revenues will be. Once we know the projected monthly revenues, we can go to your investors, dig into our own pockets, and determine the amount we will need to get this going."

"I suppose, Mort, that if we are going to do this, we need to get it going. When will you have this financial information?"

"By Sunday afternoon."

"Good. Let's meet again on Monday for lunch right here at Barneys. It'll be our lucky place to do business."

"Sounds good to me. See you then."

On Monday morning at 9:48 AM, Morton stopped by Ralph's office with a folder containing sheets of data that he had prepared over the weekend. When questioned by Toni as to what was so important that he had to work all day Saturday and Sunday in his home office, Morton replied that he had a client with some special needs and that the project would take a lot more time than he was able to spend in the office. Toni bought into this explanation and was happy that she would be able to do some of her Panetal solicitations while Morton was busy. Ralph was pleased with the level of diligence that Morton was putting behind this effort, so he too was prepared to finalize the financial side of this project.

"Mort, I've been doing some homework also."

"Great!"

"Yes, listen. I contacted the Pullman Agency, a local talent agent and told them we needed six actors. My explanation was that we were doing a documentary on nutrition and we needed some folks to assist in filming. I took the liberty to tell them that ideally we needed three men and three women of different ages. I thought that a spread like that would cover all of our bases."

"That would be perfect. When do we meet them?"

"We can meet them here in my office on Saturday morning. I have already set up the use of the conference room and set aside times. I figure we need ten to fifteen minutes for each actor."

"Okay, I'll be here."

"Look, Mort, these actors don't have to be Academy Award nominees. All they need to have is a little experience and the ability to work with our scripts."

"We are going to have scripts?"

"Of course, Mort, you know, something like this: {*Oh, my stress levels were so high, all I did was cry all night and lose sleep. I couldn't function* "actor actually sobs through this" *and I was failing at work. Then I discovered Tealation through a friend and have been drinking "Tealation-Stress" twice daily, and I am a new man, a believer*}. Well, what do you think?"

"Genius, pure genius."

"Oh shit, Mort, I love writing this nonsense and maybe you can write some too. It's like watching Benny Hinn, that televangelist who cures people. It's all a show. It's crap. I am sure he uses actors too! In fact, try to tune him in to get some ideas. Oh, and I climbed aboard the Internet Express to find a motivational speaker that has credibility. And guess what, there are millions of them. And there are some that everyone would know. I say we find one that'll do it for a percentage of the take with a guaranteed minimum, someone who people know. You know that Trump does one, but I wouldn't want someone like that because, to many, he's a joke. He's more of an entertainer. We need someone with credibility, someone that people respect, like a historian or a best-selling author or someone like that."

"I'm all over that idea, Ralph. What about the doctor or nutritionist?"

"Got that covered too, Mort. Again, there are hoards of them. We only need them on occasion, first to write an endorsement of the products, attest to doing research, and to show up once in a while at our meetings. We can get a feel for what we need to pay him or her once we meet."

On the following Saturday morning, Ralph's office was teeming with people. They ranged from actors, young and old, to nutrition professionals and motivational speakers. All sat in a waiting room until Ralph called them into his firm's largest conference room. They filed in one by one and took the available chairs. The seating was limited, so some of the younger attendees stood and allowed the older group members to sit. Morton walked around the room and handed a document with accompanying pen to each of them. When finished, he walked to the front of the conference room. Mort spoke first.

"Do any of you know why you are here?"

There was no response other than a few heads shaken horizontally.

"Good. I am about to tell you. But first, the paper I handed out to each of you is a Confidentiality Agreement. By signing this, you agree never to disclose what you are about to hear to anyone. Is that clear?"

Each nods their head with affirmation.

"If you are uncomfortable signing it, that is completely understandable, but I would have to ask you to leave the room now. There would be no hard feelings."

Curiosity likely led to the fact that everyone signed, and all were on board with what they were about to hear. Ralph walked around the room and collected the signed documents. Morton waited until Ralph had collected the papers and continued.

"My partner Ralph here and I are forming a new network marketing company. Our products are specialty teas and we believe that this will be a hit. Some of you sitting out there are candidates for our CEO and others are candidates for our nutritionist. But, for starters, several of you are actors. So, I will quickly tell you why you are here, and you can leave. Then, we will meet individually with the other candidates. All understood?"

Yes's and vertical nods filled the room.

"Okay then, actors. We will be asking you to attest to these products before audiences, both small and large. You will be randomly selected from the audience after you raise your hands on cue. If it seems bogus to you, well, it is. But we won't be the first to do this. You see it all the time; you just don't know they are actors. We will write the scripts for you so all you must do is memorize them and do the best you can. You will be paid very fairly for this. There will be no awards for this, so don't throw out anything that is currently adorning your mantels at home. If you really believe the lines that you will be spewing, then join the groups. Make sense?"

Again, heads are nodded in an affirmative manner.

"Great, we have all of your contact information, so when we are ready, we will give you plenty of notice. So, goodbye for now. Thank you for visiting with us today. You can leave through the conference room door."

The actors filed out of the door in the back and surprisingly kept to themselves all the way out. The fact that they were not communicating was a sign that they were serious about adhering to the need to keep it confidential.

Morton and Ralph interviewed each of the remaining candidates one by one. There were six altogether. In order to keep them from becoming irritated with the wait, Ralph had set up a catering service to deliver gourmet sandwiches with plenty of side dishes and a variety of drinks. They all made friends very quickly as they were called in. By mid-afternoon, the interviews were complete and all participants were politely thanked for taking the time to come in. Those who had traveled from afar were given expense forms to complete for which they would be reimbursed. After all had left, Morton and Ralph remained in the conference room in order to discuss the activities of the day.

"Ralph, I like this one guy for CEO."

"Let me guess; Bill Connor."

"You got it."

"Ralph, he looks like a CEO, walks like a CEO, has a very limited amount of sleaze factor, and speaks like a CEO. This is not his first rodeo."

"Can he stir up a crowd?"

"Oh, shit yeah. I really think he can."

"Who do you like for Nutritionist, Ralph?"

"The woman, Josephine Clarkson."

"Bingo, me too!! She has an M.D. degree, a Ph.D. in Nutrition, BUT most importantly she knows what we are trying to do here. She gets it. And she knows she can make money at this."

"Mort, I lined up an IT guy and a graphics guy. We're cooking."

"Money, Ralph?"

"On top of that too. I have a meeting on Monday with some of my high-net-worth clients. They trust me and they'll buy in. Besides, for them, the amounts we need are a fraction of what they have."

By Wednesday of the following week, "all of the ducks were in order". Funding was ready, a meeting had been arranged for all the employee contractors, and the products were being formulated. The staff was increased to include spots for every need including customer service, reception, fulfillment, meeting planner, and more. Ralph contracted for office space in Arlington, which was far enough from Colonia to be noticed. Phone service, internet, and all other services were ready to go. Tealation was only a matter of days away from being in business.

Toni and Dawn continued their relentless work on their Panetal project. Their meetings with prospects became daily events and they even began to establish goals for sales and new recruits. Both were quite convinced that their husbands looked at this enterprise as a nice diversion from that which they were doing prior to their involvement with Panetal. Neither would ever be able to explain that which they were doing prior to Panetal, but that too never seemed to trouble either Morton or Ralph. Neither Toni nor Dawn knew what their husbands were up to, and they never left themselves any additional time during the day to find out. Beyond Panetal, nothing else was a priority.

Two weeks to the day after the Wednesday when both Morton and Ralph had finalized their plans, Tealation was born, off and running. It was staffed, and strategies were in place to get it going. Morton and Ralph were elated with what they saw happening and met for a quick post-work beer.

"Ralph, we must figure out a way to get this word to the girls without them knowing who is behind it. I want them in on the ground floor so that they can see the real money rolling in. If they are made aware of the position they will be in, they'll climb all over it. Look at what they've done with that Panetal shit."

"Yes, but Mort, how do we get the word to them, and then lure them away from Panetal?"

"Let me think. There's got to be someone we mutually know that they would really trust. We could get that person to lure them in by saying something like "I can get you into a start-up that's even better than what you are doing."

"But, who's that person, Mort?"

"Not sure. Who got them started with Panetal in the first place?"

"Dawn's sister Susan."

"Ralph, do you know anyone who knows Susan who we can trust?"

"Not sure, not sure. Wait, wait, Yes! I do know someone. Susan used to work for a friend of mine, an Ophthalmologist. He's a good guy and his wife does the same sort of networking thing, only with Amway. How about I call him? His wife is cool too. We can meet with both in confidence, tell them what is going on, and then have my friend's wife lay it on Susan. She'll be all over it like a fly on a pile of dog crap. We can cut my friend's wife in too, just to make it an incentive for her to sell it to Susan."

"Perfect."

Jennifer Whiteman has been working successfully with Amway for twenty plus years. She knows the "ins and outs" of the network marketing business. She is totally aware of what makes these plans work and what makes them fail. "Ground floor" and "pre-launch" are trade words that are designed to excite people to join the fray, but unless new associates are truly on the ground floor, it can be difficult to make lots of money without exhaustive participation. When Ralph Schultz approached her about Tealation, she was skeptical. Was this just another "Amway Wannabe" or was there some merit in it? Her immediate reaction was to back off. But, instead, as a favor to Ralph and his sister-in-law Susan, she decided to research it deeper. Hours of concentration and research finally led Jennifer to believe that some teas can indeed be therapeutic. The Internet literally lent thousands of pages of information on the benefits of tea consumption. She really did not know how much of it was true, but the hype alone convinced her to take a deeper look. The financial model looked quite good, and the initial investment by the founders was strong enough to enable a marketing campaign that would make an immediate impact. After a few days of deliberation, she was in. As promised to Ralph, she would call Susan.

Susan was delighted to hear from Jennifer. It had been a while since she had worked for Jennifer's husband and had always admired her. They agreed to meet the following day at a Starbucks in a mutually convenient spot in Chicago.

"Susan, it is so good to see you again. Have you been doing well?"

"Yes, me too, Jennifer. I'm doing fine."

"Look, Susan, we could spend a lot of time catching up, but I have something that will likely interest you."

"I'll be interested to hear."

"Susan, you know that I have been with Amway for years. I've done better than one can imagine. But, I received an insider scoop about a new network marketing program that will supposedly knock people's socks off."

"I've heard that before, Jennifer."

"Hear me out, Susan. I know you're doing the Panetal thing and it is going well for you, but this is different."

"And, how is it different?"

"Susan, this one involves tea."

"Oh, geez, Jennifer."

"Forget the product for a moment, but it is a great one. I know this. BUT, if you can keep this in strict confidence, I will tell you the rest."

"I can't tell anyone?"

"Well, maybe later, but for now, only you can know."

"Go ahead."

"My sweet husband Jeffrey who you worked for has some friends who are starting this network marketing plan from scratch, brand new. These friends want to remain anonymous, but I can tell you that they are sinking a lot of money in it, and they asked Jeffrey to find them a few network marketing devotees to help them get it off the ground and be the first ones in. I'm not talking "ground floor" here Susan, I'm talking first ones, period." If you and I are interested, and perhaps a few more, we would be nothing less than founders. Does that excite you?"

"It sure does. How many are you talking about when you mention a "few more"?"

"Maybe two or three."

"Jennifer, my sister Dawn out in Colonia and her friend Toni are working with me on Panetal. They're doing great at it."

"That would be okay, Susan, and they would not have to give up Panetal."

"How soon can I tell them about it, Jennifer?"

"Immediately, but I am going to point you to some information about these teas first. That way, when you approach them, you will be well-versed."

"It sounds quite good to me. Can I really make money at this?"

"Susan, you can retire off of this. Take that statement to the bank."

"Great seeing you, I'm heading out now. I'll look forward to seeing the information. Bye and "hi" to Jeffrey. Thanks for thinking about me."

"It was my pleasure, Susan."

Susan could not wait to jump on the phone and call her sister Dawn. Her rapid-fire dialing techniques, honed by virtue of calling several Panetal prospects per hour, allowed her to reach Dawn almost immediately.

"Okay, Dawn, listen to me and listen carefully."

"Is this good news or bad news, sister?"

"Let's just say it is very interesting news."

"I'm ready, shoot."

"Dawn, you and Toni jumped all over Panetal when I introduced it to you. Now you are both doing very well with it."

"I believe we are, yes."

"Well, I got some inside scoop on a very similar type of deal, only better."

"How can it be better, sis?"

"It's better because my ex-boss's wife, Jennifer, you remember her, heard from her husband who I used to work with that two of his friends are starting a new network marketing program. And, you know that Jennifer is doing Amway for years, right?"

"Right."

"Well, Jennifer is all excited because these guys are looking for founders to help get it started, not just the typical ground floor bullshit. Founders, Dawn, founders. And guess who those founders will be? You guessed it! Jennifer, You, Toni, and Me!"

"Really??!!"

"Really!"

"What's the product?"

"Are you ready?"

"Of course, I am ready. I just asked you, didn't I?"

"Tea."

"Tea?"

"Yup! Not just your ordinary "Lipton, warm up your kishkas tea". These are an assortment of teas that will repair anything in your life, period!"

"I'll call bullshit on that."

"Well, I'll research it more, but if it hits, we are in the cashola."

"What have we got to lose?"

"Nothing, sis, that's the catch. Nothing to lose!"

"Okay, let me talk to Toni, you research the products, and let's plan to meet. And by the way, who are the investors? Whose deal is it?"

"I don't know and Jennifer probably doesn't know either. They're just friends of Jeffrey and they probably want to keep a low profile."

"Gotchya!"

The following weeks were even more hectic than when Dawn and Toni started with Panetal. They worked at a feverish pace to learn about the teas, promote, and sign on new associates. Susan, Dawn, and Toni all tried the teas for varied and different reasons, all claiming to have experienced good results. It sure is easier to sell products you enjoy using yourself than ones that are meaningless. The teas were packaged professionally, and all prospective associates were provided with sample packets. This program seemed to be accepted even better than Panetal and all three women were ecstatic with the results. One evening, Toni and Morton were out to dinner discussing life in general.

"Honey, how's that Panetal business going, or whatever it's called?"

"It's going okay, Morton."

"Just okay?"

"Well, yes. We have transitioned over to a new product line, an even better opportunity to make money."

"Really? Like what?"

"Tea, Morton, we're selling tea."

Morton immediately turned on his best poker face. He was inwardly delighted that Toni and Dawn had taken to their program so quickly. "So, will people buy this, sweetie?"

"Morton, it is flying out of the warehouse and people are signing on like crazy. And Dawn, Susan, and I are on the ground floor with this."

"Who started the deal?"

"I have no idea, but it is a friend of one of Dawn's sister's friends. Oh, it doesn't even matter. What matters is that we are in at the very beginning, and we are going to be flying high."

"Well keep me posted."

"You really are interested in knowing about this, Morton?"

"Sure, why not?"

"Well, you'll be more interested when we are running to the bank every week."

"I hope you will sweetie, I hope you will."

Within a month, Tealation was "on a roll". Toni, Dawn, and Susan used all of their existing resources in order to muster up new followers. The trio of "Pied Pipers" cut no corners in generating leads and new business acquaintances. They used their current Panetal contacts as a base for growth. When questioned why they were now touting a new program, they had prepared themselves to say that this was an entirely different concept and yet another great new opportunity. America, now seventieth in the world for per capita tea consumption would soon be moving up the scale. The rewards could be endless. The idea was genius because only a limited number of American people realized their need for tea for all the right reasons. A part of the regimen for new associates was to educate, educate, and educate. Morton and Ralph discreetly stayed on the sidelines, carefully examining every move, every initiative every sign of momentum, but at the same time, stood clear of exposing themselves as funders and founders of this new business. It was time for the two buddies to evaluate where they are with this initiative. They planned to meet at Barney's and recap the events as they saw them.

"Mort, holy shit! I never thought for a minute that it would take off like this."

"Crap, Ralph, me neither. Do the girls have any inkling that we are even remotely involved in this?"

"Not the slightest idea."

"Perfect. How does it look financially?"

"The cash is rolling in. The distribution protocols are a challenge, but my guy is catching on. We figured out a way to charge a little stipend for each check that is written. It will help to cover our bank costs."

"Won't it piss off the associates to see that we are hitting them up for a fee?"

"Yah, some, but they'll be making money and they aren't going to back out because of a small check fee."

"Okay, where do we go with this now?"

"Mort, we have a few thousand participants already, so it's time for one of those rah rah meetings. But, we cannot attend."

"Shit, Ralph, the girls will fill us in without even asking."

"Where do we have it?"

"Okay, Mort, someplace big, someplace "shiny", and someplace that has class."

"Won't that be expensive?"

"It will, but it won't matter. Look, we just need a stage, some audio, some visual, and a little food. I can get this all set up."

"So, where are you thinking, Ralph?"

"The Chicago Hyatt."

"That's impressive and ambitious."

"It'll work, what do you think?"

"If you say so. Okay, let's get it rolling. Pick a date and off we go."

The date was set and the Tealation extravaganza was planned. In just a few short months, the Tealation frenzy had picked up a lot of momentum. The Chicago Hyatt was able to accommodate twelve hundred people. The group was expected to be even larger, so prospective attendees were encouraged to get there early or accept standing room accommodations. The actors who were contracted to do testimonials were told to arrive early enough to get seats and to strategically position themselves in different locations throughout the auditorium. A set was designed as a backdrop and the large Tealation logo was attached to the burgundy and gold stage curtain. The Hyatt had prepared tables with refreshments along with personnel to guide members and their guests throughout the hotel and its auditorium. Each associate was asked to bring along at least one or two prospects. If Tealation could sign on as few as fifty percent of the new prospects attending, there would be as many as three hundred new associates on board.

Ralph and Morton had agreed that they would not make any appearance at the meeting fearing that it would tip off their involvement. Instead, Ralph contracted for a closed-circuit feed to a monitor in his office. Morton would join him as the two of them would be able to keep in close observance of the proceedings.

On the day of the Tealation meeting in Chicago, there was excitement in the air. People of all ages, sizes, cultures, races, creeds, and religion arrived by car, bus, and taxis. Many were adorned with their Tealation shirts, jackets, and another brand-identifiable garb. The halls of the Hyatt were buzzing with anticipation. The mood was elevated as people milled about exchanging handshakes and stories. The organizational staff was busy signing people in and collecting their ninety-five dollar entrance fee. With sales of products and Tealation clothing, along with the entrance fee, the expected financial draw would exceed one hundred fifty thousand dollars, far more than the tab for the Hyatt. This amount did not even contemplate the money that would come in from new associates paying their initiation fees. The stage was set and at eight o'clock the next day, the auditorium began to fill. The meeting was scheduled for nine o'clock, but the fervor for the commencement of the show was so strong that folks just wanted to get there early, hoping to get the best seats. Toni, Dawn, and Susan were some of the first ones in. Each had brought two prospects making a total of nine just from their group alone. As people entered, Toni made a comment to Dawn.

"Did you notice how many Asians and people from the Near, Far, and Middle East seem to be here?"

"Of course, silly, that's where tea is life. So, they're probably thinking that this is their way of introducing it to their cronies in the West and making a fortune off it. Let it be known that these are very enterprising people."

"I guess you're right."

Nine O'clock arrived and the room was completely full. Susan turned around and whispered to the others that not only was each seat taken, but there were people "hanging from the rafters". The lights dimmed and the buzz began. The curtains rose and standing in the middle of the stage was Bill Connor. There was no fanfare, merely a backdrop behind Bill with a curtain that had the Tealation logo and a microphone in front of Bill. Bill was discreetly expressionless. He simply stood in front of the crowd, dressed, and groomed in a most dapper way. He waited patiently for all to quiet down. Someway, somehow, this group in front of him were keenly aware that a statue of brilliance was before them and was about to share something very important, something that would affect their lives for a long time to come. The crowd quieted and Bill began to speak.

"Thank you. You have probably noticed that we have not gone through the machinations of stirring you up with loud music, fancy decorations, videos, dancing girls, and the like. I am Bill Connor and as CEO of Tealation, I am here to tell you that everybody in this room today will be participating in an event that will change your lives. If you think this is a bunch of malarkey, I encourage you to stand up and leave now. You will be respected for your decision, and nobody will ask you to stay."

Bill hesitates for about thirty seconds and not one person has moved out of their place. One could hear a pin drop.

"Okay then, let's get started. I will not be long. I am here to introduce you to people who play an integral role with Tealation. You will hear their stories. You will be invited on stage to share testimony of our products, and best of all, you will learn how you will, not might, but WILL generate significant income."

A roar emerges from the crowd and Bill with a half-smile continues to stand in the same spot and waits for the crowd to simmer down.

"I have been involved with other network marketing endeavors in the past. Some did quite well, others did not. But I am standing here today to assure you that Tealation is one that will create a huge stir in the marketplace. When you hear about our products and the results that you can experience from their use, you will be quick to understand how I can make these statements. There is nothing more that I can tell you right now other than to listen carefully to what happens here today, work hard to accomplish your goals, and enjoy the ride."

Once again, a resounding roar emerges from the audience.

"I will now have the privilege of introducing you to our own Physician/Nutritionist, Dr. Josephine Clarkson. Dr. Clarkson has years of experience in the areas of nutrition and one of the most highly touted physicians in this area. She has done considerable research on our teas, helping to formulate them, *and examining the results. You will soon hear her story. So, now ladies and gentlemen, meet Dr. Josephine Clarkson."*

Dr. Clarkson emerges from behind a side curtain and slowly moves toward the center of the stage. Bill has his hand extended towards her for a salutatory handshake. Dr. Clarkson is in her mid-40's, is dressed rather conservatively in a casual style business suit and has dark brown flowing hair that drops just below her shoulders. She has a classic look about her, dons a close-mouthed, eye-wrinkling smile, and seems extremely fit. The audience responds to her presence with a round of enthusiastic applause. It appears that Bill had set the tone for the meeting with his highly professional demeanor. Bill nods to the audience, equally nods to Dr. Clarkson, and leaves the stage to yet another polite but enthusiastic round of applause. Bill's height had created a situation wherein Dr. Clarkson must reach out to the microphone and lower it to a level that allows her to speak directly into it.

"It is a privilege for me to be here today. When the founders of Tealation first approached me, I immediately responded negatively to their offer. They respected that decision but encouraged me to take a close look at what they were trying to accomplish with their products. I was offered a fair salary to participate, but the answer was still "no". But curiosity overcame me, so I took a look at what they were trying to do. The first thing that came to my mind was that I knew of fellow nutritionists who have touted the use of certain teas and herbs to cure several varied health issues. So, I jumped on the phone and the Internet and began my research. After one week, I asked myself, "why in hell's name have I not thought of this first?" It was a no-brainer. They were definitely on to something, and I wanted to be a part of it. Salary or no salary, I was in. In just a few months, and a lot of hard work, practically fifteen hours per day, seven days per week, we had developed some of the finest tea products ever to have hit the market. We tested and sampled and can proudly say that they all work in the way they are supposed to. Just to name a few, we have Tealation-Stress; Tealation-IBS; Tealation-Heart; Tealation-Joints; Tealation-Sleep; Tealation-Energy; Tealation-Virility; Tealation-Memory; Tealation-Macular, and more. I was truly amazed, and you will be also when you see the results from their use. Certain types of these have been used in their roughest forms in parts of

Asia for thousands of years. But nobody has packaged these age-old formulas into a comprehensive, distributable format until now. Welcome all to the world of Tealation!"

Almost instantaneously the audience rises to their feet and applauds loudly. There are whistles and cheers from every end of the room. Dr. Clarkson continues to stand at the microphone and take it all in.

Dr. Clarkson continued to describe the products but kept the explanations brief so as not to take valuable time away from the testimonials and other presenters. It was time for her to invite people on stage to provide testimonials. The actors were poised and ready to approach the stage.

"It is now time to hear about our wonderful tea products from those of you who have enjoyed the benefits of their use. Judging from your letters and calls, I know that many of you have been thrilled by the results. We will limit the number of you that come up here to speak so I'll ask for a show of hands from those of you that would like to join us on stage, and I will randomly select a group to come up here and give testimonials."

Josephine Clarkson had met with the actors privately and knew who to select. She was also made aware as to where they would be sitting in the auditorium. To add credibility, it was decided that she would select at least four other associates beyond the group of actors. Hands rose, some waving with great enthusiasm, reminiscent of being selected for a try on "The Price is Right". Dr. Clarkson hesitated to shout, "Come on Down", but instead pointed to each individual that she wanted to see on stage. When selected, each approached the stage, climbed the short set of stairs, and stood beside her. There were twelve in all. The audience, with great anticipation was "all ears". The testimonials were about to begin.

"I'll ask each of you to give your name and tell us which product you have been taking and how it has changed your life. Are we ready?"

Of course, all heads nodded vertically. First up was one of the actors, a middle-aged woman who had been the first on stage.

"Hello, I am Mary Gathers. I am here to talk about Tealation-IBS. Well, this is a little embarrassing for me to share, but after what Tealation-IBS did

for me, I felt that I needed to throw humility aside and let you all know about the little miracle I experienced. I have had irritable bowel syndrome for as long as I can remember."

Almost on cue, this actor began her sniffling and dismal look.

"I never knew when an attack would strike and there were some very humiliating and embarrassing moments. There were actually times when I thought I could make it to the next restroom or to home, and even though I was close, I just didn't get there in time."

Ralph and Morton were staring at the screen in disbelief.

"Morton, really??!!"

"Hey, I had to make this seem authentic."

"Wow, okay then."

The woman continued.

"I knew where every restroom was in every store; I knew where every service station was. I was even caught speeding and was pulled over once while trying to make it home in time to relieve myself. When the officer asked what the problem was, I was honest. I simply told him, "I have to go". And, just at that moment, as the words were leaving my mouth, I exploded, sound effects and all. The officer picked up on it immediately and sent me on my way. It took a while to live that one down."

"Jeeezzuuuzzz, Mort"

"Well, yah Ralph, that one was a bit graphic."

"Then my physician of all people had heard about Tealation-IBS, and suggested I give it a try. I couldn't wait to contact a rep and within a day, I was having the tea twice a day. Within a few days, the results were amazing. I am now regular, I no longer must carry handi-wipes wherever I go, and I have an entirely new demeanor. Living in fear was quite debilitating for me. But now, I feel like a free woman. Thank you, Tealation."

The crowd stood up and applauded the woman as she left the stage. She had a "shit-eating grin" on her face, seemingly appropriate to the message. Dr. Clarkson asked the next person to approach the microphone. This was not one of the actors, but a gentleman in his mid-forties.

"Good morning everyone, I am Mike McReddy. I would like to talk briefly

about Tealation-Sleep. For years, I had trouble sleeping. I had difficulty falling asleep and I would be up two or three times during the night trying my best to fall back to sleep, but to no avail. I tried conventional medications, but they simply left me with bad hangovers. I even sleep walked. On one occasion, I awakened from a drug-induced sleep only to find my kitchen light on, the refrigerator door open and uneaten food on the kitchen table. I had enough of that and tried various supplements, all with no favorable results. It impaired relationships, it affected my work, and my health was deteriorating from the lack of rest. A neighbor of mine became involved with Tealation. She gave me a few samples of Tealation-Sleep and it worked almost immediately. I don't know what is in it, and I probably don't want to know, BUT what I DO know is that after a few days of drinking this wonderful potion, I am now "Rip-Freaking-VanWinkle". I fall asleep immediately and awaken fresh and ready to go after seven- or eight-hours sleep. I couldn't wait to become a rep and tell my story."

Dr. Clarkson thanked Mike and invited the next guest to the microphone. This time it was one of the actors, a gentleman in his late 30's wearing a pair of khaki slacks and a Tealation T-shirt. His auburn hair glistened under the lights and his bright smile was endearing enough to grasp the attention of the others on stage as well as the members of the audience. In a loud clear voice, he started.

"Hi everybody! I'm Tim Butler!"

The crown shouted back their salutatory "HI's".

"I am so pleased to be here today. I was the nervous type and suffered from anxiety. This had been happening off and on for several years. I always seemed to get nervous at the wrong time and it always worked against me. I'm telling you that it affected me workwise, socially, and in almost any situation that might lead to stress. I had a first-time date with a stunning beauty and as soon as I sat down at the dinner table, she could easily tell that I was as nervous as a National Geographic Reporter at a cannibal convention."

"Uhmmm, Mort?"

"Hey, I like analogies and similes."

"Oh boy!"

"So, my date, likely having observed beads of perspiration forming on my forehead, asked if something was wrong. I assured her that I was fine, and she shot back, that "no you are not fine, is it something I said or did? Do you not like me?" I decided to be completely honest with her and revealed my affliction. She told me that she knew of some friends that also suffered from anxiety and that she knew about Tealation. I immediately blew it off as a "medicine man approach" to my troubles. She told me that it would not hurt to just give it a try. She went as far as predicting that if I could conquer this that we would end up under the covers within weeks of my first exposure to the tea. This gave me all the incentive I needed to give it a try. So, I bought a month's supply of Tealation-Stress, and I have overcome my anxieties completely. That tea, combined with Tealation-Energy has my lady friend and I enjoying a wonderful horizontal lifestyle and I can function as normally as I could have ever imagined. I used to walk into the dentist's office and head straight for the restroom. Everything inside of me was telling me that I was in for a nightmare. I went into a shut-down mode as my blood pressure screamed for help. I can honestly say that Tealation changed my life and, if you want to change yours too, jump on board the Tealation bandwagon. Get healthy, enjoy life, and make money. Thank you!"

Once again, the crowd roared with approval. Dr. Clarkson again stepped up to the microphone.

"As you hear these testimonials, please bear in mind that the therapeutic values of our teas are real. But it is also important to note that even if you are free from any type of physical or emotional issues, there are teas that are just simply great for drinking, any time of the day, for any occasion. They make a great accompaniment for breakfast, and a wonderful afternoon beverage with snacks. Let's hear from a few more Tealation users and we will take a break."

The next testimony came from Everett Clemons, a non-actor, who resorted to using Tealation-Macular as he was having trouble with his eyesight. He had been told by a reputable Ophthalmologist that he was suffering from macular degeneration, and there was not much of a cure for it. Everett had been having difficulty reading, watching television, and reading road signs. After being ticketed for heading down a one-way street the wrong way, it was time to act. He happened across Tealation-Macular on the Internet, found an associate, and started using the product. Everett now claims that he can see almost as well as he could ten years earlier, and that even his mother-in-law was looking better to him. This comment drew a round of chuckles from the crowd. He thanked everyone for listening and walked off the stage. A few others followed Everett with their tales and the crowd never lost interest. All of this was great fodder for pushing their products and signing on new associates. There were two left on stage to provide testimony, both actors. The first of the two approached the microphone in a way one would think that he was about to deliver an "I Had a Dream speech." He stood with authority and drew his audience to him with body language and a very convincing smile.

"Greetings my Tealation friends and family."

This simple six-word statement sent the crowd into yet another frenzy.

"I am Carlos Moreno and I am the proud user of Tealation-Memory. I am only forty-two years old and I was suffering moderate memory loss. Everybody I knew told me that I am too young to forget and that it was just my imagination. I convinced myself that I was in the early stages of Alzheimer's Disease. I would go to the grocery store and even though I had a shopping list, I would still forget to buy certain things that appeared on the list. I would constantly misplace keys, my glasses, my shoes, and it goes on and on. I accidently left the dog in the bedroom because I forgotten that I had brought him in there. By the time I remembered, my wife's new shoes had been devoured, there was a giant hole in the comforter, urine was dripping from the lower bed support, and my wife's "Playgirl" magazine was in shreds covering the floor. Her immediate reaction was "do something or we shall divorce". My first response to her was not an apology, but "why in the hell were you reading "Playgirl" in the first place?" Well, I did not receive an answer to that question. I could go on and on about memory loss, but I can't remember what else I couldn't remember, so I'll just say that Tealation-Memory cleaned up my brain cells. I'm not sure what is in that potion, but I will say that it cleansed my memory chip, and I am now on top of everything. My memory is as vivid as a photograph, and I attribute it all to Tealation. So, to its creators, my hat is off to you! Thank you!"

With a huge smile and a farewell wave, Carlos bid farewell to the audience, shook hands with Dr. Clarkson, and left the stage.

"We have one more gentleman left on stage who wishes to provide testimony. We are running short on time, so I will ask him to be brief. I know some of you are getting hungry."

A man in his fifties, salt and pepper hair, and a bit overweight but with a great smile approached the microphone.

"I suppose I can be considered the last but by no means least. I'm Thomas Blazer, like the jacket. I know we are running out of time, so as Dr. Clarkson has suggested, I will be brief. My most embarrassing moments have been in the last five years with my wife of over 25 years. My virility waned long before hers had, and any remaining libido has pretty much flown out the window. My greatest fear was that she would seek satisfaction elsewhere. My urologist suggested some of the erectile dysfunctional drugs, but without the inner passion and intimate desire, the erection was just not going to happen. I spent a considerable amount of time "Googling" every keyword I could imagine that would reference my condition. I came across Tealation-Virility and thought, "what the hay"? So, I ordered some and gave it a try. For the next ten days, nothing happened, so I immediately thought that I had wasted money on yet another useless potion. Then, on the night of the tenth day, something inside of me awakened. I was already in bed reading as I usually do, and my wife emerged from her dressing area with her nightgown on. This pink ditty one was translucent, and at the sight of her moving towards me, my private companion began to stand at attention. I wondered "what in the hell is happening here?" That night proved to be the most intimate night of my entire married life and to say that my wife was thrilled would be a gross understatement. I guessed that it was the Tealation-Virility that caused this change, and as far as I can tell, I was right. I have been drinking a cup twice a day for several months now and my virility level, even at the age of fifty-four has been at its highest ever. I cannot get enough of my wife. We've been doing it on every occasion, sometimes three times a day. I have had her on the kitchen table, on the pool table, in the garden, and, just the other day, I even tagged her as she was bending over to take something out of the oven. On our last visit to her aging parent's house, I had the urge in the car just as we pulled into their driveway. So, we hopped in the back seat and ... ..."

Dr. Clarkson suddenly felt the urge to jump in and shut this testimonial down.

"Uhmmmm, I am sorry to interrupt Mr. Blazer, but we are out of time."

"No problem, Dr. Clarkson, thank you for having me."

"Mort, wasn't that last one a little over the top?"

All Mort could do was lean back and laugh out loud. Dr. Clarkson continued.

"My time with you today has expired. I want to thank each and every one of you for attending today, listening to actual testimonials of our wonderful Tealation products, and being a part of our team. For those of you who have not yet joined our family, I welcome you and wish you many years of great health and newly found wealth. It is time for our lunch break. When you return, you will see and hear how Tealation will not only change your lives from the standpoint of improved overall health, but also make your way of life financially comfortable. Thank you."

More applause followed the departure of Josephine Clarkson. Everybody simultaneously rose and filed out through the doors. The buzz was on and the only conversations that could be heard reflected accolades for Tealation. Ralph and Morton, still sitting in Ralph's office looked at one another after the monitor went blank. Ralph was the first to comment.

"Mort? Well?"

"Holy shit, holy shit!"

"Mort, the actors were great!"

"Yah, I know. But I wonder about the people who have the same ailments and what happens when they believe that Tealation has not helped them?"

"I thought about that Mort, but just like everything else in life, some things work for some, and some do not."

"You're right. Well, let's grab lunch. I am eager to see what happens this afternoon for the financial part."

"Me too."

The afternoon sessions of the big meeting were equally successful. Bill Connor specifically outlined the details of the system, from top to bottom. There were several levels of success, different modes for selling and recruiting, payments, fees, bonuses, and a rather lengthy question and answer period. For the most part, everybody in the room was on board and, not unlike Amway and Avon, the general mood was that Tealation would soon become a household name.

Two years passed since the formation of Tealation. Dawn and Toni had pretty much pushed Panetal aside and focused on their Tealation business. Each was pulling in close to twenty thousand dollars per month and the amount did not diminish as they relaxed their participation. With the residuals from Panetal and their steady income from Tealation, they were living the high life. They were asked to speak at Tealation gatherings around the country, and if it would ultimately work to their benefit, they would do it. Dawn's sister Susan opted to keep a lower profile and simply enjoyed her life of travel and leisure. There was still no reference to the original founders and the women had resigned themselves to the fact that the investors had decided to remain silent and uninvolved in the day-to-day operations of the company.

One of the bonuses to which both Toni and Dawn became entitled was an all-expense trip to the Bahamas including an island-hopping adventure on a private yacht. Both were eager to go and debated asking Morton and Ralph if they would like to join in the festivities.

"Toni, would Morton go if we asked the hubbies?"

"Not sure, it depends on what Ralph would do."

"Is it even worth asking?"

"I'll broach it with Morton tonight at dinner and let you know."

"Okay, I'll be waiting for the call."

Over dinner, Toni broke the news to Morton. Both she and Dawn had won trips to the Caribbean through Tealation and thought it would be fun if he and Ralph would go. Morton told Toni that she and Dawn had worked quite hard for this reward and though he wasn't going to speak for Ralph, he would decline. The next day, Dawn had similar news for Toni. They would go off to the Bahamas on their own. The dates were set and both women prepared diligently for the trip. Shopping for beachwear and yacht wear, whatever that might be, would be fun, and they were planning to have a blast. The day arrived and they departed for O'Hare Airport to begin their little odyssey. Both were aware that a few others had also won the trip and, since they were from other parts of the country, they would meet them in the Bahamas. This was going to be the trip to end all trips, a vacation in paradise. They were just sorry that their hubbies were unwilling to share their joy, but they understood why Morton and Ralph would want them to reap the benefits of their labors on their own.

The plane landed at Grand Bahama International Airport at 3:00 PM in the afternoon. Toni and Dawn were surprised to see a young, attractive, native Bahamian Tealation representative holding a banner with a sign saying "Welcome Tealation Family". Toni asked the bearer of the greeting how many representatives they expected and was told that there would be twelve in all. The flights had been scheduled to arrive at about the same time so that they could all arrive at the hotel together. There was a van parked outside awaiting their arrival. Within thirty minutes, all had arrived, retrieved their luggage, and boarded the van. The Grand Annona Hotel is a beautiful resort and there was a smattering of "oohs" and "aahs" as the van approached the resort. All checked into their assigned rooms only to find that each of the twelve had their own mini-suite equipped with a whirlpool tub, large flat-screen TV, a bottle of champagne, and a gift basket which included fresh fruits and an assortment of Tealation teas. Paradise had been found. Upon arrival, each associate was handed an itinerary for the trip. The first full day would be spent touring the island, enjoying lunch together, and a cocktail/dinner party on the beach. The following day would commence their sea travel on a yacht which had been reserved for the twelve associates.

Toni and Dawn met for breakfast on the following morning and were amazed by how great a breakfast could be. Fresh fruits abounded, the pastries were as good as they had ever had, and the coffee was rich, hot, and delicious. After breakfast, the same van awaited the group outside and their day began. The clicking of cameras and the continued murmurs that resembled breath-taking gasps continued throughout the day. Lunch was on the veranda of a very old restaurant that had been a local staple for many years. The service was impeccable, and the food was purely Bahamian, fresh and delicious. The beach party in the evening was no less spectacular and the abundance of fine food and drink placed all in a very merry mood. Toni and Dawn decided to take a brief walk by the surf. It was a protected area and they felt quite safe as they strolled along the break tide.

"Dawn, could you have imagined anything like this?"

"Actually, yes, and no. I knew that Tealation was doing great, just judging by the monthly stipend we receive, but I didn't expect it to be like this."

"Well, I am not going to be one to complain, that's for sure."

"But, of the thousands of associates in the Tealation family, I suppose the expense for entertaining twelve of us can't be that bad."

"I'm excited about the cruise on a yacht tomorrow. I have never been on a yacht, so I don't know what to expect."

"I don't either, but it should be fun. I don't know about you, but I ate and drank far too much. What do you say we grab a cab and head back to the resort?"

"Sounds good to me. Let's go."

At eight o'clock the following morning, the van was sitting under the portico in front of the hotel. The twelve Tealation associates lined up and one by one loaded their travel bags on to the van. Some seemed to take this cruise more seriously than others as their luggage was cumbersome. Others were traveling light, but none really knew what to expect. The van pulled out from in front of the hotel and headed to the marina. There were several boats moored there, but one stood out more than any other. It was the yacht in which this group would be doing their traveling. As they approached the yacht, Dawn commented on the appearance of it to Toni.

"Toni, would you look at the size of that boat??!!"

"It's not a boat, Dawn, it's an ocean liner."

The van was emptied and as they approached the yacht, some saw the name emblazoned on the back of it. "TEALATION I".

"Dawn, does Tealation own a freaking yacht?"

"It sure appears that way to me."

"Holy shitaski!!"

"I don't know what that means, but I agree."

The gangway was spread out from the yacht to the dock and each associate walked slowly across it to the front of the yacht. The owners of the yacht had aided in carrying the luggage. As they entered the yacht deck, waiting in a line were all the crew. Once everyone was aboard standing on the deck, the crew began to introduce themselves. One by one, they mentioned their names and their roles. There was a cook, a steward, a few shipmates, a few other hands, and of course the captain. The captain introduced himself with a clean, sophisticated British accent. "I am Bart, short for Bartholomew, Griffin. But please do not refer to me as Bartholomew. There are far too many syllables, and I am still angry with my parents for pulling that moniker out of their drawers. I will be your Captain for this enchanting journey, so find your assigned berths, relax, and enjoy the ride." Heads nodded and many shared their verbal thanks. Captain Griffin continued. "Before we embark on our journey, there are two more people you should meet. We are privileged and happy to introduce you to the founders of your Tealation family, so I will now ask them to take a break from what they have been doing, climb up to the deck and introduce themselves."

Two gentlemen dressed in sleek khaki pants, with polo shirts emblazoned with the Tealation logo and classy sandals emerged from beneath the deck to join the group. The taller of the two spoke first.

"Hello, I'm Morton Williams. And meet my partner, Ralph Schultz."

Dawn and Toni were speechless. They both were visibly shaken and were adorned with a look of astonishment. They looked at each other without saying a word, and then turned again to look directly at their husbands. While the others gently applauded, Dawn and Toni stood motionless, staring in total disbelief. Ralph was the next one to speak. He muttered only one short sentence.

"Welcome everybody to the top of "The Pyramid!"

THE END

HAIR SHRINK

A NOVELLA

BY

Stuart R Schwartz

I was named "Paul" within seconds after escaping the womb. I had no choice as this moniker was predetermined even before my folks said "I do". No, Mom was not prego at the time but she and Dad had given a lot of thought to naming their kids before they were married. A girl would have been named "Paula". I suppose that certain levels of creativity are expunged from one's curriculum when you are studying to be an accountant like my Dad, and a guidance counselor like my Mom. Our last name, predetermined long before Dad was born is Rosenblatt. So, of course I was Paul Rosenblatt. The translation of Rosenblatt is something like "the leaves of roses", or so I have been told by the German teacher at Cottonville High School in Cottonville, New Jersey. Oh, and in case you are wondering, it does not appear that any cotton grows in New Jersey. As the story goes, Frederick Cotton, a Scottish immigrant, founded Cottonville in the mid 1700's as he was the sole resident of this large tract of land that he owned. So much for my understanding that all Scots names started with "Mc". So, old Freddie's land became a village, which became a town, is slowly becoming a city, and may someday become its own State within the State of New Jersey.

You can only imagine the thrills associated with growing up in a predominately Christian community with the name Rosenblatt. Christians in Cottonville include Catholics, Methodists, Baptists, Presbyterians, Lutherans, and a few non-denominationals. How do I know this? Well, I decided to drive up and down every street one day and made a list of each type of church I could find. I was just curious, that's all. If any Mormons, Pentacostals, Buddhists, Seventh-Day Adventists, Muslims, Hindus, or any of those other faiths were represented in the community, they took off for somewhere else to worship. But, as far as I knew, we were the only Jews. I never thought to ask Dad why he and Mom chose to live in Cottonville until February of my sophomore year in high school. That was the day that I found a yarmulke duct-taped to my locker. My first thought was; how did the perpetrators find a yarmulke in Cottonville? But, on closer inspection, it appeared to be the home-made variety. Someone's living room easy chair or sofa cushion was missing a swatch of cloth because that is exactly what it appeared to be. And, it smelled from urine. I had never taken any courses in criminology, but my detective-like instincts told me that this cushion had been discarded after a four-legged pet had used it as a litter station. Now admittedly, the yarmulke was a fine and true replica of the real thing, except for the fact that most of the Jews I know do not have their name "Sharpied" on their skull cap. And, even though the intruders named me "Paulette" instead of Paul or even "Paulie", I revered this gift as a symbol of their admiration for me and my faith.

"So Dad, why did you select Cottonville as the place we should live?"

"Do you want the long version or the short version, son?"

"Short, sweet, and easily understandable."

"One of my accounting clients owned about five rental properties throughout this part of New Jersey. This house was one of them. He was having problems with some other investments and told me that he would rent the house to your Mom and me at a lower than market price if we would agree to ultimately buy the house. So we did. Short and sweet enough?"

"Yup."

My sophomore year at high school remained somewhat uneventful for the few weeks following the yarmulke incident. But, just as I thought I would be left alone and the yarmulke appearing on my locker was probably a one-time act of frivolity, the next "anti-Semitic slur" arose with the duct-taping of a box of matzos to my locker. It was immediately obvious that this criminalistic behavior was initiated by the same moron who planted the yarmulke in the exact same place. But, rather than lose my cool, I merely laughed it off, ripped the box off of the locker, put it in my school bag, and left. "Sticks and stones will break my bones, but Streit's finest will never harm me." So, I brought the box of matzos home and gave them to Mom.

"Here, Mom."

"Why did you buy these, son?"

"Actually it was a gift, Joanie."

"Paul, I have told you before and I will tell you again that you do NOT address your mother by her first name."

"It was a gift, Mother."

"Who gives matzos as a gift? Do you have a girlfriend? Is she Jewish? What does her father do?"

"No, no girlfriends Mom. For crap's sake, I'm only fifteen. Mom, it was an anonymous gift giver."

"Well, didn't someone hand it to you?"

"Actually no. It was left on my locker."

"Paul, your grammar is a mess; it was either left "at" your locker or "in" your locker. But, guessing that nobody but you has access to your locker, it was probably left "at" your locker."

"In all fairness, Joanie, it was actually duct-taped "ON" my locker. So, be a good Mom and make me some of that matzo egg thing for breakfast."

"You are in big trouble, young man!"

"Gotchya!"

So, in the Spring of my Sophomore year at Cottonville High, I decided to take steps to filter the amount of future abuse before it happened. I was to change my name. Yes, an alteration of my identity would be considered a major step in my life. It was something that had to be done. I put this strategy to a test when Mrs. Carrina handed out a quiz in Algebra class. She would take it home, grade it, and discuss the results the next morning. At the very top of this two-page invasion of the right side of my frontal lobe was a line asking for one's name and date. The left side of my brain had very little work to do for this challenge. So, on the line, I inscribed my new name. The very next morning, Mrs. Carrina stood in front of the class and called out our names in order that we would see our grades and go over the answers together as a class. When she called out "Pablo Rosales", nobody responded. Mrs. Carrina also looked quite puzzled as she had been teaching this class for almost a full semester and had never seen nor heard of this name before. So, having heard my new name called out, I sauntered up to the front of the classroom to retrieve my test.

"Paul, is this your test paper?"

"Yes, it is, Mrs. Carrina." I was smart enough not to call her Rose, her first name. That only works on Mom's but really doesn't work well on my Mom.

"I didn't recognize this name, Paul."

"That's because it is my new name, Mrs. Carrina."

"Uhmm, Paul, I don't think we can simply assign ourselves new names."

"I was wondering about that actually, but I like it and I think I will go with it for a while."

The class was muffling their intended uproar and tried taking this exchange in without a complete Vesuviacal eruption.

"Paul, I get your little joke, but let's try to not play this little game again, okay?"

Well, just for the sake of a temporary remedy to this perfunctory mind-fuck, I agreed, but my intentions were different. Pablo Rosales was who I would be and it would take an inordinate amount of coaxing to change my mind.

The use of my new name went on for a few weeks, including a new name label on the front of my locker. Let's just see them duct-tape a taco to the front of my locker. I got away with my self-assigned identity until that fateful day in May when I was called to the Principal's office. Dr. Baird sat straight up in his Principal chair behind his Principal's desk wearing his Principal suit and the ugliest tie I had ever laid eyes on. It was purple with an orange strip diagonally across it. The school colors were maroon and white, so I immediately knew that there was no element of symbolism behind this hideous accessory.

"Nice tie."

"What?"

"Nevermind."

"Do you know why you are here today, Paul?"

"No."

"It has come to my attention that you are using a name other than your own."

"Actually, I am not."

"Your name is Paul Rosenblatt. I am hearing that you are calling yourself Pancho Gonzalez or something like that."

"My name is Pablo Rosales."

"Young man, I hate to be the first one to drop this bit of news on you, but you cannot just arbitrarily rename yourself."

"I respect that you are our Principal, but let me unload this one on you. I am no longer Paul Rosenblatt."

"Are your parents aware of this little antic?"

"Well sir, it isn't an antic because it is my new name, and no, I have not yet brought this to the attention of my parents."

"When do you plan to do that?"

"Soon."

"What may I ask possessed you to do that?"

"Sir, let's say your name was not Dr. James Baird but it was say "Boris Kugelphart", how would you feel?"

"I would be proud of my name, son."

"Oh really? And if you showed up at your locker at the end of the day and a matzo ball had been duct-taped to your locker, would you still be proud?"

"Well, I am sure I would want to know who did that."

"I am very sorry to have to say this, Dr. Baird, but I could give a rat's ass who did it. I write these things off as moronic gestures by an ignorant half-wit. And you should be embarrassed that this type of ignorance abounds in the halls of your highly-revered school. But I DO find it annoying, so my name is unofficially, for now, changed. I am Pablo Rosales."

"It is obvious to me, MR. ROSENBLATT, that whatever I have to say will have no impact on you, so I will just have to give your parents a call and have this discussion with them."

"That's your call, sir. They would have found out sooner or later anyway."

"That will be all for now, young man. You are free to leave."

I am not sure what prompted me to sing a few bars for Dr. Baird as I left. Perhaps it was the constant barrage of show tunes that I had to hear from dad's stereo EVERY NIGHT that prompted me, but as I left I rang out with " I am I, Pablo Rosales, The Lord of La Mancha, my destiny calls and I go, and the wild winds of fortune will carry me onward, oh whithersoever they blow. Whithersoever they blow, onward to glory I go!"

The next day I was summoned to the school psychologist's office. I wonder what prompted that little call? Somehow I just knew. I strolled into Dr. Barnett's office at Nine O'clock sharp as directed. Dr. Barnett was a plus or minus thirty-year old woman dressed smartly in a blue pin-striped pants-suit. Her natural blonde hair flowed gently across her shoulders and down past her shoulders and the top of her back. Her features were flawless and the bright red lipstick matched perfectly with her freshly-manicured nails. In short, she was hot. I was so tempted to tell her that, but I figured that I was in enough trouble as it was.

"Paul, do you know why you are here?"

"Pablo."

"Okay, Pablo, do you know why you are here?"

"Well, I am not exactly sure but, I am thinking that it has something to do with the changing of my name."

"That's part of it."

"What's the other part?"

"Paul, sorry, I mean Pablo, I have invited your parents to join us and they will be here momentarily."

"That's lovely."

"I figured that they should know about what is going on with you."

"Do you plan to give me a clue first, Dr. Barnett?"

"No, but okay. Besides the name change matter, you have used profanity while speaking with the Principal."

"I have? What did I say?"

"Well, I do not care to repeat it, so we will leave it at that."

"Could it have been "rat's ass"?"

"Mr. Rosenblatt!"

"Rosales."

"Rosenblatt, Rosales, whatever, let's just remain quiet then as we await your parents."

Five minutes passed before Joanie and Bert tapped on Dr. Barnett's door. Joanie and Bert, as you have likely guessed are my folks. The five minute wait seemed like five hours. Dr. Barnett pretended to be thumbing through papers and I just sat and stared at her breasts. While staring, I wondered, not aloud of course, why a school psychologist would have the nerve to dress in such a provocative manner. Her business suit was fine, but the jacket was open, her somewhat translucent white blouse was tight enough that it pronounced the two lovely medium sized flesh-muffins that lurked beneath. The room, by the way, was not cold, but the perfectly placed double-nipple protuberance was looking me straight in the eyes. I truly believed with all my hard, that she was doing this intentionally.

"Come in please."

Janie and Bert walked in and sat simultaneously on the sofa in Dr. Barnett's office. It appeared that they had rehearsed the sitting maneuver as they both sat at exactly the same time, each the exact distance apart from the end of the sofa. Good job, Rosenblatts, office entrance protocol approved. Dr. Barnett greeted them cordially and thanked them for coming in. They really weren't sure why they were there, so it appeared that no clues had been offered up prior to their arrival. Dad had often said that he hated surprises. Well, this was going to be a good one. But, I was predetermined to stand my ground.

"I am afraid that there have been a few issues with your son."

"Oh?" That was Dad. He likes to preempt Mom.

"Yes, Mr. Rosenblatt. Paul here has decided to change his name."

"To what?"

"You tell them, Paul."

"Pablo, my new name is Pablo. It's Pablo Rosales. I am no longer Paul Rosenblatt, and that is the very last time I will even mutter that name."

Mom was the next to speak since Dad's mouth was wide open with surprise. "Is this some kind of a joke?"

"No, Mom, it is no joke. I made the decision and I am sticking with it. There is nothing that you can do to change my mind."

Finally Dad awakened from his momentary stupor. "This is a stupid irrational joke which we will address further at home."

"I am afraid there's more, Mr. and Mrs. Rosenblatt."

Dad had taken over the conversation. "Now what?"

"Paul here used profanities in a conversation with the Principal, Dr. Baird."

"The name is Pablo, and I do not consider "rat's ass" a profanity."

"I have heard enough, Dr. Barnett. We will continue this dialogue with our son at home."

"He sang to Dr. Baird also."

Mom's turn, "What??!!"

"Mom, I sang a few bars from "Man of La Mancha." You and Dad love that show."

"Look, son, we are leaving now. We will speak with you at length this evening after dinner."

"Ok, fine, make tamales, Mom."

"WHAT??!!"

"Just a joke, Mom, just a joke. See you later."

Dinner that night was VERY quiet. Nobody said a word. Oftentimes I would comment on dinner, usually suggesting how wonderful something tasted or how overcooked the lamb is. "Hey Mom, don't throw away the leftovers, I can wear them on my shoes for a few days to keep them from wearing out." But tonight was different. The salmon was extremely dried out, a phenomenon that occurs when you leave it in the oven for thirty minutes longer than prescribed. Mom was old school. If you didn't cook the crap out of whatever you planned to dispense from the oven, it was going to be bad for you. But, I kept my mouth shut knowing that the barrage of bullshit would fly within minutes after dinner was completed. Dad adjourned us to the family room. There was nothing going on in there either. Dead silence. No show tunes, no "Wheel of Torture", no "Jeopardy!", nothing but silence. Finally, the silence was broken. Dad's rehearsed monologue was about to begin.

"Son, your Mom and I have been thinking about what we learned about you today."

"Dad, in fairness, may I interrupt?"

"No, actually you may not."

"Just one thing, please, then I'll shut up and listen."

"What?"

"How are my grades?"

"Your grades are very good, son."

"Then I rest my case."

"What case, Paul? We are not talking about grades here; we are discussing our personal identities; who and what we are, the way we act and behave, our goals, and our lifestyles."

"Okay."

"Okay?, so do you have anything to say here?"

"Yah, there is not much to discuss. I know who I am, I know what I want, and I behave very nicely I beg to pardon."

"Calling Dr. Baird a "rat's ass" is not behaving."

"Oh, wait just one Cottonville second here. I did not call "Principal Fashion Statement" a "rat's ass". Let's make that clear. I told him that I didn't give a rat's ass about WHO was the one taping Matzos and Yarmulkes to my locker. I was just tired of being annoyed."

"Someone did that?"

"Yes, Dad, someone did that. But guess what. I will not seek and destroy. I have risen above that, so I will ignore. BUT, I have changed my name. That's final and there's nothing that will change it. Allow me to make an analogy for you Dad. You know that lovely mole that Gramps has on his nose? I'm talking about the turd-colored one with hair growing from it that Grandma is too blind to notice and too afraid of him to even make a comment?"

"Well, yes."

"Okay, Dad, let's say that by some chance you had that on your nose. What would you do?"

All of a sudden, Mom chimes in.

"I would have your Dad get it removed."

"Exactly! That's what I am saying. I have removed my mole. My name is now Pablo Rosales. So, now I have homework to do so I will adjourn to my room and say goodnight. Thank you for dinner and the lecture."

I was somewhat surprised that the next few weeks were relatively quiet around school and the household. The fact that I had changed my name had caught on in school and my parents simply ignored that matter. In fact, Mom was beginning to catch on also because after several attempts to call me down for dinner using my old name, she relented and called for "Pablo". Hearing that made me so happy, I nearly pissed myself.

Summer was summer. "Here a job, there a job, everywhere a shit job", etc. I eagerly awaited the start of school as I had made the decision to try out for the Cottonville High School football team. They were actually quite good and if I could make the team, I might be held in higher esteem by my school peers. What others felt about me really wasn't very important, but I needed some back-up extracurricular for my college applications, so why not football? I was relatively fast, I had a little size, and my strength was above average. My bedroom contained a small set of dumbbells, not the ones when my assonantal twin cousins Jack and Matt Rosenblatt visited, but the type that come in different weights. Each day, I pumped iron, or whatever they contain therein, and my arms were getting larger.

It didn't take long for me to figure out that I would not be a starter on the football team, but I would have a uniform and I would sit on the bench. I was quite sure that if our team was ahead or behind by forty points, I could possibly get in the game. But football did help me come to a major revelation. It wasn't anything that I worried much about, but I was very curious to learn that I might have some gay tendencies. How did I know this? Well, I noticed that I enjoyed spending lots of time in the showers after football practice. Why? I had an obsession with penises. I found myself staring at them in wonderment, all of the time. Of course, I was quite discreet so as not to scare off anyone from the showers. My fascination wasn't centered on the fact that these appendages were exclusive to only males. These are not items one sees every day, so I was simply curious as to the different shapes and sizes. It was interesting to note that some were long, others were short; some were skinny, others were fat; and some pointed in different directions. Others had sheaths on them which would never happen in a Jewish community. It made me quite glad that I had no recollection of the "Happy Hacker" honing his skills on my relatively young love stick. I prefer to refer to it in the context of the erotic as opposed to its elimination functions. Someday, hopefully sooner than later, I would know more about the titillating components of this particular device. So, was this obsession an indicator that I might be gay? The fact that I also could not take my mind off of Dr. Baird's headlight assembly confirmed, for the time being anyway, that the penis thing was just a temporary observational research project.

Junior and Senior years at Cottonville were fine. Almost everyone who knew me called me Pablo. I took Spanish I & II those two years and my teacher, Carolina Villas, was happy to have someone with a Spanish name in her class. She didn't seem to mind at all that I did not know even one word of Spanish when I enlisted for the classes. Everyone in the class was assigned a Spanish first name. I happily avoided that step by having already assigned myself the name Pablo.

Dating didn't take place at all until the second half of my senior year of high school. And, I wouldn't exactly refer to my interludial escapades with girls as dates. We usually went out to movies and other activities as "friends". To this day, I cannot put my finger on why these early encounters never were considered anything more than friendly encounters. After all, I did "ride the pines" in a football uniform and I was an excellent student. But, be it as it may, I knew I liked girls, and I was certain that the future was always not too far away. I was especially friendly with Eloise Hodges. I think I liked her more for her name than her personality. Eloise was cute "in her own special way" as I have heard. It was very difficult to understand her personality because she seemed to be very tolerant of everything, but yet set in her ways about what she wanted and didn't want for herself. She knew of my past and had no issues at all referring to me as Pablo whenever we did anything together. But, there was no kissing, some moderate hugging, and no words of intimacy. Eloise was a bit taller than the average senior girl, kept her reddish-brown hair cut short, and had a sharp nose that sat on an incredibly unblemished smooth-skinned face. Her lips were full and inviting, but I was not one of the invitees. She was thin with small breasts and a nicely sculpted bottom. She never dressed provocatively, but it was fun to imagine what was underneath. We did many things together as friends including the non-standard New Jersey high school stuff such as fishing, watching Independent and foreign films, classical concerts in the park, rock concerts by local bands where they allowed teenagers, and learning how to juggle. Yes, that one was strange, but there was a local guy who was a professional juggler, so he gave lessons in the park on Saturday mornings. I was a three-baller. Eloise quickly graduated to four. We spoke almost daily and were considered an "item" by classmates. But, she and I knew better.

I became a hero to Eloise because of one frightful experience. I had asked Eloise if she would drive me to the football field before the game as I had no other way to get there. I did not want to walk as I would have been late getting into uniform. On the way, at the intersection of Thomas Street and Third Avenue, Curly Manchester was driving his septic cleaning truck, presumably back to wherever it is emptied. Yes, there were still sections of Cottonville that required septic tanks as they were a bit remote to be connected to sewer lines. We usually referred to Curly as the local "honey dipper", the "Good Humor Man and his Ice Cream truck", and "The Big Dipper". Well, as Curly approached the intersection, he was presumably distracted and ran the red light. There has been speculation that he was texting at the time as the police, upon seizing his cell phone, found an incomplete message essentially saying, "Hi, Honey, Your Dip-shit boyfriend has just finished dipping the shit and is taking the shit-wagon back to …" And then it stopped. The problem with all of this was that Maria Chen, yes, she too probably changed her name, and her five-year old son Tommy had entered the intersection at the same time. Well, even though Curly tried to swerve out of the way, Maria "T-boned" the truck and it flipped over onto its side. Almost immediately, the truck's cumbersome waste matter began flowing out into the intersection. It didn't look good at all. Eloise's car was directly behind Maria Chen's, so we stopped short to take in the action. Curly was trying to crawl out of the door on the overturned shit wagon and Maria Chen seemed trapped behind the wheel. In a daze, five-year old Tommy climbed out of the car, presumably to seek help for his traumatized mother. Tommy took about three steps before he slipped into this ocean of waste and immediately went down. Tommy proceeded to slide towards the guard rail at the end of the intersection and my immediate observation was that Tommy was so small that he would slide under the guard rail and fall about twenty feet into the creek below. I could not just sit there. So, without regard for my own safety, my instincts told me that I must save Tommy. My door flew open and out I went. I ran towards Tommy, carefully trying to keep my balance in the bay of sludge, and just as I was close to Tommy, I slipped and went down also. I literally swam through the muck to get to Tommy and was able to grab him about three feet in front of the guard rail. We were both stunned. Tommy was crying loudly, and we were both covered from head to toe in septic waste. By the time we both had realized that the danger was behind us, we looked around only to find a large group of onlookers applauding the fact that we were safe. Mind you, they were applauding from a distance as I am sure nobody wanted to get close. The police and fire departments were not far behind. Eloise was out of her car screaming at me to just stay where I was. The fire department was going to hose me down. Tommy and I were literally in "deep shit". Maria Chen was pulled out of the car and thankfully seemed only stunned. She was prepared to make a mad dash for Tommy, but a savvy pedestrian grabbed her in the nick of time. She too would have become one of the doodified. So, I was hosed down and still smelled quite badly. I pretty much sat alone on the bench at the football game, but it was okay with me. Eloise had told me that what I did was "heroic".

Early one evening in May of my senior year, Eloise called me and asked if I wanted to meet her for pizza and Cokes. I hadn't eaten and

Mom wouldn't have minded me meeting up with Eloise. She and Dad liked her principally because they knew that we were merely friends and there was no fear of me marrying a Goyisha girl, a Shiksa. I had no intention of digressing here, but I often wondered if "Goyisha" was a derivation of the Japanese "Geisha" and Shiksa had something to do with the Middle-eastern "Sheiks". I wouldn't know who to ask, but I think I already know the answers. So, Eloise and I met at Tony's Pizza. It was "the" place to go for Italian food in Cottonville. In actuality, it was the only place to go. It was on that fateful night that I decided that I would put this friendship on the line and make a suggestion to Eloise which might send her out of the restaurant screaming. So, I garnered up all of the courage I could find from within and let it fly.

"Eloise, I would like to eat you."

Her immediate response was to set down her glass of Coke, look at me curiously, tilt her head, and, after a few seconds of deliberation, finally respond.

"Do you mean eat me in the same sense as a parent would say to a child, I could just eat you up, or do you mean the perverted way."

I took offense at the fact that she thought the act was perverted.

"Eloise, I do not consider it perverted. Everybody does it eventually."

"Everybody?"

"Well, I know that it is an acceptable way of showing affection."

"To whom?"

"To someone you love."

"Are you saying you love me, Pablo?"

Okay, I was sort of stuck on this one, but in my own special way, I did believe I loved her. She called me a hero. How could I not love her for that?

"Yes, Eloise, I have loved you for a long time."

"Pablo, I have always had this feeling that you cared about me, but I also was getting the "gay vibes" from you."

"Why would you say that?"

"Well, you do have some gay tendencies."

"Like what?"

"You like to arrange flowers and work in the garden. And you have asked if you could trim my hair on a few occasions. Pablo, you even asked me to go to the ballet. Straight teenage boys do not go to the ballet."

"That's not being gay, Eloise, it's just being me, Pablo. And, I am sorry, BUT straight teenage boys with CULTURE do go to the ballet." It's a very good thing that I did not mention the penis obsession with her.

"Okay, I see. Look, I'll tell you what. My parents are heading out of town Saturday morning early. I'll be alone. Come over and we can discuss it further." Before she had the chance to finish speaking the words "come over", I could feel the beginning of lower-torso levitation. I would have to wait a while before exiting the table as a full-blown hard-on was in the immediate future. Lord knows how long it would take for it to return to its relaxed position as opposed to the "locked and upright position" we hear when flying and the one I was about to experience.

It seemed to take forever for Saturday morning to arrive. I was pumped up and excitedly awaited my first journey to the mystical, magical land of erotica. I wasn't going there for any other reason than pure curiosity and my continued research of life. Eloise would be the perfect partner for this excursion and I only hoped that she was as ready as I was. I arrived mid-morning and Eloise opened the door immediately upon hearing the doorbell ring. She must have been peering out the window. She was wearing a blue sweat shirt with the name "Haul Ash Trucking" on it. Two things immediately came to mind. The most prevalent wonderment was whether or not there was a bra underneath and the other less relevant thought was whether there really was a company named "Haul Ash Trucking". If so, it was quite the clever name. She also wore tan sweatpants with a drawstring belt. Upon examination, I imagined that it might be one of those "one yank and off strings", but I would patiently await the opportunity to find out. A pair of matching tan slippers rounded out the outfit.

"Have you eaten breakfast, Pablo?"

"Yes, and you?"

"I had a little something, yes. Would you care for some juice or a Coke?"

"I'll have whatever you have."

"How about iced tea? I made it this morning actually."

"Perfect."

"Are you nervous, Pablo?"

"No, of course not. Why would I be nervous?"

"Well aren't you about to become the James Cook of the female anatomy?"

"Have there been other explorers before me?"

"With me? If there had, would that be something I would share with you?"

I really had no answer for that question. I think it was a good thing to have left it alone for now.

The iced tea was sweet and pure. It gave me a little bit of a rush, but at the same time, it calmed my nerves a bit. I was somewhat nervous about what the short term future had in store. Mom asked me where I was heading when I abruptly left the house. I told her that I was on my way to the library. I didn't think it would be a good idea to share with her that I was on a mission to eat Eloise. Some mom's just do not understand such things. Eloise was quite coy about the preliminary proceedings before we entered horizontal heaven.

"Well, Pablo, remember I told you that we were going to discuss it, not necessarily do it."

"I would not want to talk you into anything that would make you feel uncomfortable, Eloise."

"Oh, I am not uncomfortable with it at all, but I just wonder if we are ready for this?"

"I'm thinking that the longer we talk about it, the less likely it will happen."

"Let's go for it, Pablo."

"Where? Right here on the sofa?"

"Sure, why not?"

"Wouldn't a bed be more comfortable?"

"I think it's safer here."

Before I could even ask her why she was thinking that the sofa was safer, Eloise slipped over to the corner the sofa, leaned back and rested her head against the sofa's arm. She raised her legs so that she was half on and half off this lounging device. We merely looked at each other. Eloise was wearing a flirtatious half-smile and I was suffering from very mixed emotions. In a mini-second, every thought imaginable began to run through my mind. My emotions included fear, excitement, worry, and intense anticipation. Noticing that I was suffering from a mild case of discomfort, Eloise reached down to the drawstrings on her sweat pants, and while staring me directly in the eyes, slowly pulled at them until they were disengaged from their tightened state. Without a blink of the eye, she continued to look at me and reached down and slowly lowered her pants to a spot just below the top of her pubic area. I took my eyes off of her and peered down. I wasn't exactly sure, but what I believed I saw was the very tip of a heart. Could it be that Eloise shaved a heart down in pubic wonderland? The teasing continued as she stopped and hesitated.

"Are you teasing me, Eloise?"

"I believe so, yes."

"Why?"

"I'm preparing you for your little adventure."

What seemed like a minor uprising from the depths of where my manhood normally rested soon became a full-scale levitation. I was definitely prepared. Her pants were lowered to the bottom of the pubic area and sure enough, there existed a heart. It was a soft, reddish brown flaxen sea of God-woven beauty.

"It's a heart, Eloise."

"It is, Pablo, especially designed and made just for you."

My heart and loins were pounding. Eloise kicked off her slippers and they seemed to drop to the floor in slow motion. Everything was happening so very quickly, but the time was passing oh so slowly. She finally took her eyes off of me, reached down and completely removed her tan sweat pants. The skin on her legs was flawless and the small, pink crevice that existed below the heart was one of the most beautiful sights I had ever imagined. Nothing was said. I just could not take my mind off of what I was seeing. I immediately understood why the word eroticism was ever coined. It was a pure sense of anticipation.

"Do you want me to remove my pants, Eloise?"

"No."

"Are you going to take off your top?" I so wanted to see her breasts. It could only add to this mission to paradise.

"No. It wasn't the intent. Remember?"

"Okay."

"Well, Pablo?"

"Well, what?"

"Are you ready?"

"Yes, I am, I am so ready."

"I'm waiting."

I slid down off of the sofa and sat on the floor next to it. Eloise rearranged her body with legs apart so that her crotch was staring me right in the face. I had never seen anything so ravishing. The beauty of this was more than I could have ever imagined. It was the whipped cream on a hot fudge sundae; it was the first breathtaking look at the Grand Canyon; it was the gate to paradise. And, it was looking me directly in the eye, waiting, anticipating. I leaned closer and felt Eloise's hand touch my hair, guiding me into the Promised Land. My lips met the petals of this glorious perianth. They were warm and moist, inviting me to come closer, to enjoy the excursion into this inaugural interlude. Instinctively, my tongue found its way into these soft, damp lips and began to lap the lotions they produced.

"Oh, Pablo, a little higher."

I found my way a bit higher and discovered a small bump. Was this the "magic button" that I had heard about from some of my peers? I licked this spot a few times and could feel Eloise vibrating behind it.

"Yes there, oh yes, there, Pablo. Gentle, soft, gentle."

I continued and listened in delight as Eloise moaned, her breathing becoming heavier moment by moment. Her moans became louder and as they did, I felt an earthquake brewing within my own loins. I must continue what I was doing and suppress what I knew what was about to happen to me. The peak of Eloise's orgasm and my own volcanic explosion happened simultaneously, almost as if planned that way. Eloise gently pushed my head back and, as if on cue, I slid back to my sitting position on the floor beside her.

"Pablo, I need a minute to breathe."

"Me too, are you okay?"

"I'm very okay, Pablo. And you?"

"Well, sort of."

"Sort of?"

"I had a premature ejaculation."

"Premature? When was this ejaculation supposed to reach maturity?"

"Well, I don't know. I guess there was no set time."

"Did it happen the same time that it happened to me?"

"I think it did. Yes."

"Well then it was perfectly timed. We did it at the same time. It's the way it is supposed to be, silly."

"I guess so."

"It is so."

"I have a confession, Pablo."

I was waiting to hear the worst, as in this was a frequent event for Eloise.

"Yes, Eloise?"

"Pablo, this was my first."

"Really?"

"Honest."

"Well, for me too, Eloise."

"I had that suspicion, Pablo."

Eloise reached down and hiked her pants back up. She gently shook her head as I watched every hair fall back into place just as neatly as she looked before our interlude. It reminded me of a group of soldiers falling back into formation, perfectly lined up side by side.

"Hungry, Pablo?"

"Is that some sort of a joke?"

"No, I have some money that my folks left for me to eat. Let's grab a pizza."

"Count me in."

Eloise's course, "Introduction to Hetereosexuality 101" was just a one-time class. The rest was up to me through "Independent Studies". And, yes, I did my best to research the topic and practice this course on as many sessions as possible with as many "classmates" as possible. Most of this came after high school and was prevalent during my college years.

I decided to legally change my name prior to applying to college. The required age for this in New Jersey was eighteen years old. That was the easy part. The process was far more complicated than I had expected. Besides fees, there were courts, applications, documents, and a plethora of other bullshit. John Plymouth, one of my football teammates, offered to have his Dad, an attorney, assist me in the process. It would be gratis. I guessed that John felt like he owed me and to this day, I still know not why. The more I thought about the name change, I realized that I did want to be Pablo Rosales forever, but the first name, Pablo, seemed to hang out there alone, like a free balloon lost in shifting wind currents. What to do? So, I thought of several middle names that might complement Pablo and came up empty every time. Then it struck me. How important was it that Pablo be my first name? It wasn't important at all provided that everyone called me and knew me as Pablo. Without dragging you through the process of elimination that I solely endured, I came up with Juan Pablo. Genius, you say? Thank you. So, totally unbeknownst to my folks, the big court date arrived, and on that day, I officially became Juan Pablo Rosales. As far as I was concerned, I was "J. Pablo".

I was smart enough to get into practically any college I wanted, but not smart enough to receive a scholarship. The college applications went out to several schools and I knew straight away that I would be accepted at most of them. Each application bore my new name. I had predicted the level of trauma, disgust, and angst that my parents would exhibit once the mail, bearing my new name, began to arrive from the schools. It wasn't pretty and the visual of my Mom's threats to "stick her head in the oven and turn on the gas" left me hurt and dismayed. These feelings lasted only temporarily as somehow I knew she would not go through with the threat. "Mom, it isn't like I am marrying a "shiksa". That softened the blow a bit, but the receipt of an acceptance from Lafayette College in Easton, Pennsylvania was the ultimate cure of the woes. Lafayette had been the family's first choice, all the way around.

My college years were somewhat ho-hum save the occasional social interludes, but I made it through by sticking to my prearranged agenda. It comprised of study, eat, sleep, more study, an occasional weekend in Cottonville, some spectator sports, some horizontal sports with willing participants, and my quest to find decent beer. Easton, Pennsylvania isn't necessarily considered the mecca for beer connoisseurs, but I did manage to find two local pubs that had some decent draft beer. And, to my delight, nobody deemed it weird that I would drag my textbooks into the pub and study whilst indulging in a cold frothy glass of fine brew. My first year at Lafayette required that I take certain "core" classes and a few electives. I chose "Introduction to Psychology 101" as an elective, and I loved it. Prior to taking the course, I never knew how complex our brains are. The study of the mind is objective in many ways, but I believed that the subjective nature of the studies were overwhelmingly interesting. It did not take me long at all to decide that my major field of study would be Psychology. Shortly after making this decision, I was in Cottonville for a weekend.

I discussed my choices with my folks and my Mom was the first to react. "Paul, why are you taking Psychology? What can you become?"

"Who are you talking to?"

"Oh, for shit sake,

Paul, I am talking to you."

"Unless you address me by my name, I will not be answering."

Before she was able to squeeze out my real name, her entire face squinched up like a prune. And, then begrudgingly, the word left her mouth as if it were a freshly extracted molar.

"Paaaablo, why Psychology?"

"Because I find it interesting."

"What can you be?"

"Whatever I decide to be."

"That's not an answer."

"I have some things to do, Mom, I'll catch you later."

Sometimes I wonder why I even participate in conversations when the person with whom I am speaking knows what they "want" to hear, not what they "need" to hear. I never felt that I was being a jerk, though I've been called that on a few occasions. I just like to be honest.

I graduated Lafayette with honors and a Bachelor of Arts in Psychology. Never, ever agreeing to agree with Mom, what indeed was next? Who could I expect to hire me with this degree? The Lafayette part was impressive, but the major field of study, not so much. After a long, involved thought process, I decided that Graduate School would be my next course of action. It would be two full years of study, so rather than ask Mom and Dad to foot the entire bill; I would work and go to school. One of the best graduate programs in the East was offered by Columbia University in New York City. I was approved for admission within three weeks after applying.

I decided not to overload my course work for the first semester of graduate school. I could easily discourage myself by piling up hours of study and trying to work at the same time. Gina Mazza, one of my classmates in my dream theory class at Columbia told me that some of the other grad students like to find jobs that relate to their major field of study. She was in a similar boat as I was since she did not want to unload the financial burden of grad school on anyone else but herself. So, she had taken a job as a bartender at an upscale restaurant/club in Manhattan. "Pablo, if you want to practice the art of studying the mind, then become a bartender. You will not believe how drunks like to pour their lives out onto the bar." Gina and I had hit it off from day one. We sat across an aisle from one another in dream theory class and on the very first day, I made an observation that allowed me to open a conversation with her. The wristwatch she was wearing was extremely large and multi-colored to boot. It was one of the gaudiest things I had ever seen except for perhaps Mildred Hornplow's Christmas sweater. Mildred was our high school librarian. The sweater was a hand-sewn bright red dealie with a reindeer. Rather than have you try to visualize that monstrosity, I'll just move on here. So, Gina was heading for the door of the classroom after our first session when I decided to say something.

"Nice watch."

"Thanks, do you really like it?"

"Well, it roused my attention."

"That doesn't answer the question."

"It's different. I like different things."

"Does that make me different?"

"I didn't comment about the watch because I think you are different. We are studying Psych here, not practicing it, right?"

"Cute. Hi, I'm Gina Mazza."

"I'm Juan Pablo Rosales, but I go by Pablo."

"Pleased to meet you, Pablo. Are you hitting on me? It's only the first day of class, you know."

"No, I am not hitting on you, whatever that is supposed to mean. I just thought I would make small talk as I enjoy having new friends, especially when I know absolutely nobody here."

"Do you have time for a coffee, Pablo?"

"Sure."

"Good, there's a coffee shop one door down from the university cafeteria. It's cheap and good."

"Let's go."

The coffee shop was half full. Each of us had the basic "regular" coffee with cream and sugar. It was nice to know that my first friendly encounter at Columbia had at least one thing in common with me.

"So, Pablo, where are you from?"

"New Jersey."

"More specific."

"Cottonville, New Jersey, a beating of a train or bus ride from here."

"You're commuting?"

"Only temporarily."

"Then today is your lucky day."

"How's that, Gina?"

"I rented a room in a three-bedroom apartment on the West Side here. It's nice. One of the roommates is moving out in ten days. I will interview you right now, and if you qualify, you're in."

"That sounds quite good, Gina, but what makes you think that I want to share an apartment?"

"Okay then, Pablo, ride your fucking train."

I had just met this woman thirty minutes earlier and she was already dropping "F-bombs" on me. I needed to re-phrase my question and do it quickly.

"I'm sorry, Gina, I probably sounded a bit pompous there. So, let me just say that it would likely be an honor to room with you, and I am ready for the interview."

Gina didn't respond straight away to my retort. She merely took a sip of her coffee and looked at me straight in the eye. Her eyes were a sparkling emerald green with long black eyelashes. The longer I looked back at her, the less time it took me to realize that she was extremely attractive. She had a bit of an attitude, but the good news was that it had manifested itself early enough for me to appreciate her candor. Finally, she relaxed her shoulders, leaned forward and commenced asking me prospective roommate type questions.

"So, Pablo, are you straight or gay?"

The first question came as a surprise, as in "why does that matter?"

"I'm straight. Do you need proof?"

Gina rolled her eyes to that response and quipped, "Not yet."

"Are you Puerto Rican? Cuban? South American?"

"No, I'm Jewish."

"Nice, Pablo, but Jewish is a faith the last I knew of it, not a nationality."

"I'm American, Gina."

"Then why is your name Pablo Rosales?"

"It's a long story that I will share with you at some time in the future."

The barrage of questions continued.

"Are you neat? OCD? Do you cook? Do you sleepwalk? What do you watch on TV? How often do you shower? Do you have a felony record? Do your parents like to surprise you with visits? Do you have pets? Do you mind pets? In which sports do you participate, if any? Who washes your clothes? Do you have any fetishes I should know about?"

I really didn't understand why she asked so many questions, some of which were somewhat bizarre. But, after further thought, I realized that this was not Gina's first rodeo with having a roommate, and many of these questions were likely the product of past experiences. But, I answered them all and it appeared that she liked the answers. I had qualified to be her roommate.

"Pablo, what are you doing for money? Student loans?"

"Well, yes, part of it. But, I will also seek a part-time job."

"Well Pablo, remember when I suggested you tend bar?"

"I do."

"As you know, that's what I do. And guess what?! Your day has just become luckier."

"Oh? How's that?"

"One of the other bartenders, Mikhail, is moving to Europe. The manager loves me and if I recommend you, he will hire you."

"Really? How much can I earn?"

"On a good night, I haul in about three hundred dollars. You'd probably get three nights of work per week for starters, so you can figure on making about three grand a month, cash deal. That'll pay your rent and leave you plenty of extra for school, food and condoms."

"I don't need food."

"Very, very funny, Pablo. So, do you want an interview?"

"Do you conduct that interview also?"

"Ha ha, no. You'll interview with Don Meecham, our manager. He's a good guy. He will like you."

The apartment and the job worked out great. I am not sure why Gina had asked if I was neat because she surely was not. I found myself picking up after her constantly which led me to believe that she was seeking a roommate that would be her personal valet. I didn't mind as she was great to be with and a true friend. There was nothing sexual between us. She questioned my sexuality again, but not until after I was buying and arranging flowers for the apartment and trimming her hair on a monthly basis. The restaurant, The Black Talon, drew a large crowd with an emphasis on the young professional set. These were a group of people just a few years ahead of me in life that had gained their first jobs and had nothing better to do with their money than to drink heavily then head home and pass out either by themselves or with the woman or man of their dreams. I was willing to wager my nightly draw that the object of their affections wasn't quite as attractive the morning after their visit to the Black Talon. By the end of the sixth month, I was working five nights per week, pulling in about twelve hundred dollars a week and easily making ends meet financially. I had no one else to thank than Gina for helping to make this happen.

Spring arrived and I had to decide whether to continue with classes or take a break. I needed a break from my regime and decided to continue classes in the Fall. The Black Talon didn't make me rich, but it certainly paid the bills. I had stashed some of my take and decided to take a break. A lot of research led me to decide that I would escape for a long weekend to Jamaica. I told Gina of my vacation plans and was not really ready for her response.

"Who are you going with, Pablo?"

"Nobody, I am taking myself."

"You're not, you're taking me."

"I am?"

"Yup!"

"What about The Black Talon?"

"No problemo amigo mio, Don has plenty of back-up when we are not available."

The flight to Jamaica was uneventful and the all-inclusive hotel in Ochos Rios was gorgeous. We decided to share a room and when it was time to check in; the clerk asked if we wanted two Queens or a King-sized bed? Almost simultaneously, me: "Two Queens." Gina: "King." The clerk didn't have to take much time to figure out who the boss of this dynamic duo might be, and said "a King it is then."

All-inclusive means that most drinks and meals are included in the price of the resort stay. Gina likes to collect the little umbrellas and plastic palm tree stirrers that come with the drinks. At the end of the first night, the entire dresser had a full lineup of these ornaments. Needless to say, I was flying quite high and Gina was completely shit-faced drunk. I remember much of the sex, but I would be surprised if she had any recollection of it at all the next day. I had often wondered where the term "sloppy sex" had been derived, but I was now completely aware.

"Good morning, Pabbie."

"Oh God, it's Pablo."

"I said that."

"Right, what should we do today, Gina? Does the beach sound good?"

"Let's decide over breakfast which I want right here in the bed."

I listened as Gina called the room service and ordered almost everything on the menu including two Bloody Marys.

"I'm not sure I am ready for more alcohol quite yet, Gina."

"You're on vacation, Pabbie, enjoy yourself."

Up until the time we arrived at the resort, and after six months of knowing Gina, I never really knew that she had a propensity for partying. In fact, I didn't know much about her at all. She didn't share and I didn't ask. I do know that she grew up in Buffalo, New York where she was happy to have escaped because, "I got tired of freezing my little ass off every winter." Maybe she hadn't noticed that you can freeze your ass off in New York City in the winter also.

The summer after my first year of grad school was relatively uneventful. Gina and I were a couple, but I wasn't sure how to break the news that it would not be for the long term. Dad's heart, coupled with his diabetes, was not that strong, and Mom was never one to keep sharp objects in the house with which to stab herself, harikari style. But, the parents were not the only reason. Gina's laissez faire attitude about life was not synchronistic with mine, at least I did not believe so. I decided that summer that I would become a psychotherapist. My mind set was that if I became a good one, I could either go on and get my Ph.D or become a Psychiatrist. Imagine me, Juan Pablo, working with people's minds. But, it was a new goal and I would strive to achieve it. You see, one of the catalysts for making this decision was the fact that I knew how to listen. How did I learn this trait? On the rare slow nights at The Black Talon, there would always be one or more solo acts at the bar that bled their issues right out onto the bar, principally for me to listen and respond. I heard some crazy shit including the night one middle-aged executive was so down in the mouth that he told me he would head straight for the George Washington Bridge after leaving the bar and practice his swan dive. Of course, while on my break, I called the police and advised them of the proposed splash-down. They could have cared less as was evidenced by the demeanor of the officer with whom I spoke. So, I had to slide into my "you have everything to live for" speech and offered to buy him a few drinks if he returned the following night, which of course he did.

Psychotherapy required extra course work and post graduate on the job training. It wasn't going to be easy, but I knew it was what I wanted to be. Gina didn't follow course and decided that she would be more inclined to do social work. She actually seemed perplexed that I would pursue this direction.

"Are you going to try to change me, Pablo?"

"From what to what?"

"From whatever you think I am now into whatever you think I should be."

"Psychotherapists don't change people, Gina. They help people make adjustments to their character so that they can live better, and enjoy life."

"How can I possibly live better than I am now?"

"I am not exactly sure, Gina and I am not a psychotherapist yet, so let's move on to the next subject". That new subject, by the way, was what and where we would be eating that evening.

The course work for Psychotherapy was rigorous at Columbia but I found a way to make it through. I graduated with honors but it would take more courses and some training to be licensed as a therapist. I decided to become licensed in New York though I knew that the competition for work would be stiff. New York City had become home for me, and even though I had no idea whether or not there would be a future with Gina, I became so used to being around her; I just didn't want to think about moving away.

The Psychology department at Columbia placed me in my first real job which was a part of my training. I would work in a crisis management center called The Meade Center, taking calls and meeting with prospective patients by phone. For me, there was no face to face intervention. The State of New York subsidized our clinic and the patients were referred by doctors, hospitals, churches, schools, and by other referral bases. The calls came in quite frequently and each situation was different. There were so many different scenarios, so all of the training in the world might not have prepared me for what was to come.

"Hello, you have reached Pablo Rosales at the Meade Center. May I have your name please?"

"I'm Dianne."

"Hello there, Dianne. How may I be of help for you today?"

"My minister, William Codden, told me to call here." She told me this in a manner in which I was supposed to know who her minister is.

"Oh, I see. Is there a problem?"

"Yes, there's a problem."

"Okay, Dianne, are you going to share this with me?"

"Are you Puerto Rican?"

What in hell? Why would she ask me that straight out of the box?

"Dianne, thank you for asking, but I am unable to share my personal background with you."

"Oh really, Mr. Pablo? So, I guess I am supposed to pour out my heart to a phone robot and I can know nothing about the person I am speaking to?"

"Let's chat about what the issue is, Dianne, and then we can get to know one another a little better."

"My boyfriend repeatedly belittles me and has now threatened to beat me."

"Your minister suggested you call Meade about that?"

"Yes. He told me that you deal with such situations."

"How long has this gentleman been your boyfriend?"

"Too long and he is not a gentleman."

"I see. Do you know what may have provoked these incidents?"

"He calls me stupid and is always criticizing me."

"Why do you stay with him?"

"I don't know. Maybe he is all I know."

"Perhaps it is time to give the relationship a little rest. Maybe you would meet someone who appreciates you more than this fellow."

"I have tried that, Mr. Pablo, but I miss him when he is not around."

"Have you sat down and talked to him about the way you feel?"

"I tried that, but he always starts yelling at me and calling me names."

"What types of names does he call you?"

"Do you really want to hear this?"

"It will help me help you evaluate the situation."

"He calls me "pea-brain", "pancake tits", "tea-sipper", "shit for brains", "sister of Satan", and other similar niceties."

"Do you enjoy tea?"

"Of course, I do, all kinds. I try to have a cup or two or three daily."

"Dianne, it appears that you may have some self-esteem issues and you allow him to push your buttons. We can work on that but you might consider going your separate ways for a while. If you do, you will have to be firm in your convictions and stay the course. In the meantime, leave your email address after I disengage the call. You will hear a tone, and what follows are instructions for leaving your email address. I will be sending you the titles of a few books that will help you through this."

"You want me to read, Mr. Pablo?"

"Yes, but they are brief, more like pamphlets."

"Okay, when will we speak again?"

"Let's set something up for a week from now and we can resume our chat. In the meantime, try to ignore the name calling. He may have some insecurity or other types of delusional issues which he takes out on you. Okay?"

Okay, bye."

Dianne was one of many similar type calls. I was enjoying the diversity of the situations and almost felt comfortable lending advice. I knew that the calls were being recorded, so I had to try my best to hide the sarcasm, the cynicism, and the smart-ass remarks. Gina would pound me day after day wanting to know about my calls. I wanted to share, leaving out the names to protect the client's privacy and on some occasions I did, but for the most part, I simply refused to discuss these.

My first suicide intervention call was a doozy. I was totally unprepared for it, but I did my best to follow protocols until the frustration set in.

"Hello, thank you for calling Meade Center. How may I be of help?

I sat awaiting a response and there was nothing.

"Hello? Hello? Is someone calling?"

Finally I heard some sobbing, so I waited. Then, after a minute or two of waiting, the gentleman on the other side spoke up and said "hello?"

"Yes, this is Pablo Rosales. Are you okay? What is your name?"

"Bill, Bill Jameson. No, not really. I am not okay."

"Please share."

"I was just released from the hospital and I am still hurting."

"Would you like to tell me what happened?"

"I was hit in the head and face by a ceiling fan."

"Did it fall on you?"

"Yes, it did."

"I am truly sorry to hear that. And you were right under it when it fell?"

"Yes, I was."

"What type of injury did you sustain?"

"It knocked me out cold and I suffered a concussion. There are multiple cuts and scratches."

"Was anyone there to help you when it happened?"

"No, but when I came to, I had my cellular phone in my pocket, so I called "911". They arrived but the front door was locked, so they had to use some device to open it up."

"Well, I am glad they were able to get to you."

"Is there something you wanted to speak with me about?"

'Well, yes, I guess."

"Go on."

"There were a lot of questions asked when they found my noose attached to the ceiling fan."

"Whoa, wait, wait. You tried to hang yourself?"

"Yes, sir."

"Oh, my Goodness. And you failed because the ceiling fan couldn't hold the weight?"

"I suppose so."

"How much do you weigh?"

"About two hundred and twenty-five pounds. When I kicked the chair out from under me, that's when the fan came straight down and knocked me out."

'That's awful."

"Yeah."

"First of all, I am not sure why you decided to tie the rope to the ceiling fan. Why not go outside and find a tree?"

"Aren't you supposed to be trying to talk me out of doing this?"

"Well, yes, but a ceiling fan? How reliable can that be?"

"There aren't any trees near my apartment, and I didn't want to freak anybody out when they saw me hanging outside, so I tried to do it privately."

"If you were successful, would you have really cared about freaking someone out?"

"Yes, I did care. It wouldn't be good for people to see that. I mean what if they just had finished lunch or were on the way to lunch? Oh look, Bobby, there's some guy that looks like he turned blue hanging from a tree. Oh yikes, Sammy, let's skip lunch."

"Okay, I get your point. Why would you have done such a thing?"

"I'm a loser."

"Nobody is a loser, Bill. Everybody has something to live for."

"My girlfriend broke up with me last week and she called me a loser as she turned and left. I watched as her extraordinarily large butt was passing through the doorway and thought to myself, perhaps she is right."

"Let me see if I've got this right. You hanged yourself over a woman? And one with a huge butt to boot? How old are you?"

"I'm 28, and I did it because I realized that she might be right."

"Okay, listen to me, Bill, you need to come in here for some sessions. Do not try this again and I will tell you why. But, first, do you have any passions?"

"Passions?"

"Yes, like music, hobbies, anything like that?"

"I like to feed mice to my snake and nurture him. I take the snake, his name is Claude, on walks through the park."

"Okay, there's a major "yikes" on that. What type of snake, Bill?"

"Claude's a Boa Constrictor, but he's not as big as most of them."

"Who would have fed Claude had you killed yourself?"

"Not sure, but I am sure somebody would have adopted him."

"Bill, there's not a lot of folks out there who are willing to adopt a snake. In fact, I have never heard of a snake rescue. Look, you have a lot to live for, and I have some ideas. Will you come in and chat?"

"Okay."

"But Bill, I need you to promise me that you will not do anything to hurt yourself before you come in."

"When would I go there?"

"Tomorrow morning, first thing. You might want to leave Claude at home though."

"Okay, I'll be there. I won't hurt myself."

I learned that Bill, the snake charmer, showed up and met with one of Meade's advanced counselors. But, I did not learn this until after Meade George, our CEO, Founder, and Leader, called me into his office for a chat. Sorry for the digression, but why do people name their offspring with a last name for a first name and a first name for a last name? The question was purely rhetorical, but I had seen this on many occasions.

Meade George was a gentleman in his mid-forties with an unusual look about him. His hair was a bit disheveled as one might expect a Psychiatrist's to be. His head was very thin and I wondered how his glasses stayed on his face without falling off. In fact, I did notice that Dr. George continually pushed his glasses up the bridge of his nose in order to keep them in place. Why hadn't someone invented glasses for people with skinny heads, and while they were at it, fat heads? I was interested in knowing why I had been invited into his office until he began to speak, and then the interest waned dramatically.

"Mr. Rosales, are you aware of why I called you in to meet with me?"

"Sorry, sir, no, I haven't a clue."

"Mr. Rosales, did you speak with a Mr. Bill Jameson yesterday on our crisis intervention line?"

Oh my God, he was referring to our snake aficionado.

"Yes, I did sir. We had a decent conversation. In fact, he will be here today if he hasn't arrived already."

"Mr. Rosales."

"You can call me Pablo."

"Let's stay with "Mr. Rosales" for now. Are you aware that we record and monitor the calls?"

"I am."

"Then why in HELL did you suggest that Mr. Jameson hang himself from a tree?"

"Oh, I didn't at all. I was merely ... ..."

"You did, Mr. Rosales, and that is totally the opposite of anything we stand for or believe in."

"May I just explain myself?"

"You may but I cannot assure you that it will have any favorable impact on me."

"Dr. George, Mr. Jameson failed in his attempt to take his life. He failed because he tied his noose to a ceiling fan. I was merely asking why he hadn't thought about the potential instability of a ceiling fan. I didn't at all suggest he hang himself again. I was curious as to why he didn't hang himself from something more stable, like a tree."

"You are a graduate from one of the most prestigious post-graduate Psychology programs in the country and yet you felt compelled to ask one of our crisis intervention patients why he did not hang himself from a tree?"

"You don't understand, sir."

"I understand perfectly, and it just does not work with me, Mr. Rosales."

"Look, Dr. George, the guy is coming in, he promised he wouldn't hurt himself, and I feel the call went quite well."

"Mr. Rosales, there are too many young people who would give up a lot to have an opportunity like this. As far as I am concerned, you blew your opportunity, so I am afraid we will be suspending you effective from the time you walk out of my office."

"Does suspending mean that I might be able to return sometime?"

"I'll give that serious thought, Mr. Rosales, but don't get your hopes too high. So, you are excused now and thank you for coming in."

"Yah, you're welcome, Dr. George. Good bye."

My world came crashing down in just those few minutes with Dr. George. Did I really make a mistake with "Jake, the Snake"? I didn't think so, but there was no sense arguing with Dr. George. That interlude may very well have been a dagger in the heart of any hopes to become a licensed therapist. But, the more I thought about it, was it really what I wanted to do in life? Did I really want to sit and listen to people's troubles all day when I had enough of my own? I didn't think so. The only person who could come to my aid was Gina. I took the long walk down to Central Park and sought a bench on which to dwell while I pondered my future. I would call Gina in the evening and ask her advice. I did know that my future as a therapist might very well have been permanently stalled. Any prospective employer would learn of my brief stay with Meade Center and call there for a reference. In short, I was screwed.

I can think of no place better than Central Park in New York City for people watching and contemplation. The park offers a little bit of everything. The unexpected moments of solitude are highly welcome though they only last for a brief while. I was able to find a vacant bench just under an American Elm tree. The bench was spotted with bird droppings, but none of them appeared to be too recent. The sight of the droppings was more of a turn-on than a turn-off as I had always heard that good luck followed those who were recent victims of a bird poopering. So, my feathered friends, eat up, and feel free to unload on me. All sorts of people went by, likely represented by several different cultures. The park was for everyone as it should be. I was surprised to see as many mid-day joggers as I did. And, there were bikers, skateboarders, and rollerbladers also. A young couple in their twenties went by me on rollerblades. The male was a natural, the female was a beginner. I knew this by seeing the terror in her eyes, especially when she was coming right at me. I prepared myself for a horizontal launch, but felt assured that the boyfriend would steer her clear of me, which he ultimately did. He waved a "sorry, but I've got this" wave, and I smiled a "no problem, I was ready for you" smile back at him.

A woman who I guessed was in her mid-forties was heading my way with a large Rottweiler on a lead. Both wore friendly smiles, and though I should not be afraid of this breed, I felt a nervous chill run through me. As they approached, I looked up and winked at both.

"Nice dog."

"He's just leaving puppyhood. His name is "Momozono", named after one of the Japanese emperors from the 1700's. We call him "Moe". He's gentle, so if you would like to pet him, feel free."

This one sentence raised so many questions, but I decided to leave it alone.

"Moe, Moe, come."

In a nano-second, Moe was literally in my face. I was quite sure that he was expecting a treat, and, if I could help it, my nose wasn't going to be a part of the feast. My new friend was quick to hand me a treat that I could serve up to Moe. I asked Moe to sit and he quickly obliged.

"I'm Suzanne. And you?"

"Pablo."

"Are you here daily?"

"No actually, I am a Central Park virgin. And you?"

"Well, I'm not a virgin, oh, to Central Park that is. I was feeling down and decided to take Moe for a walk in the park."

She was feeling down. I immediately imagined that I had stumbled across a prospective "patient".

"Sorry you are feeling down."

"It'll sound stupid but I had my hair cut this morning by someone new and he butchered it. That's why I'm wearing a baseball cap."

"Let me see."

"Oh no, I can't show you."

"Who am I going to tell? Do you think I'd call the folks over at Vogue Magazine and report you?"

"I guess not."

Suzanne removed her cap and I took a look at the mess she had residing under her hat. It wasn't good. I had to be as polite as possible as the repercussions of being honest and agreeing with her was far worse than patronizing her.

"Oh, it isn't so bad, Suzanne. Turn around."

Suzanne did a pirouette and lo and behold, it was actually crooked in the back. Her stylist must have had his head tilted to the left when he cut the back end. Yes, she had been hacked.

"Well, I am sure you can find someone good to do it next time."

"Yes, I will return to my original hairdresser. I was told that this other guy was good and not terribly expensive."

"You get what you pay for, Suzanne."

"You're right, Pablo. Next time I will know better. I'll be on my way. It was nice to meet you. Oh, and by the way, do you work in the city?"

"No, I'm a student at Columbia and just taking a break."

She would never have picked up on this lie, so I didn't feel at all uncomfortable about exaggerating my status.

"I see, Pablo. Perhaps we shall meet again out here sometime."

"That would be great. You and Moe have a nice day. Bye, Moe!!"

With nothing else to feed him, Moe didn't even turn around to snort goodbye. I was okay with that.

As Suzanne sauntered away, I made an immediate and bold decision. Screw therapy, I shall become a hair stylist. It was time to leave the park and prepare my consultation with Gina on this subject.

Gina answered my call on the first ring. I knew how prompt she was answering the phone and only worried if she didn't answer immediately. I had been lectured on this worrying detail in the past after I questioned why she hadn't answered promptly. "I was in the shower, Pablo, for craps sake. Stop worrying about me. You have programmed yourself to hear my voice after the first ring. Stop that." I apologized more often than not for my insolence, but we understood one another which was paramount. I invited Gina to meet me at Fiore's Restaurant. We both loved the place for the same reasons; great food and wine at reasonable prices. I also loved the place because our usual server, Teresa, had huge breasts. I managed to be discreet when I ogled them. If I hadn't, I would have had my Spanish/Jewish ass kicked with regularity. We had our favorite table in the rear corner and Teresa had our wine on the table before our asses even hit the seat. It made us feel special to know that we were regulars and were treated with like dignity. I decided to get right to the point.

"Gina, I was let go by Meade Center today."

"What??!! Why??!!"

"I'll give you the brief version."

"Please do."

"Well, I was working the crisis intervention phone lines and I took a call from a fellow who had tried to commit suicide by hanging himself from a ceiling fan."

"Oh, Pablo, that's horrible! But, a ceiling fan?? What was he thinking? If he had any size at all, nine out of ten times, it would have come crashing down."

"My point precisely."

"What did you say to him?"

"I inferred that he might have tried hanging himself from something sturdier, like a tree."

"You did not."

"Yah, I did. Dr. George had been monitoring the calls and called me in on it."

"And fired you?"

"He suspended me, same shit."

"What are you going to do, Pablo?"

"That's what I wanted to discuss with you, Gina. I have made a decision about what I want to do going forward."

"And, that is?"

"I will go to Cosmetology school and become a hair stylist."

"Sure you will, and I will become an astronaut."

"I'm dead serious, Gina."

"Holy Kamote, Pablo!!"

"Kamote??"

"Sweet potato."

"Oh."

"So, Pablo, how are your parents going to take this news?"

"No way will I tell them. Are you kidding me? They'd hire a hit man."

"They will find out eventually."

"I have time to figure out a way to be deceptive."

"Okay, Pablo, you obviously wanted to tell me because you want my feedback. So here goes. You have certain passions, some of them leaning towards being artistic. I know it makes you happy. I may be wrong, but I truly believe you went to college in order to placate your folks. You are intelligent, skilled, and have a wonderful quirky personality. I say follow your passion and let it fly."

"I knew there was a reason why I love you, Gina."

"Add that reason to the list. It'll be even harder to get rid of me."

I had no plans of "getting rid" of Gina, but I was happy to receive her vote of approval. I had to move quickly as I wanted nothing to stand in the way of my decision. Having studied a list of cosmetology schools, I settled on one in mid-town Manhattan. I liked the fact that it was far more expensive than most for several reasons, the most prevalent of which was the fact that they likely had highly skilled instructors. Also, their name, Blythe Cosmetology Academy, was highly recognized in the industry and their placement services were unequalled. I would be able to pay tuition and all of my living expenses from my income at The Black Talon where I was raking it in.

Beauty School, as it is commonly known as, was a "piece of cake". The written exams were quite easy as they tracked the sample exams from the test book, word for word. My styling techniques were already imbedded in my mind and hands, so all I really needed were the basics. The classes lasted forty weeks. The requisite number of hours was one thousand. I would have been able to complete the courses sooner, but I was in no hurry. The school attracted all types of people and I was quite sure that I wouldn't want my hair done by anyone who had a tattoo across their forehead and neck, several piercings in various parts of the face and body, and multi-colored hair. But, I suppose there was a market for that too. The teachers liked me because I came across as totally committed and never second-guessed my instructors or peers. There was a clinic where the public was allowed to visit and get a significant discount on their styling. I was the star of the clinic and several of the patrons referred their friends and family. They were told to ask for Pablo. The tips were often greater than the cost of the cut and style. I graduated with honors and was presented with a plaque with my name engraved on it. The licensing process was expeditious and I was now ready to become a bona fide stylist.

Gina took me out to dinner when I received my license. We decided to head downtown to Little Italy and popped into Angelo's for cocktails and a bite. The place was packed, but to my surprise, Gina knew a maître' d, so we were seated immediately. A bottle of Valpolicella arrived and I was ready to dive into that as soon as it was opened. The server suggested that we allow it to breathe, and I suggested that it had breathed long enough. "It can breathe in my stomach".

"Pablo, what will you do with your license?"

"Hang it where I am working."

"I knew that smartass, I mean where will you work?"

'Ya know, Gina, I don't know."

"Go for the gold."

"What?"

"The gold, Pablo. Go work at one of the high-end salons. That's where you will make the money."

"I can't just walk into a salon and say, "here I am, hairstylist extraordinaire, Juan Pablo Rosales at your service". They won't' know me from Adam and I have no following."

"Why not? Look, I will research it for you. I get all of those girlie magazines and I'll make a list. We will write a script that you can follow when you go in. Ask for the owner or manager and let the bullshit fly. You have a certain charm about you, Pablo, you're charismatic. And, you carry that Latin flair, even if it is by name only. I'm telling you, it'll work."

Gina did go right to work and came up with a list of hair salons, mostly in mid-town Manhattan in New York City. Some were downtown in "trendy" neighborhoods, but the list was long enough to keep me busy. I decided to begin my quest on a Wednesday. I knew how busy the salons could be on a Friday and Saturday. I preferred to be in midtown as it meant less travel and more prestigious neighborhoods. The first five salons that I visited were a complete bust. I found it difficult to find a decision-maker and when I did, the first, almost standardized, question was where had I worked and do I have a following. I was terribly polite and turned on the charm, but the "Juan Pablo Charm Machine" was either malfunctioning or completely ignored. I grabbed a quick lunch at Blimpie's, sprayed some mint breath saver into my mouth and began to pound the pavement once again. A combination of nerves and the belly-bomb that I had inhaled at Blimpie's were making me feel ill. But, I had to continue my quest. I was now on Madison Avenue, somewhere in the neighborhood of the "50's streets" when I stopped in front of a boutique wine and cheese shop. It was time for me to window shop. It became immediately apparent that most of the wines sold here were not within my budget. Boxed wines would soon be over my budget. I began to turn and walk away but noticed a decorated door just to the right of the wine shop window. Written on the door in a beautiful gold-leafed script were the words "Palais de Cheveux". My limited knowledge of French led me to believe that I had stumbled across a hair salon. I backed up several steps so that I could look up at the windows. The second and third floors were definitely housed by hairstylists. I could see some people through the window, a nice little marketing strategy. I checked to see if this place was on Gina's list, but it was not. My bold move followed. I ascended the steps slowly almost turning around. What if they only hire French people? Am I dressed appropriately? Should I be honest about my experience? Is it wrong to try to start at the top rung of the ladder? Is the Blimpie sandwich going to explode thereby creating one of the greatest embarrassments of my life? I made it to the top of the stairs and walked through another door. A reception desk appeared right before me. Sitting behind it was a smartly-coiffed woman in her mid to upper twenties. As soon as she greeted me, I knew straight away that she was French.

"Good afternoon and welcome to Palais de Cheveux. How may I help you? Do you have an appointment with us today?"

"Well, actually, no I don't. I was wondering if I could speak to someone about a job."

"Are you a stylist?"

"Yes."

"Please have a seat across the way. I will call Francois from his office and he will speak with you."

"Thanks!"

I had a seat and looked around. The place was busy and it was classy, perhaps a little too upscale for a rookie like me, but I figured that I should at least hear him out. Francois, pronounced "Fran-swa", approached me. I knew it was he the moment he walked through a door and entered the reception area. Francois was a man in his 40's, with thin, wispy hair, and a tight smile that could have easily been transformed into a grimace without any effort at all. In a moment he was before me. I stood to greet him. We exchanged handshakes and pleasantries.

"Hello, I am Francois. And, how may I help you today."

"Well, I am here seeking a job."

"I see. Are you a licensed hair stylist in the State of New York?"

"I am."

"Okay then, can you start right now?"

"What?"

"Are you able to start right now?"

"Uhm, yes."

"Good, I'll get you an apron. You can do the paperwork later. One of my shampoo girls left abruptly this morning and I am stuck. Do you shampoo?"

Francois' offer wasn't at all what I expected. Fortunately, we had to learn every facet of hair service at the school's clinic. I could shampoo with the best of them. But, was this the way I wanted to begin my career? It didn't take me long to realize that I was standing in the middle of what might have been the fanciest salon in New York City. All frogs, excuse the expression, must start as tadpoles. Thus, I decided that I would give it a go. Eventually, I could prove my worth as a stylist and to be able to say that I worked at Palais de Cheveux would be enough to make me happy until the big day arrived, assuming it would.

The first afternoon at Palais de Cheveux didn't end until 7:00 PM. I must have washed about 15 heads of hair. Each client would be special to me and I did my best to make them feel comfortable. I could tell which ones wanted to be engaged in conversation and which ones wanted to be left alone. When I returned home that evening, I pulled the cash out of my pocket and laid it on the kitchen table. I had no idea how much I earned. When a patron handed me cash, I merely stuffed it in my pocket without even looking. I folded the bills out neatly and counted out ninety-five dollars. Holy shit! I had made ninety-five dollars from just shampooing and that was only from tips. It did not include my salary which was small but adequate. I could only imagine how much the stylists were raking in. Gina showed up at about 8:30 PM. I had already eaten, but I warmed some leftovers for her.

"Any luck today, Juan Pablo?"

"Indeed there was luck, Regina."

"What do you mean?"

"I have a job."

"Already?"

"Yup!"

"Where?"

"Palais de Cheveux."

"Bullshit!"

"I do."

"How the f...??"

"I walked in, I was approached by the manager, he handed me an apron, and off I went."

"Pablo, that happens to be the swankiest salon in the entire city. I purposely left it off the list as I never expected they would hire you. In fact, I thought that they only hired French people."

"I told the manager my name was "Jean Paul.""

"You did not!"

"No, I did not. It so happens that they had a shampoo girl leave abruptly in the morning and they were desperate for a quick replacement. I walked in just at the right time."

"I'd take a job sweeping floors in that place, Pablo."

"Well, I'm hoping that I won't have to do that, but at least I have a start. I need to be there tomorrow at 8:45 AM."

"Good for you. Get out some wine. I am always looking for an excuse to have a glass of wine. A New York Met's baseball pitcher making it past the 5th inning is no longer a viable excuse."

"Coming right up."

I became a very popular shampoo guy quite quickly. I did not perform an ordinary shampoo as one might have expected. Head and neck massages were included and I didn't rush my patrons in and out of the chair as some others might do. The water temperature was always perfect and the shampoo used by the salon was the "good stuff". One woman even asked me if she had to leave the chair. I told her to come back more often. After several weeks of washing hair some clients even requested me when they called for their appointment. Francois was also pleased. He offered me lunch on several occasions and gave me a slight raise in pay. Francois wasn't one to throw out compliments but he went out of his way to tell me that he liked what I was doing. And, beyond all this, I was making good money. But, after a few months, I knew that I no longer wanted to be a scrubber forever. I had keenly observed several of the stylists at work and was convinced I could do as well if not better. It was time to show my prowess, but how? I came up with an idea, so I approached Francois.

"Francois, may I run something by you?"

"Sure, let it fly."

"My friend Gina asked me if I would style her hair. Would you mind if she came in and I did it here?"

"That would be fine, but it would have to be at a time when you are not busy washing."

"I can get that covered for the amount of time that it will take."

"Okay then, Pablo, sure, have her come in. I'll make a station available for you."

The second phase of my plan was to prep Gina for this visit to the salon. Our dinner conversation that night included my plea for help.

"Gina, I want to style your hair."

"What's wrong with it?"

"Nothing, but it is part of my plan."

"What plan?"

"The plan to graduate from behind the shampoo sink and into a work station."

"My hair is fine."

"It's not, but let's not argue about it."

"No, no, Pablo, what's wrong with my hair?"

"Okay, Gina, it's too long, your ends are split, the color is drab, it doesn't fit your face and it makes you look eight years older."

The eight years older statement is what drew her attention. No woman I had ever known wanted to look older than she does.

"Really, I look old?"

"No, not old, just older than you are."

"So, you think you've learned enough that you can transform me?"

"Oh yeah, in fact, you will leave the salon looking five times more gorgeous than you already do now."

"You think I am gorgeous, Pablo?"

"Of course I do, but you will be even hotter."

"When?"

"Friday afternoon."

"I'll be there."

My plan was to impress the crap out of Francois. I had told Gina to show up looking disheveled and she obliged. The sweatshirt and ragged jeans added to the presentation. When she arrived, I introduced her to Francois. He immediately gave her the once over glance and nodded his head vertically. He designated a station for me and off we went. Gina loved the shampoo and murmured some sweet words of approval. The process had just begun. I wouldn't allow Gina to see what I was doing until I finished. I was about to transform this pauperesque woman into a princess. We moved from shampoo, to color, to cut and style, to blowout and finish. Two hours later, I allowed Gina to turn around and look in the mirror. The gasp was loud enough that it could be heard on the New Jersey side of the Hudson River.

"What, Gina?"
"Oh My God, Pablo, Oh My God."
"What?"
"It's absolutely amazing. I freaking LOVE it!"
As I had hoped, Francois was standing right behind me.
"Pablo, very impressive. Why didn't you tell me?"
"Tell you?"
"Oui, votre travail est magnifique."

I had a pretty good idea what that meant. But I had no idea what was coming next.

"Pablo, I will need you to wash hair this weekend as we will be busy, but starting next week, you will have your own station. Congratulations!"

I immediately turned around to look at Francois. Gina also spun around and simultaneously with that maneuver; the tears began to rush out of her eyes. I was overwhelmed with joy and the rush I experienced from hearing that statement was nothing like I had ever known. My career had commenced.

The only clients I would see from the beginning would be walk-ins or people who called in for the first time. And, that was fine with me. There was no need to be slammed with work when I was basically an apprentice. But the clientele list grew quickly. It was rare that someone left my station unhappy, and the referrals poured in. Before it I knew it, I was seeing at least five new people per day, men, women, and children alike. I was one happy stylist.

Hairstyling includes many phenomenons, not the least of which is the need for people to share their lives with the stylist. Some were silent through the entire process, but others "spilled their guts" out to me as soon as their butts hit the chair. It was almost as if there was a shingle hanging from my chair that said "J. Pablo Rosales, Hair Stylist Extraordinaire and Therapist". The ability to listen and often comment on what I was hearing fit in perfectly with my training, both as a stylist and as a therapist.

One client, Mindy Goldfarb, came in once every two weeks from

Long Island, New York. Mindy was about forty-five years old and did everything imaginable to look younger. Creams, lifts, high-end makeup, and hair colors were part of her vast repertoire. Mindy would pile through *Seventeen Magazine* in order to find a "young looking hairstyle" in which to transform her. I tried on several occasions to convince her that looking classy rendered her far younger looking than to dress and make herself up like a teenager. I knew that Mindy had a fifteen-year old teenage daughter because Mindy had commented on how she and her daughter had been mistaken for sisters. She reeled at my comment that it must have been a dark place. But, I was making her look better than awesome, so she would take my tongue-in-cheek jabs at her. Mindy opened up to me one Friday afternoon when she appeared to be somewhat distressed.

"Pablo, it is no secret that you are a therapist too."

"Not officially, Mindy."

"Well, you're trained, aren't you?"

"Yes, my secret is out."

"May I ask you a personal question?"

"Sure."

"Can we keep this confidential?"

"Of course. I took an oath never to reveal any conversations I have with clients."

"You did?"

"Well, sort of."

"Okay, then here's my question."

"What would you say if I told you that I caught my husband looking at porn?"

"Was it gay porn, Mindy?"

"No."

"You're good then."

"What do you mean by that, Pablo?"

"Mindy, it is not unusual for men to look at porn. In fact, all men look at porn."

"No they do not."

"Do you know of anyone that doesn't?"

"Sure, I've asked and they say no."

"Then, whoever "they" is are lying."

"Well, I think it is wrong, Pablo."

"Wrong or not, Mindy, he's okay. Look, you are very attractive, so don't get the notion that he is seeking a substitute. It's a curiosity thing. Men like to see sex even if their own sex lives are active or inactive. In fact, I am willing to bet that if you asked any of your lady-friends if they would watch it or participate in anything erotic, you would be surprised with what you hear."

"I never thought about that, Pablo. Do you look at porn?"

"I already told you that all men look at it. I have an active sex life, so I don't seek it or crave it but if it jumps in my face, I'll take a look."

"May I ask you if your sex life is with a woman or are you gay?"

"You just did ask me. Is it something you must know?"

"Not particularly."

"I know you are dying to know, so the answer is that I am not gay. I respect the choices some men and women make, but I am straight."

"Do all men cheat on their wives too, Pablo?"

"Of course not, especially in this day and age when you never know what you are "sticking your business into." I also think that smart men know the consequences of cheating."

"Oh yeah, if I ever caught Howard cheating, I would cut his balls off and hang them on the fireplace mantle as a constant reminder."

"Mindy, I have to believe that Howard would not be there to be reminded if you did that."

"Maybe."

"Listen, Mindy. We're almost done here, but let me leave you with this. You don't need to worry unless there are signs that Howard is unhappy. If you are unhappy, and I am getting some vibes that you are, then it is time for both of you to have a chat, either amongst yourselves, or with a marriage counselor. Also, don't try to be anything other than what you are. I am sorry but dressing up like a teenager, asking for styles that make you look younger, and spreading crap on your face is not the answer. You want to be loved for what is inside, and that's more important than the way you appear. Your self-esteem will force you to look and dress smart, but carry some class about you. I don't want to lose you as a customer, but I will tell you straight out that what you are trying to achieve cosmetically is classless."

"A big "ouch" on that, Pablo, but I hear you. You won't lose me. In fact, I appreciate your honesty."

The next time Mindy came in, she had her fifteen-year old daughter, Marcy, at her heels. Marcy was just the opposite of Mindy. She was terribly unhappy that she looked like a teenager and wanted to be identified as an "adult". Whatever she was doing wasn't working. Sometimes you can read "brat" without having to hear as much as one word. This kid was a brat with an attitude. She had plopped herself down on the empty chair at the station next to mine.

"Pablo, I'm not so sure I like what you're doing with Mom's hair."

"Isn't it more about what Mom likes?"

"Well, you're the artist here. You should be directing her."

"Sorry, Marcy, but this is what your Mom asked for and this is what she shall receive."

"Pablo, are you gay?"

Mindy had heard enough from her little offspring and chimed in.

"Marcy, that's terribly impolite. That's enough."

"Well, he seems gay, Mom."

We obviously needed some clarification here. It was time for me to speak up.

"Mindy, it's okay. I can handle her. And, Marcy, why do you feel it important to pry into my personal life?"

"I was just wondering, Pablo."

"You were just wondering. Well Marcy, are you a virgin?"

"What??!!"

Mindy drew an astonished look and seemed aghast that I would jump in with that. Mindy looked at me and then at Marcy, deniably seeking an answer.

"It's none of your business, Pablo, and why would you ask me that?"

"Marcy, have you ever heard the expression, "If it walks like a duck, quacks like a duck, and looks like a duck, there's a good chance it is a duck". Ever heard that before?"

"Yeah, Dad uses that at times."

"Okay then, if it walks like a tramp, dresses like a tramp, talks like a tramp, and acts like a tramp, there's a good chance she's a tramp."

"Oh My God, Mom. Why did you bring me here?"

That was a question that I wanted to ask myself but hesitated. The "gay" comment had set me off. Marcy was alarmed and Mindy was visibly shaken. They finally left and I can't say that I was unhappy to see them leave. Mindy would continue to see me but Marcy never reared her horrid head again. Mindy was quiet for the most part on her latter visits. I attribute the muted interludes to her not wanting to hear what she needed to hear versus what she wanted to hear.

As time marched on, I became busier and busier. I did a lot of listening, and when appropriate, I would share some thoughts that might render comfort or understanding. But there were some discussions for which I had no answers. Yes, I was a psychotherapist, but my only training had been "on the job" in a hair salon. I was totally unprepared for Eddie Montgrove's latest offering. I had been cutting Eddie's hair religiously each month, usually at the beginning of the month. He was quiet but once in a while he would want to talk sports or work. Eddie was in his mid-30's and had a nice job as an investment banker for a private equity firm in mid-town. Though most of his income was from commissions, he had his hands in several buy/sell deals, so he did quite well financially. Most of my male customers were good tippers, but Eddie was exceptional. One Tuesday afternoon, Eddie was in my chair and was unusually quiet.

"Eddie, are you okay?"

"I'm okay, Pablo, but I've been having some problems."

"Anything you want to talk about?"

"I didn't want to talk to anyone about it, but I know that you studied psychology, so I will share it with you."

"Not sure if I can help, Eddie, but I am happy to listen."

"I wouldn't want anyone else to know about our conversation."

"I am sworn to secrecy."

"I have had problems with intimacy for the longest time."

"What sort of problems?"

"I have had girlfriends and was close to becoming engaged once, but every time I get close to becoming intimate, I just do not get aroused, and I am not sure what is going on. I mean the women I meet are attractive and I am sure they are sexually active, but nothing happens."

"I haven't dealt with this type of issue before, Eddie. Is there anything in your past that might contribute to this lack of intimacy?"

"Well maybe, Pablo."

"Do you think you might be gay?"

"No, no, not at all. It really isn't that. In fact, I love women"

"Anything else you can think of, Eddie? You know that there could be several underlying issues that could contribute to this."

"Do you think it might have anything to do with the fact that my sixth-grade teacher, Ms. Haggerty, had her way with me? I was only about 13 or so back then and I had no idea what was coming.

"That's quite young to be having sex, Eddie."

"I know, I know."

"Do you and Ms. Haggerty happen to stay in touch?"

"Actually no. Ms. Haggerty left the school and moved away shortly after our affairs."

"Oh my, did she move because of these interludes?

"Well, I really don't know. But, as young as I was, I was very remorseful about it, and I know it must have had an impact on me. She was highly unattractive, and borderline obese at the time.

"Why did you go along with this, Eddie?"

"Uhmmmm, I don't know." I was immature and afraid. But, if I get close to another woman, these events pop into my mind."

"Eddie, I think your issues are a bit deeper than anything I might be able to help you with."

In graduate school we studied Abnormal Psychology, some of which included inappropriate sexual conduct. The studies included several pages on incest, nymphomania, and other related issues. I recommended he visit with a psychiatrist, one who might know more about this type of behavior. There were other abnormal psych cases, many of which blew me away. How many people out there are so screwed up? The answer my friends is MANY.

Janice Walter began seeing me for cut and color about two months after I began at Palais. Janice was an extremely attractive woman in her late twenties. She had long, flowing dark brown hair. Her eyes were hauntingly beautiful and it almost seemed that she was partially Asian. I honestly didn't know much about her as she really never said much when I was working on her hair. When my face was anywhere near hers, I could detect a faint smell of alcohol. And, this happened at any time of day, even in the morning. I originally thought that the scent was left over from the night before, but the more I saw her, the more I noticed that she was tipsy all day. One day Janice showed up for her three o'clock PM appointment. Once again, she smelled of alcohol. I wasn't sure what her beverage of choice was, but my gut told me that it was wine.

"Uhmmm, Janice, have we been drinking today?"

"We, Pablo?"

"Just a figure of speech. Okay, have YOU been drinking today?"

"I had a glass of wine at lunch."

"One?"

"What?! Are you the wine cop? Yes, one glass."

"Okay, Janice, sorry I asked."

All of a sudden, out of the blue, Janice broke into tears and began to bawl. So, here I was trying to cut her hair and her head is bobbing out of control, she's sobbing out loud, everyone in the salon is looking over at us, and I had no clue how to console her.

"Janice, are you okay?"

The crying began to wane, she grabbed a packet of tissues out of her purse, and slowly but surely, she was recovering from this little episode.

"Pablo, I'm sorry, but I'm a fucking mess."

"Want to talk about it, Janice?"

"I've been drowning my sorrows, Pablo."

"Well, not to be rude, but I think your sorrows have been hanging around awhile."

"It's gotten worse. I have some major problems."

"Such as."

"I'm an addicted gambler."

"I see. So you're a pathological gambler? I know something about this."

"I've heard that term, Pablo."

"How long has this been going on?"

"Do you really want to know?"

"That's why I asked."

"Ever since I was a young girl, Pablo."

"Wow, that's a long time."

"Oh shit yeah. As an example, when I was ten years old my neighbor Barbara, who was also ten, would walk her dog with me when I walked mine. We would bet one dollar on whose dog would pee first. My dog, "Clit", usually won and "Dick" couldn't beat him. But Barbara did not know that I had cheated."

"Wait, wait, Janice. Hold your thought on the cheating thing but did I hear you say that your dog's names were Clit and Dick?"

"Yah, I know. It was a coincidence. See, Barbara's family gave all of their pets' boy names. Their cat was "Tom", their other dog's name was "Ralph". As for me, my Dad insisted that we name our dogs after Roman emperors. Our dog "Augie" was named after Augustus; "Claude" was named after Claudius, and "Clit" was named after "Clitorius"."

"Uhmmm, Janice, I hate to break this bad news to you, but your Dad was jazzing you. There was no Emperor Clitorius. Are your Mom and Dad still together? And what is it with people naming their dogs after Emperors?"

"No, they're not together."

"Yah, imagine that. So, how did you cheat?"

"Right before I met Barbara on the corner, I made Clit drink a ton of water. I just stood over the bowl and told him to drink, drink, drink.

So, I knew that he would be pissing on everything in sight. And, by the time I got to the corner, he was ready to unload."

"And you think that this was where it all started?"

"I don't know how it all started, Pablo, but I knew it was in my blood and it has never left me."

"And, that's why you're a fucking mess?"

Janice hesitated before answering my last question and began to sob again. I waited patiently, messed with her hair a bit, and offered her some water which she quickly declined by shaking her head horizontally. Finally, over her tears, she spoke again.

"I'm in trouble, Pablo. I need to gamble, but I lost my income stream."

"How much money do you gamble in a month's time, Janice?"

"Oh, I'd say about fifty thousand dollars a month."

"FIFTY THOUSAND DOLLARS!!??"

"Yes, about that."

"Where in hell do you get that kind of money to gamble? Are you going to tell me that you earn that money from gambling?"

"No, I steal cars."

"Holy shit, Janice, Holy fucking shit!"

"Yah, and my connection got busted and I do not know what to do."

"Your connection?"

"The guy who takes the cars off my hands after I steal them."

"How much were you making a month?"

"On a decent month, between eighty and a hundred thousand."

"Oh My God!! How did you do the stealing thing? It's all kind of bizarre to me."

"I had a system and an accomplice."

"Do tell."

"Are you really sure you want to hear all of this?"

"Yes, I'm sure."

"Okay then. I would steal the cars in New Jersey. I had two sources, a few upscale restaurants and a few filling stations. I had accomplices who worked as valets in the fancy restaurants. We knew when the busiest times were at the valet. The cars would get backed up and the patrons would leave the keys in the car, usually when the car was running. When the valet was taking the cars to their spots, he would run his arm across his brow, and that was a signal for me to go in and take one. Obviously, I couldn't go to each restaurant too often as they would definitely catch on to me."

"Sorry to interrupt, Janice, but some of those places have cameras."

"Oh yes, most do now. But, I have a disguise. You would not recognize me. When I am "working", I wear a blonde wig, a beret hat, and sunglasses. As soon as I pull off with the car, I find a place to change back to my usual look. I also change the license plates on the car. I have an extra set of plates from New York. The police are out looking for a blonde driving a car with New Jersey plates on it. So, I stay a step ahead. I also take cars from busy filling stations. I have attendants that help me. The attendant would take off his cap and wipe his brow when the customer leaves the car to go inside the convenience store at the filling station. Then, as if he was an actor, he will pretend to chase me down the street after I pull out. It is all staged perfectly before I move in. I throw these guys a few thousand a month, so they are happy for the extra work."

"What do you do with the cars?"

"I was getting to that. I stay in New Jersey for a while. Most of these stolen cars are taken directly to Queens or Brooklyn, New York because that's where the "chop shops" are. The cops get notice of the theft almost immediately so I hang low for a while in the Garden State. When I feel like it is time to head over to New York, I drive up to the Tappan Zee Bridge way up north. It is unlikely that the cops will be waiting for me up there. From there, I drive down to Queens where I meet my "connection" at a designated meeting place. I have no ideas where the cars go from there. But, he has my cash waiting for me when I arrive. I call in ahead with the make, model, serial number and condition of the car before I leave New Jersey. Oh, and I usually take Hondas, Jeeps, and other cars that bring in more money rather than the high end stuff. But, I have had a few BMW's, Jaguars, and Audi's. Heard enough?"

"Wow, yeah, wow! I almost wish you hadn't shared all of this with me."

"Well, you asked, Pablo. Now can I count on you to keep this our little secret?"

"Of course, but what happened to your connection in Queens?"

"I haven't the foggiest notion. All I know is that I received an anonymous call a few days after my last drop. It was a guy with a gravelly voice and a thick New York accent. He told me that my connection was busted and that they would no longer need my services unless I heard from him again. He disengaged the call before I had a chance to say even one word. I tried calling back, but the phone was out of service."

"That's one wild story, Janice. How are you feeling now?"

Once again the sobbing commenced and my thinking cap was firmly attached to my skull. How can I help this mess of a young woman? I waited once again for her to settle down. Finally, she was able to speak.

"Pablo, I want to change my life but I am unable. I hate myself for what I am and what I have done. I want to have a man in my life, maybe children, stop all of these bad habits, and be a normal person."

"They are not habits, Janice; they are addictions. Are you addicted to alcohol?"

"I am, Pablo."

"Okay then, Janice, let's start with that. This will be super tough but you will have to wean yourself off of the alcohol. Do you have a close friend, one who loves you and understands?"

"I do, my friend from grammar school, Penny Lemieux."

"Call Penny as soon as you get home, meet her, and tell her about the alcohol, and NOTHING else. Got it?"

"Okay, yes. Why?"

"You will need her to go to Alcoholics Anonymous with you. Try it out, don't give up on it and when you feel that need for a drink, also think about what you want out of life. Don't let this addiction stand in your way."

"I'll try it out, Pablo."

"Call me on my cellular and let me know how it is going. As for the gambling, it's a bad addiction that is hard to stop. I'll do some research on it and get back to you. You may not be able to go "cold turkey" on it, but there are some solutions."

"Thanks, Pablo, I appreciate you. There is something about you that told me to spill my guts to you. I can't put my finger on it, but I trust you implicitly."

"Okay Janice, I'll be in touch."

The only cures for gambling are cognitive behavioral therapy and support groups. I found some therapists and a few support groups. I was not completely sure any of it would work, but I felt some sort of compassion for Janice and wanted to help her in any way I could. Within a few days, I was able to point Janice in a direction. I wasn't sure if it would help, but at least it was a start. I was becoming aware that I had done the right things in my life. I wanted to reach out and help people, but I did not want to be a therapist. My mini-bouts of depression, or as I would coin it, "mood swings", did not need to be further exacerbated by other people's problems on a full time basis. I was a self-proclaimed "hair shrink", and I was happy to leave it that way.

Things were going well for quite some time until a new customer named Morgan Hamersley hit my chair. She seemed perfectly normal to me for the first three visits. When she left the salon, she was always beaming with delight. Morgan was thirty-two years old, and intelligent. She was some type of International Consultant for manufacturing and worked for a private agency that facilitated relationships between local vendors and foreign manufacturers. Morgan kept her naturally blonde hair short-cropped as she "didn't want to have to mess with it" in the mornings. It's easier to do that if you are a natural blonde as there are no roots to cover up. I didn't have to do any exploratory anatomical visits to learn that she was naturally blonde. Hair stylists just know these things. Morgan loved dogs and would chatter away about dogs as well as other animals throughout her entire visit. She attended dog shows, walked other people's dogs as a favor, and volunteered at the veterinarian and at pet shelters. On her fourth visit to Palais, she seemed a bit irritable but I decided not to comment on it. She was not as chatty as usual and kept frowning as I trimmed and snipped away.

"Can you hurry, Pablo? I have to get to the hospital."

"Are you okay?"

"I am but my boyfriend is not."

"Oh sorry, Morgan, I hope it isn't anything serious."

"He'll survive."

"May I ask what happened?"

"You can ask, Pablo, but there's something wrong with the way you're cutting my hair today."

"What??!!"

"It's shorter on one side than it is on the other."

"Morgan, it looks quite even to me."

"Then you need glasses, Pablo."

I was not expecting this from the usually mild-mannered Morgan, but I would play "pretend" with her until she settled down. Her face was turning red and blotchy which often accompanies anger. Something was amiss here and it wasn't my styling.

"I'll get it perfect for you, Morgan."

"Hurry up."

"Okay, what's going on here?"

"I need to get to the hospital. I told you that already."

"I'm going as fast as I can. And what happened to your boyfriend?"

"He got hit in the skull with a cellphone and it cut him over his eye and did some damage to his eye."

"My God, Morgan. How did that happen?"

"He is usually quite good at dodging flying objects, but this time he didn't see it coming."

"May I ask if this particular flying object was one that had recently left your hand?"

"He pissed me off."

"So, you felt compelled to toss things at him."

"That's how I vent."

"May I suggest you find other ways to vent?"

"It's none of your fucking business, you hair hack. Let me out of here."

I asked no more questions and sent Morgan on her way. She had exhibited all the signs of being bipolar. My prognosis was confirmed on her next visit as everything was fine and dandy as if nothing had happened at all. She was sweet, attentive, and loved her "do". She left a nice tip and went merrily on her way. She left me wondering if she was diagnosed with the bipolar disorder. I really did not want to be subjected to this angst again. As time went on, the same pattern continued. She would be the sweetest, most charming client I could have ever imagined. Then, on unexpected occasions, she would blow up. How did she keep a job and a boyfriend no less? I decided to confront her with the big question. I wasn't going to wait for a blow up. I would drop the "Q-bomb" on her when she was at her best. The time finally came. She was in a sweet, fun mood until I popped the question. I tried to ease into it, but there's no easy way to ease into asking someone if they are fucked up beyond all recognition.

"Morgan, I've been meaning to ask you something."

"Sure, Pablo, what's that?"

"Well, you are usually so sweet and docile. Then, once in a while, you seem to "fly off the handle" so to speak."

Before I could get another word out, her face immediately turned a bright shade of red and I even detected an element of steam leaving her nostrils, not unlike how I would envision Satan's sister.

"What are you implying, mother-fucker?"

Heads turned as her voice was raised. Her stare could have frozen a charging bull.

"I wasn't implying anything, Morgan; I'm sorry."

"Mind your own business, you amateur piece of hair crap."

"Hair crap, Morgan? Hair crap? What is that supposed to mean?"

"I come here because it is convenient. My five-year old niece could cut hair better than you."

"I hope she's licensed, Morgan."

"What?"

I wasn't going to allow this exchange to escalate, so I told her that I was going to finish up and send her off. She got up as soon as she felt like I was finished though I really wasn't. As she departed, she threw a one-hundred dollar bill on my chair.

"That's too much, Morgan."

"Shut up, you piece of shit. Go home to your gay lover, asshole."

She left. I was exasperated. I was pissed off, but I was cognizant of what she was. But why one-hundred dollars? Was there a hidden message there? I had Morgan's email address and decided to write to her.

"*Morgan, I am sorry for the confrontation that you and I had at the salon today. I didn't mean to set you off like that. You have always been nice to me. I cherish you as a client and do not want to lose you. It doesn't have anything to do with money at all. It's just that I know what you are capable of as a human being, and I want to be there for you. I do not want to be your enemy. It is difficult for me to say this but I do have some background in human behavioral issues, and I want to share something with you. For starters, I am not licensed or qualified to diagnose you, but I believe that you may have some bipolar characteristics. Don't hate me for suggesting this. I would not have even taken the time to write this if I didn't care about you. You may want to get evaluated. If it is negative, then I sincerely apologize. If there is a diagnosis, then you can receive some treatment. I have brushed aside your taunts and the slurs. I don't believe that you really mean them. And, for the record, I am not gay. If I were, I would continue to stand proud. Please feel free to write me or call me at any time. Juan Pablo Rosales.*"

I did not hear back from Morgan and she stopped coming to the salon. It bothered me. I hesitated to call her as I was not inclined to receive yet another lashing. Time passed and six months later, almost to the last date that I saw her, Morgan came sauntering into the salon. She was not on my schedule for an appointment. In her hands, she bore a carefully wrapped gift. The paper was bright shining silver with a huge blue ribbon bow. A card had been placed under the ribbon.

"Hi, Pablo, here's something for you. I will see you soon."

I couldn't imagine why she had showed up and what was inside the box. I looked up at Morgan and was surprised to see her only leaving the salon. I opened the card first and inside it was a note.

"*Dear Pablo, several months ago I left the salon in a huff. I was quite pissed off at you and everything else around me. I received your email and became agitated even more. How dare you to pry into my personal life and try to tell me what was wrong with me. I did not feel the need for your advice and I resented you for a few weeks. Then, one evening I had a knock down, dragged out episode with my boyfriend. I hurt him physically and emotionally. He walked out on me forever. I was crushed. I reached out for him and I was totally ignored. My world came apart, Pablo and everyone else was to blame besides me. In the following weeks, my closest friend Marisol and I met for lunch. She suggested that I see a therapist. She had visited one and claimed that the visits had helped her. Marisol believed that even a few visits with her therapist would be helpful. I blew off the notion, but the very next morning, I was on the phone with Edna Deering, Marisol's therapist. I will not bore you with the content of those meetings, but Ms. Deering felt that I needed to see a doctor, which I did. After four sessions with Dr. Camille Tonelli, she prescribed some medications for; yes you guessed it, a bi-polar condition. I began taking the meds, embarked on an exercise regime and a new diet also prescribed by Dr. Tonelli. I now feel like a new person. I will eventually be weaned off the meds and hopefully it will work. This note and little gift is my way of both apologizing and to say thanks for awakening me. You are a special man, Pablo and I am quite stupid for not hearing you out sooner. I am also sorry for inferring the "gay thing" and I must say that even though I do not know your social situation, if there is a woman in your life, she is one lucky girl. Your faithful and admiring client, Morgan.*

I believe in one of life's rules that if you can make at least one person happier than before, you have accomplished something that money can't buy. I didn't have to do much to help Morgan, but the benefits of my education had paid off to some extent. I opened the gift. Inside the box was a stuffed animal, a rabbit. Around its neck was a ribbon with yet another note. I opened the note slowly and had no idea what it could have said. The note was written in long hand in script so small, it was difficult to read, but I did.

"*Hello, my name is Clover. I am your lucky rabbit. For centuries, rabbits have been known to bring luck, happiness, and wealth to their companions. Promise to keep me by your side, love me, and always be loyal. Your life will be fulfilled if you can keep these simple promises."*

I picked up Clover and held her close to me. I didn't care at all if anyone was watching. I looked the rabbit straight in the eye and said, "I promise."

The luck commenced the very next day. Upon arrival at the salon each day, the first thing I do is to take a quick look at the schedule to see who will be visiting that day. Janice Walter, the "gambling drunk", or perhaps the correct order of that description should have been "drunken gambler" was my eleven o'clock appointment. I could hardly wait to hear of her most recent escapades. Janice had also been out of touch ever since I recommended Alcoholics Anonymous and some gambling support groups. Both addictions would be hard to conquer, but I had hoped for the best. Janice walked through the salon doors at exactly eleven o'clock as scheduled. She looked vibrant, wore a huge smile, and practically ran over to me. The bear hug was unexpected but welcome.

"Pablo, I'm so sorry that I have been out of touch. I had lots to do."

"May I ask you how things are going, Janice?"

"They're going, Pablo, but I am not "out of the woods" yet."

"Gonna tell me?"

"Of course I am going to tell you. Let's get started with the hair first. I look like crap and I don't wear wigs any longer."

"Does that mean that you have quit your job stealing cars?"

"I have. It wasn't helping me accrue Social Security benefits if you know what I mean. Plus, my "connection" wasn't providing health insurance coverage either."

"Yah, Janice, one of the hazards of being a criminal."

"Thanks for classifying me, Pablo."

"How else would you classify it, Janice?"

"A professional thief."

"Sure, Janice, that sounds a lot classier."

"Well, Pablo, I have been going to Al-Anon meetings religiously each week. I went "cold turkey" a month ago, and to be honest, I don't miss it. The hangovers, the lack of sleep, the cost of good wine, and my health just didn't need it any longer. And, guess what!! I'm fine with it. It makes me wonder if I was really an alcoholic. Perhaps I just enjoyed it in large quantities. But, regardless, I am off the juice now. I have a bit of a coffee addiction now, but it's probably a lot safer."

"And, the gambling?"

"The gambling is a different story. I have attended support groups and have stayed away from the bookies. I even deleted all of their phone numbers from my phone. But, it's in my blood and I can't shake it that easily. I have plenty of cash reserves to carry me, but I have to think about getting a real job. Gambling is all around us at all times and it is a promoted habit. You see it everywhere. Even business offices have "pools" of some type or another. Ya know, Pablo, it's funny, but the gambling for me is not about the money or the prospect of earning riches from it. It's just the thrill of winning that turns me on. Sometimes I would go to the store and buy twenty of those mega-dollar lottery tickets. The chances of winning are about one hundred and fifty million to one. In other words, there's no chance or perhaps an extremely thin chance. I wouldn't look at the winning numbers until the morning after the drawing. That way, I could stay up half the night thinking about how I would spend my new-found riches, deciding where I would go, what I would buy, and who I would also make rich. But, I never won, so what would I do, Pablo? I'd buy more tickets for the next drawing just to increase my odds. Is there any logic to that? Of course not. But, in my mind, the rush I received from it outweighed the odds. I'm a sick puppy, Pablo. I will beat this though. Count on it."

"It's a step ahead, Janice. Are you going to keep me posted?"

"Of course I will. You were one of the catalysts I needed to get this behind me."

"So, I assume you won't be stealing any more cars?"

"No, I won't but I must tell you something funny. Last month, I had a date and I asked him to take me to one of the upscale restaurants in New Jersey from which I stole cars. My date knew nothing about my past antics. The waiter was very engaging and liked to chat us up, especially since it was a quiet night. He was telling us about how one of his patron's cars was stolen from right out front of the restaurant that past Saturday night. The valet had been busy and someone just walked up and took it. My immediate thought was that I had a competitor, but not really because I was out of the business. I asked him if that happened often. He said that it hadn't happened in a long time but there used to be a hot blonde with sunglasses that would steal them with frequency. They just couldn't find her and he had been incredibly intrigued about the "hot blonde" and how she could have pulled it off so often and so easily. I wanted to burst out laughing, Pablo. I was a legend."

"Maybe you have a protégé, Janice."

"I haven't trained anyone, and I'll keep my secrets to myself for now."

It had been great to see Janice again and I was quite happy that she was on the path to recovery. I just hoped that it would stay that way. My co-career as a "hair shrink" had taken hold and I wondered how many others I had helped to improve their lives but had no way of knowing. Eddie Montgrove stopped coming into the salon and I was curious as to whether he still had issues with intimacy. It's hard to imagine what type of emotional impact one experiences from having fucked animals. And, there were others, most not as bizarre as Eddie's interludes, but many were curiously really messed up. The world was spinning down a funnel cloud of lost hope, emotional distress, schizophrenia, and despair. Was I the anointed messenger of hope and the tour guide to the land of reason? Show me the way, Pablo, take me there. Tell me that I have every reason to live. And that became my mission. I was the self-appointed hair shrink and I was the best there was. My clientele grew to the point where I simply could not take on any additional patrons. I was making a shit-load of money. And, the powers that be, namely Francois and his nearly invisible bosses, took note. Francois approached me one day after a long day of styling and listening to troubles.

"Pablo, it is quite obvious that you have become our most popular stylist."

"Thanks, Francois. Do you think it's my good looks?"

"Hardly. But, we would not want you to ever leave us. You are our matinee idol here."

"Why would I leave, Francois? This is my home away from home. In fact, I am here more than I am at home."

"Well, that's good news, but just to be sure, we are raising your commission rate, and by a unanimous vote, the owners have decided to offer you a five percent ownership share in the salon."

"Oh wow, Francois. That's amazing. But, I'm not French."

"Let me tell you why that doesn't matter, Pablo. The name of the salon is French, I am French, many of the stylists are French, and even the receptionist is French. But guess what! The owners are two Jewish guys from Brooklyn."

"Figures."

"They love what they see in you and how you have favorably impacted the salon. Plus, it wouldn't hurt for the two Yids to have someone of Hispanic descent as a partner, even on a limited basis."

"Okay, Francois, I'm not going to slide into any details here, but I too am Jewish."

"No shit?"

"Yeah, no shit. But, let's just leave it at that."

Francois just chuckled, turned around and walked away. I couldn't wait to tell Gina about this latest turn of events.

Gina was so excited to hear this latest news that she suggested we celebrate with dinner and fine wine. I could always count on Gina to rationalize food and booze. But, I couldn't complain. I was always on board for a good time, even after a long day in the salon. And now, I was a salon owner, if only on a small scale. So, party time, rear your ugly face!

Mom and Dad had learned to accept my name, my avocation and my lifestyle. They even had decent comments regarding "Gina, the Goy". I have to believe that the gifts I poured on them, coupled with the fact that some of their friends were still supporting their grown kids, enabled a stronger relationship between us. Mom would throw her arms up in the air and say "what am I going to do about my little Paulie?"

My only answer to that was … … … …."It's Pablo, Mom, Juan Pablo. Take note."

Life continued in as uncomplicated a manner as I would have liked. But, there were some very interesting roads traveled including work, the folks, and Gina. Hair Shrinks roll that way. Perhaps I will chronicle much of this in future compositions.

THE END

CPSIA information can be obtained
at www.ICGtesting.com
Printed in the USA
LVHW040201040522
717810LV00015B/341/J